Rachel Greenlaw grew up in North Cornwall, surrounded by wild moorland. She studied English with Creative Writing at Falmouth University before moving to an island in the middle of the Atlantic, where she lives with her husband and two children. Her debut, *One Christmas Morning* was shortlisted for an RNA award. Rachel can be found on Instagram @rachelgreenlaw_

Also by Rachel Greenlaw

One Christmas Morning
The Woodsmoke Women's Book of Spells

Killmarth Trials duology
The Ordeals

YA
Compass and Blade
Shadow and Tide
Starlight and Storm

Praise for Rachel Greenlaw

'Sizzling and addictive romantasy.'
Sunday Post

'A rich romantasy ideal for fans of dark academia.'
Mirror

'Captivated me from the very first page. It reminds me of why I love writing and why I love reading. It's magical and grounding at the same time, otherworldly and natural. I absolutely treasured it from beginning to end.'
Cecelia Ahern, *Sunday Times* bestselling author

'The magic system is captivating, and the ending will leave you yearning for the second book.'
Express

'If you like your romantic fantasy books thrumming with magic and atmosphere, *The Ordeals* will have you hooked from the start . . . The multi-layered magic system draws you into this dangerous, dark academia world and the central mystery keeps you guessing. Bring on the sequel.'
Culturefly

'What a wild ride! Rachel Greenlaw's romantasy debut combines captivating world building, a seriously twisty plot, and a steamy romance. I thought I knew where this was heading, but boy was I wrong. The way the layers of this story unfold made it impossible to put down!'
Demi Winters, author of *The Road of Bones*

'A magical college with death games, a murder mystery, and dangerous magic? Yes please! Deliciously dark with high stakes and a sizzling hot romance, *The Ordeals* is not to be missed!'
Tessonja Odette, author of *A Rivalry of Hearts*

'Clever, exceptional.'
Milly Johnson, author of *Together Again*

'An atmospheric and cosy read, sparkling with enchantment.'
Natasha J. Hastings, author of *How to Charm a Viscount*

'Modern magic meets perfect prose. I read this in one day. It is an absolute masterpiece and one of my favourite books of the year. It incorporates magic in a modern way that feels natural. You will love meeting the Woodsmoke women as much as I did.'
Frost Magazine

'An evocative and compelling story about lost love and the magic of coming home.'
Sunday Mail

'The characters are so raw and relatable and the mystery so intriguing that I hated slipping out of this magical world and back to reality.'
Kate Robb, author of *This Spells Love*

'Otherworldly, beautiful, and completely captures the imagination.'
Muddy Stilettos

'Spellbinding and starry, the Woodsmoke Women cast a spell on me.'
M.A. Kuzniar

'An enticing read.'
Belfast Telegraph

THE DIVINES

RACHEL
GREENLAW

HQ

ONE PLACE. MANY STORIES

HQ
An imprint of HarperCollins*Publishers* Ltd
1 London Bridge Street
London SE1 9GF

www.harpercollins.co.uk

HarperCollins*Publishers*
Macken House, 39/40 Mayor Street Upper
Dublin 1, D01 C9W8, Ireland

This edition 2026

1
First published in Great Britain by HQ,
an imprint of HarperCollins*Publishers* Ltd 2026

A catalogue record for this book is available from the British Library.

HB ISBN: 9780008741358
TPB ISBN: 9780008741365

Set in Bembo Std by HarperCollins*Publishers* India

Printed and bound in the UK using 100%
Renewable Electricity at CPI Group (UK) Ltd

FSC
www.fsc.org
MIX
Paper | Supporting responsible forestry
FSC® C013604

For those who are never ready to turn that final page.

Part 1

Hell is empty and all the devils are here.
~William Shakespeare

Chapter 1

Aftermath

The maze is riddled with tricks and traps. As I search for the monsters, the blade strapped at my thigh scrapes inside its holder with every footstep. Knox is just in front of me, Alden a few steps behind and we move as one, like shadows through the twists and turns between the hedges. I'm restless. Unmoored in the sea of death surrounding us in the aftermath and I keep reliving those final moments as our world tore apart, just four weeks ago, when the Cold Ones attacked Killmarth.

The great hunt is upon us, and we must fight.

'DeWinter, do you sense anything?' Knox asks quietly, glancing over his shoulder. 'This mist is dense.'

I cast my awareness out, past the hedges, through the drifting spires of fog. I try to sense any threads or glimmers of magic, of anything that isn't as it should be in this place. But we are alone in the maze on the edge of Killmarth, the site that served as the location for our second Ordeal. Which can't be right. 'The gargoyles at the entrance said three entered before us, they mislead at times—'

'But they never outright lie,' Alden adds at my back. I shiver, his tone, quiet and serious, kindling something deep under my skin and for a moment, I picture where we would be at this moment if the cold ones hadn't invaded Killmarth that night. If the great hunt hadn't begun in earnest over these past weeks. In my new bedroom in Gantry, probably. It's early still, sunlight just gilding the tops of the hedges of this maze, and I would be stretched out beside him, his hands roaming slowly down my sides, soft kisses dusting my clavicle, a moan escaping my lips as his fingers flutter under the band of my—

'Oh, but you smell *good*,' a voice says from an opening in the hedge on my left, as a figure steps through the mist. Spotless suit, ruthless gaze, a cruel smile twisting his mouth.

A cold one.

Alden doesn't hesitate. The hedge explodes around the monster, snaring it within heartbeats. I surge forward as Knox covers the other opening, in case any others spring an attack whilst we're focused on this one. I whip the blade from its holder at my thigh, pressing it against the foul monster's throat and it grins at me, eyes manic as it struggles against the bindings Alden formed around its chest. 'A blade? Surely by now you know—'

I stab it with the wooden stake I'm carrying in my other hand, driving it through its chest. 'That you die when that thing you call a heart is staked?' I whisper, as its eyes widen before exploding in a plume of ash. I dust myself off, placing the stake back in the holder strapped on my other thigh. 'Well aware. The blade is just a distraction.'

'You're getting faster,' Alden says as he wields his botany magic to push back the hedges to the sides of the opening.

'More ruthless, you mean,' I say with a sigh. 'Let's find the other two and get back. Breakfast is calling.'

'Watch out!'

I spin, finding two more cold ones either side of Knox and as one lunges he ducks, coming up with a stake in his fist. Alden throws out his hand, a branch clawing out of the hedge on the opposite side to skewer the second cold one through the back, straight into her heart. She stares at us, blonde hair hanging in a limp sheet around her grey cheekbones, staring pitifully before disintegrating into nothing but ash. I rush forward as the cold one Knox is grappling with grabs the stake, flicking it behind him.

'Now it's just you and me, wielder—'

But the cold one doesn't get a chance to finish. I've already plucked my iron blade from its holder and thrown it. It rips into the cold one's chest and as it breaks its grey skin, I twist my fingers, focusing on the iron of the blade, imagining it turning into something else. Wood. My magic twists from my fingertips, spearing the blade, now embedded in the cold one's chest and before it can even blink, it shatters into dust. The blade, now made of wood, although a twisted, rather brutal version of its former self, clatters to the ground and we are left in ringing silence.

We all stare at each other, breathing quickly as the mist rolls away entirely within the maze, revealing the dawn.

'Just as we practised, DeWinter. Nice,' Knox breathes, flashing me a grin. He toes the blade with his shoe. 'How many attempts?'

'Many, many attempts,' I say, shaking my head. 'Bloody hard getting an object to change into a new material and actually *keep* it that way.'

'Stone still eludes me,' he replies. 'Too stubborn. We should probably work on that.'

A slow clap echoes down a passageway between the hedges as they peel back like curtains, revealing Professor Hess, flanked by two others. Ezra Darley and Caroline Ivey. Ezra Darley, the Collector, the man I believed was my uncle for many, many years . . . who it turns out was lying, all along. My keeper, my boss, my trainer. I sneak a glance at Knox, his *actual* nephew and find the faintest trace of a smile as he nods to his uncle in greeting. They get on well, though I have no idea why or how. Clearly Knox sees something in him I don't. The last time I spoke to Ezra alone was just before the massacre in the Keeper's Hall. And we resolved nothing.

I already know Ezra Darley is a complete bastard but Caroline Ivey, on the other hand, with her almost silver eyes and sharp cheekbones, is an enigma still. Working for the Crown, she has watched over the Ordeals this past semester, keeping an eye on hopeful scholars with promise. And now we are full scholars, Alden, Knox, myself and now . . . just fourteen others. She seems to have stayed on as less of an observer, more an assembler. She's here representing the Crown, and she expects Killmarth to supply her with the very best wielders for the great hunt. Older, more experienced scholars have already been reaped for the Crown's forces, the attacks coming in waves across Kellend and Theine. But for us freshly minted scholars, we are still in training. Staying in reserve in case we are needed.

The three of us were selected this morning for this illusion to show her how we would handle coming up against the cold ones again. If we could work together as a team and if the training plan that Killmarth had hastily put together was working. I look uneasily over her shoulder, to Killmarth College, proper. Tessa was meant to be here too, but she didn't leave her room. Has only left it, actually, when one of us has dragged her to training or lectures or to eat something since four weeks ago when Greg and three other scholars were murdered by the cold ones. We've covered for her so far when she doesn't show for something, but I'm just waiting for the moment Caroline figures out she's not just occasionally absent. And what the faculty and Crown will do about it. It's a bad patch this week. She's sequestered herself in her bedroom for the past two days and I haven't been able to tempt her out.

'Well done, well done,' Hess intones, ceasing his clapping and bringing my focus back to him. 'Of course it's what we expected of the three of you. Sophia, you are beginning to wield alchemy with intent. Excellent.'

His eyes are bloodshot, ringed with fatigue, hair a shock of unbrushed red. My heart twists as I picture him, holding my mentor, Hester Lewellyn, as she died. The first person to truly believe in my wielding, who was teaching me above all, how to value myself. I swallow, pushing back the image of her glassy eyes, the blood speckling her lilac dress and nod to him. He cared for her too, beneath all that quiet restraint was a pile of love letters charting their shared secret history. When she died, I wasn't the only person who lost someone. 'If we're done here, I'd like to get breakfast. Professor.'

'You have an hour,' Caroline says softly, flicking a tiny leaf off her scarlet coat sleeve. 'We require your presence in Darley Hall for a meeting of your team. Tell no one.'

Alden frowns. 'Darley Hall . . .'

'Is the ideal place for a meeting that cannot easily be . . . interrupted,' Ezra says, crossing his arms. 'Where is Tessa Godolphin this morning? She was meant to be here.'

'She's studying,' I say quickly, holding his gaze. I keep my features relaxed, blinking slowly but I don't miss the tell, a slight quirk of his mouth. He knows I'm lying through my teeth.

'See that she joins us,' Caroline Ivey says, tilting her head slightly. The light catches the thin scar on her cheekbone, the mark she will carry forever of the massacre in the Keeper's Hall. Her almost silver eyes land on mine. 'One hour, don't be late.'

Chapter 2

Death Becomes Her

'Tessa?'

I reach for the handle, pushing the door open. It gives with a creak, revealing a room shrouded in darkness. I can make out the slump of her shoulders, her silhouette against a thin gap in the curtains. She's sat in an armchair before the window, the place she's returned to almost every day since that night, looking out. As though the sea in all its restless glory may one day bring him back to her.

'Tess, it's been two days since you've left this room. We talked about this. You're barely eating—'

'I'll eat when I'm hungry. And I'm not hungry,' she says, voice a feeble scratch of sound that cuts deeper than a scream.

I wince, taking another step towards her. I wonder how long she's been sat there, when she gave up on all hope of sleep. She's barely been sleeping. It's the nightmares which wake her as soon as she closes her eyes. Over the years, I have learned to live with nightmares and still find sleep. But for Tessa, this is new. Loss, grief, becoming a version of herself she does not recognise. Witnessing something she cannot now un-see. 'He wouldn't want you to be like this. Greg wouldn't want this for you. Have a bath, I'll run you one. Come down to the hall for some breakfast. Just . . . leave the armchair. Please.'

She draws in a deep, shuddering breath and my heart twists. I rush forward, drawing my arms around her as a sob rattles in her chest. 'I can't do it. I can't . . . believe he's gone. It's not right. None of this makes any sense.'

'I know,' I say, closing my eyes, and rest my forehead on her shoulder. She slumps back, tremors running through her body and I pull her closer. 'Please just come and eat something. Please. Have a cup of tea with me.'

She sighs and I think she'll refuse, like she has done every time over the last two days. Before that, she seemed to be operating in shock, and I could coax her down for a meal, or a lecture, or a training session. Even if she did just stand at the side, horror glazing her unfocused eyes. But now, she's barely moving. She's unravelled over the past two days, sinking beneath the surface of her grief. I'm afraid she'll wither away, that she'll drown in the mire of that day.

Finally, she nods. 'All right.'

I help her into the bathroom, run the taps and soon have a hot bath for her to step into. I close the bathroom door and assemble an outfit for her, laying it all out on the bed. Then when she's dressed, I neaten her hair, pinning the curls into a bun at the nape of her neck, just as she likes to wear it. I stare at her reflection in the mirror above the dressing table, silvered at the edges, but her gaze is cast down, unseeing. 'There's something else. We've been summoned to a meeting in Darley Hall.'

Finally, her gaze lifts. 'By who?'

'Caroline Ivey and Ezra,' I say. 'We've got about half an hour for breakfast.' I brace her shoulders, turning up the corners of my mouth in what I hope is an encouraging smile. 'It'll be fine. We can get through this. I won't leave your side.'

Her gaze drops again. 'If I must.'

⋆

Tessa manages about three spoonfuls of porridge and a few slices of apple. I ply her with tea, hoping she will at least drink something as I eat as much as I can. The session this morning in the maze left me ravenous. I haven't seen Alden and Knox, but I figure they've gone to another hall for breakfast. We're sitting in Godolphin, Tessa's house hall, and it's so different to Gantry. Where Gantry is severe and stripped back, Godolphin is comfortable and chaotic.

Colourful woven rugs layer the cold stone floors, a haphazard collection of art plasters the walls and the breakfast is set up along one long side table in tureens that stay piping hot. Tables are scattered throughout with comfortable, upholstered chairs, some striped, some plain, some patterned. Everyone is chatting, relaxed despite the storm cloud hanging over Killmarth and the notable absence of the most senior scholars, chosen by the Crown to fight. But for the remaining Godolphin scholars, this is the one space they can take a pause and be their true selves.

If it wasn't for the attack, I expect the atmosphere would be livelier. Masquiers tend to gravitate towards creative pursuits; painting, sewing, pottery, theatre. It's a discipline of honing and self-expression, of mirroring the world around them and making sense of it, and I suppose this space and their interests are a reflection of that.

Professor Silver wanders in, chatting with a librarian as they both help themselves to mugs of tea, racks of toast and pots of jam and butter. They scoop everything up, still talking quietly together and grab a table in the corner. It's only when Professor Silver's gaze shoots up, landing on me and Tessa that I realise most of the scholars in this hall are talking about us. Silver nods briefly, going back to her conversation, but those around us keep stealing furtive glances.

Even a month later, they're still talking about Greg and what I did in the final Ordeal. I eat a little more, sip my tea but when I hear the words 'attack' and 'werewolf', I push back my chair and stand abruptly. Tessa looks up at me with those soft, hopeless eyes, so unlike the person caged inside right now. I would give anything to bring her back to life. But the only way of doing that is to tear Greg from the arms of Death herself. And that is beyond an alchemist. It's beyond even the gods.

'Come on, they'll be waiting for us,' I say, smiling encouragingly. She closes her eyes briefly then pushes back her own chair, taking my arm as we leave Godolphin Hall and its whispers.

As we cross the courtyard, there are few scholars milling around. All eating breakfast at their halls or studying elsewhere or just absent. Taken away by the Crown to bolster the forces fighting back waves of cold ones. I don't know whether it's still a secret that Darley is being used by the professors or not, and honestly, I do not care to keep their secrets right now. All that's on my mind is keeping Tessa going, propelling her forward. And finding out how on earth we are going to fight these creatures, what Ezra and Caroline want specifically from us, now the great hunt has begun.

I push open the door of Darley, finding a figure there awaiting us.

Dorothea Parnell.

Ruthless gaze that misses nothing, stern features harbouring a slight sneer and hands clasped before her, wool skirt and grey jumper blending all together to give her the appearance of an apparition. The head housekeeper, who first showed me into Hope Hall as a hopeful scholar. She sighs through her nose, regarding us, and it doesn't escape me that she barely ever blinks.

'Touch nothing, follow me and keep your curiosity in check,' she says in her grim, monotone voice. 'Darley Hall is unstable at best, portals appearing and disappearing at will over the years. Hopefuls and scholars have entered here on a dare or a whim and never stepped back out,' she says over her shoulder as we ascend the staircase. 'Of course, you will not know any of this. It's been unstable since my late husband fought against the cold ones in these very rooms and won, but at great personal sacrifice.'

I shuffle behind her, glancing back every now and again at Tessa to ensure she's still following. Her gaze is on her boots, not even a spark of interest in her. So different to the determined Tessa I know and I wish I could wind time back, tell her and Greg to leave the Crucible before we crossed that courtyard at Alabaster House.

Parnell opens a door at the end of the corridor on the first floor, where we overheard a secret meeting two months ago. It seems so strange that it was only a matter of weeks in the past that Tessa and I broke in here, determined to get ahead in the Ordeals and discover the secrets within this hall. So much has changed.

'Ah, the other two you mentioned. Shall we begin?' Edmund Locke says, leaning against a table. The last time I saw him was in the depths of the Morlagh, parting ways as we ventured back to the portals which would lead us here, to claim our victory over the first Ordeal. He seems hardened, none of the humour and pithy remarks from the night we shared in his family's hunting lodge. As though the great hunt has already stripped Alden's older brother of some of his humanity.

Gathered around are all the people I suspected would be here, and also a couple I did not. Knox Darley and Alden Locke stand near the window, arms crossed, features unreadable. I dart a look at Alden and he nods to me, even that small gesture sending a fizz of electricity through my veins. Then there's Hess, sat in an armchair, no less haunted than in the maze this morning. Caroline Ivey is sat with her legs crossed next to him.

Then there's Ezra Darley and stood next to him . . . Frances. And beside her, Belle, the masquier from the year above who tried to trick me in the masquier Ordeal. I frown at Frances and she raises her shoulders, features pinched with anxiety. Ever since the attack she's been keeping a low profile, avoiding the rest of us. But as she essentially outed herself as a werewolf when she transformed and fought the cold ones in the massacre, I expect she's just trying to avoid the likely prejudice that will follow her. Werewolves exist mainly on the fringes of society in the three territories. It's unusual for anyone to grow up and learn restraint, even to the point where they can control if they turn or not on the full moon. Almost unheard of for a werewolf to also be able to pursue a normal life as a wielder.

'Let's begin,' says Caroline. 'You all know Knox and Alden, but Sophia here has been kept in the shadows by Eddie for his own reasons. And Tessa Godolphin has been recommended based on her promising performance in the final Ordeal.'

'And these two?' Edmund asks, indicating Belle and Frances. Belle smiles at him like a cat. No . . . actually, rather like a wolf—

'Werewolves,' Caroline says in a clipped tone that brooks no debate. 'Outstanding control. They're from the same pack.'

'They can both turn at will?' Ezra asks.

'We can,' Belle says, raising her chin. 'And *we* are people, you don't need to treat us like pets that perform for treats. You can address us directly.'

Knox chuckles, quickly turning it into a cough behind his fist as Parnell darts him a murderous look. Belle flicks me a small smile, which I return. Well played indeed, hiding in plain sight for so long at Killmarth.

'Any more introductions needed? No? Good,' Caroline says, rising from her chair and crossing to a blackboard in a wooden frame on a set of wheels. In one deft stroke, she erases the few chalk markings scratched across it and sketches a rudimentary map of the three territories with a stub of chalk, before drawing three crosses on the border line between Theine and Alloway, then a further series of crosses across Kellend. She turns on her heel and stabs the chalk at one of those crosses, marking a place just north of the capital city of Dinas Tar. 'The simple fact is, we are at war. A secret war, but war nonetheless and I can say with absolute certainty, we are losing.'

I assess the array of crosses and bite my lip.

'Each one of these marks represents where the Crown have deployed our teams of wielders, not only to deal with the cold ones, but also to deal with an emerging situation with Alloway. We are depleted, and we are overstretched.'

'What's the situation with Alloway?' Alden asks.

'Fion,' Ezra answers, and I don't miss the hint of aggravation in his tone. 'An Allowayan sleeper agent, planted in Kellend to rise up through our own pipeline of schools to gain a place as a scholar at Killmarth College. Then tasked with gaining the trust of her professors, before destroying it from the inside.'

'Thereby weakening the territory for the next great hunt,' Caroline adds. 'Of course, thanks to Ms DeWinter—'

'That threat was neutralised in the final Ordeal.' Ezra nods. 'However, it has created a . . . situation.'

'The Allowayans are pissed?' Knox asks.

'Not the way I would phrase it . . . ' Caroline's mouth twists. 'But yes, they are calling it an act of war. They firmly deny any allegations of purposeful plotting against the Crown and Kellend and are declaring her death a move against them.'

'What absolute rubbish,' Knox mutters, crossing his arms.

'Yes, I quite agree.' Caroline shrugs. 'But certain members of the Allowayan leadership have rather seen this as a way of rallying the people against us. Which has successfully divided our forces and meant we do not have enough wielders on the ground in our own territory to fight the latest waves of the great hunt. We were already diminished compared to eight years ago, but now . . .'

'In a matter of decades, wielders will be wiped out,' Edmund says to our left, putting his hands in his pockets. 'Unless of course, we get a lot better at fighting back against the cold ones. Or . . .'

'Develop a weapon deadlier than any blade or stake,' Caroline continues.

Edmund nods, reaching to the table behind him and picks up a small, glinting glass bottle, no bigger than my thumbnail. Alden steps forward, frowning. 'What's that? I can sense it, it seems . . .'

'Strange?' Caroline supplies. 'It's an antidote. In development still, named after the wielder who first began the work, Henry Nocturne.'

'The nocturnal,' Ezra says quietly, eyeing the milky, glowing liquid within.

'I hear Nocturne was one of *your* marks that you collected for your map,' Caroline says, raising an eyebrow at him. 'Met a chilling end. Didn't think to intervene? Surely you must have been watching him.'

'I was too late,' Ezra says, removing his reading glasses to blink at her. 'I collected him for my map to keep a friendly eye on him. But a cold one got to him in the last great hunt. I was . . . otherwise engaged. Protecting an asset.'

I think back to the last great hunt, the cabin in the Morlagh, this man, Ezra Darley, the Collector sat before that door, day and night. Dolly smoothing back my hair, telling me stories whilst we were cooped up inside. Then the drive back to Dinas Tar, and the silence afterwards. As though I had dreamed the whole journey and never visited the vast sprawl of northern forest in Kellend at all. I'd almost scrubbed it from my memory when I stepped through that portal into the Morlagh Woods on the first Ordeal.

Protecting an asset . . .

I pinch my lips together. He means me. I glance at Knox and find him watching me, as though he's working something out too.

And it only occurs to me then . . . Ezra Darley has just admitted he doesn't just collect marks for the purposes of blackmail and extortion. He collected Henry Nocturne to protect him . . . to keep a friendly eye on him. I shake my head. It must have been to benefit himself, somehow. I cannot believe any of those marks on his map were collected for altruistic purposes.

'When you say antidote, what do you mean?' Alden asks, still staring at the potion in the glass bottle. 'An antidote for what?'

'Vampirism,' Caroline says.

There's a ripple of shock around the room and even Tessa raises her gaze to stare at the glass bottle. 'You mean to say . . . the cold ones can be *cured*?'

'That's the theory, at least,' Caroline confirms. 'The nocturnal antidote Edmund is holding is the result of carefully piecing together Henry Nocturne's research. Over the past eight years, botanists have been tasked by the Crown with recreating his theoretical vision for a cure and making it possible. The team are almost there. What we lack though is a key ingredient.'

'What key ingredient?' I ask, eyeing the liquid. It appears viscous, as though it is bottled moonlight itself.

'We're not sure. When Alden says he senses it's strange, that's what our team of botanists also describe it as in their reports. A complex set of ingredients that produce an elixir that is unlike any other. It bears no similarities to any of our botanist-made healing potions or tinctures, which I suppose is what Locke means by "strange". And when we have tested it—'

'On cold ones?' I ask.

Caroline nods. 'On cold ones, it appears to curb the bloodlust a little, but only for very short spans of time.'

'You— you captured them? To test it?' Tessa asks as her features harden. 'Where are they?'

'Kept safely for the purposes of research only,' Ezra says cryptically. I meet his gaze and wonder if they are marked on his map as well. I wonder, for the first time, who else he is following and for what purposes.

'And whilst we develop this elixir and search for that final, elusive key ingredient, we need recruits, wielders like you, who can protect Kellend,' Caroline says. 'This is not the first great hunt. Nor will it be the last, if we do not stop them. But in the meantime, we have to fight back.'

'Which is where we come in,' Knox mutters.

'You all have specific skills and showed promise in the Ordeals. You all bring something to the table. Something the Crown needs now,' Caroline says. 'Hess has put you all forward in a team, and you will be called upon when the time is upon us to act. We would not usually call up such green scholars, but with our forces divided, you have a golden opportunity to step up for the good of Kellend, and the Crown.'

I suppress a snort. This golden opportunity rather sounds like they're getting desperate, raking the territory for wielders they haven't yet called upon.

'We will train you, arm you, prepare you,' Edmund adds. 'This is the whole purpose of Killmarth now, after all. You've been in training sessions for the past few weeks with the others, but now we need you to work as one team. To bond, to fight together.'

I look around at the others. My new team, whom I must bond with. Who will have my back, and I theirs if we're called upon. None of us are properly trained. None of us, if I'm being honest, are ready. My gaze lands on Hess, and he looks away. He knows it too.

They discuss tactics with us, training regimes and drills so that we are prepared to leave at any moment, as needed. All to fit around our studies and our time as scholars here at Killmarth. As Caroline talks, I sense Tessa drifting further away in her thoughts and reach down, clasping her hand, hoping to keep her anchored.

As the meeting concludes, leaving me with more and more questions and very few answers, I feel a hand land on my shoulder. Looking up, I find Ezra's gaze boring into mine and can't help narrowing my own eyes. 'Yes?'

'Stay behind a moment,' he says quietly. 'I have something to discuss with you.'

Chapter 3

Anatomy of a Team

I wait until the others have left, nodding to Alden when he looks at me questioningly to reassure him. Then after Hess has created a portal, sending Edmund back to Morlagh Manor, he and Parnell shuffle out, the meaning of her piercing gaze clear. Stick to her rules. Touch nothing, disturb nothing. Leave Darley Hall as soon as possible.

Rounding on Ezra, I cross my arms. 'Well you certainly kept your cards close to your chest, didn't you?'

He shrugs, unperturbed, and takes a seat. For the first time, I see the true marks of tiredness, the deep grooves of shadow surrounding his eyes. But it doesn't fill me with sympathy. 'Secrets are kept that way for a reason. As you're now aware, the Crown did not know of *your* existence either.'

'I'm sure Caroline is thrilled about that.'

'I can deal with Ms Ivey,' he says softly. 'You on the other hand, I believe are quite volatile. Even with Hess's tutelage—'

'Tutelage! I've barely spoken to the man—'

'You will need guidance, coaching, mentoring—'

'My mentor is dead,' I say. 'Hester Lewellyn . . . she . . . she . . .' I swallow, staring at the floor, furious with myself for cracking. For showing any of my real emotions.

'I am sorry for your loss. Truly,' Ezra says quietly. 'Too many have been taken from us. I bear the weight of them too. Believe me. But we must discuss what sparked in your veins, what you now realise you are. An alchemist. A powerful, but very much untrained wielder.'

'No.'

He blinks quickly. 'What did you just say?'

'You're about to say you'll be my new mentor, aren't you?' I grit out, all the sorrow and grief spilling through the cracks of me moulding swiftly into something else. Something keener, harder. 'Well, I refuse. You kept me in the dark for too long. How can I possibly trust you?'

Ezra stares at me for a moment, an emotion flitting so swiftly across his features, I almost believe I could have imagined it. 'Sophia, I don't wish to quarrel with you. I simply need to mould you into the alchemist the Crown needs.'

'To what end?' I ask.

'To the bitter end,' he says. 'The end of the hunting in our world. Or until the end of us.'

'But Hess—'

'Is a broken man. The Crown does not wish to overburden him at this time.'

I take a breath, levelling him with a look, summoning up all the fear, the rage, the loneliness he instilled in me, ever since I was a child entrusted to his protection. I know the shape of his training. I was honed by him for years and it cast me into the deepest shadows, until I no longer knew what I was, or what I wanted beyond freedom. 'I won't be a burden on Hess, he can train me. Or Silver. I'll even accept *Parnell* as a mentor over you.' Then I turn on my heel and leave the room.

★

I slink through the corridor on the third floor of Gantry, unlock my bedroom door and close it behind me. It's a slight upgrade on my room in Hope, the bed is a double and the bathroom is nicer, and even though it's full winter now, it's warmer. Cosier. There's a soft rug underfoot and a bookcase that I've already placed a few library books on, as well as some of Hester's books. The day after the attack, when we were moved out of Hope Hall to the castle proper to be less cut off, Hess left a pile of them for me outside my door with a note saying simply, *She would have given these to you. They are yours now.*

I run my fingertip over the spines, remembering her floor-to-ceiling bookcase, the history spilling from the pages and pull out a random title to stare at. It's a heftier tome, the complete works of an alchemist who specialised in creating what they call bridges and portals as two separate endeavours when crossing between two points, or what Hess simply refers to as portals. I do wonder if Hess is ducking his responsibilities of training me, as the only alchemist on the faculty. As if he just can't summon up the will right now to do much except go through the motions, or . . . more likely, he can't stand to be alone with me, her final mentee.

I understand it, I really do. But I know that if it was Lewellyn, if this situation were reversed and Hess was the one who had died, she would have gathered herself together. She would have stood up, calmly, with a stoicism I would marvel at, and chosen to fight. She would have begun my true training immediately and saved her emotions for later. She would have accepted what was at stake, even as her heart crumbled. We're all mourning. But I need Hess more than this book on the theoretical work of portals. I need him to step in so I can legitimately push Ezra Darley and his offer away. I need him to fight past his grief, delay the moment when he falls apart completely for just a little longer. Just like I have.

There's a knock and I call over, 'It's open!' just as Alden walks in. He eyes me carefully as he closes the door and I place the book back on the bookshelf.

'So . . . an elixir,' he says, leaning back against the door and crossing his arms. 'They kept that quiet.'

'Annoyed you didn't know?' I ask.

He raises an eyebrow. 'No. It's merely a comment. Even Edmund guards the Crown's secrets well. Something ruffled you?'

'It's just . . .' I throw up my hands. 'Ezra wants to mentor me. He wants to train me and I said no.'

'You said no.'

'Aren't I allowed to say no?'

He shrugs. 'You have every right.'

'There's a "but" there, isn't there?'

He moves to sit down on the edge of my bed. '*But*, you have to train. After the final Ordeal, we know you have untapped potential and with the great hunt underway—'

'Treat me like your girlfriend and not an asset, please. Don't see me the way they do.'

'Girlfriend?' he says quietly, a small smile flickering on his lips.

I open then close my mouth. 'Yes.'

'Which makes me your . . .'

'Boyfriend,' I say, smiling, and wander over to him. He opens his knees and I stand between his legs, wrapping my arms around his neck as he peers up at me. His eyes catch the light from the window, fracturing into chestnut, oak, caramel . . . I could stare at him for hours. 'I'm frustrated. I was hoping Hess would step up. I can't stand to work with Ezra. It took everything in me to get away from him, and now he's here. Like I didn't risk my life to escape.'

'And you're grieving. Hester, Greg . . .' he says. 'I don't see you as an asset. Well, not in the same way *they* do . . .'

I chuckle, lowering my face to his and kiss him, relishing the distraction, even if it's only temporary. 'What exactly makes me *your* asset, Locke?'

'Hmm,' he says, kissing me again before wrapping his arms around me and falling backwards onto the bed. I gasp, tumbling onto his chest, my hands trapped behind his neck still as his gaze sweeps over me slowly, as though drinking me in. Instantly, my heart matches the steady thump of his, calm and rhythmic. 'Maybe this . . .' he says, moving his hands down my back, spreading them over my thighs and gripping them through the workout leggings I'm still wearing. 'Or this . . .' His hands move up to my backside, squeezing gently and I bend my mouth to his jaw, nipping kisses along it. 'Maybe just all of you,' he says, his voice a gentle rumble that warms me right to my toes.

I pull back slightly, tracing the planes of his face, taking him in. 'I love you, too.'

He growls, low in his throat and flips me so I'm beneath him. 'We have twenty minutes before our next lecture, DeWinter, and I think you're distracting me on purpose.'

'Can't we stay here? They won't miss us,' I say, grinning as he kisses me again, closing my eyes as the weight of his body settles over me. 'Just a few more minutes . . .'

He's quiet for a moment and I look up at him. 'What is it?'

'I'm just thinking about what I could do to you in *just a few minutes . . .*'

I chuckle, but the sound is swallowed up by his lips, his kiss deepening deliciously. I open my mouth, allowing his tongue to sweep inside, and arch my hips slightly, pressing into him. I feel him respond, swelling against me, and all I want is to pretend we're anywhere but here. Lock the door and forget the great hunt, Killmarth, lectures . . . everything. My heartbeat quickens as he runs a hand down my side, his fingertips grazing my skin. I shiver. He's all deep kisses and heat, the curves of us melding together and everything outside this room dissolves. His kisses trail down to my throat and I moan softly, wanting more than anything for time to stand still.

He groans, breaking off the kisses and buries his face in the bed next to my shoulder. 'You'll be the death of me.'

I grin, arching again, and he rises, leaning on his elbow to stare down at me beneath him. 'Stay here tonight.'

'Is that a command or a request?' he says, smiling down at me.

'Both? No. A command,' I say. I check my wristwatch and wince. 'All right, we really do have to get a move on.'

He nods, rolling off me, and I get up, tidying my hair, peeling the workout clothes from my body, and cross to the bathroom. 'Tonight,' I toss over my shoulder with a wink, as I lean my naked hip against the doorframe, feeling his gaze burn into my skin.

'Tonight,' he agrees readily.

★

The day passes in a blur, Tessa's seat empty beside mine. I try to focus, reminding myself that I fought to be here. I completed four Ordeals, I danced with death and somehow, walked away with my heart still beating. I push away all thoughts of the cold ones, Ezra, Lewellyn's final moments, Tessa's grief . . . and I make notes. I listen to the professors. I try my hardest to forget the war beyond these walls.

Even in the midst of turmoil, Killmarth carries on with its scholarly endeavours. And as a freshly minted scholar, along with the other first years, we gain an introduction to each type of wielding. It's botany this afternoon, a few hours to inhale the scent of green and loam in the glass structure in Fetlock. Professor Grant, our esteemed head, leads us through a workshop on how botany can be used to heal. Charlotte, one of the botanist wielders, coaxes a collection of seedlings into faster growth, biting her lip in concentration as she pauses their acceleration before they begin to wane and wither away.

Grant's keen eyes flash in my direction before she nods to Alden. 'Locke, your turn. A demonstration on Frances. Make a small cut on the back of your hand if you will, Frances, that's it, staunch the flow, that's it . . . now Locke, talk me through a poultice you would make, laced with your magic that will accelerate healing.'

'Then apply it?' Alden asks.

'Precisely.'

Alden blinks quickly, then moves forward as Professor Grant wheels back, everyone gathering close to watch him grab a pestle and mortar, a bottle of boiled, clean water, Epsom salts, a bowl and a tiny bottle of oil. As he begins selecting leaves to shred, explaining their properties and how they will act together to draw out infection, speed healing and reduce inflammation, Knox leans in closer to my ear. 'Makes sense they've selected him for the team.'

'Do you think they'll assign him to work with this team of botanists developing the nocturnal?' I murmur back, watching on as Alden makes a small joke, Frances smiling, and offering up her cut hand.

'Perhaps,' Knox says. 'I was more considering the kind of situations we'll find ourselves in. A botanist with a good grasp of plant lore and application for healing is useful, yes?'

I pinch my lips together. I hadn't considered the attributes we are all bringing to this newly formed team, and why. 'A botanist, two alchemists, a masquier, two werewolves . . .'

'Who are also adept wielders . . .'

'The healer, the portal makers, the what, thief? The brawn.'

'Or spy.' He shrugs. 'And all of us trained in combat.'

'Knox, something to share with us all?' Grant asks quietly and I look around, finding her eyes not fixed on him, but on me.

'Merely making an observation to DeWinter here about how good Locke is with his . . . hands.'

The group of scholars titter quietly, glancing at me, and I battle the flare of heat in my cheeks. Grant clears her throat, looking away, and Alden continues on, his audience recaptured as his magic weaves over Frances's hand and the poultice.

'Are you sure you were included in the team for your strength as an alchemist, Knox?' I mutter.

He smiles knowingly. 'Sleight of hand, I would say. Draw lots of attention in one direction, say with the snap of moonlit jaws . . .'

'Whilst you slip a stake beneath their ribs?'

'Exactly.'

The rest of the afternoon trails away into a candlelit supper in Fetlock, surrounded by plants and botanists, before I take Alden's hand, lead him back to my bedroom in Gantry and finish what we started. I tug at his pullover, and with an easy grin, he shrugs it off, discarding it on the floor. Then I move to undo the buttons on his shirt, but he captures my hands. 'One for one?'

I chuckle. 'All right. But I get to choose.' Then I kick off one of my brogues and he laughs. 'Now the shirt.' I tip my face to his, his fingers caressing my jawline as he kisses me softly, my heart fluttering within the cage of my ribs. I kick off my other shoe next, as he's stood before me, shirtless, his lean frame muscled from all the training we've been doing over the last semester.

'Socks next, or are you feeling brave?' he murmurs.

I raise my chin, keeping his eyes pinned to mine as I undo the buttons on my trousers, sliding them slowly over my hips. His eyes travel down, watching as the waistband skims my thighs and pools around my feet. 'I'm always brave.'

He leans in, kissing me again, unbuttoning my own shirt slowly as I reach for his belt buckle. The heat builds beneath my skin, the longing for him. I've wanted him all day. 'Watching you wield earlier, creating the poultice to heal . . .'

'You like watching me wield?' he asks, undoing the final button before bringing his hands up to my shoulders to drag the shirt slowly down my arms. His movements are controlled, slow. Methodical. And I find it's driving me wild. My blood hums beneath my skin, hot and thrumming, as heat pools between my thighs.

'I like watching you work with your hands, Locke,' I tease, my pulse racing faster, the ache in my core growing more insistent. 'Now your turn, trousers.'

When we're down to our underwear, I draw him to my bed, the contours of his body moulding with mine as he kisses me, still feather light. I run my fingers down his arm, the one that bears the scars from our final Ordeal. The threads of silver, the burn of intense magic that covers his skin from shoulder to wrist. We are so fortunate to be here after all that has happened and I don't take him, or us for granted. I sink into the warm light of his touch, taking it slowly, allowing him to coax me until I'm ready, even as I twist the sheets in my fists, the anticipation overwhelming all other thoughts. I gasp as he enters me, as our bodies twine together. 'Like this?' he asks.

'Yes,' I manage, matching his rhythm, building in tempo as our control breaks. He rocks against me, every fibre of my being alight at the sensation of him, every fibre begging for more, more, more. And Alden, generous as he is, complies with wicked abandon, pressing deeper and closer and harder until I can no longer tell where his body ends and mine begins. His mouth finds mine, hot and wet, and I taste the salt of his sweat on his lips before I catch his lower lip between my teeth, nipping, drawing out a low growl, the friction between us delicious and overwhelming. And then we are both falling, tumbling over the edge together.

I fall asleep in his arms, listening to the waves beating the rocks outside the window and wonder how many nights we'll get like this. When it's just me and him, tangled together in the soft candle-light of my room, safe within the walls of Killmarth. If we'll both survive.

Chapter 4

A Fine Night for a Wedding

The bells clatter and clatter. I'm running, running from something, something with teeth and a shadow vaster than the world and the air is so heavy, I can't make my limbs work. There's a portal up ahead, in a sea of darkness, the intense imprint of that shadow almost consuming me whole. I gasp, but find I can't breathe, everything is turgid and wrong, I try to scream, grasping at nothing, that portal disappearing beyond my fingertips, even as I'm reaching, reaching—

Air floods my lungs as I fling myself upright.

But the bells are still clattering, the shadows still looming and as I flatten my palm against the cold wall, I know I'm at Killmarth.

But the bells . . . the bells aren't in my nightmare. They're real. It's the alarm bell in the Keeper's Hall, chasing me awake. And we're no longer in reserve; this is a call to arms. To fight.

'Alden,' I croak, shaking his shoulder before bolting from my bed and stubbing my toe. I swear, the jolt of pain setting my teeth on edge as I pull on my underwear. 'Alden!' He stirs, then swears as well.

'An attack,' he says, rising swiftly, grabbing his shirt to pull on. 'I'll meet you in the courtyard.'

'Unless they're in Killmarth again,' I say, crossing to look out of the window. But all is still, full night wrapping the panes of smoky glass.

'It won't be here. They never attack twice in the same location.' He bends down to kiss my temple then walks swiftly to the door. 'Bring all your stakes. And Sophia . . .'

I look up at him. 'I know.'

'Nothing foolish.' He grips my arms, kissing me again, this time on the mouth, deeper. Harder. When he breaks away, he searches my eyes. 'I can't lose you.'

'I promise,' I whisper before he releases me, heading once more for the door. I pull on a shirt, a jacket made of supple fabric I can move in and thick close-cut leggings. Before pulling on my boots, I turn up the collar on the jacket, feeling the phantom bite of those teeth from a month ago. This will be the first time I work with my team outside of training and my entire being is fizzing and sparking. I don't know if we're ready. But we have to be.

Suppressing a shudder, willing the phantom sense of that jaw clamped around my throat to subside, I hurriedly strap a stake to each of my thighs and rush out of the door. Scholars are moving through the dimly lit corridors, either dressed as I am or shepherding other scholars to the common rooms. We have been instructed to assemble in those if the attack bells ring, unless we've been told to be in the courtyard. We're all divided into teams now, some on alert, some in reserve and if one fails . . . I swallow. Another team will be ready to take their place. Most of the senior scholars are still in the field and the scholars that are still at Killmarth are on a rotation.

This time, I will be in the first team to respond.

'DeWinter, what a pleasant evening for it,' Knox says, falling into step beside me as we make for the staircase. He turns briefly, casting a glance at a young man stood in the corridor, watching us leave. Knox ruffles the back of his head with his hand, a pensive look crossing his features. 'Blake is worried.'

'I hope you told him you'll be back by breakfast,' I say, smiling at him. 'He can save us seats in Gantry.'

Knox huffs a small laugh. 'Your optimism is either misplaced, or naive.'

We take the stairs two at a time, passing the other landings. 'You don't think we're ready?'

'Not in the slightest,' he says quietly, eyes flitting to meet mine. 'They're calling us up because everyone else is exhausted. You can't wield from an empty well.'

'Fall into your lines!' Caroline calls in her clipped, icy tone as we enter the courtyard. 'Knox, DeWinter, so glad you could join us.'

I get into place behind Tessa, who is trembling. I almost tell her to sit this one out, but as I glance at Caroline and Hess, I realise that's not an option. And knowing Tessa, she would never admit to being too weak right now for a fight.

I look back, seeing Alden, Frances and Belle, all stood in line before one mirror. Knox, Tessa and I are in front of another. 'Only one Darley on this one?' I ask Knox softly.

'He's probably already there,' Knox says through the corner of his mouth. 'Most likely the person who raised the alarm.'

'Oh. Of course.' He wouldn't sit this out at all. He'll be there already. I keep finding it hard to marry up this Ezra that Knox knows, who works for the Crown, who defends Kellend . . . with the Ezra I grew up with. The Collector.

'Remember, no isolating yourselves. Stay with your team, cover each other, communicate. Another team is already in place, sent by the Crown. A fuller response is being prepared,' Hess says, striding towards the mirrors. 'This will be triggering after the attack on Killmarth.' He blinks quickly, turning to the mirrors. 'But you have the advantage. We are surprising them this time. Use every weapon at your disposal. Act without mercy.'

Hess holds his palms out to the mirrors and gold threads blast from his palms. I squint as the light burns my retinas, knowing that no one else here can see what I see. His wielding. His alchemy magic at work. The mirrors settle into distorted images of another place. A lawn before a great, sprawling house, chairs and tables and strings of beautiful, delicate lights. Flower arrangements, a platform swathed in white . . . and people everywhere, screaming. Cold ones viciously attacking them.

'Oh gods . . .' I say softly. 'It's a wedding party.'

'Scholars, with me,' Hess says. 'For Killmarth, for Kellend. For the Crown.' Then he charges through, magic blasting from his palms like lightning.

Tessa growls and shivers, as though shucking off her own skin, her masquier magic agitating the air surrounding her. Then she pounces through the portal and on the other side—

She becomes a werewolf.

Stake in hand, I follow her through. Into a field of night and blood, into a world echoing with terror. I land on one knee, hand hitting the ground. Then I look up, assessing the terrain. Cold ones are everywhere, feeding or chasing their prey, and as I watch, two more werewolves leap out of the portal on my left side. Belle and Frances. They make quick work of a cold one, Belle digging her claws into the woman's shoulder blades, Frances ripping out her throat. I take a breath then race over, raising my stake to drive it through her heart. Dust plumes around me and I find myself staring into a werewolf's eyes . . . Belle's eyes, flecked with ochre, before she grunts and chases after her next kill.

The ground is littered with bodies. The wedding guests like rag dolls, suits and dresses and furs slashed with blood, unseeing eyes raised to the stars. Fireworks suddenly fizz and pop, reigning over the night sky, and I glance up, seeing a dusting of gold stars pluming overhead. Then more crackle, another flying into the air with a high-pitched scream before bursting in a cloud of red. There's a pile of them, all ready for a display, flames licking at their edges in the centre of the lawn. One ignites, flying sideways and narrowly misses Tessa as she leaps, hitting a hedge and exploding in a frenzy of blue and smoke.

This should have been the moment for toquay and delight, instead it's chaos. Another massacre. A cold one darts past, clawing for a guest who's trying to flee. He fastens his arms around the man's suited back like a lover, dipping his mouth to his throat . . . and bites. The air unleashes from my lungs as I begin moving towards them, a throb of panic erupting in my mind. Fireworks continue lighting up the lawn and the bodies in flashes of colours, whistles and booms puncturing the screams, adding to the confusion, the dissonance. When I reach them, I'm too late, the cold one taking one look at my stake and releasing the body of the man, his teeth pink from the blood, mania in his eyes. He bolts into the night, another firework illuminating his path towards the house, where I've no doubt more victims await.

A scream catches my attention, and I see the bride, dressed in white and lace, veil thrust back from her forehead, already bloodied. She's being herded by three cold ones. They're playing with her, I realise. She releases a ragged sob, holding out her hands as vines twist out of them. But the three males simply bat it all away before a single vine can ensnare them. I swear under my breath, knowing I've already broken the first rule. I haven't stayed with any of my team. I'm isolated. Alone. Looking up, I see Alden and whistle, pointing at the bride. He nods, approaching from the other side, and I close the distance, licking my lips.

I have to do something. I have to save someone. Anyone. All around us are the sounds of the battle, the howls and tearing from the werewolves, the feral gnashing of the cold ones, the shrieks of the wedding party as they're caught and drained, or fighting, wielding as best they can. And more fireworks, the explosions ringing like bombs in my ears, frying my nerves. But I have to block it out. I have to save one. Just one.

They won't have the bride.

I sneak up behind the first on silent feet, gripping his shoulder before swiftly staking him through the back. His head cracks backwards, greying hair brushing my fingertips before he is nothing but ash in my hand. Alden grabs for the second, slicing at his cheek before driving his stake through the cold one's chest. But the last one is too quick. In a hiss of hate, he clutches the bride's throat and simply . . . snaps.

Her eyes fasten on mine the moment her bones sever, and I feel the rush of air part my lips as the light dies in her eyes. My heartbeat drums in my ears, the shock pinning me in place then in a sudden, impossible rush, the last cold one is before me.

'Oh, it's you,' he says, grin horrible and wide.

'The fuck you're having her.' Alden growls and raw magic blasts into the cold one's side. The cold one smacks on the ground, his limbs splaying out at awkward angles. Then he looks up, dazed, to find Alden bearing down. 'Stay *put*.'

I watch in disbelief as Alden doesn't just stake him . . . he carves him up. It all happens so fast, blood splatters on the grass, the cold one begging, pleading . . . before Alden whispers something I don't hear, smashing his stake through the cold one's chest. Ash pools on the ground and I look back at the bride. She reminds me of Dolly. So frail now. Lifeless. 'Alden,' I croak, staggering over to him, and pull him up. 'We have to keep moving. There are more here. More people . . .' And I haven't saved one of them. I look around, finding the same scene, playing out across this lawn. Then

I realise. These people, this wedding party, they're not just human, there are many wielders.

All the wielders are botanists.

There's a yelp and I see in a flash of fireworks, a werewolf being herded. Five cold ones, two with their arms fastened around her sides, another moving in for a headlock. I find my feet, beginning to run, the scene so sickeningly familiar . . . then as another firework whistles, launching skyward, a crack. Her body slumps, the cold ones scurrying away like spiders. When I reach her, it's already too late.

Frances is dead.

Chapter 5

Hollow

The world turns dark and far away. Her fur is still warm as I place my hand on her head, as I brush my fingers over her ear. She's dead. Frances, with her blonde curls, who we saved from being poisoned just *weeks* ago, who was part of our team, one of us . . . she's just . . . dead. Dead like Dolly, like Greg, like Hester. Reality crashes in as I retract my hand, staring around at the carnage. Fireworks still explode, dusting the dark with lurid light. The hedge along one side of the lawn is alight, the flames creeping ever closer to the main house. Cold ones, in swoops and flashes, fight the guests still left and my team. Belle, across the lawn, throws back her head and howls in a cry of mourning. I stagger to stand as my gaze lands on Alden's, his eyes on Frances. That'll be us if we don't fight. This isn't training, this isn't an assignment, it isn't even an Ordeal. I need to get my shit together or I *am* going to die.

Vine and thorns twist from the outstretched hands of three guests a few feet away, magic blasting as they wield. Questions blare in my mind about who they are, why they're all botanists, but before I can even verbalise one to Alden, I spot Ezra near the house, combatting two cold ones. He trips one, slashing at an ankle, and stakes the other, a cloud of ash and dust hiding him from view in the flash and bang of a golden rain firework. The wedding guests are too scattered, clutching wounds, eyes wide and frightened, but there are cold ones leaving, as though in a managed, planned retreat.

'Belle and Tessa are herding them all onto the lawn, there,' I say to Alden, grabbing his arm as I see them snapping at the retreating cold ones, blocking their escape from the lawn. My mind snaps from confusion and overwhelm into focus so suddenly, it's jarring, but I have a plan. Just one . . . save *just one*. I'm flailing, this is all too much, and it's a shit plan, a desperate plan, but I have to do something. *Save just one.*

'Where's Knox? We can take them out if we stay in that spot.'

Alden nods, assessing the lawn quickly, and scans for his friend. 'Over there.'

We surge forward, helping Knox take out a female cold one, red hair glinting under ravenous eyes. I quickly relay the plan and he agrees, moving with us. I can't see Hess anywhere, but with Ezra by the house, it means the wedding party, or those who are left, can stagger inside and shelter. I only hope Ezra has cleared the house itself and secured it.

Then we await our prey. Belle and Tessa snap their wide jaws, cold ones stumbling back . . . right into our path. We take out three, making quick work of them, and I glance up, finding Tessa just a few feet away. But she's no longer in the form of a werewolf. Now she's herself, a stake in each fist. And I've never seen such hate.

She grips one by the collar, forcing him to the ground. Then she stakes him through the throat, pinning him in place, a gurgle of blood choking him. She whispers something I don't hear, head bent low, and as she pins his arms either side of his chest with her knees, she drives the stake in. Slowly. I watch with growing horror as the stake finally rips through his body, his flesh decomposing to nothing but dust. When she rises, her gaze locks with mine. Blood spatters her cheekbone like a gash. But her eyes . . . her eyes are hollow.

Empty. And I realise these monsters took more than Greg from her that day. They carved away a piece of her soul.

I approach her carefully, taking her hand in mine, and lead her past the dying, the blood, the final cold ones that the others are picking off. I lead her to the edge of the lawn and I wrap my arms around her. 'I'm so sorry, Tessa.'

She catches sight of Frances, still slumped on the ground. And her body shakes and shakes.

*

Killmarth is calm when we return through the portals. A breeze of ice and salt moans through the courtyard, a gull crying overhead as it wheels through the night. I take Tessa back to her room, waiting for her while she rinses away the blood and dirt of the battle. I wish there was a way to wash all her pain away as well. But when it's soul-deep like this, it can't be bandaged or stitched. It might always be this way. She might never find her way back to the self she was before. I can still feel Frances's fur on my fingertips, the spectre of it whispering as my mind bleeds fireworks and glinting teeth. The booms and fizz and shrieks eclipse my thoughts, dragging me back to that lawn and I'm frozen again. Frozen, like in my nightmares, except it was real. It was all real.

A gentle knock startles me and I stand up to open the door, smoothing my hands over my jacket, willing the tremors to calm. Alden is standing there, still as blood spattered as I am. His eyes are dark, swirling and troubled. 'Ezra and Caroline have called us all to Darley.'

'When?' I ask, glancing over my shoulder as Tessa walks back into her bedroom. Her features are listless as she pulls a thick camel-wool jumper from a drawer and puts it on. I half close the door, blocking her from view, and murmur, 'She's tired. She needs rest, food . . .'

'She needs something no one can give her, Sophia,' Alden says softly. 'You know that as well as I. Ten minutes. I'll see you there.'

Only Knox and Tessa have freshened up, the rest of us still in the clothes we wore to fight the cold ones. Tessa walks in ahead of me, taking a chair in the furthest corner, and I can't help but study every movement. Worry for my friend, for her heart, is ringing as a warning in my ears, slowly increasing in intensity. She's still in shock. Right at the beginning of her grief, and now she is being asked to draw herself together, lock it away in a chest, and fight. I know we are at war, but I can't help but fear for the toll this will take. That is, if she survives. Frances flashes again in my mind and my stomach lurches.

'As you all will have gathered, the cold ones ambushed a wedding, a secret wedding in a manor house to the west of the Pendle Woods,' Ezra says with lethal calm. 'We have rushed the few who survived the attack to the Crown's own botanists and medical team in Dinas Tar. But this attack was planned, swift and brutal in its execution. Even with our intervention, few will make it to see the dawn. If any.'

I shiver and cross my arms. Now I've stopped, the cold has seeped into the marrow of my bones and I can't seem to get warm. All I can see is the bride I failed to save. Frances. That man in a suit as he slumps into the grass.

'The Crown thanks you for your service,' Caroline adds, eyeing us. 'And we would not usually have called you all in straight after for a debrief without giving you a chance to rest. However, we believe we have been compromised.'

Ezra clears his throat. 'I track every person of interest to myself and the Crown and fortunately, I was able to raise the alarm and ask

Caroline to assemble a team of you to intervene alongside me. But that kind of coordinated, premeditated attack was similar to what unfolded here. And that wedding was secret for a reason, only those closest to the Crown knew of it.'

'Eddie . . .' Caroline says, as though in warning.

'It's better they know, Caro,' he says. 'Every guest at that wedding was either a close family member or a member of the special botanist team working on the elixir, our cure for vampirism. Our strongest, most lethal weapon in our fight against the cold ones and their hunts.'

A ripple of unease runs through us all.

'And their research?' Knox asks quietly.

'What they carried with them to that wedding, gone,' Caroline says, blinking quickly. 'Their laboratory is still intact, their older, established research is heavily guarded. We are waiting on word from the medical team working on the few survivors so that we can speak to them individually. And ascertain if any of them can still work, if any of them will survive, or if we have lost the most vital part of the project. The wielders themselves.'

'We suspect an Allowayan agent may have been planted in the team,' Ezra says with undisguised bitterness. 'Be aware and be careful. Tell no one, not even your fellow scholars about the events that occurred last night. Where there is one mole, there may be more. Perhaps they were in that team of botanists. But we can't rule out the possibility that it was one of us.'

*

'We have to talk about what happened,' I say the next day to Alden. He's sitting with his back to me and I note his shoulders stiffen. 'When that cold one came at me, you were . . . brutal.'

For a moment, he says nothing. Then, 'I couldn't bear it. He was going to hurt you. And you . . . you'd frozen.'

I release a breath, going to him. Wrapping my arms around him, I place my head on his shoulder and sense some of the tension leave him. 'The great hunt, the cold ones . . . we weren't meant for this. Any of it.'

He dips his head, closing his eyes. 'When I watched him step towards you, it was like he was all of them, all wrapped up in one monster. The one who killed my father. Greg. Lewellyn. Those hopefuls that had just become scholars. And all I felt was rage.' He brings his hand up to mine. 'I want vengeance so badly, and carving up that bastard was all I cared about. I have these moments, these times when I cannot control how much I loathe them. What they've taken from me, from all of us . . .'

I close my eyes, pressing a kiss to his throat. 'That's what I'm afraid of. That they'll take your humanity as well. We will avenge them all, Alden, I promise. But not at the cost of becoming monstrous ourselves. Look at Fion. How twisted she had become, how single-minded in her pursuit of glory.'

'I'm not like her.'

'No. But I wonder who she might have been without all that hate instilled in her. All that loathing in her heart. I wonder if she might have been like us.'

Chapter 6

A Garden of Graves

The gravestones glitter with pale frost in the morning light gilding the cemetery. Wards have been placed around the whole churchyard on the outskirts of Marazia for the funeral, just inland where the cliffs give way to a patchwork of fields. Killmarth is across that short stretch of ocean, the path through the sea enclosed by the frothing tide. As I look up, I can see the steam train chugging away from the station, steam exhaling from its sleek black body, like an animal finally unleashed. So long ago, it feels that I made the journey down here. My fingers find the space where that bracelet used to be. Before I broke it, not realising freedom also meant the end of the Collector's protection.

It hasn't changed anything though. I'm still a tight ball of bitterness.

The small church, formed of granite stonework, rises up from the landscape like a grey tooth, as though it is nothing more than an outcrop of the rock found everywhere along this coastline, that was mined and honed in dedication to the gods. Stained-glass windows depicting their valour and benevolence stretch across one side, facing the dawn. One for each of the main gods, Gallant, Aline and Argus, all depicted with their faces upturned to the stars and sun, wearing gowns and robes to symbolise their divine reign. The Attestations is kept on the altar at the centre of the church, rows of pews fanning out around it. We sit, listening to the rise and fall of the sermon, and I twitch incessantly throughout, longing to leave. It's only when we are allowed out into the blush grey day that I feel I can breathe again. Such a small space cannot contain such a swell of stifling grief.

Greg's family especially are gaunt as crows, standing here now in the graveyard. I can hear every sniff, every throat that catches, every scrape of a fingertip over the order of service. It is as if the very world is holding its breath, crowding in to bear witness alongside us. But it isn't until his father begins to weep that I want to run out of the graveyard, away from that church protruding like a solitary tooth, away from the gathering of sorrow, and never return.

Tessa stands beside me, the soft breeze lifting a winding curl from her temple. Her eyes are no longer hollow. They're set. Dark, hard pebbles that bore into his gravestone, like she can chip his name away and carve someone else's there instead. It's almost worse than the hollow void she has been since his death. Now, that void is filled with something that isn't Tessa. And I don't know how to bring her back.

Frances's family did not want to inter her body to the earth here. They took her away silently and no one has spoken of her since. Like a severed limb, the phantom shape of her remains, worrying at all of us, an aching absence that we can't fill with grief or rage. It is hard to mourn a sudden absence.

'We give his body to the land, so it may feed the world . . .' the vicar says, her kind eyes drifting over all of us congregated.

I chance a look to my left and Alden glances at me, before his hand finds mine, squeezing my fingers.

'. . . Aline will greet Greg in her gentle fields . . .'

There's a shuddering sob, then another and I see Hess turn on his heel, walking away across the graveyard.

'. . . just as Gallant and Argus will measure his soul and find the great and good in the weight of it. And so, to the land, to the sky, to the journey . . .'

Tessa brings a handkerchief to her face, dabbing at a solitary tear.

'We commit you, Greg, for it is their will.'

The vicar steps back as members of his family grip shovels, beginning the labour of putting his soul to rest. It hasn't been safe until now for us all to gather here, so many wielders, so much blood pulsing with magic. The wards woven around this graveyard and church are intricate. Strong as steel. For the length of this service, no cold ones will break in.

I breathe in the loam, hidden amidst the sharp frost and it takes me back to that night I buried someone I loved more than anyone in this world. Dolly. I close my eyes, forcing away the image of that night. The cold rain on my skin, the hopelessness in my heart. And when I open them again, I find Ezra staring at me. As though he knows what I picture and who I am remembering.

'I'm going to put some flowers on Hester's grave,' I murmur to Tessa then slip my fingers from Alden's grip and walk around to the other side of the graveyard. It's freshly dug, this grave, but her family wanted a private gathering. Only her brother, her father and a cousin present. I expect to find Hess there now, but he's over by the wrought iron fence, facing the cliffs. Staring out to sea. I don't disturb him. Instead I draw out the small posy Alden coaxed for me from seed in Fetlock, asphodel and rosemary. The flowers of regret, and eternal memory.

'A fitting choice,' a voice says behind me.

I don't turn. That voice, on the other side of the vault, an iron-clad will between me and freedom that followed me through my childhood nightmares for years. 'She deserved better. They both did.'

I don't need to say her name. He knows who I speak of. Dolly

Love, the eighty-year-old chain smoker with a thin grasp on illusion, a better grasp of cards and the fiercest heart I've ever known.

'More like her will die if we do not end this, Sophia.'

I sigh through my nose, feeling my patience ebb away. 'Not here. Not now.'

'When, then?' he asks quietly, stepping up beside me. 'When more people die? When another of your *friends* dies?'

'I will not give you power over me again,' I say through gritted teeth.

He snorts. 'Do you think I wanted to be your guardian? Do you think I asked for the charge of a girl I barely knew? All I needed was to protect you. That bracelet kept you safe.'

'It kept me subservient,' I hiss, snapping my gaze to meet his.

He doesn't blink, only smiles sadly. 'Fine. I am already the villain in your story. But know what you are choosing this time by not allowing me to train you. Your magic is strong, yes. But you do not know how to access it at will. You do not know control, or how deep that well is—'

'Hess can teach me.'

'Hess is a damn shell,' Ezra growls, flashing his anger for the first time before he takes a breath. 'There is a mole in Caroline's team. Alloway threatens our fragile peace. The great hunt is not over and our best asset has been damaged, possibly beyond repair. We need alchemists. We need *strength*.'

'I can create bridges. I can manipulate nonliving matter.'

'You didn't wield once in the attack on the wedding,' he says. 'Not *once*. Why?'

'I . . . it was dark. Confusing.'

'Then you must learn to thrive in chaos, Sophia. Have I not taught you to adapt?'

I close my eyes, tipping my face to the sky, and feel the first soft touch of a snowflake. When I open my eyes, the churchyard has darkened, the sky above muffled in white. Snowflakes drift down, growing more frequent, and I breathe in the pure scent of winter. 'This conversation is over, Ezra. We are at a funeral.'

'Just . . . think on it. If you change your mind, I will be in Darley at midnight.'

He turns, stepping away, and the words tumble out, unbidden. 'I froze.'

He pauses.

'At the wedding, I froze. It can't happen again, I know that.'

He says nothing.

'I need to make sure.'

His lips part. 'Of what?'

'That I don't freeze again,' I say. 'Not ever again.' Then I look at him. 'But I don't trust you, Ezra. I think there's us, then there's the Crown, and there's you. And there may come a time that you have to pick just one, and I don't trust you to pick us.'

He swallows, looking at me, and in his eyes I see I'm right. We both know it.

With one final glance at Hester's grave, I go back to Tessa. He doesn't follow.

★

But later, the questions without answers loop through my mind. I lie awake, staring at the pattern of moonlight and shadow on the ceiling, thinking about Tessa. About Greg. About Hester Lewellyn and Professor Hess. The memory of Alden from the night of the wedding surfaces. How he carved that cold one up slowly. Purposefully.

In the pursuit of peace, will the cracks of war appear within ourselves?

What matters most, my pride, my integrity . . . or those I love?

Just how far would I go?

The questions chase me from my bed at quarter to midnight. I pull on my boots, wrapping a coat around my nightdress. With only a candle in a sconce to light my way, I hurry down the corridors of Gantry and cross the courtyard, slipping between shadows. I find him in the room we use for meetings. Waiting in the dark.

'I have one condition,' I say. 'After this is over, after we've defeated them, I will no longer be considered an asset by anyone. Not by you, Caroline, the Crown . . . I will be free to do as I please. To study, to learn. As I choose to.'

Ezra Darley shrugs. 'Agreed. When the great hunts end, we will all be free to be who we were meant to be.'

He pauses, and in that space between words, I sense another man. One with dreams, with friends, with a life teeming with hope for the future. Then he blinks and it's lost, the shutters drawn down once more on all that he may have been.

'Now, let us begin.'

Part 2

Abandon all hope, ye who enter here.

~Dante Alighieri

Chapter 7

Fury is Better than Fear

Confusion and chaos are the weapons he wields. And Ezra Darley is a relentless foe.

'Ah, fuck!' I hiss as a weighted ball whistles past my ear, followed by a bar weight rolling at my unprotected ankles. I duck, roll and come up in a crouch, my back to the wall. Sweat glistens along my hairline, heart racing under my training vest. Knox vaults to the side, narrowly missing being bludgeoned as well before slamming up against the wall a few feet away. And Ezra just raises an eyebrow, utterly impassive from the other side of the gym.

'If you're always on the defence, you'll get yourself killed,' he calls across, over the soundtrack of off-beat, shrieking music he's set up from alchemist-made speakers. The gym of Killmarth in the basement is our training ground today. And he's simulating an attack, combining sensory overload with a completely random set of obstacles to overcome. The lighting is low, the shadows stretch like overfed cats and there's a storm cloud brewing in my temples. When the cold ones attacked us here at Killmarth, I used my power to move stakes through the air . . . but it was in the moment. I've tried and failed to budge a single object since, and yet Ezra is able to control every damn piece of nonliving matter in this gym with cold precision. 'Use your magic. Push them away, or better yet, turn them on *me*.'

'I'm . . . trying to.' I pant through gritted teeth, as, with the merest flick of his index finger, a set of smaller balls used for bat and ball games roll across the gym floor, hitting my side in a torrent. I push out my magic, pleading, *begging* each of those balls not to hit me, but no use. 'Gah!'

Knox manages to leap out of the way in time, wielding so the balls aimed for him change from weighted balls and bats into a flurry of bubbles. I glare at him and he shrugs. 'Be quicker and you'll get fewer bruises.'

'Fury is better than fear, Sophia, but only if it sharpens you,' Ezra intones. 'Knox is neither furious nor fearful. What does that tell you? You cannot always rely on crude wielding or raw magic. Use your well wisely.'

I swipe at the balls with an out-flung arm, asking them to change into something harmless, cotton wool, fluffy as clouds . . . but they just bounce off the floor, rolling away, stubbornly the same as before. I swear again, frustrated with myself. In moments of high stress, of panic, I'm finding it harder and harder to wield at all.

'You've only had a taste of what the cold ones are capable of. You will have to learn to detach in an attack, to leave your heart behind and when one of your friends dies, which they will—'

'Why are you saying this—'

'—it won't rattle you so much that you stop *moving*. The moment you stop is the moment you're dead. We had great hopes with the elixir, perhaps foolish hopes . . . but now our wielders, particularly our alchemists, are really our only defence. You must be better, Sophia. Stop being so polite with your power and *command it*. Don't ask these objects to change their nature. Imagine that is what they already are. Tell them, tell yourself, that is what they are.'

I dodge another weighted ball and this time I force my will into it. I wield, amending its very nature, telling myself it's simply a ball of wool. It rolls across the ground, unravelling, a long length of green wool trailing across the gym. Knox smiles, distracted, and a similar weighted ball pounds into his side. 'That's it!' he says, coughing and rubbing his hip. 'You're getting it.'

I look at Ezra, but his features remain impassive. Unimpressed. 'It's a start.' Then he waves his hand, the wool gathering itself back up, turning into a weighted ball. 'Cold ones crave the blood of an alchemist the most. That's why our numbers are dwindling, they're simply picking us off first in each great hunt. We're a feast of magic to them. An alchemist's blood is the most potent. You must always be aware, always ready to wield. To defend yourselves.'

'So I'm a weapon and a target?' I say, dodging a rattle of weights as they roll across the gym floor, Knox doing the same before he wields, successfully turning half of them into more bubbles. The other half he has to leap and hop over, before one takes him out. I grunt as I run, hopping over the last one, then reaching for a bar bell I wield, telling it to change entirely. That it's a stake, a wooden stake. The cool metal warms to wood in my fist and I thrust it up at Ezra's exposed throat—

To find an iron blade awaiting it. 'Better,' he says, shortly before a handful of tennis balls bludgeon the side of my head. I retreat, wiping the sweat from my forehead, and narrow my eyes. He's so damn calm. It's infuriating. I glance over at Knox and see he, at least, is a little more ruffled than usual. 'All right, we'll call time for today,' he says, checking his watch. 'You've got a lecture with Hess in half an hour. Knox, you need the practice. Sophia, don't skip a single training session. It could be the difference between your life or theirs.'

Ezra leaves me to clear up the mess of the gym and I wave Knox away, knowing he didn't get a chance to eat breakfast this morning and I did. I'm grateful for the sudden silence as the chaotic music cuts out. The lights glow brighter, banishing the shadows, and the weight pressing on my chest diminishes. I can breathe again. I blink, slightly dazed, and mutter curses as my gaze flickers over the practice weapons, weights and equipment littering the ground. His one stipulation is that I tidy up and wield until each object is exactly the same as before. Exactly.

It takes me fifteen minutes to get the gym back in order before I pelt up the staircase of Gantry to change and clean up. By the time I reach the lecture hall on the floor below, the other eight scholars are waiting, all alchemists. As is Professor Hess. He doesn't say a word as I cross the front of the room, spying Knox with a vacant seat next to him. I slip in beside him with a grateful smile but he doesn't even turn to acknowledge me. He's tapping his pen on a notebook, which I notice is thick with marked pages and notes. He places an index finger on an underlined word and I nod, understanding. Tactics. This is his playbook, the one he's taken with him across territories whilst working for the Collector, his uncle.

Hess clears his throat and I pull out my own notebook and fountain pen, trying to relax my aching shoulders and ignore the throbbing storm in my temples. I may be a stronger alchemist than illusionist, but I'm learning it still takes its toll.

'All right, now we have a full complement, let us make a start.' Hess flicks his fingers and a piece of chalk levitates, writing on the blackboard behind him. My eyes widen at the incredible control, the perfect penmanship as the chalk writes, 'The Great Hunts and Our Response'. He claps his hands and the chalk pauses but does not drop. 'Two lessons. Firstly, the control and movement of nonliving matter. As alchemists, some of you are now adept at changing the state of nonliving matter. Some of you can even create portals, manipulating your environment to create a bridge from one point to another. But this . . .' again, the chalk moves, writing out his points on the blackboard as a neat list, 'is another skill. Sophia, you were able to do this in a moment of intense pressure using your raw alchemy magic during the . . . the . . .' He swallows, blinking quickly, and I wonder if he's about to break again, if the eggshell of his mind is still coated in fissures. But then he takes a breath, composing himself. 'You commanded a series of spikes to volley through the air in the Keeper's Hall, pinning your enemies. Do you know how you did it?'

I shake my head.

'Could you do it again now?'

'I wouldn't know how,' I say honestly, thinking about what Ezra said earlier in training, how I must learn to wield with intention. With complete command.

'All right. Darcy, you're up. I know you've been practising with books . . .'

I look around the sparsely populated lecture room and catch the eye of the red-headed woman I saw on one of my first days here as a hopeful. She's still just as glamorous, her lips a sweep of maroon, eyes outlined in kohl, vivid auburn hair twisted up with a pencil, tendrils hanging around sharp cheekbones. She skips to the front, pouting as she expertly wields, a stack of heavy books levitating above her upturned hand. After a moment, she begins to frown, breathing more heavily until finally she grunts and the books thump on the floorboards. 'I can't manipulate them for long, they don't want to move, it's not a natural state.'

Hess wags his finger. 'Exactly. It's a short-term command, a tactic for a weapon mostly, to enable it to reach its target. It's a complex form of wielding, because you are commanding each atom not to change its natural state into another material, but to *move*. Your magic will deplete faster as it's wrapping around each and every particle, forcing motion. Darcy, you may return to your seat.'

She nods, seeming a little paler, and scoops up the pile of books before sitting back down.

'Senior scholars, I expect you to practise. Knox and Sophia, you'll be covering this in your training with Ezra. Now . . . on to the next subject of this session. Our response. The Crown have instructed the faculty to take a different approach this semester. Previously, we would not have even broached this subject until your third year. The great hunts are not widely broadcast to the public and as such, the response is a controlled one. But needs must, and unfortunately for you, you are all needed.' He hesitates, eyeing us all, and the piece of chalk writes on the blackboard behind him, just one word. Asset. I shiver, a full-body response to being regarded as such.

'As you are no doubt aware given the number of scholars surrounding you today, our numbers are few. Which is why every single one of you is regarded as a valuable asset to the Crown. With the . . . attack.' He swallows, turning to the board and plucking the piece of chalk from where it hovers in the air. 'And the immediate aftermath, we find ourselves in need of alchemists at every level. You have all been put into teams and you will all be called up. I'm afraid there is little time for rest over the coming weeks, and we ask that you attend every training session. Now, the tactical approach to working with your teams . . . Yes, Darcy?'

'Where are the others, professor?' she asks. 'One of the librarians is an alchemist, she's absent, and there are two others in my year, then one third year . . .'

Hess swallows. 'Those three are missing in the field, I'm afraid. Our librarian has been reallocated by the Crown.'

Missing in the field . . .

'You mean dead, don't you?' Darcy asks bluntly. 'Not missing. Dead.'

Hess flinches then nods. 'Most likely. Bodies not yet recovered.

But given that it was on the border with Alloway, and with their policy of not taking and holding prisoners—'

'Ruthless bastards,' another scholar mutters, dashing his pen on the desk before him. 'We should all be there, beating them bloody.'

'No, Soames,' Knox says quietly. 'We should all be here, as the Crown wishes, listening to Hess and preparing to be useful assets in the fight against the cold ones.'

Before Soames can retort, a scream rattles the windows. Shouts echo around the courtyard and we all begin scraping back our chairs, rushing to look out of the three large windows that overlook the courtyard. A portal, a shimmer of air, has been slashed across the centre and as we watch, a woman wearing the white and blue of the medical wing dashes out of the Keeper's Hall, holding a whistle to her lips. She blows it three times, succinct, ear-piercing blows, and I wince. There are already three bodies on the ground. Caroline is there, a tear in her trousers, blood in her hair . . .

I press my fingertips to my mouth. One of the bodies on the ground is missing its head entirely. Two women are screaming, blood drenching their combat uniforms.

'Shit . . .' Knox says softly beside me as Ezra leaps from the portal, followed by half a dozen other wielders, before he closes it swiftly. More medical staff flood the courtyard, Caroline directing them over the moans and screams of the wounded, the man missing his head just chugging blood over the ground. Soames turns and rushes for the door, hand clamped over his mouth, and I look at Knox. 'It's his cousin. Graduated two years ago.'

'Gods,' I breathe.

'All of you, stay put unless you are called for. I have to . . . I must . . .' Hess crosses to the door and closes it behind him. I stare down at the courtyard, the chaos as stretcher bearers emerge from the Keeper's Hall, as Professor Grant appears, instructing her staff calmly. The warning bell begins to clatter and some of the senior scholars around me look at each other, nodding.

'That's us,' Darcy says, smoothing down her clothes. 'The rest of you, into the common room you're assigned to if you've not been tapped for this wave. My team, with me.'

Knox tugs on my arm to pull me away from the window, to the common room where we'll gather until instructed otherwise. But before I turn away, Ezra glances up at the window, meeting my gaze. He's in charge of all of this now, I realise. He's practically managing the response to the great hunt now the Crown's forces are so divided between here and Theine's border. I'm under his command, yet again. Only this time, it's not just my liberty at stake. It's everyone's. His mouth twists in a grimace before he shakes his head, then continues calling orders. The teams readying for the response begin filtering down to the courtyard, just as the wounded and dead are carried away. I walk to the door as the bell clatters and clatters, feeling like my body is somewhere far away.

Chapter 8
Fireside

My team is not called up. A week flits by, each day consumed by training and lectures. The only time I have for Alden is at night, his limbs tangled with mine, both of us passing out from exhaustion. I search for Tessa when I can to check in on her, reminding her to eat, needing to know she's all right after the funeral. She reassures me she is and although I know she's really not, it's only the passage of time that can heal her fractured heart. I just wish I could give her more of my own time.

★

Something hard connects with my jaw. A picture frame. I groan, disorientated, and duck quickly behind an armchair, pressing my back into it as I gently touch the side of my face. He wielded from the other side of a damn door and sent a *picture frame* smacking into my face. 'Um, ow?'

'You felt that, did you?' Knox's muffled voice says dispassionately from behind the locked parlour door. 'Maybe try *moving faster*, DeWinter.'

'Asshole . . .' I mutter, shooting a glare at the door. We're in Alabaster House, which apparently isn't just used as a safe house and a place for hopefuls to gather for the Crucible. It's also used as a training ground. And this morning it's, in fact, a battleground. Me versus Knox Darley, and so far, he's absolutely owning me.

'Think outside the box, Sophia . . .' Ezra says from the corner of the parlour, watching me. 'Knox doesn't know exactly where you are in this room after all . . .'

'I know, I know, a moving target isn't a dead target.' I huff a breath, swinging to the side as a lamp hurtles across the room, shattering over the fireplace. He's been practising since that lecture with Hess. But so have I and now, I do the exact thing he doesn't expect. I vault for the door, unlocking it as I'm moving, forcing my will into the metal of the lock and twist. The door springs open and Knox raises his eyebrows in surprise, just as he's bludgeoned by a pile of leatherbound hardbacks. He shouts, covering his head, as I sprint past him, swinging through the hallway for the staircase. I leap up them two at a time, then fall flat on my face. The stair beneath my foot has simply disappeared.

'Really?' I gasp, forcing movement into my limbs as the stairs disappear, one by one. I find myself leaping for wooden stairs before they vanish, just as I reach the landing. I pant, crouched at the top and look down at him, a grin spreading over my face. 'Now how are *you* going to get up?'

But my grin is extinguished immediately. Because the stairs didn't vanish . . . they moved. Right to where he's standing. He steps up, and in a burst of golden light, wields so that the step moves through the air, towards me. I swear, scrambling back, and move to the one room I haven't checked yet, that until now, he's guarded. Damn he's a strong wielder. But I bet he'll burn himself out . . .

'Remember, Knox, if she finds the paperweight before you can conceal it . . .'

'She gets first pick of our next training exercise,' Knox says bitterly, his voice unnervingly close. 'But Ezra, you're forgetting—'

The paperweight I'm seeking flies over my head, straight into Knox's outstretched hand. 'She's still scrambling around, searching with her eyes, not her magic. She hasn't figured out yet how to cast out her awareness, to sense nonliving matter around her with her power. Objects she can *manipulate.* And DeWinter, this paperweight is made of silver.' He throws it in the air, catching it deftly. 'You need to learn how to distinguish between the different kinds of nonliving matter that you can manipulate then *only* manipulate that one thing. It's about fine tuning. It's about turning your surroundings into a weapon, as much as the one you wield in your hand. Until that day comes . . . I'll always beat you.'

I sit on the floor and groan. 'Fine, you win.'

There's the sound of wood reforming, cracking and shifting before Ezra ascends the newly formed staircase to stand beside his nephew, looking down at me. I'm struck by the uncanny resemblance between them, the twin grins, which are quite clearly very much a Darley trait.

'Your choice then, Knox,' Ezra says, clapping him on the shoulder. 'Sophia, best get practising, yes?'

★

On a rare day when the bell does not clatter, when all the teams of scholars are at Killmarth, I attend a lecture given by Hess and Silver on specific tactics.

'Now let's discuss team dynamics and how best to utilise the skills of each wielder type,' Silver says. 'Masquiers, how many of you in this room can successfully transform into a werewolf?'

A smattering of hands are raised, Belle and Tessa the most confidently. Silver smiles. I wonder if she knows Belle's secret. 'Good. Belle, a demonstration, if you please.'

Silver backs away as Belle shakes and transforms between blinks into her majestic werewolf form. Then Silver claps once, drawing everyone's attention back to her. 'I need every masquier able and willing to do this at will. Belle and Tessa will begin your training now. Werewolves, we've found, are an excellent addition to our teams but their nature is sometimes volatile. If every masquier can change into this form, we will no longer need to call on them.' The masquiers all murmur, packing up their things and slinging satchels over shoulders, pushing back their chairs. The room is a third lighter as Belle and Tessa transform back into their true selves, leading them out. 'The hall, Belle. All Godolphin scholars will take lunch in Gantry or Fetlock instead today.'

Hess clears his throat as Silver excuses herself, following the masquier scholars to the hall to work with Belle. 'Now on to the rest of you in a team. As you've no doubt gathered, we're bolstering each of your teams with werewolves. Up to this point, every team has been made up of two masquiers, some with the capabilities of Tessa and Belle, among others. You'll also have had at least one botanist, capable of some degree of healing, an alchemist and an illusionist. You've all been given close-combat training, but botanists are especially good at noncontact defence of your team, especially in woodland areas. Alchemists, you've performed admirably in the field, learning to change other objects into stakes as needed to bolster supplies and trick your opponents. Illusionists, the level of misdirection and camouflage you have wielded has been integral to saving lives in an ambush. You have all formed close bonds with your own team, figuring out ways to work together as one. But from now on, given the losses . . . we will be combining teams.' He eyes Knox and crooks his finger. 'Knox's team will pair with . . . Soames. Soames? Ah, there you are.'

Soames gives Knox the dirtiest of looks as he shuffles down to join Knox and Hess at the front of the room. I glance over and see Alden crack a grin at Knox, who covers his mouth with a cough.

'Now, those in Knox and Soames's teams, raise your hands.' I raise mine and scour the rows, seeing Darcy raise hers, along with some other third-year scholars. We're being paired with a far more advanced team, who I know have already suffered two losses. 'Field training will be held in Godolphin for you, the whole afternoon.'

I frown. 'The entire hall?'

'That's right. Apart from the dining hall and the private sleeping quarters, Godolphin is being turned over to training. Operating in enclosed spaces successfully is vital in case we have an attack in some of our more populated areas.'

'Like Dinas Tar,' I murmur, picturing those tightly packed alleyways I dragged Dolly through that night.

'I'll run through the other paired teams and assign you a space for field training. Charlotte? There. And Danson?'

As we're filtering out for lunch before an afternoon of field training with our newly expanded team, Knox taps my shoulder, then Alden's.

'Games night, our team only. Eight o'clock, Fetlock third common room.' He winks at Soames, who bristles and brushes past us. 'Not the new lot. Just us. About time we kicked back, don't you think?'

★

The thought of a night with the people I actually care about gets me through an afternoon of training with the third years. Darcy, Soames, Peters and Felix. Their illusionist, a woman called Fiona, died in their last skirmish. I find Soames irritatingly observant, Darcy a keen study and Felix a nervous botanist, down to the permanent shake in his hands. Darcy confides that Fiona was his girlfriend, and he tried to save her, but she bled out. Apparently he was the best botanist in their year only two weeks ago. Faculty are still deciding on whether he should even stay on at Killmarth. I think of Tessa and all the covering we did for her in the early days after Greg's death. I wonder if the faculty were having the same discussions about her. Peters makes up for Felix's temporary shortcomings, wielding his botany as a healer far better than Alden, but they're a mixed bag.

When I enter the common room at eight o'clock, I find it bathed in firelight. Knox, Belle, Tessa and Alden all lounge across a scattering of sofas and armchairs, the rugs and upholstery all mismatched shades of cherry, plum and forest green. The paintings and photographs on the walls depict past scholars who used this space, arms slung around each other, grinning at the camera. Some of the paintings are artwork by scholars as well, or donations from family collections to furnish the common room. I release a breath, toeing off my shoes as I sink into the sofa next to Tessa. Knox pours me a glass of velvane and the octagonal tumbler is passed along, hand to hand until it reaches me. That first sip slides down my throat too easily, all toffees and smoke, and I raise my gaze to find Alden toasting me. The memory of the first time we met, at the Pickled Gargoyle flashes in my mind and I grin back, taking another sip.

'Good to see you at a couple of lectures this week,' I say to Tessa, nudging her shoulder. 'Not drinking tonight?'

She shakes her head, glancing at me before her gaze lands once more on the flames in the fireplace. 'I want to keep a clear head. Me and Belle are doing more training with the other masquiers first thing.'

'Fair enough.'

'About the last few weeks . . .' Tessa hesitates, then grips my hand with hers. 'Thank you. For trying. For pulling me out whenever you could. It's felt like . . . like drowning. Or a deep well. And it's just me alone, in this muffled silence.'

'I'll always pull you out, Tessa. I love you,' I say, smiling at her. 'And it's still raw. You're grieving.'

'There's grief and then there's absence,' she says, reaching for a mug of tea on the side table next to her. 'Now I'm doing something about it, it feels better.'

I guess she means throwing herself into training with the other masquiers. I open my mouth to ask her more, glad she has a purpose, when Knox rises from where he's sitting.

'Shall we toast?' he asks, raising his glass. 'To us, and to Greg and Frances. May they be remembered through our actions.'

'To Greg and Frances,' we all say back and I take another sip of the smoky green fire in my glass.

'Now . . .' Belle says, unwinding her legs from her armchair to grab a deck of cards. 'Who wants to play for flor?'

'I'm game,' Alden says, leaning forward.

'Me too,' says Knox.

'When do you ever turn down a game of cards?' Alden says, chuckling as Belle shuffles the deck.

'What can I say, I just love the game.' He shrugs. 'Tessa? Sophia?'

'I'll sit this one out,' says Tessa, as I move closer to the coffee table by the fire and accept the hand I'm dealt.

'Sure?' I glance back at her.

She winks. 'I'm good. You play.'

We all throw a few cheap flor coins in the centre, the copper and tin rattling together in a pool. I bet big on a round of pokerface and lose all my flors, laughing hysterically as Knox, of course, sweeps them all towards him, victorious. Alden subs me for a game of brig and twist, Belle dealing the cards with swift precision as we're all passing the velvane around, when the bell begins to clatter.

We all freeze.

It continues, a ceaseless, awful sound that I have come to loathe and fear. I look up at Alden, sobering up instantly, the warmth of the night draining away, and sigh.

'Well, shit,' he says. 'Good thing our team is in reserve—'

The door slams open, Hess outlined in the doorway. We all turn to gape at him. 'I'm afraid too many of the Crown's forces have been called to a skirmish in Theine. We need you, prepare yourselves. You're not all shit faced, I take it?'

'Quite sober,' Knox says smoothly, running a hand through his hair.

'Excellent, excellent,' Hess replies, distracted and harried. My jaw drops as he nods to us, then disappears.

'Well shit, indeed,' Belle says, already heading for the door. 'Fucking figures, the one night I've actually enjoyed all semester. See you in the courtyard in five. And Knox? I'll be winning those flors back. Don't even think about dying.'

'Wouldn't dream of it.'

Chapter 9

Once More unto the Breach

The corridors are rife with scholars. I see Tessa just in front of me, her head bobbing in the sudden deluge of bodies, and call out to her, wanting to check she's all right. She barely said a word all evening, didn't join in the card games . . . an unnerving sense creeps over me, that everything isn't all right with her.

I change in record time, strapping the holders to my thighs for the stake and blade. Now I'm more adept at changing a blade to wood, I prefer the weight of a blade in my hand for close combat. I catch my reflection in the mirror and find a different woman staring back at me. Someone I don't recognise, someone hardened and cold. Someone ready.

The corridors and staircase in Gantry are deserted as I stride through them, entering the courtyard encrusted with frost.

'Places, scholars,' Professor Grant says, her voice projecting over the clang of the bell's insistent chimes. I fall into a line behind Darcy, snaking out around the edge of the courtyard, and peer around her, searching for Tessa. A hand lands on my shoulder and I look up, finding Alden frowning down at me.

'You good?' he asks.

I nod, placing my hand on his. 'I'll see you on the other side.'

Caroline has her fingers threaded in front of her as she moves to the centre of the courtyard beside Professor Grant, intense silvered gaze sweeping us all. 'Wielders, you will be joining others in the Pendle Woods. A large cluster ambushed a school on the edge of the woodland . . .' She swallows, her breath catching, as I reach up, covering my mouth with a hand. Darcy gasps in front of me and I catch Peters looking back at her, features limned with shock.

I reach back for Alden's hand, gripping it tightly, as Caroline continues, outlining the strategy, how we will encircle them, and take out as many as we can. His gaze snags on mine, rage and despair and a deep-seated hate. He wants to kill. He wants to tear them apart. But as I stare at him, he releases a breath and dips his head in the smallest of nods. He remembers.

We line up before the two mirrors, portals Hess has hastily created. He stands to the side, shadows permeating his eyes as we step through, one by one. Into the wild heart of Kellend. I step through and breathe it in, the scent of loam and green and cold. The woodland is white with snow, luminous and beautiful, the air stinging every inch of my skin that's exposed.

Belle transforms, quietly shaking out her wolf form to prowl through the forest. This place is silent. Deadly silent. The snow muffles everything, every footfall, every whisper.

Until a cold one explodes from the thicket.

I twist in an arc, stake gripped in my fist and skewer him in the chest. His eyes flare wide in surprise before he collapses into dust at my feet. But I didn't miss the smeared blood on his white shirt. The blood that was not his.

'Stay in a pack,' I hiss to the others. 'They'll try and pick us off.'

Then chaos erupts.

Three cold ones swing down from the trees, lithe and effortless as they land in the snow. The woods are alive with them, all in white shirts, all smeared with wielder blood. They're frenzied and cackling, high on the feast they've already consumed.

'Stay in formation!' Ezra calls across, appearing on our right flank, drawing three metal stars from a pocket, all with wood at their centres. He manipulates the stars, sending them flying at three cold ones, bursting from a clearing to his left side. Each one finds its mark, burrowing into their chests. His movements aren't practised, they're intuitive, I realise. He's fought them so much, he can anticipate their next move. 'They're heading for a portal, we need to cut them off.'

I weave through the trees, keeping Alden and Peters on my left, Tessa just ahead on my right, Belle, a shadow of teeth and fur, to the far right. Darcy, Soames and Knox bring up the rear. Unleashing my blade from its holder, I wield, using it to dart between the trees, cutting at ankles to stop the cold ones in their path. It works once, twice as I topple two, then two more, leaving them for Alden to stab through the heart, dust pluming in shrieks as they're ended. Then he wields, using branches to trip and trap them, each of us working in turn to disarm and eliminate. Felix does the same, working with Knox, and I hear the distant cries as the werewolves pick off any that are bolting from the main group of them. For the first time, we're working as one, exactly as we've trained, and a flare of hope, of victory unfurls in my chest.

Belle howls and my heart catches in my throat as I whip around, finding two pinning her down. 'No,' I breathe, already charging for her, picturing Frances, picturing Greg. 'Not again.'

I wield, darting my blade between them, hacking off a hand with a firm slice of magic. The cold one roars, blood spurting from his wrist, and he drops Belle, turning on me. 'Eat dust, you leech,' I hiss, wielding again, twisting the blade around in the air behind him. His mouth cracks into a grin, just before it pierces his spine. Leaving him clutching at the hole in his throat. I waste no time, rushing forward to stab him through the heart, and watch in grim satisfaction as he disappears into dust.

Belle snarls and I glance over, seeing she's pinned the other one to the ground. A young woman, blonde hair splayed around her, pleading like she's afraid. 'End her, Belle. We need to keep pace with the others.'

Belle doesn't need telling twice. She rips the heart from her very chest, tossing it aside. I stake it and the cold one is ash under Belle's paws. She chomps, shaking her head back and forth before leaping away, into a clearing. I check Alden is still on my left and nod to him, noting his torn jacket. 'You all right?'

'A flesh wound,' he replies, continuing on. 'Keep moving, DeWinter.'

I dash forward, senses on high alert for any more attacks. But like phantoms, they've bled away into the snow and ice once more. But one of us is missing . . .

I can't see Tessa.

'Alden, have you got eyes on T?' I ask quietly, my words almost swallowed up by this chilling woodland. 'I can't see her.'

'Shit. No. Not for the last few minutes . . .' He leans over, repeating the question to Knox and Darcy, who both shake their heads, stepping to the front. We all walk into a clearing, ringed with trees like silent sentinels.

In the centre, Tessa stands over a cold one. I sigh in relief, beckoning to her. 'T, get over here. You're too exposed. We can't split up, remember?'

She looks over at me, then down at the cold one, panting and pleading at her feet. It's a young woman, about the same height as Tessa, dark curls tight around her forehead and cheekbones. Perhaps once she was beautiful, perhaps if she wasn't a killer, she still could be. But all I see is a near-dead monster that Tessa needs to finish off.

Yet instead of killing her, Tessa crouches down, running her gaze over the vampire's body as she whimpers. I realise the cold one has been staked to the ground, twin blades driven through her shoulders. Nausea claws up my throat and I shudder. This, this right here is what I've been afraid of, I realise. Tessa's grief spilling out into cold-blooded revenge.

Now I'm doing something about it, it feels better . . .

'Tessa . . .' I say, hands out, approaching slowly. 'You just need to stake her, then move on. There are more here, more we can take out.' I swallow, ignoring the desperate pleading of the cold one. 'You're not like them. Don't do this. It's not who you are.'

She blinks at me, straightening, and smiles sadly. 'I don't know who I am any more, Sophia.' Then the glow of gold surrounds her as she wields her masquier magic. And in a heartbeat, she transforms into the perfect twin of the cold one she's staked to the ground. But it's when she opens her mouth that I freeze. 'No, please help me, please . . . hmm,' she says, cocking her head to the side, considering. 'Do I sound like her?'

I draw in a breath, unease prickling over my skin, and stride forward, plunging my own stake into the cold one's heart. She moans softly before turning to dust. When I stand, Tessa's already gone, running across the clearing to the other side. I press my hand into my chest, turning to the others, still at the edge of the clearing. Darcy's eyes are wide with shock, none of us have even raised this as a tactic. No masquier has trained to transform into one of them. 'You have to be careful. Don't— don't hurt Tessa.'

Then I take off after her, Alden calling out behind me. But all I can hear is my own ragged gasps and Tessa's voice, melding with that monster's own.

Chapter 10

Girls Don't Want Flowers, They Want Revenge

'Tessa!' I call softly, swearing under my breath as I stumble over a hidden tree stump, crashing into the ground. With a groan, I push myself up, ignoring the cuts on my palms, the cold snow seeping into my clothes. 'Tessa!'

But she doesn't answer. I keep moving, not bothering to wait for the others, terror creeping up on me, until it's blaring like a siren. I don't know what she's doing. But this wasn't our plan. She's never once suggested that she could wield and become a cold one, that her masquier abilities stretched that far. This is not a tactic we've discussed, not in our team, not with Caroline or Ezra, not with anyone. The fact that she will have been practising, alone, cultivating a perfect version to blend in amongst them . . . what is she planning? If she gets close to them and then exposes who she really is, they will tear her apart. I'm afraid for her. But more than that, I'm afraid of what's inside her, driving her to do this.

I catch sight of her, the slight glow around her from her wielding marking her out in my sight between the silent trees. 'Please, stop!' I cry, eyes darting everywhere, hoping I'm not being followed. I'm completely vulnerable, horribly exposed. If they attack now, I'm screwed. My team are far behind me and the woodland holds an eerie quiet. But I can't abandon her. I have to know what she's planning.

She flits between the trees, always just ahead of me and I realise she's tracking one of them. A cold one. Why is she stalking him and not getting close enough to take him out? I hurry forward, keeping the stake gripped and ready in my fist as the trees thicken, masking her from view. Desperately, I rake through the undergrowth, cages of twig and bramble and snow guarding her path. I get desperate, slashing at the tangled thorns, pushing my way through, aware I'm too loud, too obvious.

Then all at once, I find the edge, a clearing coming into view. And I flinch back. Through the branches laden with snow and frost, there is a portal. And surrounding it, perhaps fifty cold ones.

My very breath stills as I watch them, hidden by the trees surrounding me. In sharp relief, to me at least, stands Tessa. Amidst them now, as though she is truly one of them, limned in gold light. She's wielding so precisely, if I could not see her magic, could not sense it, I would believe her one of them. A monster. A vampiric being from another world. Just watching her, so vulnerable, so exposed, if one of them should realise, should turn on her—

I close my eyes, trying to calm my jumping heart. When I open them again, I realise they're all smiling, laughing. *Congratulating* one another.

One of them standing beside the portal laughs heartily and raises a fist. They all mirror him, raising a single fist in the air, and even Tessa does the same. I watch in disbelief and revulsion as they all cheer, clapping each other on the back, exchanging kill counts in excited, booming voices. All of them are wearing white shirts splattered with the blood of wielders. Children. They attacked a damn school. I clamp my jaw, wanting so desperately to stride out into the clearing and set my blade against each and every one of their throats, before staking them in the withered excuse they call a heart. I want to detonate. I want to scream my rage until the clearing is a furnace and take them all to meet their maker.

But Tessa . . .

I grit my teeth, my entire being shaking with sickened fury.

'What a feast we have enjoyed!' the man standing beside the portal roars, grin practically splitting his face under glittering, cruel eyes. 'But with some of them on our tail, we must away. A spectacular hunt. May it give you all strength and that of your line, until the next time.'

'Until the next great hunt!' one calls and the others all call it back, lifting their fists again. Nausea roils in my stomach and I brace a hand against my middle. They celebrate this? They are not just vampiric creatures, here to sate their hunger, they truly are monsters. There is no humanity in these beasts.

Then I notice how the portal ripples, how it does not seem to be anchored to anything tangible. It's simply hanging there, a passageway through the air. Marking the doorway to the bridge that crosses to their world. It ripples more, then settles, presenting an image of a world that is not all snow and ice and hulking trees. A hall, dark, save for the scant light of candles and wall sconces. And shadowy figures near the edges, as though awaiting their return.

One of the cold ones steps through, then another, all of them surging towards that portal. I take a step forward, not knowing what Tessa plans. Will she begin killing them, here and now? Will she transform into a werewolf and maul whichever cold one she can clamp with her jaws? I have to reach her. I have to stop whatever madness she is planning.

But then I realise . . . she is edging forward as well. Straight for the portal, through which they all step. Heart in my mouth, a strange thrumming in my ears, rather like the wings of a trapped bird, I can only look on in horror as she takes her turn stepping through . . . and disappears into their world beyond. I clamp my hand over my mouth, a small, strangled scream escaping.

And five pairs of eyes snap to the undergrowth where I'm hiding.

There's a sudden breeze, strands of my hair ruffling as it streams towards them through the trees. They all sniff, one of them sighing with guttural delight. They've scented me. A few more drift through the portal, until it's only these last five. Five male cold ones, all smiling at the very place where I'm standing on the edge of this clearing. One sniffs the air again and chuckles before putting his hands in his pockets. 'Come out, come out, pretty wielder,' he says in a sing-song voice. 'We won't bite.'

'Hard,' another says, and they all laugh, creeping forward.

I push through the branches, standing my ground on the tree line. 'If you want my blood, come and take it,' I say, gripping my blade in one hand, stake in the other. Then I smile as well, releasing the stake from my grip, and wield, letting it hover beside me, just as Hess taught us. I catch a flicker on the edge of the clearing and my smile only widens. 'Don't be shy.' Darcy enters the clearing on the other side of the portal, twin stakes in her hands and a snarl in her throat. Two turn, assessing her and begin stalking to her side of the clearing, then as I side step, she does too and I nod to her. We're going to herd the bastards.

Two come at me at once, faster than I can track. But out of my peripheral vision, I see the snapping jaws awaiting them, the looming creature that has found her quarry. Belle pounces, a low growl in her throat, leaping from the other side of the clearing. She makes short work of one of them and I spy the fifth, running for the portal. I grit my teeth, sending the stake at my side like an arrow after him. But he steps through the portal, just as the stake slips in behind him, the portal disappearing in an implosion of alchemy.

'No,' I murmur, walking forward, focusing on the place where the portal just was. But I'm distracted by a gasp across the clearing and see Darcy on her knees. Her gaze locks with mine as the cold one pinning her down snaps her neck to the side. She slumps over, dead, and he clamps his jaw around her throat, the blood pulsing in vivid spurts. Belle howls, finishing off the second she's fighting. The other cold one who went after Darcy quickly melts away into the woods. My heart judders as my mind catches up with what just happened, what that cold one that is left in the clearing is doing, drinking Darcy's blood. I fling my blade, wielding so it becomes a wooden stake, then guide it through the cold one's back. Right through its heart. He explodes in a cloud of ash, Darcy's body falling into the snow. And the portal . . . it's gone. Tessa, she's just . . . gone.

I give Darcy's lifeless body one agonising glance before throwing myself at the spot where the portal was, pushing out my magic, trying to recreate the bridge that has just been broken. I wield, forcing everything into it, picturing that darkened room, those monsters, any scrap I can cling to that might open a portal here and build a bridge to where she is . . . but nothing happens. Not even a flicker of that place, their world appears.

I sink to my knees, staring at nothing. Alden calls my name, sinking down beside me, shaking my shoulders. When I turn to him, all I see is panic, horror. The mirror to my own. 'Darcy, they killed Darcy,' I say.

'Where's Tessa?' he asks urgently.

'Gone,' I say, my voice sounding very far away. 'Tessa is gone.'

Chapter 11

Survivor's Guilt

'She stepped through a portal with the rest of the cold ones. Back to their world.'

Alden's features shatter. 'Oh gods.'

Belle comes to stand beside us, transformed back into her human form. 'Are you sure? All I could smell was cold ones,' she says, helping me to my feet. Just then Soames and Peters crash through the undergrowth, barrelling for Darcy. Knox has her head cradled in his lap, gently lifting her body out of the snow. Every single one of us is reeling. First Frances, now Darcy and— and Tessa . . .

'She wielded, she's been practising, imitating . . .' I say, running a hand down my face. I'm in shock. The world seems at once echoey and too loud, but also distant and soft, as though I'm no longer here, as though I've floated away and I'm staring down at us all in this clearing. I attempt to gather my scattered thoughts, to focus on Tessa. If she can even change her scent to blend in, maybe she won't be discovered straight away. Maybe there's still time to save her. Unless she plans on slaughtering as many as she can, unless she doesn't even plan on staying hidden, staying alive . . . or worse, what if she doesn't have a plan? What if the sum total of her planning was wielding so convincingly that she made it through that portal, and now she's winging it in another world? Alone.

'Ezra,' I croak. 'Where's Ezra?' There's no one else in moments like these and the realisation that I need him hits me. No matter my own pain, my own feelings, he is the one who could fix this. He knows more about the cold ones and their great hunts than anyone.

'He's gone to the school,' says Knox, walking over to us. 'He's creating a portal to take any wielders there directly to the Crown's healers. Any survivors, that is.'

I close my eyes and shudder.

'We've done all we can here, scholars,' Hess announces, entering the clearing. 'Back to Killmarth. Any wounds that need looking at, please report to the medical wing on your return. And Sophia?'

'Yes?' I say, desperate hope shining through all the horror.

'I am sorry,' he says, his gaze connecting with mine. And it's as though it's not just about Tessa, but about Hester as well. About him checking out on my training at a time I needed him to step in as my mentor. But his eyes are cloudless now, sure and strong. Then his gaze sweeps over Soames and Peters, the body of Darcy they are carefully holding away from the cold, cold snow. 'All of you, I am so sorry for your losses. May they both find peace.'

★

I slam my fist into my bedroom door. All I can see is Tessa's eyes as she looked up from that cold one she'd pinned to the cold ground. Then her back, limned in golden light, retreating through that portal. Now I've practised, I can see a masquier's wielding clearly, in a way I couldn't before. I just hope that no one she encounters has the same sight as me. She must have planned this. Must have practised and practised in the confines of her room to get the imitation of a cold one exactly right. I drop my forehead against the door, the cool wood a balm to the heat raging inside me. I'm furious. With her, but mostly with myself. For not seeing the twisted shape her grief had taken, or the plan forming behind her eyes.

Although I'm glad he's got his shit together after weeks of going through the motions with lectures, I'm also extremely pissed at Hess for choosing his moment of clarity to refer to her like she's already dead. I don't want condolences, I need a solution.

Sliding down to the floor, my back to the bedroom door, I look over at the bookshelves. I need to find Ezra, or Caroline . . . I just need *someone* to care enough to make a plan with. We can't abandon her and give her up for dead like Hess clearly already has. My gaze snags on the book Hess gave me on my shelves, the one about bridges. I get up, crossing to it, and begin leafing through the pages. A bridge . . . from our world to theirs? In a frenzy, I snap the book shut, placing it back on the shelves and shove back my hair. I can't even read the words, my mind is in turmoil. The longer she's there, the longer she has to maintain her wielding . . .

How long until she's discovered?

A plan, I need a plan. The strategic nature of my mind clicks into place and I examine my options. I can't think clearly enough to read a book right now, I need to speak to someone who already knows how to create portals. Perhaps to their world, and not just within our own. Reaching for the door handle, I fling it open and stride off in search of Ezra. I may not trust him, I may not like him, but he's the strongest alchemist I've ever met and even though he's a calculating bastard, he doesn't just give up without a fight. If anyone can give me hope, it's him.

After searching the Keeper's Hall, the various dining halls and common rooms, even Darley, I almost give up. But then I remember what Knox said, that he was returning to that school for survivors. I head straight for the medical wing and find him there. He watches me quietly, eyes older than stone, as a botanist stitches a wound on his shoulder, with wielding and the finest thread. I'm taken aback for a moment that he's injured. He doesn't even flinch, just slumps against the wall, sat on a stool in the far corner as other botanists busy themselves with the other patients. Every bed is taken. There's even a line of wielders with minor injuries lined up, waiting on a bench.

Some of them, I realise, are survivors from the school. My breath catches, some of them are so young. I turn questioning eyes on Ezra and he shrugs. 'The Crown didn't have resources for all of them. There has been a wave of attacks today across Kellend as well as that skirmish on the Theinean border. I had to bring some back through a portal here instead.'

Some. There must be forty wielders in this room, many of them gangly limbed teenagers, with big, ghostly eyes. They've seen too much. Experienced far too much. All of them.

I swallow and nod, gaze landing on a boy. He can't be older than thirteen, poised and wary as a new fawn, cuts and bruises riddling his skin. He's sat up, staring at nothing, clutching a red ribbon in his fist. A girl's hair ribbon. 'How many?' I say quietly to Ezra.

'What?'

'How many in total did you save?' I ask carefully, eyeing the other beds, the bench with them lined up, staring at nothing, a few adults dotted amongst them. Their teachers.

He sighs and nods his thanks as the botanist finishes up his stitching and moves away, to the next patient. 'Not nearly enough. A few dozen students managed to hide. That one over there clutching that ribbon fought off an attack on his sister . . . she's with the Crown's best right now. We're hoping she survives the day. Most of the teaching staff were already dead when I arrived, defending their students. It was a massacre.'

I fight back the tears, throat suddenly thick. 'I need your help.'

'Of course you do.'

'Tessa walked through their portal,' I say, folding my arms to hide the tremors. 'Before I could stop her, and it closed up.'

'My condolences,' he says, wincing. 'A good family. Promising masquier.'

'She is more than just a . . .' I take a breath, reminding myself to stay calm, measured. I don't want condolences from this man. I need action. 'She's in their world, and I need a way to get there. I need to form a portal and create a bridge between worlds.'

'Would that I could help you, Sophia . . .' he says, testing his shoulder by rolling it gently, then wincing, 'but it can't be done.'

'It can't?'

'Wielders have gone through before, but only ever used portals made by the cold ones during a hunt.'

I cling to this scrap of hope, taking a step forward. Perhaps their knowledge combined with anything I can glean from that book in my room . . . 'Where are these wielders? Can I speak to them?'

'I'm afraid not,' he says. 'No one who has entered a cold ones' portal has ever returned.'

*

We sit in glum silence in the hall of Fetlock. There are few botanists here at dinner, most of them amongst the plants in the glass tower, or in the basement laboratories. Several senior scholars have been drafted to help in the medical wing as more casualties are brought in through portals created by Hess from other parts of Kellend and the border. So Alden, Knox, Belle, Blake and I snagged the nicest table, moving the tureens of food into the middle so we could help ourselves. Not that we've eaten much. The wild field pie is delicious, but I can't bear to even finish the helping on my plate. Knox has produced a bottle of velvane and we're all drinking morosely, each in our own private nightmares of the great hunt.

'Survivor's guilt,' Blake says, topping up our tumblers before pushing his specs up the bridge of his nose. He has the carefully tousled hair, white shirt and maroon wool pullover vest of a decidedly well-tailored scholar. But it's his kindness that makes him shine. I can see why Knox gravitates to this illusionist. 'You've seen the death, the blood and yet you've all come away alive and well. It's only natural. But you must remember, all of you will be needed next time. If you hadn't survived, who would defend Kellend in the future?'

Knox reaches for his hand and squeezes it. 'What would I do without you?'

'Drink a lot more, I'd wager,' Blake says, features creasing into an affectionate grin.

Belle downs her tumbler in one, features gaunt, and Knox leans over to refill it. 'Do you think it'll ever be over?'

Her question is met with marked silence. I sip my velvane, feeling the flush of warmth cascade through my veins. 'I have to get her back. There has to be a way.'

'Tessa?' asks Belle.

I look at her and nod. 'Ezra said only the cold ones have created the portals that lead to their world. But I can't help thinking . . . what if one of us can? There has to be some method to it.'

'You opened a portal in the final Ordeal,' Alden says, a contemplative frown pinching his forehead. 'You shouldn't have been able to, yet you did. Ezra says no one has returned from their world, but were any of them alchemists who did what you did, with no training?'

'I doubt it,' Knox says quietly. 'My uncle is clever, but some things outfox even him.'

‘What if . . .’ I say, untangling the knots of my thoughts, smoothing them out. ‘What if we need a cold one to figure it out? If they can create portals to travel back and forth, maybe I can get answers from one of them.’

‘It would stand to reason,’ Alden agrees. ‘Not sure where we would find one now though. They’ve all returned to their world until the next wave. There will just be some stragglers left behind.’

‘If the pattern follows previous hunts, they’ll launch another wave soon,’ Knox adds.

‘But maybe we could get in touch with someone else in the Crown’s forces, someone still out there . . .’ Belle says slowly, a glint in her eye banishing some of the shadows. ‘If there *are* any stragglers . . .’

‘We might be able to smoke them out,’ Knox adds firmly. He glances at Alden. ‘What about your brother?’

‘It’s a possibility . . .’ Alden considers. ‘I’d have to get a message to him, well, I’ll have to locate him first.’

‘Wait . . .’ I say. ‘We don’t need a straggler, do we? Caroline and Ezra told us they’ve kept cold ones to test the nocturnal on. Remember?’

Knox’s gaze slices to mine and he places his glass back on the table. ‘If they’re still holding them somewhere . . .’

‘We need to find out if they kept any alive and where,’ I say, sitting up a little straighter. Finally, a way forward. Not stabbing in the dark.

Alden nods. ‘I’ll start working on my brother, see if he knows anything about the nocturnal project. Where we might find a cold one.’

‘I’ll go through that book on bridges . . . see if I can glean something.’

‘I can hit the library, see if there are any other resources we’ve overlooked,' Knox offers. 'If I start asking my uncle, he'll get suspicious. Best stick to the research he won't question.'

'Oh, I'll join you,' Blake says quickly. 'The library is my church, after all.'

'I thought *I* was your church,' Knox grumbles.

'A different kind of worship,' Blake chuckles, eyes darkening.

'Bridges,' I say. 'Just any information on bridges, or portals. I've got a book in my room I can check through too. Thank you, all of you. For not giving up on her.'

Belle's features soften. 'We all care about her. If we can find her, we will. In the meantime, I'll figure out wielding to appear as a cold one.'

I blow out a breath, feeling something close to hope. We just have to get to her before they do.

Chapter 12

An Old Friend

Tessa and Greg haunt every corner of this library. Drinking in the scent of leather and wood polish, the crisp, caramel pages of the volumes and the darkness between the stacks as they march off to the distant archive rooms, I am enveloped with heartache. Every moment we studied here as hopefuls is imprinted in my memories and I cannot, *cannot* accept a world in which Tessa and I will never study here together again.

I take a deep breath as Alden's hand slips around mine. The warmth and connection ground me and I flash him a quick smile. It's only been two days since she vanished through that portal, but it could be a lifetime. We've made little progress and I'm clinging on to hope like a lifeline as I read every page of the book Hess gave me. 'Just like old times.'

'Except you're not looking for poisons.'

I smile, letting him swing me round to plant a soft kiss on my mouth. 'No. And yet it's more of a needle in a haystack than cramming for the Ordeals. Any luck with your brother . . . ?'

'None,' he says, hiding a grimace. 'If we want to find out where they were developing the nocturnal, we'll have to find another source.'

I tap my teeth, thinking of who might know . . . but I'm drawing a blank. If we have to search for a cold one left behind in Kellend, it could take weeks. Tessa likely doesn't have that long.

'But then Blake, Knox and I got talking. We began to wonder if we've been too focused on the wrong question,' Alden says, tugging on my hand. 'What if, instead of locating where they were developing the nocturnal . . . we just need to identify where the Crown have laboratories. There are only so many locations, and it would have been in Kellend . . . we know it's not here at Killmarth . . .'

He pulls me down the stacks, to the dimly lit edge of the library, where the doors to the archive rooms line the wall at the back and I smile, realising what he means. 'You think the Crown would disclose that kind of information though?'

'No,' Alden admits. 'But the records in the archives here are extensive. And if you were developing an elixir and needed to test a vast array of plant life, wouldn't you raid the stocks they have in the poison garden? And wouldn't the esteemed and scrupulous housekeeper have kept notes of which deadly plants had been sampled and sent elsewhere?'

Stepping inside, I see it's already occupied.

'We have a breakthrough,' Blake says, practically vibrating out of his seat. 'I befriended a member of the groundskeeping team, someone who's been here for many years. She said there has only been one occasion when samples have left Killmarth from the poison garden, so Alden pulled the records. For research purposes, he's studying the poison garden for his third-year thesis, did you know?'

'How studious of you to have already decided on your thesis,' I murmur to Alden and he winks.

'You see why we all get on so well?' Knox says, sauntering in. He places one slim volume on the table beside Blake. 'Where else would I find people as calculating and resourceful as I? The final record. Process of elimination, you see, DeWinter. There's only one year now we have not checked.'

Blake reaches for it, leafing through the pages, scrutinising every one. I look on, barely daring to breathe . . . then his eyes alight in triumph. 'There. There! Twelve specimens couriered to the Nocturne research facility. This has to be it, what else would be named after Henry Nocturne? Address . . . gods. Highhelm.'

Blake swivels the book so we can see it, and I bend down, running my finger over the record. 'But Highhelm . . . that's the palace. On the edge of Dinas Tar.'

Knox nods slowly as it dawns on him, on all of us. 'They were developing the elixir in a research facility inside the palace itself.'

'Nowhere safer,' Alden says.

'You suspect they're keeping cold ones there. Experimenting on them,' I say, tapping a fingernail on the book, my heart beating faster and faster. If they're still there, if they haven't disbanded the facility entirely and moved the cold ones they're testing on . . . 'That place will be more heavily warded than Killmarth.'

Belle sticks her head around the door. 'Ah, here you all are. You look guilty as sin.'

'Not just yet,' I say softly. 'But we soon will be.'

Belle closes the door carefully. 'You've found something.'

I nod. It's a lead. Even if it's a dead end, we can't ignore it. 'Knox, Blake and Alden have.' I glance at Knox. 'I think it's time we join forces on an assignment.'

'What do you propose?' Knox asks.

I lean forward. 'We break into this lab in the palace and find out what they've been working on. And *who* they've been working on to refine their elixir. Then we take them and use them and their knowledge to figure out how to open a portal to their world.'

'Sounds dangerous,' Belle says.

'Exactly,' I say. 'What wielder would be foolish enough to break in and liberate one of them? If we're careful, they'll never suspect us. They might not even realise before it's far too late.'

'And if they've been moved?' Knox says.

I shrug. 'It's up to you. It's a risk, a huge one, I'll understand—'

'We're going,' Alden says firmly and Knox nods.

★

We gather at midnight in Darley Hall, the one place we're least likely to be disturbed. An illusionist, a masquier, two alchemists and a botanist. I nod to Knox and he throws back the sacking cloth from the floor-length mirror we found stacked in the corner. We need a bridge from here to the palace grounds. But first, we need a map of the palace itself.

'And you really think your contact will have intimate knowledge of every passageway and room of the palace? Enough to sketch out a map for us?' I ask Knox dubiously.

'I can guarantee it. Care to wager?' Knox asks, raising an eyebrow and staring me down.

I shake my head. I've played cards with the best of them, I know when to hold a bet. 'Well, lead on. We're all curious.'

He cracks his knuckles and holds out a hand to me. 'I might need a boost. And you'll have to focus on the same place as me.'

'Where?' I ask, taking his hand.

'Corner of James Street. You know it?'

I frown, my memory stirring, showing me a place I'm all too fond of. But it can't be . . .

'You're picturing it?' he asks, beginning to glow gold as he calls upon his alchemy magic to create the bridge.

'I am,' I say, drawing upon my own, focusing on the mirror, the bridge we need from here to there. I picture us all stepping through, to that shadowy street at midnight in the city I grew up in. The city I know like the back of my hand. 'But where this person, this contact will be, if I'm not mistaken—'

'The Pickled Gargoyle,' Alden says at my side as the mirror swirls then clears, revealing the place we created a bridge to. 'Your old stomping ground, isn't it, Sophia?'

I shoot Knox a look, wondering if that first time I met Alden, when he was the person I overheard speaking to Alden, wasn't his first visit to my local haunt. 'Apparently it's someone else's too.'

Knox merely smiles and nods to Blake. 'You still all right? You don't have to come, no one would expect you to risk yourself and your place as a scholar. You can stay behind if you prefer.'

'I'm all in,' Blake says, reaching to peck Knox on the cheek. 'You know I've been wanting to meet this elusive ex of yours.'

Ex?

Knox chuckles, releasing my hand now there is enough magic to sustain the transformation from mirror to bridge, and brushes his lips against Blake's knuckles in a kiss before stepping through, into James Street, beyond. Blake goes after him, then Belle, leaving Alden to smile mysteriously at me before I step through last, breaking the bridge. We do not want anyone to come across the mirror in Darley Hall and raise the alarm.

The Pickled Gargoyle is exactly as I remember, the swinging sign depicting a tipsy gargoyle, the dark, squat windows giving away nothing of the inside and the deep-green door, which is closed against the winter chill. Knox walks in first, a wash of light and laughter spilling out like toquay into the cobblestone street. I wade through the honeyed light, straight into the thick of a crowd of scholars. Everyone in this bar is half cut, full of misplaced swagger and bellowing voices, and the loud music is a jarring throb in my ears.

'Not quite the same without a velvane or two inside you,' Alden says and I shrug, watching as Knox shimmies to the bar. Where Pewter is stood watching him, a polishing cloth thrown over one shoulder. I wave to Pewter but he doesn't even look my way. The only person he's got eyes for is . . . Knox.

Wait.

'Is Pewter Knox's ex?' I ask Alden in disbelief.

Alden nods. 'You know him too?'

'Apparently everyone does!' I say as Belle rushes over, reaching over the bar to clasp his hand. His eyes flicker to hers, lighting up as he grins. 'And here was me thinking I was special.'

Alden laughs. 'Small world. And Pewter has that way with people. Especially ones he wants to keep tabs on.'

I frown in confusion as the sea of scholars parts and I'm able to shuffle to the bar. 'Pewter!' I call over, elbows on the bar. 'Long time.'

He turns that grin on me. 'Long time indeed! Looks like you fell in with the wrong crowd.'

'They're not all bad,' I say, laughing.

'Velvanes all round?' he asks, beginning to line up the octagonal glasses. 'I'm guessing this isn't just a social visit? Knox?'

'Sadly, not,' Knox says with a wince. 'Can anyone cover you for a while? We need your help.'

'If this is Crown business—'

'It is,' says Belle. 'But I won't say no to the finest velvane in the city.'

'Nor me,' I say.

He eyes us all quietly and turns to Knox. 'Have you told them?'

'No,' Knox says, accepting a glass of velvane from him. 'I thought I'd leave that up to you to decide.'

Pewter chuckles, shaking his head. 'I'd call this an ambush by anyone else. Can't ever trust a Darley.' He pours the rest of us our drinks, then one for himself and chucks it back, grimacing before wiping his mouth. 'Shall we adjourn to upstairs?'

He calls over another member of bar staff, a young woman with fiery hair and a north Theinian accent. Then he beckons us all to the door set by the alcoves at the back of the room and we all whisk up a narrow flight of stairs to the office on the first floor. He leans against the window ledge and we all crowd in, standing awkwardly as he folds his arms. 'What are you after then?'

'A map,' I say, stepping forward, and dart a look at Knox. 'Of the palace. Apparently you're the man who would know. And after that, answers to my own questions, Pew.'

His features soften. 'About me being tasked to keep eyes on you?'

'Let me guess, by the Darley not currently present . . .' I say, gritting my teeth.

He nods. 'Sorry. Part of my job. The old man wanted you to get the hint about Killmarth . . . but at the right moment. I figured you were ready, even if he didn't think so. And with the map thing . . .' He runs his hand over his jaw, looking at each of us in turn as the sequence of events that led me to Killmarth, all my careful spying and evading, believing I was being oh, so clever flashes in my mind . . . when really Ezra knew all along. Bastard. 'I could help you with a map of the palace. But I would need a damn good reason.'

'And I suppose you know because you work for the Collector too,' I say, a little edgy. Now I'm connecting the dots, realising the bastard knew everything, set it all in motion . . . I don't know what to make of it. Apparently his only complaint is that I tried for a place at Killmarth before he deemed me ready.

'No, wrong there. I only helped him out when our goals aligned,' Pewter says with a small smile. 'I grew up in the palace. Still serve the Crown, actually. You're looking at the first cousin, once removed, of our dear Queen herself and a spy for the Crown.'

Chapter 13

Go Big or Go Home

'Well fuck me . . .' Blake mutters.

'Apparently he already is,' Pewter says, nodding to Knox. Belle snorts, covering it with a cough, and mutters something about mixing business and pleasure.

'Jealous?' asks Knox, raising his eyebrows. 'Not like you.'

'Not at all,' Pewter says smoothly. 'Merely a statement. So you want to get inside the palace? To a specific part of the palace, I presume? Any reason why you can't go through the official channels and must sneak inside?'

I glance at Alden and he nods. We can trust Pewter. I mean, I do wish I'd known he was keeping tabs on me, that does sting a bit, but then I should have expected it of the Collector. Of course he had eyes on me at one of my favourite haunts. Everything in my life was controlled. 'We need to gain access to a secret lab and potentially liberate a cold one we suspect is being kept there to find a way to enter their world and rescue a friend of ours.'

Pewter blinks quickly and whistles. 'You never were one to mince your words, Sophia. Go big or go home, I suppose. Lovely to see you, anyway. And you, too, Blake, great to finally meet. Good luck.'

'Thanks?' Blake says in confusion.

'He means with me,' Knox says dryly. 'Any more sussing out and stalling you want to do? Are you going to help us or not?'

Pewter smacks his lips. 'Fine. Just because they're all with you, doesn't mean the Crown can trust them. For all I know, you could be leading them into the palace for a hostile takeover.'

'Well for a start, Knox is not the leader . . .' Alden says.

'I am,' I say, thrusting up my chin. 'And before you ask, no. Ezra does not know we're here. This is personal. It's for a friend.'

Pewter eyes me for a moment. 'Which friend?'

'Tessa Godolphin,' I reply, then explain what happened in the Pendle Woods. 'She— she lost someone recently. Someone very important to her. I believe she's gone to their world to seek revenge in the most explosive way possible. But there's no current plan to get her out alive. The professors and the Crown have given her up for dead.'

'Hmm,' he says, nodding. 'Sounds about right. There are unavoidable casualties in war and all that. I've always thought that's a load of shit, but those in power do like to keep their hands clean and a bird's-eye view of it all. Details, like individuals, are sometimes below them.' He claps his hands. 'Well. I need parchment and ink. If it's one of the laboratories you seek, you're going to have a rather interesting night.'

★

Knox and I choose the office door to create the portal. Or more accurately, the threshold between the office and stairwell. I think about the bridge, the path we'll all need to step from here to there. But I only have what Pewter has *told* me about the palace to sketch the portal on the other side and point the bridge to. I hope it's enough. I've never really considered what would happen if we all got trapped on a bridge. Isn't it basically just . . . space? A tunnel between two points in time? I roll back my shoulders. This is an assignment, not the time for scholarly musings.

'Remember, you'll have three minutes. The guards rotate on that floor and there's a short absence. Maybe longer if one of them needs to take a piss,' Pewter says. 'Don't get caught, for the love of the gods. It would really mess up my night.'

'And ours,' Knox points out. 'I have no intention of being caught. Sophia?'

'Ready,' I say, nodding to the others, all thoughts of being nothing but a collection of cells drifting, trapped between two points in space, swept aside. 'If it goes to shit, just return here, all right? Don't wait for anyone. Save yourselves. Pewter will get you on a train back to Killmarth tomorrow.'

'Where we'll just have the delightful Parnell to deal with . . .' Alden says.

I shrug, hiding my grimace. 'The only gaping hole in the "if this all goes to shit" plan. Knox, one of us has to make it back here to open a fresh portal to Killmarth. You can sacrifice yourself to save me, don't worry.'

Knox's chuckle is dry as kindling. 'Remind me to never say yes to one of your schemes again, in that case.'

I take his hand and call upon my magic once more. And in my mind, I picture the place Pewter described. A small sitting room, floor-to-ceiling bookshelves in gelder wood, a shabby, neglected air, the furniture and books seemingly assembled in a bizarre concoction of styles and tastes from various eras, a window overlooking the palace kitchen gardens. And a wall sconce, beside the bookcase, which flickers with flames. I close my eyes, concentrating, feeding my will into this vision of a room on the first floor of the palace. The seat of the Crown.

'Looks like you've located it,' Alden says quietly, voice shining with a note of awe and unmistakable pride. I open my eyes and find the swirling mist clouding the mirror parting to reveal the first-floor sitting room for visiting dignitaries from the entirely fictional territory of Frim. A sitting room unused, except for odd pieces of furniture and books to be squirrelled into and discarded. And most importantly, glimmering with threads of illusion.

I turn to Alden and wink. 'Can you keep up is the question, Locke?'

He grins at me, a glint in his eyes. 'Always, DeWinter. Lead on.'

As the threshold ripples then settles, I release Knox's hand. Then I step over, into the most heavily guarded and warded building in Kellend. The bridge we've created is through the door leading into the sitting room, and all is quiet. Drenched in a lunar glow, the room is silvered and expectant, as though awaiting unexpected visitors. The wards snap, pushing me backwards, but I'm ready. After shoving my way through the gates of Killmarth, the Collector's bracelet shattering from my wrist in a pool of the blood that forged it, I know wards are only as strong as the wielder that created them. And between Knox, Alden and I, we possess a vast well of raw magic.

Knox places his hand on my shoulder once he's through, grunting with the effort to not be shoved back into the office above the Pickled Gargoyle. Then Alden does the same, shoving his way in, gripping my hand. I'm already coaxing the wards, telling them we belong here, that we're meant to be in the palace tonight. The combined will and magic of Alden, Knox and I not only convinces the wards to let us in, but they reform around our bridge, leaving a tear for us to exit through. The threshold to our bridge holds.

Tentatively, Belle and Blake shuffle through and Blake immediately begins to wield, crafting the illusion of a vacant sitting room to any suspicious guard. We've timed it perfectly and within the three minutes of the guard change, we're all through the portal and dressed in illusion.

'Belle, if you will . . .'

Belle wields, tailoring her clothing to the uniform of the guards, described in detail by Pewter. She stands on one side of the door, ready to deflect any curious attention, or worse. Blake crafts the illusion of another guard to stand on the other side of the doorway, so Belle doesn't look shifty standing there by herself. Then it's my turn. I walk over to the wall sconce, dancing with flames, and narrow my gaze, skimming over the bookcase to where one book stands impossibly straight, amid a shelf of haphazardly stacked volumes. I grip it and pull. And like a lever, a mechanism behind the bookcase clicks, and it swings forward, revealing a passageway beyond.

There's the sound of footsteps outside the doorway and I snap round, all of us freezing, waiting. But it's only one of the palace guards, walking slowly past, gaze sweeping over the room before continuing. I release a charged breath and raise my eyebrows to Knox. With Knox and Alden at my back, I cross into the passageway and hope to gods that Pewter remembered the layout of the rest of this place accurately. Because if not, we'll attract the wrong attention. And I'll have set us all up for at the very least, punishment. At worst, a spell in the Crown's prison.

The passageway is cold and full of echoes, every footfall creating a cascade of staccato sounds. Knox draws a match from a pocketbook, lighting two candles for himself and Alden. They send flickers of light over the old stone, highlighting dancing shadows that leer and disperse. I keep my hands free, stretched in front of me, ready to wield. I do not trust this empty, echoing silence.

When we reach the end of the spiral staircase, three doors greet us. The temperature has dropped noticeably, the damp cold of winter seeping through the walls. I turn to Alden and Knox, features pensive in the soft glow of candlelight. 'Thoughts? Pewter didn't say which door.'

'He might not know which one was being used by the botanists,'

Alden says, crossing to the first. He places his hands on it, frowning slightly. 'This one is made of newer wood, I can feel the embers of life still sealed within it.' Then he moves to the next. 'This one is ancient. Beyond, I sense nothing. No life, no light, no energy.' Then the last. 'And this . . . behind this door is teeming with life. And magic.'

'All right,' I say. 'Looks like we have our winner.'

We enter the room beyond, finding the door unlocked. It's the laboratory we were seeking, filled with plant life, windows down one side of the roof that when we look, open out onto the sky, a grate above them. This space is washed in silver, just like the sitting room above by the moon's glow. It's ethereal and strange, yet wondrous. The variety of plants lining the walls is immense, some tiny and glinting in their beds, some towering with clutching tendrils, aching for the open sky. Alden takes a deep, unhurried breath.

'Their research,' Knox says from the far corner, where he's plucked a folio from a shelf stacked and indexed with similar ones. He flips through the pages, whistling. 'Meticulous research.'

I cross to a board, pins holding photographs, notes, a calendar . . . the collected detritus of a tight-knit team. Reading a note, then eyeing the photograph of all of them stood together, right outside in the palace grounds, my heart twists. Most of them lost at that wedding, a team that worked so diligently as one.

'I can sense something other than plants down here,' Alden says softly, frowning. 'Although not in this room.'

Knox clears his throat, holding up the folio he's reading. 'Might it have something to do with the research subject mentioned here? Apparently . . . they're kept in the room next to this.'

We all look at the wall, dividing this lab from the room next to it. 'A cold one?'

'Yes,' Alden says, cracking his knuckles. 'Must be what we're looking for. It seems different to the cold ones we've fought though. I suppose you wouldn't even consider getting behind me, would you, Sophia?'

'Absolutely not,' I say, flashing him a grin. 'Illusionists first.'

He chuckles and we move back into the corridor. I call on the well of magic within, then release the stake I carry from its holder. I'd rather not turn our only lead in getting to Tessa to dust, but if I'm dead, then I cannot find her.

Knox wields, parsing apart the lock, transforming it into nothing but air. The door swings open with an ominous creak and a breathy laugh escapes from the darkness within. I swallow, steeling myself for a fight, and step over the threshold.

'Alchemist, alchemist, botanist . . .' a voice breathes. 'And a hint of an illusionist too. What an interesting night this is turning out to be.'

'Knox, light,' I murmur and he obliges, lifting a candle to flicker across the room. It's just as cold as the winter night outside, but that doesn't seem to bother its occupant. Chained to the wall beneath another roof light window, he sprawls on a bench, eyeing us with delight. Fair with dark red lips and even darker eyes, he's not like any cold one I've seen before. Around our age, perhaps a little older, but no greying to his skin or hair.

'Oh gods,' Knox says before taking a step back towards the door. The candlelight gutters as I frown at him.

'What?'

'That's not just any cold one. He's not from their world,' Alden says, voice strained.

'How do you know?'

Knox swallows. 'Because that's the Crown Prince.'

Chapter 14

Werewolf Carnage

The man smiles at me and winks. I shudder as he delicately sniffs the air and runs a pink tongue over those deep red lips.

'I thought the Crown Prince was ill. A sickly young man, kept far away from court and society life . . .' I say.

Alden shrugs. 'He hasn't been seen in public for years, that's true. A recluse, or so the Crown claim.'

'Last I heard, he had been sent to the mountains to the east of the Pendle Woods for a long period of recuperation and recovery,' Knox says calmly. 'For his . . . illness.'

'Well, now we know what the mysterious illness is,' I reply, keeping the stake in my hand raised. 'Looks like he's been turned.'

The Crown Prince suddenly sniffs louder, eyes flaring wide. 'It's you that smells so good, isn't it, alchemist? Must be the combination of magic in your blood, that seasoning of illusion . . . so vibrant. Positively tingles on the tongue, I imagine.'

'Great to know I smell so nice, never heard that before,' I sigh, glancing at Alden. 'Thoughts?'

'We probably shouldn't kidnap the Crown Prince?' Alden says.

'Definitely a difficult one to explain away if we're caught,' Knox agrees.

'But nevertheless . . .' I say, scenario after scenario flitting through my mind. We could leave him, but then we wouldn't have a cold one. And every day that passes could be the one that sees Tessa dead. But if we take him . . . how will we get him out quietly? And if we are caught . . . I bite my lip. No ready explanation springs to mind. But now he's seen us. All three of us . . . he'd be able to identify us again.

'Listen to me carefully,' I say. 'Do you know how to create a portal into your world?'

'Depends,' he replies, crossing one leg over the other.

I frown. 'On what?'

'What's in it for me.'

Knox rolls his eyes before stepping outside to check the corridor. I can guess what he wants. But if I let him feed on me, will he tell me? Should we even leave him here now he's seen our faces? Before I can make a decision the tumble of my spiralling thoughts is interrupted. By a loud alarm bell.

'Either that's because of us, or the others have done something they shouldn't have,' Alden says. 'We better move.'

Alden darts to the door as the peal of the bell seems to get louder and louder, an unending shriek that pierces my skull. We're out of options. 'Do you want to come with us?' I ask the Crown Prince. 'What's your name? Not your royal, official name. Your chosen name?'

'Andry,' he says with a wicked grin. 'And I haven't had an invitation that good for some time.' He proffers the cuffs and chains binding him to the wall. 'A little help, alchemist?'

I tap my teeth, gaze darting over the links and the cuffs. Something tells me that freeing Andry completely would be more than a little foolish. Surely he was kept chained for a reason. 'Alden, Knox?'

Knox appears again in the doorway, frowning. 'Don't tell me . . . he's coming with us, isn't he?'

'I need you to understand me, Andry,' I say, acting quickly.

Striding to the wall, I place my hands either side of the chains anchored to the stone and shunt my magic into it. The huge bolts shrink, falling away to rattle either side of him and I shove him hard in the shoulder, slicing the air with the stake to hover over his chest. Then I lean closer, watching his pupils expand. 'If you try to escape, I will stake you. If you bite anyone, I will stake you. If you cause us any trouble—'

'You'll stake me,' he says quietly. And far too calmly. 'We should probably get going, shouldn't we, alchemist?'

I yank the chains upward, passing the end to Knox, who nods grimly. Alden's features darken, but he says nothing, waiting until we've passed, me in front, Knox and Andry being led behind, before bringing up the rear. I hear Alden mutter something threatening to Andry, who merely cackles, and I wonder if his mind has fractured in this cold, dark place. If he has in fact, not seen daylight for a very long time.

The shrieking alarm bells cut off when we're halfway up the spiral staircase, dousing us in eerie silence. I swallow, drawing my blade into my other fist as I surge upward, knowing full well that if we're trapped down here, I won't be able to get the others out. And even with Pewter's everything's-*really*-gone-to-shit exit strategy and directions to a secret passage out to the grounds, I don't fancy their chances of getting out of this palace unscathed.

Or ours.

We get to the sitting room upstairs and find it unnervingly empty. The window is open, moonlight flooding the room like a search beam and a sudden howl has me racing to the window to peer out.

'Shit . . .'

Just beyond the kitchen gardens is a huge, hulking shape. A werewolf, darting back and forth across the lawns at the edge of the Great Wood, the woodland to the north of Dinas Tar, owned by the Crown. I frown. If I didn't know any better, I would say this werewolf is . . . frolicking?

Andry covers his mouth with a hand, whispering and giggling behind it, eyes wild as they drink in the sitting room, then the view out of the window. Knox keeps a stake poised between his shoulder blades, the point hovering in line with his heart and the links gripped in his fist. Alden sweeps up the staircase to stand beside me and chuckles darkly. 'Looks like Belle is enjoying herself.'

The room seems to squeeze and I clutch my chest, the breath beaten from my lungs as magic glints around us. Then a figure appears in the far corner, the room relaxing. The alarm bells begin pealing again. The figure shivers, stepping forward into a shaft of moonlight, and I see it's Blake, looking no worse for the illusion he wielded. 'The guards started poking around the room, so Belle decided to enact plan B.'

'Werewolf carnage?' I ask.

Blake nods. 'She leapt through the window, transforming before she even hit the ground.' He removes his glasses to polish the lenses on the sleeve of his shirt. 'Quite impressive. The guards set off the alarm and all left pretty quickly. Lots of shouting about securing the golden eagle, whatever what means. Thought I'd better conceal myself though. I don't think this palace likes any form of wielding, fairly sure that was me triggering the alarm.'

'Could have been the presence of this one,' I say, pointing to Andry, who is now leaning against the window, watching in glee as the guards race back and forth, shouting to one another as Belle leads them towards the tree line, then back up the lawn, snapping at their heels in obvious delight. 'We better leave. Belle knows to get to the meeting place.'

'She's clearly having far too much fun,' Alden says.

'Well at least someone is,' Knox mutters as Andry sniffs at him and grins.

Knox and I carve a bridge out of the doorway once more, the portal rippling before it settles, revealing an anxious-looking Pewter clutching a tea mug, leaning against his desk. I take one of Andry's chains and Knox and I step through with him, then Blake, leaving Alden to swiftly cut through after. Then I collapse the portals, watching as the bridge dissolves into nothing, all of us blinking and contemplating what we've just done.

'Well bugger . . . you didn't tell me you were going in to kidnap royalty,' Pewter says, aghast. 'Andry . . . haven't seen you in years. Thought you were in some poncy mountain resort . . .'

'Eight,' he says, grinning a touch too maniacally for my liking. 'And most definitely not some mountain resort, although that does sound *divine*. They didn't like me seeing anyone on account of, well . . .'

'You being turned into a vampiric, wielder-blood-thirsty monster?' Pewter supplies.

Andry shrugs and giggles in that high-pitched way that sets my teeth on edge. 'I should have mentioned, but I'll need some elixir soon. Next dose due in a few hours, takes the edge off. You're all smelling a little *too* good . . .'

'And I suppose you're thirsty too,' I say, eyeing him warily. 'When was the last time you fed?'

'If you're offering, I wouldn't say no, wielder . . .' he says, canines flashing in the light from the lamp on Pewter's desk.

'I don't think so,' I say, jerking my chin. 'Sit there, stay quiet and we wait for the last of our team. Don't try anything reckless or I'll take you back to the palace myself.'

He shudders but sits, remaining still and quiet. Belle appears an hour later, before dawn graces the city, exhausted but unharmed.

Knox and I create our final bridge, back to Darley Hall and I wonder if this was a stroke of genius, kidnapping Andry, or a fuck-up on a colossal scale.

*

A few hours chained inside one of the attic bedrooms of Darley leaves Andry sulky and taciturn but the rest of us rested and ready to tackle the biggest hurdle of how to keep him secret in a college full of perceptive wielders. Alden, Knox and I assemble in Darley the next day, in the corridor outside his attic bedroom whilst the others carry on as usual with lectures and studying, all of us acting as if we hadn't gone on a night heist to steal the Crown Prince.

'He's going to have to stay here,' Knox says, leaning against the wall, arms folded. 'Fortunately I did manage to pilfer something else in that lab . . .' He draws a charcoal-coloured folio out from inside his jacket and opens it. 'The ingredients and methodology for the current mix of elixir. The one that, as Andry puts it, takes the edge off. Should make him more malleable but won't actually sate him.'

'Nice one,' says Alden with a nod, taking it from him. He flicks through, nodding quickly. 'I can mix this in Fetlock, it'll take a few hours . . .' He glances at Andry. 'You can hold on that long, yes?'

Andry stares back stonily. 'I thought I wouldn't be chained to another wall when you sprung me from that decrepit dungeon.'

'We gave you a window and a bed. What more do you want?' I say.

'Freedom.'

'In Kellend?' I say and tut. 'Tell me. How would I reach your world?'

'My world? This *is* my world—'

'The cold ones' world.'

A slow smile creeps across his features. 'I wondered when we'd get to it. The real reason why you liberated me.'

I sigh. 'You can tell me now, or I can withhold the elixir Alden makes until you do. And this . . .' I say, extracting a vial from my pocket. I spin it in my fingers, the ruby liquid glinting in the low light from the window. 'This is what you really want, isn't it?'

He licks his lips, eyes fixed on the blood. 'There's magic in that.'

'You can sense it?'

'Of course I can. It exudes power.'

'Interesting,' I say softly, glancing at Alden before tossing it to him.

Andry catches it, wrenches open the cork stopper and downs it before closing his eyes. 'Delicious, your blood, alchemist. Best I've tasted, oh . . . ever.'

I frown. 'Why do you think it's mine?'

'The taste . . . it smells like you. The scent, taste, texture, along with the unique patter of your heart, they all combine for us into individual, unique food sources. You smell as you taste and your heartbeat sounds, like lavender, honey and copper with a hint of sea salt.'

Foreboding trickles down my spine as I nod to Alden and Knox to leave the room. When we've secured it, I turn to them both, whispering urgently. 'If his sense of smell is that keen, it's only a matter of time before *they* sense Tessa.' I don't mention what I'm most afraid of. That we may very well be far too late.

Chapter 15

From the Shadows

The elixir at least stops Andry talking about how good I smell. But when we begin to ask him more questions about his nature, how he was turned and his interactions with the other cold ones, as well as how they create bridges between their world and ours, he becomes remarkably less talkative.

Which really pisses me off.

'You know these are all the same questions those other wielders asked. Repeatedly,' he says, glaring at us. 'And I'm sure you'll do exactly the same as they have, keep me exactly as I am, just a font of knowledge for you to use. I bet you have no intention of trying to help me, or free me—'

'We want nothing more than a fully functioning elixir, just as they did,' I snap. 'But only when you no longer need to sustain yourself with wielder blood will you be allowed to go free. Did they tell you *that*?'

'Perhaps,' he says, looking away.

'And why did you clearly not cooperate with them?'

'Because if I ever got out, the others would turn on me. Instantly,' he says quietly.

'Interesting that you know that,' Knox says, a smile ghosting over his features. 'What *others* are you referring to?'

He chuckles, wagging his finger. 'You're cleverer than they were.

Always asking the same questions, trying to wear me down like water over stone. But your mind is built differently, isn't it, alchemist?'

'Flatterer,' Knox says. 'But still unhelpful.'

'I wonder if he responds to anything else,' Alden says.

'Like pain?' Knox replies lightly.

Andry's eyes glide lazily to meet mine. 'I might respond if I'm given the right incentive. A vein will do the trick, alchemist. Just open it up and I'll answer your questions.'

'Not happening,' I say, my blood heating. We're getting nowhere and I'm so done being nice to him. He's the only thing standing between me and Tessa. And yet he's still playing these games. 'A friend is in danger and I need you to answer these questions. Please.'

He sighs, slumping back and I hold my breath. Perhaps that was enough, perhaps I just needed to explain why—

'Sink to your knees and say please again with a juicy vein for me to nibble on, then maybe—'

Before Andry can react, I pull out my blade and sweep forward, gripping his hand to place on the arm of the chair he sits in and stab it straight through. He cries out and my stomach twists with nausea. It was instinct. Brutal instinct, driven by pure desperation and fury. I can't believe what I've done. This is the part of my training with the Collector I always shied away from, always tried to avoid. He breathes heavily, moaning with pain, and I have to hide my shock . . . it was barely a thought and now my blade is through his *hand*.

'How do I create a portal to their world?' I say, enunciating each word with careful clarity, pushing my shock, my nausea aside. I need him to hear me through his own screaming pain. 'Is there a specific method they use for bridging two worlds?'

He pants, his moans of pain becoming a hum, deep in his throat, then he laughs, throwing his head back, even as his body convulses.

I grit my teeth and twist the end of the blade, hating myself for this. 'All right, all right . . . vile, *vile* wielder,' he spits, whole body writhing. 'You need me alive.'

'Do we?' I ask softly. 'Or shall I find myself another cold one . . .'

He hisses and I smile wickedly, forcing myself to play this role. 'If I tell you, will you let me go?'

'Perhaps. If you tell me what I need to know. And if it leads to a cure.'

He hisses again, features contorted from the pain. 'When I say you need me, I mean quite literally. I've seen them open a portal. I was with a group of them for a time in the last great hunt . . . it took a couple of them. Linking hands and working together. As one. That's how they return to their world. I didn't step through. We were ambushed and I was captured by the Crown. I do wonder sometimes what life would have been like if I had stepped through though . . .'

'Sharing magic . . .' Alden murmurs, frowning at Andry as he trails off. 'Any specific location?'

He sneers at Alden. 'Surely you would know *that*, Alden Locke.'

Alden blanches and turns to Knox. 'The Morlagh Woods would be one. Not far from where I found my father.' Then his gaze meets mine. 'I'll wait outside. I've had enough time with our future king.'

I jerk the blade from Andry's hand and he cries out, then cradles it to his chest. A fresh wave of nausea sweeps through me and I have to bite back the 'sorry' before it crosses my tongue. 'Can you heal him first? Enough that he stops bleeding?'

Alden nods, crossing the room to stand before Andry. Then he holds out his hands and says quietly, 'I hope for your sake and that of Kellend's that if we manage to turn you back, you've retained some of your humanity. Sneering at the loss of my father's life is ugly and cruel.'

He wields, his botanist magic stopping the bleeding, knitting the sinew and muscle back together. Andry bites his lip, blinking quickly, and shudders.

Then Alden turns to me. 'It'll leave a scar. But he won't bleed over the furniture.'

I watch him leave then glance at Knox. His features are troubled, arms crossed over his chest. I take a breath, looking back at the cold one we've ensnared, revulsion churning in my gut. But not at him, at myself. I know I would have gone further. He doesn't care about helping us to save a friend, his sole focus on feeding. Perhaps this is what becoming a cold one means, the humanity, the soul being stripped away from a person. Until all that's left is a greying, ravenous shell. But he's not the one who just stabbed someone's limb for information.

I crouch down, until our eyes are level. 'I don't want to do that again, but I will. And now we've lost your healer. Tell me exactly what you saw when they opened the portal. Even if you didn't cross over, you must have seen something through it. Maybe they will have talked about their home. Tell me exactly where you were and be *specific*.'

'Or what?'

'Or we do this the hard way,' I say, smiling at him. 'I've got all day, Andry.'

He swallows, cowardly eyes darting from the blade in my hand to the stake strapped at my thigh. 'All right, alchemist. Bring me some parchment and a pen. I'll share what I know. But I want protection. If they know that I've shared this information with you—'

'You won't be leaving the wards of Killmarth until we can guarantee that,' Knox says.

He grumbles but acquiesces. 'I never received such harsh treatment in the palace . . .'

After he's finished writing down everything he can recall about the portal, I leave the room, finding Alden leaning against the wall beside the door. I hand him the parchment and nod. He rakes his gaze across my face and I try to summon up a smile, but falter.

'That was tough,' he says, opening his arms for me to walk into. I lean against his chest, closing my eyes and trying to banish the image of the blade going through his hand. The blade that I was holding.

'It was either you, me or Knox that had to go in hard,' I say with a sigh. 'There was no way he would talk otherwise. Knox can turn torturer next time. I don't have the stomach for it. It was a shock for even me . . . I don't think I can do it again.'

'Good thing it was you, really,' Knox says, joining us as he locks the door. 'Alden would have carved him up.'

'Smug prat.'

I push away from his chest, the sound of Andry's cry of pain still lingering in my ears. He's smiling but I catch it, that hint of shadow at the corners. He's thinking about the hunt at the wedding, I'm sure of it, when he went too far. That and the night he found his father, deep in the Morlagh. 'Well, we got what we needed,' I say. 'And if it works out, he will do in the end as well.'

I don't voice aloud that an eventual victory for us all doesn't erase it. The horrors of war and the lengths we will go to end it. To survive.

★

I enter the room in Darley Hall at midnight, when most of Killmarth is slumbering for the next training session with Ezra. Knox stands beside him, arms crossed, just as Ezra's are and it strikes me again how alike they are in build and stature. The same small twist of a smile alights their features as the door snicks shut behind me, and Ezra extends a hand, indicating the long table, set with lumps of metals, glass, and other nonliving matter.

'An alchemist's worktable. We are going to work on fine-tuning your wielding,' Ezra says. I go to take my place before the worktable, so the materials are within reach, but he shakes his head. 'No, no. You'll stand over there, in the corner, and you will wear this blindfold.'

Knox passes me a length of cloth to wrap around my eyes. 'To tune one sense, we must extinguish another.'

'All right . . .' I agree, taking the cloth and walking to the farthest corner of the room. 'Up until this point, it's just been instinctive though.'

'Exactly,' Knox says smoothly. 'Ezra ran through the same training with me when I sparked. Some materials you will find do not bend to your will as readily as others.'

I nod, stepping into the corner, and tie the blindfold around my eyes. It eclipses all light, leaving me into total, muffled darkness. I falter, not knowing how to discern the differences between glass or silver or clay at this distance. 'How will I know, though?' I ask, feeling a little unanchored without knowing exactly where Ezra and Knox are in the room. 'If I can't see—'

'Send out a thread of your magic and learn to sense the differences,' Ezra replies, sounding very far away. 'Now, I want you to turn each and every lump on this table into silver. We'll start there to find your baseline.'

An hour later, the threads of my magic are crackling across my vision. A web of wielding, gold and glittering, criss-crossing over the table on the other side of the room in my many attempts to change the state of each lump into silver. My first thought was to find the silver itself, wrap my magic around it and feel for any discernible property that would indicate how it was different to the others. I compared it to the lump next to it. And found something subtle, something hard to define. A taste, a sense of the vibration of its true self. Then, satisfied, I began the intricate work of changing each and every lump of matter to be identical. I found that each type of material needed a different type of coaxing. After the first explosion, I flinched back into the corner. But Ezra and Knox only chuckled.

'Keep going, Sophia,' Ezra said. 'That was only the clay.'

But an hour in, and I was beginning to feel hollowed out, an insistent drumming in my temples. It wasn't about the raw magic I could thrust into each lump and force it to change. It was all about fine-tuning, coaxing, listening . . . and I was already growing weary. Pushing up my blindfold, I assessed my progress. The gold had splayed out in a puddle of cooling metal, the glass a scatter of fractured pieces and several other metals had just rolled over a bit. But amongst my failures, lumps of silver gleamed. I stepped forward, touching each of them, sensing that they now felt like the original lump of silver.

'Not terrible,' Ezra says. 'You're most attuned to other metals and wood. Glass, clay and stone need more work. Knox, care to do the honours?'

'Sure.' He waves a hand over the table and I sense threads of alchemy magic weaving around each lump. Until it's a table filled with silver, other than the stone which remains stubbornly as itself, although now I see small glints, veins of silver threading through it. He puts his hands in his pockets and nudges my shoulder. 'You did better than my first attempt, DeWinter. We'll get there.'

'Tomorrow night, we'll attempt—' Ezra begins.

'Er, I can't,' I say, with a casual shrug. 'Study club. Knox is tied up too, aren't you?'

'Afraid so,' he says and clears his throat. 'The following night, uncle?'

'Of course,' Ezra says, nodding to us. 'Of course.'

★

The following night, the depths of the Morlagh sway with unnatural shadows. Maybe it's the ghosts of the past, maybe it's the clouds sweeping overhead, or perhaps it is just my imagination made flesh. I find I see the silhouettes of cold ones everywhere now. Belle transforms immediately, stalking alongside us, alert for other werewolves, or worse. The moon hides, the stars are few and I can barely see two steps ahead. Constantly scanning back and forth, eventually my vision settles and I can make out the shape of the crooked, wintry woodland around us.

Knox and Alden brace Andry on either side, Blake has stayed behind in case this all goes to shit. If we don't make it back by dawn, he'll tell Hess where we are. Although by then, there might not be much of us left to scrape off the forest floor.

'Always told myself I'd never return to this particular clearing,' Alden muses as we walk, the cry of a small animal echoing off the trees.

'You all right?' I ask.

'I will be,' he replies and I wish I could see more than the faintest whisper of his features. The dark really is all consuming tonight, a wintry depthless sort of dark. 'You don't have to do this,' I say quietly. 'You can turn back now, it's too much. Going back there.' I think of Dolly, that house, that alleyway. I don't think I'd be able to set foot inside that place.

His hand reaches for mine and squeezes. 'I can do this. Don't worry. T is my friend too. Mourn the dead, protect the living, right?'

'Right,' I choke out, hating that I've pushed and pushed for this. We're all here tonight, wandering the Morlagh because of my single-minded desperation. I'm planning to launch myself into a dangerous, deadly world and I'm expecting them all to just join me.

I breathe in the frost, sipping the cool air as we reach the location marked on Andry's rudimentary map. It's a space that perhaps thirty or so could gather in comfortably. The perfect place to form a portal, bridging their world and ours. 'So their portal locations are a match to ours?' I ask Andry. 'How do you know for sure?'

'I overheard one of them talking about the woodland in their world. How it had to be pinpointed exactly, so it wasn't splicing a tree or a building on the other side.'

This notion of another world, a distorted mirror to our own with pinpoints that it's possible to line up, like a twin map, to match a place there with a place here is dizzying. I think of Hester Lewellyn and wonder what she would have made of this. I miss her. Another name, another person stripped too soon from the landscape of my life.

Tessa cannot be another.

'Here,' Andry says, staring round. 'They were standing here, after they turned me. Talking about taking me back, which house I would belong to, who would get to keep me as currency, a hostage—'

'Houses?' I ask, rounding on him. 'First time you've mentioned this. They're split into houses?'

He shrugs, a grin bloating his face. 'You didn't ask.'

I summon all my self-control and smile at him. 'I'm asking now.'

His smile falters, eyes flicking to my blade, then back to my eyes. 'The ones that travel here seem to be from the main houses, few lesser houses. As though they have the power to cross over, the means to. And they feed to further their line, their house. The wielder magic they consume passes to their entire line, trickling down and down. The head is the most powerful, but the vampiric dregs of the house still benefit. It sustains them. The house with the most potent blood rules over the others, setting the rules for each hunt, and who will get to go on the next.'

Knox runs a hand down his face. 'Figures. Wielder blood feeds them, gives them strength and in turn, their house is sustained . . . even elevated. Which is why we're not overrun. They can't all cross over.'

'Which means there will be far more of them in this world we're walking into than we've ever seen here,' Alden adds.

'And some of them will be desperate,' I say, contemplating. 'Especially if they've never joined a hunt. Or they don't belong to one of the more powerful houses. They'll be feeding to sustain themselves in their own world, on whatever source is there. Vampiric elitism . . . deep joy.'

Knox shivers. 'Well, shall we get on with it, DeWinter? No time like the present for a little jaunt into the gaping maw of death. I for one cannot *wait*.'

'I've known worse odds,' Alden supplies.

'I haven't,' says Knox. 'It's definitely Tessa's round when we finally get to that pub in Marazia.'

'Five rounds, at least,' I mutter, calling upon my magic. I hold my hand out to Andry and raise an eyebrow. 'No bolting, no nibbling. Or I'll take you back to your mother.'

He chuckles breathlessly. 'This is entirely your funeral, alchemist. I'll not stand in your way.'

I grasp Andry's hand, trying not to shudder at the dry, cold feel of his fingers clasped in mine. Knox nods on the other side, Alden keeping a firm grip on the back of Andry's neck. Then I picture it. Another woodland, another world.

Their world. The one I glimpsed through the portal before Tessa disappeared into it.

For a moment, nothing happens as our raw power suffuses the clearing. Glowing and glimmering, gold and honeyed in my eyes, we create sunlight. We create a false day. Then the air in the clearing ripples, every hair on my skin standing on end. And before us, another clearing appears. Another place, another world.

The cold ones' world.

'Well, you've succeeded,' a voice says from the edge of the clearing. The blood freezes in my very veins as, at the sound of a finger snap, a pale light hovers at the fingertips of a man leaning casually against a tree.

Ezra Darley.

'Now tell me, scholars, why you have the missing Crown Prince gripped like you're about to sacrifice him to some eldritch god . . . and why the fuck you've got a portal open to another world?'

Chapter 16

City Lights

'We were wondering when you'd show up.' I smile.

'Knew you'd be suspicious,' Knox agrees.

'Study club was the worst cover story we could come up with at short notice,' I say. 'And we needed you here with us.'

'Without you telling the entire faculty, or the Crown, what we were up to.'

'Had to be out here, away from Killmarth,' I say.

Ezra crosses his arms, watching us quietly. 'I'm assuming you're planning to cross into their world to find your friend, Tessa Godolphin, yes?' he finally grits out.

'Correct,' Knox says. 'We knew we couldn't hide it from you entirely.'

'We just ask that you don't stop us,' I say.

He runs a hand down his face and groans. 'Well played, both of you. Well played.'

'What, you're not going to apprehend these— these scholars for kidnapping a member of the Crown?' Andry explodes.

'Oh, shut it,' Knox says, exasperated. 'You're barely a member. And you're asking the wrong person to give a shit.'

Andry mutters darkly about bringing back capital punishment as Ezra steps forward, eyeing the portal. Then he turns to me. 'Who are you planning on taking with you, Sophia?'

I hesitate, gaze flicking to Alden and Knox. 'No one,' I say, raising my chin. 'I needed them to help me create the portal and secure this area. But I'm going alone.'

'What?' Alden says.

'I can't risk any of you. Ezra's told us already, no one has ever returned from there. Not one wielder. Whoever leaves here and crosses that bridge may never return.'

'And you think, what? That you're expendable?' Alden says and I don't miss the quiet fury in his words. He thinks I'm sacrificing myself, like in our final Ordeal.

'She's my friend and I will find her,' I say softly. 'I didn't realise what she was planning, didn't pay attention. I should have. It's on me.'

'It's on all of us,' Ezra says. 'No one knew what she was planning and we've lost a damn good wielder. I don't want to lose any more, not tonight. Not any of you.'

'Which is why I need you to open the portal here when—'

'No, Sophia,' Ezra says. 'If you cannot be swayed from your recklessness, I will go with you. I'm not losing a single one of you, and I mean that.'

'And if you think I would let you walk through that portal without me . . .' Alden says.

I run a hand down my face. 'I can't let you—'

'Then don't,' Alden says. 'I have free will. As does Ezra. We know the risk, we know what we're willing to do. Look at my father. Look at what he did. He fought to the end to try to end this. As did your parents. All of us, every time we fight for the Crown, for Kellend, for our world, risk *everything*.'

My breath catches and I blink furiously. 'You're impossible.'

'He's right though,' Knox says.

'Well, I suppose I'm first then?' Ezra draws a stake, melded with whirls of iron. 'Let's get this over with. Knox, I assume you're staying put?'

Knox nods. 'To reopen the portal on this side and guard Andry, yes.'

'Good.' Ezra nods. 'After we've gone, tie him to a tree. If we're not back by dawn, alert the Crown.'

My gaze flickers to Alden's and I take a deep breath as the reality of what we are about to attempt hits home. It could end us.

'Belle?' I call softly. Belle appears, eyes glowing in the dark as she approaches. She transforms as she walks, shaking off the fur and fangs until it's just her, stalking across the clearing.

'No sign of anyone for miles.'

I nod. 'Good. That's good. Guard the perimeter and at the first sign of trouble . . .'

'Hotfoot it to Morlagh Manor.' She smiles and places her hand on my shoulder. 'I know. Please don't get murdered.'

'We'll try our best,' says Alden, nodding to Knox. 'See you in a few.'

'Remember, tell her rhyn's on her,' Knox says before looking away. 'But seriously, be careful. You too, Ezra. Sophia, I like you too much already. Don't make me go to the Crown at dawn.'

I grip his shoulder for a moment and Belle transforms once more, padding in slow, threatening circles around Andry. She snaps her jaws as he releases a skittish yelp.

Then Ezra takes a breath and marches through the portal. I step forward, taking Alden's hand and we walk after him, into the one place we shouldn't. The heart of enemy territory.

And when I turn to look back, I cut my hand through the air, just as Knox does the same on the other side. He holds my gaze as we collapse the bridge, the portals dissolving. We cannot risk a cold one discovering we've opened it and crossing over to our world . . .

or realising we've crossed into theirs, and hunting for us. Though, it will make returning to our world that much harder. If we can return.

*

The woodland is similar to the Morlagh as we walk through it, stepping as carefully as we can over branch and snow. Silence is cut short by several prolonged animal cries that set my teeth on edge, then the sound of a tussle, before silence reigns once more. The air nips at my exposed skin, the tip of my nose already numb from the chill.

'Look, through the trees,' I murmur, pointing to the east. Lights dance between the branches, winking softly in the distance. 'A town or city?'

'There's a town close to the Morlagh, to the east of where we would be in our world right now. But it's small. This looks much bigger . . .'

'Interesting.'

'Perhaps where they come from when they use this portal location to our world?' Alden says as we tread carefully through the frost and snow.

'Makes sense. It's just so strange that this is a whole other world. A distorted mirror of our own . . .' I say. 'If it wasn't overrun with cold ones, I'd feel some sense of wonder right now.'

'Same,' Alden says.

'Less chat, you two. Keep your wits about you,' Ezra murmurs up ahead. 'Remember this entire world is a death trap. They cannot know we are here.'

I glance behind us and wince. Our footsteps are marked all too clearly through the snow, if anyone is close by, it wouldn't be hard to track us. But we don't have time to sweep every footfall away. 'Let's get away from the trees, find a path or road where there are other tracks. Or the snow has melted.'

'Agreed,' says Alden.

We trek through the trees under a midwinter sky, finding a track where the trees thin. I try to figure out what Tessa would have done, where she would have gone. Would she have followed the other cold ones to that city? Or stuck to the woodland surrounding, stealing food when she could and finding shelter? I shiver as a cold wind whips my hair from the back of my neck, clawing its way beneath the collar of my jacket. No. She would not have survived long out here. And with her masquier wielding, disguising her as one of them, she may well have made it to that city. She may well have begun exacting her revenge on any cold ones she could for Greg's untimely death.

'You're thinking of going to that city, aren't you?' Alden asks.

I shrug. 'I don't fancy our chances of not freezing to death out here. And if Tessa made it that far, she might have left a trail.'

'Of death?'

I snort. 'If we're lucky.'

'Well, best we move now, before any of them detect us. Maybe we can blend in,' Ezra says and I blink in surprise. He's . . . agreeing with my strategy?

'Or maybe we'll be like a fine banquet and attract the attention of every cold one in that city,' I say with a sniff. 'But I don't see any other way.'

'Decision made.' Alden nods and flicks me a grin before whispering so only I can hear, 'If we die tonight, I just want you to know that you look really hot.'

'Vampire hunters turn you on?' I ask coyly.

'Just you,' Alden says, brushing a strand of hair behind my ear. 'Whatever you're doing.'

'You can show me exactly how turned on by me you are once we get out of here,' I say breathily, relishing the distraction as we move closer to the city, away from the line of trees.

'Locke, DeWinter, let's focus, shall we?' Ezra says softly, glancing back at us. 'No wielders have ever returned from this world. Let's keep that front and centre as we navigate this place. I would like us to be the exception, not the rule.'

The risk. Such a risk he's taken for Tessa. No, not just for Tessa. For me. For all of us. The realisation jolts me and I don't know what to make of it. For a moment I picture my parents, wondering if they crossed this way in their final mission. If they saw these woodlands, that city in the distance. I take a breath, shaking off the thought. Ezra's right, I need to focus. But I can't help wondering if he is shoving his own pain aside. My parents were his friends, just as Tessa is mine, but he wasn't able to save them. He never had the chance to rescue them from this world.

He was just landed with me.

Maybe this is about my parents, or maybe it's about me. But for this first time, I want to ask him more, to understand a little better. If we return, perhaps I'll find a time to ask.

The track is mercifully empty and as the clouds part, the sky reveals a scatter of jewel-like stars to light our way and a moon . . . a moon very unlike our own. 'A blood moon,' I say, gazing up at it. 'It's actually crimson . . .'

It bathes the world in red, dressing the snow and frost in shades of vermillion. I wonder for the first time if this world is part of our universe, or parallel to it. Running just one step away, only accessible by creating a bridge. And if there's this one, what if there are others? What if the cold ones are not the only beings to find a way to create a bridge to our world?

'Sophia, look at this,' Alden says, kneeling suddenly. I drop down into a crouch beside him as he brushes away the snow crusting the top of a carved stone marker. 'It looks like a distance marker, but there's something carved beneath it. I can't quite make it out . . .'

Cold settles in my bones as I pick out the words, piecing them together. 'One mile, Astrum. City of Aline.'

'Aline? The goddess?' Ezra says, frowning as he falls back from his position at the front, scouting to stare at the marker.

'It can't be the same, can it?' Alden says softly.

I brush my knuckles over her name and look up, narrowing my gaze on the lights and buildings up ahead, calling to us like a beacon. 'Well, well. How interesting.'

'What's more interesting is why three travellers would be on this road on the night of Aline's feast and not in Astrum, celebrating with their houses,' a voice says from behind us.

I gasp, whipping round with a stake in my hand to find a figure, dressed all in red. A hood covers their face, bathing their mouth in shadow, but I catch the smile dancing there. The smile of a cold one, finding their own feast.

A bell begins to toll, slow and steady, emanating from the city, Astrum. The cold one slips back her hood, revealing a cruel, pale face, angular features and a glinting blade in her hand. 'Far from home on a night like this, Sophia. I wondered how long it would take you.'

Chapter 17

Dipped in Toquay

I blow out a breath and throw back my head, cackling. 'Tessa, you scared the shit out of me . . .'

She grins, dropping into a bow. 'I couldn't resist. Alden, Ezra.'

Ezra nods stiffly, then turns his back on us, monitoring the dark.

Alden grins. 'Good to see you, T.'

Then I sniff, close the distance between us and throw my arms around her. 'Tell me this isn't a trick and it's really you.'

'It's really me,' she says, hugging me back. 'You brought the muscle, I see.'

'Best compliment you've ever given me,' Alden says, chuckling before I step away and he sweeps her into a hug as well. 'We must stop meeting like this.'

'In imminent, mortal danger?' she asks, looking up at him.

'Exactly.'

'A touching reunion,' Ezra says suddenly, turning towards us, steel in his gaze. 'Ms Godolphin, we have risked our very lives to bring you home. Time to return, scholars, and we will discuss your actions on the other side. Our odds grow increasingly worse the longer we remain here. I quite prefer my blood to stay *in my veins*.'

'It's not far, just a short way into the woods,' I say to her, gripping her forearms. 'I can create a portal, and—'

'Go back so soon?' she says softly.

Ezra exhales sharply. 'I will keep this brief as I do not want to *drag you.* But we are leaving. Your selfishness could still end the life of not only me, but those you love. Do you really want that?'

'Of course not, but that city—'

'Will remain a mystery for another day. Or did you want your family to grieve you like you, yourself, grieved all too recently?'

She casts her eyes down. 'I admit, I was not thinking beyond my need to avenge him.'

'Clearly,' Ezra says abruptly. I can tell he's not just pissed, he's furious. 'We're leaving. *Now.*'

'Wait.'

Ezra clamps his jaw, steely gaze flickering with fury. 'Wait?'

'See this for what it is, an opportunity,' she says, her own gaze hardening. 'Return if you wish, but I have gathered information, intelligence that the Crown could only dream of possessing. This world, the people here . . . I have only just begun. This world is not all we thought it might be.'

I frown as her gaze lingers on the skyline, drenched in red from the moon's eerie crimson glow. 'What is it then?'

She swallows, her eyes landing on me. 'There are cold ones, certainly. But there are also others. Other . . . species. Werewolves, elvish, even those that have gills and can live underwater. And humans. There are people too.'

'People like us? Wielders?' Alden asks.

Tessa nods. 'They're clever. Smarter than us. They've found ways to not be the target of the cold ones. There are laws, there are houses and packs and . . . factions. A hierarchy. If they kill a wielder here, or take their blood without consent, they're killed. Along with their immediate line, anyone they've turned and anyone that turned them. Like I said, it's not the place we believed it was. When the cold ones hunt in our world, it's to feed, but it's also for sport. For glory. And because they are not permitted to hunt here in that way, not permitted to *kill* to feed, Aline does not allow it.'

Frost trickles down my spine. 'If the cold ones don't hunt in this world, then what do they consume? How do they sustain themselves here?'

'With this,' Tessa says, producing a bottle and a vial. 'One is to curb the bloodlust so they don't suddenly get the overwhelming urge to attack another creature. The other is a potion, it resembles blood and holds a whisper of magic in each bottle. It sustains them, feeds them, but doesn't sate them. They vie for a place on a great hunt to finally feel sated, to drink pure blood, as they call it. And to feed those in their house. To make them stronger. When they feed, the magic trickles down through their bloodline, sustaining all in their house. The lowest members get the least. They can exist on this, they call it toc. But it's a thin, miserable existence.'

I shudder. 'But some of them die when they hunt.'

She shrugs. 'For them it's worth the risk, for the glory of the hunt. For the strength if they return. They are usually elevated in their houses. But then of course, they've tasted pure blood and everything else is ash. Then they're desperate to win a place on the next great hunt.'

'And the cycle continues . . .' Alden says. 'How did you find out all this?'

'I listened. I learned,' she says with a smile. 'I broke into one of their manufacturers. And I also kidnapped one, bound him to a tree in the woodland, and carved him up until he talked.'

My stomach churns with nausea, picturing Tessa as the torturer. Picturing myself as I calmly stabbed Andry's hand with a blade. 'This vial, the one that curbs their bloodlust and the potion, toc, the one that sustains them, what's in them?'

Tessa shakes her head. 'I don't know. That was my next thing to learn of. But the formulas are closely guarded, from what I can glean. They're both produced by one house only. The Ravens.'

I cross my arms over my chest, the cold seeping beneath my jacket as the clouds drift overhead once more, blotting out the moon. Snow begins to fall, spinning in lazy drifts, then thicker, quickly blanketing the road. At least our tracks will no longer be visible. 'We need to return, then parse through all this.' I hold out my hand, squeezing hers. 'Please come home, T. Come home with us.'

Her features, the features of the cold one, soften as she squeezes my hand back. Then she sighs. 'There's still so much to learn here though, I've only just scratched the surface . . .'

'Don't even try it,' Ezra suddenly snaps. 'We are returning. Now. Enough of this selfish foolishness. Your friends could have died to help you. They could still.'

She flinches away from him, but I hold her hand firmly in mine.

'You walk with us, *now* and perhaps I won't lose my temper. But I will not risk Sophia for another moment. Do we have an understanding?'

My name on his tongue chills me to the bone. I stare at him, the tone of his voice now triggering every bad moment from my childhood. Every terror, every night of loneliness. But right now . . . it's about protection. Protecting all of us. 'He's right, T,' I say, looking at her. 'You're risking all our lives. Please.'

Alden says nothing but as my eyes flick to his, I know he'll do it. He'll knock her out if he has to, sling her over his shoulder and carry her home. Maybe she realises too, or maybe Ezra has finally got through to her, but she relents. 'All right. Let's go home.'

★

We find the clearing, the woods swaying eerily in the trembling breeze. The whistling through the trees is a long, throaty scream and I can't help flinching as the moon paints the shadows red. The crimson, splashed over the dead white snow, is stranger now than when we first arrived, when it was moonless.

I take Alden's hand and focus on the middle of the clearing. 'Let's get out of here. Ezra?'

A small smile, which on anyone else I would believe is pride, washes his features and he gestures to me to take the lead. 'I'll support you if you need a boost, but this is your show. Get us out of here, alchemist.'

All right . . .

I call upon my magic, the raw well at my centre. The cold has drained me physically, the wielding of creating the bridge to arrive here has depleted that well. My vision dips and fizzes as I blink steadily, narrowing my gaze as I remind myself I am steel. I *can* create another portal. Alden's magic pours into my veins through our linked hands and I gasp softly. It's honey and toquay, it's sunlight and stars. The molten heat flows into that well and I plunge into it, drawing it all. Then I release a breath and picture the Morlagh Woods. I picture our world, silver moonlight, a woodland of lichen and creaking, ancient trees and *home*. I step forward, tasting tea on my tongue. Tasting velvane. It's so visceral, so perfect, and I push all that honeyed magic out into the clearing.

And I carve a portal out of air.

But . . .

Nothing happens. The blood-lit air doesn't ripple, doesn't sway. The woods whistle and scream and my magic . . . does nothing. I grit my teeth, trying again, calling on more and more, scraping the very edges of that well—

'Sophia,' Alden says, from somewhere far away. 'Sophia.'

I gasp, releasing his hand, and look at him. 'I can't . . . it's not working. When Andry said we would need him to get *here* . . . he never said about returning. I just assumed you needed a cold one only to get into the cold one's world, but for ours, I thought I could just create the bridge back, because it's into *our* world, not theirs . . . he must not have known . . .'

Alden's eyes widen, but he's not looking at me. He's looking past my shoulder, to where Tessa stands. I turn slowly, foreboding sinking its claws into me. Tessa is standing there, but two others are with her now. One either side, a glinting blade at her throat. Ezra murmurs a curse, beginning to circle, that glinting stake held in his fist.

'We knew you'd be back,' the cold one on the right says, a woman with red hair that slips down one shoulder, greying skin gaunt against the vibrant hue. 'When we sensed the portal location being used . . .'

'We knew you'd have to return, eventually,' the other adds, another woman, with spiked dark hair, eyes huge and dark as beetles. Then she sniffs Tessa's throat, chuckling quietly. 'Clever, clever wielders . . . a masquier, yes? Never known one of you to be able to change into one of us so convincingly. Only one element miss—'

I don't let her finish.

With the magic still fizzing at my fingertips, I twist the stake out of its holder with my will, alongside the blade strapped to my other thigh.

And I unleash them.

But the cold ones are quicker.

The blade pierces like an arrow, cutting the air where the cold one with red hair stood, striking a tree at her back. The stake hits the other's arm as they twist, launching through the air to the right. Tessa uses the chance and bolts, reaching me in a few steps and skidding to a halt beside me and Alden. Ezra swears again, weighing them with his gaze. He's hesitating, calculating. The risk here is greater, because it's not just about killing these vampires. We risk being trapped here. To open the portal, we need one of them alive.

'They're different here,' Tessa says urgently. 'The ones that hunt, they're nothing compared to the ones I've fought.'

The woman with red hair draws twin blades from sheaves along her back, smiling at us. 'The ones blessed with a place on the great hunt are sated. But those of us left behind, we're so constrained, so surrounded by the blood of wielders that we're not allowed to even taste . . . and we *hunger*.'

She pounces.

Faster than I can track, faster even than that cold one who killed Dolly, she launches at Alden, just as the other one darts for his other side. He leaps away from me and I turn, grasping at thin air. Grasping for his hand, but he's tumbled away. Fear grips me as I round on them. 'Alden!' I cry as they hustle him towards the tree line. Then I'm running towards him, Tessa at my side, as Ezra's warnings of a trap buzz in my ears.

As though in slow motion, he falls into shadow.

And I can no longer see him.

Chapter 18

One of Us

My heartbeat slows, pounding like a drum. Each beat marks a lifetime as I run to him. His name lodges in my throat, a whisper, a prayer as a snarl rips from those shadows. And the trees surrounding us explode into life. I shield my face, ducking swiftly as a web of new life twists towards those shadows. Tessa screams, the sound echoing all around us, and I reach for her, glancing to check she's all right.

She's no longer wielding. She no longer appears to be a cold one. It's Tessa I find, crouched beside me, handing me a blade, eyes filled with fear and awe. Just as mine are.

There's a roar, but it's not the sound of those monsters. It's Alden, beating them back.

We rise, waiting as the trees bend inwards, branches like claws, clutching for their prey. I smile, heart receding to its usual, steady rhythm as Alden emerges. Ripped shirt and jacket, chest exposed and bloodied, but whole. Alive. And behind him—

The cold ones. The limbs of the trees encasing them, thrusting them forward into the clearing. Alden twists his wrist, beckoning the trees forward with his wielding. 'We need one of them, don't we? Last time, we used Andry.' Then he waves his hands at them. 'Take your pick.'

Ezra chuckles at our backs as I shake my head in wonder. The trees are aglow in my sight with his golden magic. The monsters snarl and snap as the trees strain from their roots, dragging them onward to where we can open the bridge. I reach for Alden's hand, feeling him sag slightly, his breath harsh and a little too quick. He's hurt. They've hurt him.

Then I see where he's bleeding. A bite mark, on the side of his throat. 'Alden . . .' I breathe, eyes widening in horror. 'They bit you, they—'

Then with a crack, the cold one with red hair breaks free. I gasp as she wrenches back Alden's head and between blinks, opens a vein in her own wrist, mashing it against his lips. 'Drink, wielder,' she hisses. 'You want one of us? *I'll make one for you*.'

'No,' I gasp, ripping him from her grip. But with another crack, the other cold one breaks free, hands clawing for Tessa.

She stands her ground, slicing at the monster, eyes darting to mine. 'Open it! Grab the other one and bloody *open it*!'

Ezra's stake whistles past Tessa, striking the cold one in the chest. But with a vicious cackle, she rips it back out and I stare in horror. Ezra splutters, raising his hand as every stone in the clearing is dislodged from the earth. They burst through the frost and snow, hurling for the cold ones and Tessa ducks away just as they tear through the vampire's flesh.

I lunge for the other cold one, slashing at her throat so she's gasping like a fish, other hand pressed to the gash. Then I grip Alden's other hand, stare into the space where I need the portal to appear, and shove.

'Ezra, I need— *I need you*!'

His magic suffuses my veins. I cry out with the pain of it, the searing raw magic like blades of lightning as I bridge our two worlds not with wonder, but with brute force. Then when the air ripples, when the portal appears, I kick the cold one away, letting her gasp and bleed on the ground. Tessa yells, leaping through the portal, and I push Alden after her, before turning for Ezra. He's making quick work of the other cold one, now a heap of torn flesh, spearing her with a stake.

'Ezra, now!' I cry and his gaze meets mine. And I see it. The pain of grief, of loss, the sorrowful, dark heart of him. I swallow, beckoning to him, needing him in this moment to not be a human being. I need him to be the ruthless monster I've grown up with. I need him to walk past me, through that portal and not look back. He braces my shoulder, staring down at me, and I shake my head. 'You first, alchemist.'

He sighs, not wanting to leave before me, forever the person who goes last. 'Your show, Sophia. Your show.' Then he steps over the threshold of the portal and I cast one last look at the clearing, checking no other cold ones plan to follow us. Eyes. Dark, hungry eyes emerging from the tree line.

Oh gods, oh gods . . .

I leap through myself.

In the Morlagh, I tumble into the snow, then whirl, dizzy, stars imploding in my eyes and slash my hand through the air. Collapsing the bridge, cutting off any possible pursuit for now. Then I fall to the ground, limbs impossibly heavy, breath a thready rasp, dragging up my throat. Darkness eclipses my vision completely as every glint of magic in my well is gone.

★

The remaining hours of the night come in fits and starts as I wake then fall back into oblivion. There is snow, soft as powder, cold seeping into the very marrow of my bones, the limbs of trees, restless and bristling. Then a house, a sprawling, lonely, lovely house, candlelight, a female voice, commanding and kind. Then oblivion rushes in once more and I am left to struggle towards the light.

'. . . gave too much.'

'Why you were all out there . . .'

'. . . would have done the same. If it was Father, if it was me . . .'

'Of course, but the risk . . .'

I try to grasp those voices, follow the ribbon of their words into wakefulness . . . but it's like clawing up through a lake. A dark, murky lake with water as viscous as oil. When I do manage to open my eyes, thin daylight filters through a window. The sky is a pearly blue, framed by heavy curtains, and when I angle my head against the softest pillow, I find a canopied four-poster bed and a fireplace crackling with flame. There are twin sofas in front of it and Alden sits on one of them. He's wearing the most casual outfit I've ever seen him in, a simple navy blue jumper with a hole in one arm and the kind of trousers the ground staff wear at Killmarth. I wince when I notice the bandage on his neck.

'Where are we?' I ask and wince again. My voice does not sound like my own. It's a wisp, a faint breeze of sound and even asking that question drains me. My eyelids are weighted, leaden, dragging me back towards that still, deep lake. But I fight against it, needing to know where we are. 'Did I collapse the bridge in time? Did the portal close?'

'It did,' Alden says, rising to cross the room to me. He sits on the bed, reaching out to smooth the hair back from my forehead. 'Thanks to you. We're at Morlagh Manor, my family home. My mother and brother are seeing to the others.'

'Andry?'

Alden smiles humourlessly. 'He tried to bolt. Knox tackled him, knocked him out and hauled him all the way here. He's chained in the attic and Mother is trying to reason with him. He's better around her, more malleable. He remembers her from before he was turned.'

'That's good,' I say, my eyes already closing. 'We got Tessa out, didn't we? That's good.'

'Sophia . . . I have to tell you something. Try to stay awake this time.'

'This time?' My eyes flutter back open, watching him.

He swallows. 'When we were escaping, I was bitten. And one of them managed to feed me a drop of their blood. Apparently that's all it can take . . .'

Suddenly, I'm wide awake. 'What are you saying?'

'We can't know for sure, not until the next moon turn, but according to Andry . . .' he says, eyeing me carefully, 'as with werewolves, the change seems to happen slowly, then solidify after a full moon's turn. But I may well have been turned. Into one of them.'

★

It takes me another full night and day to recover enough to leave the bedroom. Alden's mother has discussed a cover story with Ezra, and he in turn has spun some tale about a secret assignment which he has called us all away on. All bullshit, but we'll deal with any suspicions over our absence from Killmarth later.

As I descend down the main staircase, my legs shaky, muscles still weak, I take in the entrance hall of the Locke family seat. There's a shabby, haphazard sort of comfort about it, with a polished honey-coloured wood staircase, armchairs and sideboards along the edges next to a jumble of rain boots and coats, walking sticks and umbrellas by the front door. There are paintings and sepia-toned photographs lining the walls, all mashed together and the air smells of pine and cedar, and something warm . . . I realise it smells like

Alden. I'm greeted by three dogs, all with thumping tails and soft eyes.

Alden's different here. His rugged good looks simply make sense in a home like this, lingering at the threshold of a place given over to the wilds, where ancient trees grow and creatures of legend roam free. I can see him now, finishing at Killmarth College, having developed his ability to wield as a botanist. A time when he can return here, manage the land and woodland, spend time in a huge greenhouse, bursting with new life, and fill his days with loam and green.

Perhaps if it weren't for the cold ones, that would have been his future. Perhaps it still can . . . I glance at him, worry gnawing at me. If somehow he's wrong about that bite. He went there for me. He crossed over because I did, because I could not leave Tessa there. I could not lose someone else I loved deeply. He took the risk, but it was for me. And now . . . I swallow, panic clawing at me. Now he may suffer a fate worse than dying.

Raised voices float up from downstairs and I realise they're all arguing. About us. Alden sighs, catching my eye, and smiles faintly. 'It's been like this since Ezra returned a few hours ago.'

'Ezra's here?' I ask, trying to stifle the panic over that bite. There has to be a way out of this. My fault. It's all my fault, what's happening to him, the risk he took . . . 'Of course he is.'

'He has opinions. But so does my mother.'

I look at him. '*Oh*. She's a match for Ezra.'

'You could say that.'

I release a breath, straightening my shoulders as we reach the bottom of the staircase, trying to maintain some semblance of normalcy for Alden. 'Suddenly, I don't mind him being here.'

We enter a room off the entrance hall, another fireplace greeting us with a wash of warmth. Outside it's still a stark world of white with the permanent drifts of midwinter snow, but inside, this lounge is a cosy haven. Sofas and armchairs are scattered throughout, smothered in mismatched cushions and blankets. There are side tables with stacks of books, framed photographs and oddities, a paperweight in the shape of a gargoyle, a vase of jewel-like long feathers, a jar of corks stained with the contents of the bottles of toquay they once stoppered. The walls are lined with bookshelves and paintings with a writing desk by the window, piled up with pens and ink pots and letters. If this room were a person, I would instantly want to be friends with them.

And on the sofas by the fire, everyone sits or sprawls, with only one person standing, hands clasped behind his back, a scowl on his features—

'Darling, at last,' a woman says, standing quickly and striding across the room. Her smile is open and warm, dark hair cascading down her shoulders, the same shade as her son's. She's the most beautiful woman I've ever seen. Not because she's obviously pretty, but striking. Broad shouldered, tall and sturdy, with a strong nose, expressive eyes, full red lips and a slight flush to her cheeks. Alden's mother, Celia Locke. She takes my hands in hers and I find a pair of eyes just like Alden's, warm brown with flecks of caramel staring down at me. But I don't miss it, how her gaze flicks to Alden, the fear at the edges. 'Glad to see you on your feet. Come, come, tea and cake. Sit by me. Tell me all about yourself.'

Ezra snorts. 'We don't have time for this, Celia. Your son could be on the verge of becoming a murderous monster, just like our Crown Prince. Thanks to your absurd and highly dangerous rescue,' he says pointedly and I can't help agreeing with him. I should have gone alone. He didn't condone it; he didn't want to go. I effectively forced his hand. 'We need a solution, fast. We need to fix the nocturnal elixir so it doesn't just curb the bloodlust. We need the cure.'

Chapter 19

Lab Coats and Midnight Drinks

Ezra draws a vial from his pocket, holding it up to catch the winter light. The nocturnal.

'What do you propose?' I ask, Celia's hands dropping from mine. She flashes me a sad smile, moving back to take her place on a sofa, and I have to stop myself from glaring at Ezra. She's the mother of the man I love, and this is the first time I'm meeting her. If this first impression sticks . . . I swallow. It's not a great start. I've rebelled, spearheaded a mission to rescue my friend, taken her son with me and in the process, he's been bitten by a monster. It might take a full moon turn for the complete change, but even now, he could be turning. The instincts to hunt, to feed, to thirst kicking in. I've brought danger into her home and risked the life of her son.

She should despise me. She shouldn't graciously welcome me here, Ezra's right. Because the man I love, the man I've fallen for so completely might even now be changing into a monster. And it's all my fault, not Ezra's. Mine. He's the person I've always thrown it all at; my resentment, my anger, my sorrow. He moulded my stubbornness by being the wall I could throw myself against, repeatedly. And it's almost worse that I've seen the chinks in his armour, the way he's so utterly human. How he cares, deeply. It's harder to hate someone you understand.

'What I propose, Sophia, is that we either use the blood of Alden, or the Crown Prince you foolishly *kidnapped*, the repercussions of which could catch up with all of you at any moment. Or did you think I wouldn't suspect you when I was given the assignment by the Queen herself to track down his kidnappers and bring them to her alive for her to deal with? There are surprisingly few alchemists able to craft portals. You're lucky your particular brand of wielding is not well established yet.'

I remain silent, his gaze about as warm as stone. Foolish indeed. Of course he would have realised it was me. He would have been there in the Morlagh, following us whether Knox and I gave our stupid reason for not attending a training session or not. He's been keeping tabs on me. And I've been so *obvious*, it's a wonder I'm not already languishing in the damn Crown's dungeons. I was the one distraught by Tessa's disappearance; I was the one who wanted to open a portal to find her—

'I must correct you there, uncle,' Knox says, crossing one leg over the other. 'Sophia was only one component. Or did you think her strong enough to open and close every portal, and create a bridge from Killmarth to the palace by herself? You saw how we worked when we crossed over to their world. I believe you overestimate her.'

I gape at Knox, who raises one finely manicured eyebrow at me. Gods, he's always been the most intelligent of all of us. Touché. Thank the gods he's on my side.

'Be that as it may,' Ezra says softly, 'we are left in a dire situation entirely of your making that now must be reversed. And I cannot, in good faith, tell the Queen that I had no knowledge of any of this when it inevitably comes to light. So we must ensure that before that day comes . . . we have something to offer her other than painfully drab excuses. Not that we have any real chance of creating a cure when the Crown's best botanists have been working on this for years, but we are left with no choice but to try. Celia, Edmund, may I request a room given over for the use of a temporary laboratory? We may not have much of a chance of finalising the cure, but you'll need to test each stage of development on Andry. It's the only way now of developing it in time to save Alden. The Queen will be far more willing to accept the fact you kidnapped her son, and not condemn you all, if you return him to her cured.'

Celia works a response around in her mouth, fear flashing again in her eyes before nodding. 'First floor, at the back of the house. My-my husband's lab has not been touched in many years.' She takes a breath, eyes landing on Alden. 'It seems as good a time as any to revive his old equipment.'

'Excellent. Thank you, Celia,' says Ezra. 'Then I will leave you to your work. I expect Knox has enough of the stolen files from the Crown's lab to continue the work?'

I cross my arms. 'What makes you think he would have them?'

Ezra stares right at me. 'I know each of you better than you know yourselves. Knox here values knowledge above all else. He never would have left such valuable documents behind. Now I must go and convince Caroline and the Queen that I am doing my utmost to recover her son and buy you the time you need. Discreetly.'

★

Over the next few days I regain my strength, the well of magic within me refilling. Celia and Edmund ensure we are fed and rested, but most of our time is spent in Alden's father's laboratory. Knox determines that we must first establish a baseline for taking the elixir to the next level, to the cure. Samples of mine, Andry's and Alden's blood are taken, and mine is also compared to Tessa's in case our wielding abilities mean the results differ. Knox pores over the work of the botanists alongside Alden, oil lamps burning long into each night. The elixir doesn't alter mine or Tessa's blood, as expected. But with Andry's, it reduces certain components for a time, with Alden's, we can begin to identify those components within his blood. Seeing the sample data makes me nauseous, he's already changing on a molecular level. Now we need to develop the nocturnal so that it doesn't just suppress those components in his and Andry's blood . . . it eliminates them entirely.

Alden tries wielding first, using his botany magic to change the nocturnal to match the potion from Astrum. But it doesn't work. He just shrugs, hiding his disappointment. 'Had to check it off the list.'

Around midnight, when the others have drifted off to their respective rooms, Alden and I find ourselves alone. His father's lab is lit by candlelight, shadows flitting over the walls and equipment. It's a cosy space, filled with glass tubes and a scarred, long worktable, as well as a sink, cabinets and a selection of old lab coats, with patches sewn on the elbows. He looks up at me and stretches, before glancing at the clock.

'You know, my father and I used to have a bit of a ritual when I was home from boarding school.'

'Oh?' I ask, setting down the notebook I've been scratching notes in.

Alden points to a cupboard by the sink. 'A midnight drink. Mother never knew, or if she did, she never let on.' He slides off his stool and goes over to the cupboard, pulling out a few jars and then rummages for the milk. He turns to me and smiles. 'Brought it up from the kitchen earlier. Would you like a cup?'

I smile warmly back. 'I would.'

Alden begins the process of measuring out various powders in a beaker, then pours the milk in, mixing it around. He carries it over to a Bunsen burner, setting it in a holder to heat gently. I move to stand beside him as he draws two mugs towards us. 'It would always be just the two of us, our secret. Not even Edmund bothered coming in here when Father was working on his experiments.'

The milk and powder begin turning a gorgeous velvety brown, and I smell something sweet and rich. Hot chocolate. 'You made hot chocolate with him.'

Alden holds up a finger. 'Not just any hot chocolate. Father figured out a few added ingredients to deepen the flavour, and it was the drink I thought about every term at school. I will warn you, no hot drink will ever compare to the midnight drink.' He smiles teasingly but I catch it. The edge of sorrow at the corners. I lean into him, so our bodies are close, and he turns off the Bunsen burner, before pouring out the drink into the two mugs. 'There, you try.'

I draw it to my lips, blow on it and watch the steam curl away. The first sip I take warms me down to my toes, and Alden's right. It's the best hot drink I've ever tasted. I grin at him. 'He sounds very wonderful.'

'He was,' Alden agrees. 'He really was.'

'I'm sorry,' I say, looking up at him. 'If I hadn't dragged you all to their world, you wouldn't be here trying to finish the nocturnal. We'd still be at Killmarth.'

'And Tessa would most likely be dead,' he says gently, gaze fixed on mine. 'I don't regret what we did, not for a moment. I would do anything for you, just as you did for me in the final Ordeal.'

'It's different—'

'It's not though,' he says. 'You walk into fire, I walk into fire. I'm never waiting for you to see if you step out of the other side. I'll be right there, walking with you. Of my own free will.'

He takes my cup from me, placing it further down the worktable, and braces his hands around my hips. Then in a smooth movement, lifts me onto the workbench. I squeal, dropping my arms around his neck. 'The perfect height, Locke.'

'Fancy that,' he murmurs.

He tastes of hot chocolate when I kiss him. Opening my legs, he steps between them and my heart cranks up a notch. Every place where we touch, I melt. This kiss, this moment of quiet in the sea of uncertainties surrounding us is everything. He's my touchstone, my home. I place my hands on the worktable and he places his on top, leaning into me. I arch my hips, warmth pooling at my core, that delicious flutter of heat spreading through my veins. Our kisses deepen, lengthen and I lose myself in this midnight.

But I want more.

He groans, moving one hand to cradle the back of my head, twisting his fingers in my hair, tugging gently.

'You taste sensational . . .' he whispers against my lips.

I move my hand, accidentally knocking over a test tube and it cracks. I flinch, realising I've cut my finger, and notice he's suddenly gone very still. I glance at my hand, a small bead of red welling on my index finger. I can almost feel his desire as a tangible thing in this lab. Without thinking, I bring it to his lips, offering it to him. 'Make it better?'

He takes my finger in his mouth, licking off the bead of blood. His eyes darken with an almost animalistic desire. Then he turns his head away, closing his eyes. 'I can't— this—'

'It's all right,' I say, cupping his cheek, drawing his gaze back to meet mine. 'Remember I love all of you. We'll figure this out.'

He kisses me again, harder than before, slipping his hands under my jumper and shirt. I gasp as his fingers raise gooseflesh over my skin, as he runs them up and down my rib cage. I continue kissing him, feeling the heat building between us, and reach down, unbuckling his belt. I stroke him with my hand, teasing, as his own hands undo my trousers, lifting my hips to slide them down. He groans again and the sound reverberates all through me. He's already close. I guide him inside me, angling my hips, and lean back, bracing myself on the worktable. He thrusts, one hand under my shirt, massaging my breasts, the other reaching between my legs, rubbing in slow circles.

'Harder,' I gasp, throwing back my head. I burn for him, for his touch, for the intense pleasure, the unfurling at my core. Each wave builds until I'm writhing under his touch, as he's driving inside me, then I shatter all around him. He thrusts, climaxing as well and the ripples of heat keep coming as I ride the wave until I'm spent. I lie back on the worktable, panting, and look up at him. His eyes meet mine, wicked and molten with desire still, then run down over my body slowly. Unhurried.

'Lab work has suddenly taken on a whole new meaning,' he says with a cheeky smile.

★

Tessa and I opt to forage together over the following days, determined to find all the plant life mentioned in the Crown's botanists' research. The first step is to replicate what they have achieved so far, so we understand every step of the process, every ingredient. The next is to elevate it. There's something missing, we're all sure of that, but what . . . we're uncertain. And when compared to the potion that Tessa swiped in the cold ones' world that is used to curb their bloodlust, we find there is a difference. Almost as though theirs has the potential to be a complete cure, but it's diluted.

'It doesn't just calm the bloodlust, but also the thirst entirely. Only, it's temporary,' Knox says, eyeing Andry as he wolfs down a plate of chicken pie and seasonal vegetables. Celia stands in the doorway, watching him.

'But you only have the small amount Tessa was able to take,' Celia says. 'Which means you need to replicate that and figure out what the difference is between your elixir and their potion. And whether whatever component is missing simply needs to be of a higher concentration . . .'

'Or if it is indeed only one component,' Knox says, pushing his hair back from his face. There are dark shadows under his eyes, the lack of sleep telling on his skin. But I've seen him watching Alden. He'll be damned if he lets his friend slip away before his very eyes. 'And we've tested against every plant in the vicinity. Alden, is that every strain in Kellend?'

'Every plant specimen from the main groups,' he says, also watching Andry. I've noticed how sometimes, there is a tremor in his fingertips now. Only sometimes, and only when he's with all of us. I worry that it's his desire for wielder blood, already taking root. 'But we haven't exhausted our world yet. There are different specimens we can gather in Theine—'

'And Alloway,' Knox says, gaze flicking to Celia. We all grow quiet as her features shutter. If any of us travel to Alloway, we are putting ourselves in very real, mortal danger if we are found. The skirmishes on the border have become even more intense in recent days.

The front page of a newspaper Edmund brings back from a meeting in Dinas Tar blazes with the words 'Theine Alight Over Night' with a sepia-toned image of a city skyscape ablaze. Knox became very still as Edmund read out the article, then abruptly left the room. The city was somewhere he had spent some time last year, I found out later. Close to the border, but it was clear the war was gaining momentum.

Knox spent all that day trying to contact his friends there, dialling number after number, a tilted glass of velvane never far from his lips.

'The cold ones have allies in Alloway. Or at least, sympathisers,' I say, thinking of Fion and her crusade to be Argus reborn. 'If there is an unidentified component, a plant used in the cold ones' potion, it may well originate from there or at least be something of a similar variety. It would make sense.'

'It would also make sense why the botanists working for the Crown hadn't developed their elixir into a full cure,' Knox agrees. 'If they hadn't yet looked beyond Kellend for the missing component. They've already eliminated so many plant species according to their research, and the state they had got the nocturnal to was impressive.'

'Impressive maybe, and highly methodical. Maybe they could have got the go ahead to gather and test plant species from other territories. Maybe they were working on that but it was deemed too risky. But it's not too great a risk for us,' Tessa says. 'It's not as though we have anything to lose.'

'Except for our heads,' I point out.

'Do they still behead wielders?' Andry muses with a chuckle. 'Delightful territory. So friendly.'

'We're shooting at shadows,' Knox growls, massaging his temples. 'There's too much we don't know. Too many assumptions being made. We know the components of the nocturnal so far, we know they are all plant based. But we know little about the potion Tessa was able to swipe. This is all conjecture, not fact.'

I sigh. He's right. We're following rabbit trails, trying to cut corners based on speculation. 'Take another sample of his blood. Just to be sure. We need every piece of evidence, we have to analyse all the data available to us right now. Is it one component, or more? Is it a plant, or something else? If we take a risk, if we go into enemy territory to gather specimens, I want it to be a calculated one.'

'Spoken like a Darley . . .' Knox says, casting me a look and I nudge him.

'The only good thing that came out of my years living with the Collector. I can scheme like a Darley,' I say grimly. 'Let's give it two days to gather more evidence and form a plan. No more risks without gathering all the facts first.'

'It's one missing component,' Andry says quietly, sitting back. 'Between your nocturnal elixir and their potion, it's only one thing you're missing. You're close, I'll give you that.'

We all freeze, staring at him. Finally Knox speaks. 'Are you fucking with us, prince?'

He shrugs. 'Believe what you like. I want you to find a cure. I want you to get the nocturnal right, because then I'll be free, yes? No longer a monster?'

'That's right,' I say quietly. 'Do you know . . . what the missing component is?'

'Wrong question,' Knox says smoothly, leaning towards him. '*How* do you know?'

'The scent.' He grins, drawing in a great lungful of air, then exhales. 'I can place the number of notes, like a melody. The nocturnal needs fine tuning, it's off by one note.'

'Interesting,' Celia says from the doorway. 'Alden, can you sense the same?'

'Not yet,' he says, eyeing Andry. 'Perhaps I will soon.'

'Can you tell what's in their potion and what's in the nocturnal?' I press. If he knows, if he's been holding out on us . . .

'Not exactly,' he says, 'so you can stop acting like you're going to stake me, alchemist. They're both a mix of plant life. You've been on the right trail. I'm a botanist, just like Alden here. Never thought to ask, did you? If I'm a wielder as well. I didn't attend Killmarth, never got the chance, so I suppose it's not *widely* known . . .'

I stare at him, keeping my frustration in check. Just. 'Then if we find the missing component and we enhance the entire nocturnal formula—'

'Now you're getting ahead of yourself.' Andry chuckles. 'Who says a full cure is merely more concentrated ingredients? Perhaps a catalyst is needed?'

'But—'

'I can tell you about the subtle differences between the nocturnal and the potion your friend Tessa brought back,' he says, crossing an ankle over his knee. 'Not how to develop it into a full cure. Would you make three cakes by tripling the ingredients? No. Not necessarily. One can hope, I suppose. I certainly do.'

'All you've told us is that it's one missing component, not multiple,' Knox mutters.

Andry wags his finger. 'And that it's plant life. That's quite a lot to go on, isn't it? Best get cracking.'

★

Two days sees the end of the semester at Killmarth and the beginning of the lastwinter break as well as our surety that we need to cast the net wider. We need to explore the plant life of Theine and Alloway. The war is mounting each and every day, but we hide our deep worries under casual jokes and discussions of our research. But it's there, like a spectre. The risk we are taking with our plans and schemes.

With all scholars going home for a rest and to celebrate the darkest nights of the year with festivities, before the world begins to warm once more, Blake arrives at the door of Morlagh Manor. We leave Knox and him to their reunion and when Knox has brought him up to speed, he doesn't hesitate. 'I'm Theinian,' he says over dinner. 'It makes perfect sense for me to be the one who goes to gather there. I know the terrain.'

'And I know the territory better than most after my year on assignment,' Knox says, leaning back in his chair.

'Looks like we have two volunteers for Theine,' I say. 'Which leaves Alloway. Tessa, Alden?'

'Never been, always wanted to,' Alden says.

'Liar.' I grin, hiding my twist of anxiety at what we are proposing. What we are planning. 'Tessa?'

'Well, you need a decent masquier,' she says, polishing off the last of her toquay in one gulp. 'Sounds like we're celebrating lastwinter abroad.'

'Holidays all round,' Knox says, rubbing his hands together. But the jollity is off, we can't quite meet one another's eyes.

'Celia, may we trespass on your goodness a little longer and leave Andry in your care?' I ask, raising my eyes to meet hers for a moment. I hope she realises what I am not saying. An apology. A plea that we may begin again, after this is all over.

'Of course,' she says, nodding, and I don't miss the worry that darkens her gaze before she summons a smile. 'Edmund and I will guard him. And the laboratory.'

'Possibly don't mention anything yet to Ezra,' Knox says. 'I've got a feeling that travelling to the heart of a territory that despises wielders probably wasn't part of "figuring it out".'

Chapter 20

Love is a Person, Love is a Place

That night, we celebrate lastwinter early. Celia gathers her finest gowns and Alden and Edmund furnish the men with black tie. We drink golden toquay, play games in the lounge by the light of the fire and allow Andry to join us, chained of course, but he doesn't seem to mind too much. Celia goes to the kitchen to stir the mulled berry toquay, and I take the opportunity to help her. When I walk in, I find a room with a high ceiling, a stretch of windows overlooking the gardens, a sink beneath, and a huge oven with hotplates warming a pot. The scent of spices and berries permeates the air, and I drink it in, smiling at Celia as she turns to me.

'Thought I'd give you a hand,' I say, stepping over the threshold. The low light from the lamps glints off copper pans and glassware, the island counter at the centre strewn with baking dishes, flour, wooden spoons and hastily dropped tea towels. 'Are you doing this all yourself?'

'Alden helps, when he's not in the lab,' Celia says, stirring the pot of mulled toquay and sniffs. 'Isn't it divine? My grandmother's recipe. So you grew up with Ezra?'

The question, snuck in at the end, catches me off guard as I busy myself tidying the kitchen island. 'I did. But not just him . . . two other people that worked for him.' I swallow, setting out a tray with small tin cups. 'Dolly. Dolly looked after me mostly.'

Celia nods, her back to me. 'She died, didn't she? Recently. I'm very sorry for your loss.'

A lump suddenly forms in my throat as she looks over, nothing but kindness shining in her eyes. 'You've done well. I know she would be very proud of you.'

I swallow, not quite trusting myself to speak, and help her ladle the drink into the tin cups. I set them on a tray and her hand brushes my arm. 'Thank you.'

'For what?' I manage. Surely all I've done to this woman is bring her pain and drama.

'For Alden. I haven't heard him laugh so much or talk so freely since he was a boy. Since before his father died.'

'I—' I nod and smile. 'I love him.'

Celia's face brightens further, her lips curving into a full, radiant smile. 'I know. I can't tell you how happy it makes me, knowing he is so loved in this world.'

I bite my lip and turn to her. 'It's my fault though, what happened to him. What may still happen. He wouldn't have even been in their world if it wasn't for me.'

'We don't blame you,' a voice says from the doorway. I turn and see Edmund standing there, arms crossed, features troubled. 'He crossed over there of his own free will to save a friend. Ever the hero.'

'Just like your father,' Celia whispers, her breath hitching.

Edmund's eyes shine and he smiles at her. 'You're right though. He hasn't been so happy since before our father died. It's just such horrible timing, that he finds happiness now.'

'Seeing Andry, all I can see is what my son is becoming, what he will be if this cure is never completed . . .' Celia's hands tremble and the tin cups all clatter together in a discordant rumble. She takes a breath. 'But we all have to pull together. We can't change what has happened, but we can change the outcome.'

I nod. 'We can.'

'Guilt is a poison, Sophia,' Edmund says suddenly. 'It'll kill you slowly. We all wish, more than anything, that we had gotten there sooner that night when Father died. But this time, we can get there sooner. We can save him. That's what I'm clinging to.'

'The last threads of hope,' Celia says. She blows out a breath, nudging me with her shoulder. 'Love is uncomplicated at the end. There is only ever one path, one choice. All the others are so clearly false.'

I pick up a tray and we step back through the corridor then into the lounge, and I hear it as she does. Her whole home, echoing with laughter. Edmund grins, moving to stand beside Alden, just as Celia begins passing around the tin cups of mulled toquay and my heart swells. One path. She's right. Since I've met him, there really has only ever been one.

After the mulled toquay is handed out and Celia settles next to Alden to talk quietly by the fire, as Knox, Blake, Edmund and Andry play a heated game of cards, I fall onto the sofa beside Tessa, tucking my feet up under the folds of gold material. Her eyes are pensive as she watches the others and I'm aware of the world behind them. All the memories and thoughts, the myriad of moments that make her who she is. And how entwined Greg was within them.

'He would have been playing cards right now,' she says. 'He would have been sat right there, next to Knox. I can almost . . . almost picture him.'

I look over at the group of them and fit that image of Greg beside them. His goofy red hair, his lopsided grin, how he'd be laughing right along with them. And my heart aches. I reach for Tessa's hand and squeeze it. 'None of this is as it should be, is it?'

'No,' she says quietly, her fingers tightening around mine. 'But I realised something, when I was there in Astrum. When I was watching them, the cold ones, the other creatures. The ordinary people, going about their days, the groups of cold ones, scheming in their houses. I realised that I had him. I had . . . it. What the cold ones will never have.' She takes a breath. 'Love. I had Greg, I had his love for such a very long time. Not long enough, it never would have been enough. But I felt it. I knew, right down to my very cells that he loved me, and that he always would. That's special. That's something I'll always have.'

I rest my head on her shoulder. 'Always.'

'And I'll always have you,' she says. 'When I left you in that forest, when I walked through the portal . . . don't think it didn't cost me. I don't regret going, but I loathed having to walk away from you. Having to leave you behind, because I know what that feels like, now. Greg has gone on, and I'm left in the after.' She brushes her hand down my cheek. 'I won't leave you again like that, not knowing if I'll survive. Not intentionally, anyway. I knew— I knew, deep down you'd come after me. That you'd find a way and pull me back out. That was selfish. I knew you'd walk into mortal danger for me and I took that for granted. I took you for granted, you and your heart. That's not what a friend does, and I'm sorry. I'll be better. I'll be the person Greg saw when he . . . when he looked at me. I won't walk away from you again.'

I sniff. 'You better not. But I forgive you. I love you too much to do anything but forgive you, T.'

She chuckles. 'You know what I realised, over there, what shook me out of it, and made me start to miss him rather than be so furious? I need to be more Greg. Whenever life was utterly shit, he would be an absolute long clown, and I couldn't help smiling. He wouldn't want me avenging him. He'd want me to ache a little less over time and smile a little more.'

'Be more Greg,' I murmur, smiling as well. 'That sounds like it should be our team slogan.'

★

During a heated game of stick or twist, I leave them all to it, drifting upstairs in the long gown of shimmering gold that Celia lent me. The twisting straps, low back and slit up the side remind me of the dress I wore for the Ordeal of Lies and as I step out onto the upstairs balcony adjoining one of the guest suites, glass of gold toquay in hand, I shiver under the frosted starlight.

Leaning against the stone rail of the balcony, I lift my face to the stars. The sharp cold slices over my skin, too hot from sitting beside the roaring fire. I take a sip of toquay, allowing the bubbles to pool on my tongue before swallowing it.

'I always loved stargazing from this balcony,' Alden says and I smile without turning round. 'There's something about the clarity of the night sky here, always so much crisper and more defined in the north.'

'As though we are closer to the stars,' I murmur, glancing at him as he comes to lean on the rail beside me.

He flicks me a smile, then moves closer, smoothing my hair back behind my ear. Where his fingers brush my skin, warmth shimmers and I shiver, my heart beating a little faster. Gods, he looks hot tonight. The black tie, the way he tilts his gaze upwards, taking in the expanse of starlight . . .

'Are the others still downstairs?' I ask lightly, angling my body towards his.

He smiles, turning to face me, eyes smouldering in the velvet dark. 'No one will disturb us here, if that's what you're asking.'

'Oh,' I say, reaching out to find his belt loops, and pull him a little closer. 'That's good to know. After the other night in the lab . . . I've been waiting to get you alone again.'

'Naughty,' he says, chuckling as his lips dip to my throat and he trails kisses over my skin, so softly, so slowly that I groan. Wanting more. He braces his hands against my hips, pressing his thumbs into the whisper-thin fabric. 'You know this dress leaves you very . . . accessible.'

I gasp as his hand reaches down, finding the slit in the fabric, running up the bare skin of my thigh. As his other hand still braces my hip against his body, his mouth tracing the lines of my clavicle, his fingers work up in sweeping circles, brushing along the softness of my inner thigh.

I reach up, running my fingers along his jawline, tracing the contours of his face. The cold night air, the feather light touch of his fingers, the desire within me . . . gods this feels good. 'We've been working too much.'

'Far too much,' he agrees, his voice almost a growl and my whole body purrs in response.

Still just a whisper of touch, he moves his fingertips in those achingly slow circles. I shiver, heat and cold colliding inside me, as his fingertips just brush the sensitive part of my inner thigh. 'Alden,' I moan, moving to press my body into him. 'Don't tease me.'

He chuckles against my throat. 'Why not? I want to hear you cry my name.'

I gasp again as his fingers reach further, as they skim over my very core, as he cups me with his hand, shifting me so I'm pushed up against the balcony. His eyes lift to mine and all I see is desire. Deep and molten as a lake. Then his fingers find the edge of the lace of my underwear, plunging beneath to stroke gently, sending waves of heat all through me. My stomach clenches as his fingers work me and I move my hands to the buttons on his trousers, not wanting to wait a moment longer. But he growls into my ear, 'Not yet. Not just yet. I want you wet and ready for me. I can hear . . . I can sense your pulse racing. Your scent . . .'

My hands still, then move up to his head, tangling my fingers in his hair. His mouth finds mine again and I groan in pleasure. There's nothing else in the world but him and the starlight above us. Time ebbs, and I feel that delicious ache building and all I want is him. More of him.

His lips coax mine open, leaning my body back further over the balcony, tongue moving to claim me. His fingers keep stroking, the heat in my core building and building, then his mouth releases mine as he draws back slightly. I catch the glitter in his eyes, the hunger that isn't entirely . . . Alden. That is primal and full of thirst. Then with a soft groan, he lowers his head to nip at my skin, just above my clavicle. I gasp, the slight sting melding with the aching sweetness of his touch between my thighs.

He licks my skin where he's nipped at it, drawing a bead of blood to the surface. 'You taste . . . gods. You're addictive. Put your arms around my neck.'

I obey, hearing something primal in his voice, something deeper, darker. Then he lifts me until I'm straddling him, until I'm balanced on top of those railings, my thighs open to him as he frees himself from his trousers. He pushes my dress aside, the lace of my underwear, then in one swift movement, plunges inside me. I cry out, my voice carried away on a sudden breath of the wind. I expand to encompass him as he moves inside me, adjusting until he's holding me firmly, grasping my hips to keep me steady. There's something more commanding about him, and I wonder if it's being here, away from Killmarth, away from our lives as scholars, or because of the change in him. How he's turning, even now.

I look into his eyes, finding nothing but desire. Eclipsing all else. He thrusts again and I cling to him, feeling the building of all that heat he coaxed with his fingers hardening to a molten ache. He thrusts up, angling his hips, and I see stars and light as he finds that spot, the place that will unravel me. He thrusts and thrusts, the sharp cold of the air streaming deliciously around us.

'Does that feel good, Sophia?'

'Yes,' I manage, barely able to form thoughts let alone words. He stills slightly, a devilish smile on his lips.

'Do you want more?' he asks me, holding himself taut, stealing the friction I wildly crave.

'Yes please. More,' I beg as I try to push him deeper, but he frustratingly stays just shy of where I want to feel him.

'I like when you beg for me,' he whispers against my ear, before he angles his hips, somehow thrusting deeper and I gasp. 'How about now?'

'Gods . . .' I say.

'No, Sophia. My name,' Alden growls. 'I want to hear *my name* on your lips when you . . .'

He thrusts again and the ache, the deep ache is almost unbearable as I cry his name, as I come completely undone.

He groans as I tighten around him, thrusting twice more before he shouts, the air echoing with his pleasure. I pant, clinging to him, feeling the eddying sweetness after climax. He brushes his lips over my searing hot skin before pausing on my throat. Where he . . . where . . .

'I— Did I bite you?' he asks quietly and I blink at him.

'I think . . . maybe you did,' I say, my eyes not leaving his. 'Do you . . . desire me in that way as well now?'

For a moment, a shadow passes over his features, then gently, he eases himself away from me, helping me down from the balcony rail. I walk on shaking legs as he guides me back inside, leading me to a lamp where he can examine my skin. 'Shit,' he says, running a fingertip over my skin. When he shows me, it comes away red. With my blood. Within moments he's wielded, healing my skin once more and I guide his chin to look at me. His eyes are troubled, dressed in darkness.

'You didn't hurt me,' I say softly. 'I trust you, Alden. We'll figure this out.'

He nods, blowing out a breath, and runs his fingertips down my cheek. 'I can stay away from you, if you prefer. I can't lose control, not with you—'

But I place my lips over his, kissing him firmly. And when I shift back, I ensure his eyes are fixed on mine once more. 'Control is only found through *practice*, Locke. Maybe we should try again, until you master it.'

His answering smile lights a flickering flame in my core as he nods. 'To our chambers then, DeWinter. If I am to find restraint, I mean to ravish you.'

Chapter 21

Stranger Woods

We assemble in the entrance hall the following morning. Knox and Blake, Alden, Tessa and I, a divided group with the same assignment; to gather plant specimens and hope to find a cure. With the revelations Andry chose to share, that the potion Tessa stole from Astrum is made of plant life and that the nocturnal elixir is one component away, we know this is the best way forward. It's still nagging at me, that the nocturnal will be a diluted version, a replica of their potion that curbs bloodlust. Even with the final component, we will still need to figure out what makes it a full cure.

But one step at a time.

We've received word from Belle that she is well, home with her family for lastwinter. She knows to cover for us, should our absence from Kellend be noted. I hope the Crown do not turn their enquiring gaze on us, or Morlagh Manor. But we cannot be too careful.

'Do you remember I told you about the lastwinter balls we used to have here, before my father died?' Alden asks me, brushing my knuckles, and I nod. 'Next winter, I will throw one. Open the house again and celebrate our victory over the night.'

'And I will be at your side,' I say softly and lean closer to him to whisper, 'wearing that gown of gold.'

He chuckles, eyes glittering as our gazes meet. 'I shall look forward to it.'

Edmund carries in two mirrors, setting up one next to the other. Knox and I work on them together, creating a bridge to a location in Theine and then one into Alloway. I summon up the raw well of my magic, wielding alongside him, focusing on the portal I wish to create and picturing the places Knox has described in detail. We first create a portal to Theine, the portal on the other side opening to reveal a kitchen in a safe house. One owned by the Darley family. The next, the one to Alloway, was a little more challenging to pinpoint. We had to pick somewhere not too close to a heavily populated area, somewhere that a portal could open unobserved.

We chose a forest to the northeast, far from the lush farming regions of the middle and south, in the more mountainous, rugged region where there are fewer known towns. A forest, we reasoned would hold more plant species, left to grow in the wilds. And if we have to wield, we are less likely to be caught. It's far from the border conflicts, far from any known outposts. We should be able to forage undisturbed and unobserved.

Armed with two reference books by a botanist with classifications of Allowayan plant species, a magnifying glass, a collection of vials, cloth bags and notebooks to record what we collect, it feels like a research module being undertaken in the field. For the first time since completing the Ordeals, ironically, I feel like a true scholar. The scholar I aspire to be. Perhaps one day this will be my reality, going on research trips and writing papers to prove my theories. It's something I can hope for if we are successful.

'Ready?' I say to Alden and Tessa as the mirror image of a forest glade reflects out at us from Celia's floor-length mirror.

'Ready,' Tessa says and nods to the others. She walks through first, ready to wield if necessary, Alden after her.

Just before I step through, Celia reaches for my hand, curling my fingers around something small. 'In case anything happens, show this and it might work.'

I look down at the pendant in my palm. A depiction of Argus, wrought in silver. 'Thank you.'

She smiles sadly. 'It was my husband's. May it protect you now. If any Allowayans find you, you are devout believers, remember. You love the gods, their word is truth. You abhor wielders.'

Impulsively, I wrap my arms around her. 'I'm sorry none of this is as it should have been. When we return, I would like to begin again. As your son's partner, first visiting your home.'

She releases a breath. 'You are exactly what I hoped for, Sophia. I promise. We have no reason to begin again. Just return, all of you. Safe and whole.'

I step away from her, ducking my head so she does not see the glistening corners of my eyes. To be accepted into her home, to be worthy . . . in all the years I was the Collector's creature, I never felt I belonged anywhere. Always a shadow at the edges, always longing for a place in this world, a family that was mine. Now in these people, this woman, I suddenly have that. And I still do not feel that I deserve it. I drop the pendant into my pocket and smile at her and Edmund. 'Thank you.' Then I cross through the portal, into Alloway.

The scent hits me first. Even in the depths of winter, the forest still smells of the trees that populate it. Hinderlegs, with black bark and bowing branches, they reach up as giants to the sky, bowing over about ten metres from the ground. It creates a spider web of darkness all around us, like a woven cage. Barely any light filters through, and barely any snow. The forest floor smells almost herbal and rich.

Tessa whistles quietly, pulling out a compass to check which direction is true north and points. 'The mountains are this way, which means that to the east and south . . .'

'How far?' I ask, standing from the rock I was perched on.

'Two miles. Not far.'

'Lead the way,' Alden says, shouldering his pack.

*

The following day, we leave with the dawn, the world still oddly quiet. 'Barely any birdsong, no cries of creatures in the night,' I say, eyeing the surrounding trees. The cottage roof has collapsed in on itself a few feet away, one window smashed, like a bruised eye. And yet even with the quiet, the solitude, I can't help feeling still that we are being monitored. That we are not alone out here, in the wilds of Alloway.

We make good progress over the course of the morning and when we break for food, catalogue what we have gathered so far. 'Four species we cannot readily identify in this region,' Tessa says, tapping her pen against her thigh. 'I say we leave here, take back what we've gathered and if needs be, identify any other regions of interest.'

'I agree,' I say, stretching. 'A bath would be very welcome.'

'An actual toilet as well . . .' Tessa says, wrinkling her nose.

I grin, opening my mouth to comment on modern plumbing when I catch a flash in my peripheral. A dart of white between the trees, bigger than a bird, but smaller than one of the wild creatures we thought we may encounter . . . I catch Alden's eyes and his flare wide in understanding as I continue talking, bending towards my pack as though to get something out. Then I stand, throwing my blade . . . and it simply disappears.

'Now what are three wielders from Kellend doing all the way out here?' a voice says and I whip around, Alden and Tessa leaping into defensive positions.

A woman steps from between the trees the other side of the clearing, from where I threw my blade. Yet she has it, pinched between her fingers. A smile graces her lips, a strip of white hair curling around her face. Her eyes glitter menacingly and in that instant my blood runs cold. 'How long have you been tracking us?'

'Long enough to know you shouldn't be here. Do you know what Allowayans do to wielders? You'll be lucky if your families even receive word of your deaths,' she says, securing my blade at her own belt and patting it. 'I'll ask you one last time. What are you doing in my territory?'

Chapter 22

In for a Flor

Tessa growls, the sound vibrating in her throat as she transforms between blinks, leaping for the woman. Alden weaves to the left, disappearing amongst the trees, and I twist my wrist, cloaking the clearing with an illusion of impenetrable dark, for her at least. We've trained for this, in the team training sessions, in the dawn groups within the maze, in the gym between lectures. And now, we move on instinct.

Predictably, the woman lunges for Tessa. As Alden bursts from the trees, tackling her to the ground, she rolls, faster than any human should be able to move, whispering something as life blazes from the soil. Plants shoot up, enclosing Tessa, then Alden and I rush forward. I will my stake to become something else, something made of metal. Something unbreakable. There is no time for the complex weaving of alchemy that Ezra has been training me in, to only use a small amount of my power to change an object's state. Instead, I force raw power into it, changing it quickly, leaving me breathless.

It transforms in my fist and I bring the steel blade to her throat. She stills. 'It appears we are not the only wielders in your territory,' I say with lethal calm. 'Release my friends. We need to talk.'

For a moment, she freezes and all I can hear is the rattle of my own heartbeats. Then she sighs, seemingly deflating, and the twisting, coiling plants disperse. Alden coughs, thumping his chest and blinking at her steadily. 'Not just a wielder. A botanist.'

Tessa rises swiftly, narrowing her gaze on the woman. 'A botanist with secrets.'

'Drop my blade,' I say and she glares at me before releasing it to thump on the ground.

'All right, all right,' she says, shaking her head. 'You win.'

I watch her as she draws a breath, face set in a picture of acceptance. Of passive surrender. And I make a decision. The steel blade in my hand glints for a blink, transforming back into the wooden stake it was before. I place it back in its holder and hold my hands up, showing her I bear no weapons. 'Are you Allowayan?'

She doesn't answer straight away, instead eyeing us all in turn then nodding sharply. 'I am.'

'And you live out here?' Alden asks.

'Alone?' adds Tessa.

'As you see,' she replies.

I press my lips together, weighing her up. She's clearly not a scout, nor is this an ambush. Curiosity, then? Or does she want something from us? 'You're not trained in combat. But nor are you completely helpless.'

She snorts. 'Is that a compliment?'

'Merely an observation.'

'You remind me of . . .' She blinks, looking away.

'Who?' Tessa asks, slipping a little closer. 'Who does she remind you of?'

The woman blinks furiously, sorrow flickering over her features. 'Hirzelle. My daughter.'

'Is she close by?' Alden asks. 'Where are your people?'

I know the answer before she speaks.

'Dead,' she says. 'All dead and gone. Thanks to the rulers of Alloway and the sycophants that follow *them*.'

I look to where she is pointing, and find the pendant Celia gave me for protection in case we are caught, hung on a chain just below my clavicle. 'The gods.'

'You followed us when you spied that I wore this?' I ask, touching the depiction of Argus, wrought in silver. 'Why?'

'Why do you think?' she asks bitterly. 'No friend of the church is a friend of mine.'

'You would have killed us,' Tessa says quietly. 'You meant to track us out here, then end us.'

'Hirzelle was the last to be rounded up, murdered for her gift,' the woman says, raising her chin. 'After that I vowed to avenge them, all of them. To kill any follower of the church and their teachings.'

I sigh and glance at Alden, who stands back, still assessing this stranger with lethal calm. 'I am so very sorry for your loss. We are just here to collect plant specimens, then we'll leave your territory. We do not follow the church, this—' I point at the silver pendant, 'has done its job though. It was given to me so if we met any Allowayans they would not immediately suspect us for what we are. And turn on us.'

The woman smiles for the first time. 'Not worked as it should then, has it?'

'Not really,' I admit. 'But I never expected to find an Allowayan who is also a wielder. Nor one who doesn't follow the church.' Then I stand, holding out a hand to her. 'Truce? My name is Sophia. This is Alden, and Tessa.'

'Amaria,' she says, squinting at me.

*

She begins walking with us, taking her time to open up as Alden eyes her warily. But as the afternoon dwindles, the air damping down, burrowing under our collars and sleeves, she tells us her story. Of how she came to be here, so far from any towns in Alloway, deep in the wilds. She tells us of her struggle to hide hers and her daughters' gift for so long. Then how one person suspected in their village, and the hunt raged from home to home, smoking them out. They escaped at first, but on the run, one daughter fell ill and succumbed to a fever, leaving her son-in-law and grandchildren, none of them wielders, to lead better lives without her. Then her other daughter was caught. Tried in a trial and shown no mercy.

That was the day her rage burst like a dam.

She gutted five men of the church, watching the light leave the eyes of every single one of them and a price was placed on her head. 'They were not men of the gods. All they wanted was control and power.'

'So you really live out here entirely alone?' Alden asks her as night begins to fall.

'Well . . .' she says, pointing to a place beyond the trees. 'Not entirely.'

I gasp as lights begin to trickle through the leaves and branches. But not the light of lamps or lanterns . . . magic. The honey-dipped light of a wielder. The others cannot see it and they look at me, baffled. Then the sound of a nocked arrow pierces the quiet, before a gruff question is spoken in Allowayan, into the night. Tessa and Alden both freeze, hands loose at their sides, ready to wield. But Amaria calls back and looks at us. 'Your choice. Come with me, have a bed for the night and meet the elders. Perhaps you will get some answers. Or stay out here, and perhaps you'll stumble upon the plant species you search for. Or maybe you won't.'

I look at her and she shrugs, walking forward, into the gloom and calls back over her shoulder. 'Your move.'

I glance at Alden then Tessa. 'In for a flor . . .'

Tessa snorts. 'They better have something decent to eat, that's all I'll say.'

'Alden?'

'I'm not sure I trust her . . .' He swallows, gaze flicking to mine. 'But I have to try anything. And if Amaria is right and they have information that can help, I have to take the risk. But if there's the slightest hint of danger—'

'We're out of there. I promise,' I say firmly. I don't want to take any risks, not after everything we've been through. But Alden, even now, is changing. By the next moon turn, according to the Crown botanists' research, the transformation will be complete and I don't know if we'll ever be able to reverse it. We have three weeks. No stone can go unturned. I led him into their world, I held every life in my hands when we crossed over. If I could, I would go alone into the dark. But I do not want to risk leaving them out here either. It is our move, but there's also only one move to make. So I step after Amaria, placing my trust in this stranger and my instincts and hoping to gods I'm not wrong.

Chapter 23

Grumpy Gargoyles

We break through the tree line to find a ruined castle before us. A ruin . . . surrounded by a high wall with gargoyles perched atop it. The wall extends for some thirty feet, towering above us, the gargoyles' claws clicking on their stone perches as they eye us warily. Amaria is stood on the other side of a gate, one with curling vines made of silver. She clutches the gate, staring out at us and bites her lip. 'There is no other way, I'm sorry. You'll be judged by the gargoyles that guard the wall.'

'And if they don't like our answers?' I ask, gaze snapping to hers.

'They'll tear us apart. Limb by limb,' Alden says. 'Not quite like the gargoyles used in the Ordeals, these ones.'

'Or across Kellend, to guard manor houses and stately homes before they were banned,' adds Tessa, swallowing. 'These are the originals. They were bred to become almost like pets in Kellend and Theine.'

'But here . . . left to the wilds?' Alden clicks his tongue at one leering down at him. 'Vicious creatures. I'm surprised they've even agreed to guard this castle.'

'Be nice to them,' Amaria says, eyes darting upwards. 'They haven't fed for a while.'

I notice two have moved to lower perches, claws scraping against stone as they take up their new positions a little closer to us. I take a small step back, wondering if we should just make a dash for it. If I've just made a fatally wrong move.

'Don't show them your backs, either,' Amaria says. 'They take umbrage. The last stranger who stumbled across this place ran and . . . well. They didn't make it very far.'

I suppress a shudder and plant my feet, staring up at them. These gargoyles are different, Alden and Tessa are right. Larger than the Kellend variety, they have hooded brows over mean little eyes, bat-like ears, full sets of sharp teeth and at their backs . . . wings. Tucked in close. Ready to spring into the night sky and soar.

But beyond those gates, there is so much magic. Woven through every stone of that ruin, glimmering and glinting, moving like a thousand entwined streams. Whoever these elders are, they are master wielders. 'I would bet anything that the ruin we can all see isn't a ruin at all,' I murmur to Tessa and Alden. 'Riddled with magic. I would bet anything it's an illusion, but it's so intricate, I can't discern what it truly is.'

'You think it's worth it?' Alden asks softly, eyes darting to a gargoyle to his left, lowering itself onto a closer perch as it shows Alden his teeth. 'I will not risk you both.'

'Chivalry might not get you too far here,' Tessa says dryly. 'But I appreciate the sentiment.'

I take a breath and nod. 'We know the rules. Three questions, no more.'

'Actually, we get to ask the questions, wielder,' the gargoyle above my head grates out. 'And if you answer with an untruth, we get to suck the meat from your bones.'

'Excellent,' Alden mutters.

'Three questions?' I ask.

'Three. One for each of you,' the gargoyle confirms.

Tessa rolls her shoulders. 'Well, let's have them then. Before the suspense kills us.'

The gargoyle above my head snarls, a forked tail whipping out to curl underneath its perch. Despite myself, my heart thumps a little harder. I'm not sure we would outrun one of them, let alone a dozen of these creatures.

'Do you intend to harm anyone beyond these walls?' the first gargoyle asks, eyeing me with quiet malice.

'No,' I answer quickly, meaning it. Tessa and Alden quickly follow with the same response. For a moment, the night air is drenched in silence and all I can hear is the beat of my own heart, shrieking like an animal in my ears. Then a gargoyle to the far right shifts, clicking its claws and I expel a short breath.

'Second question,' that gargoyle says, gaze boring into Tessa. 'Are you agents of Alloway?'

'Absolutely not,' Tessa says and Alden and I quickly state that we are not as well. Again, there is a moment of silence in which I wonder now, if they are conferring. If there is a silent way they communicate between themselves.

'Final question,' the gargoyle closest to the gate says, tail whipping out, then curling into its side. It eyes Alden, who meets its gaze steadily. 'Are all of you . . . human?'

I hesitate. How do we answer this question? If Alden says no, will they let us through at all? Or worse . . . will they turn on us?

'My companions are both entirely human,' Alden says. 'But I am not. I was born human but bitten by a cold one and forced to consume a drop of its blood very recently. I am turning. Changing. By the next moon turn, I will be entirely vampiric in nature. No longer human.'

The wind suddenly whistles through the trees at our backs, and I may imagine it, but there's the sound of footsteps. Of creaking

Then Alden talks, explaining what happened to him. How we no longer have the luxury of time, when we could do with months or years, we have merely weeks. For a time, we just eat, finishing our food, then as though Jevynn and Kadie have come to a decision, Jevynn begins.

'Now you have shared your truth with us, we will share ours with you,' Jevynn says. 'You should know that every person in this hall is a survivor. From raids mostly, and they came here with nothing. Every one of them a wielder, magic sparking, betraying them to Alloway. Some of them had families that exposed them and ran for their lives. Some have lost mothers, fathers . . . children. We survive because we stay hidden and secret. This is a refuge.'

'You never wanted to cross into Theine or Kellend? To seek asylum?'

'Some have,' Kadie says. 'Some were successful in crossing the border, but most were caught. We remove the location of this place from their memories before they leave.'

'It seems cruel, but we cannot risk a trail leading back to all those who have chosen to remain in safety here.'

I look around at the people gathered, some now clearing plates and bowls, some reading, or chatting, or pulling mending onto their laps. I count a hundred people, all ages. But all Allowayan. I don't like to think of what they have seen, what their journeys were like to reach this place.

'Magic divides,' Alden says.

'*Power* divides,' Jevynn replies. 'Some territories, like yours, embrace magic. But ours . . . well. The rulers of Alloway have our territory in a firm, unyielding grip. They say the cold ones do not hunt here, because the gods conquered our hearts and minds. That magic is blasphemous and the gods will punish us if we harbour

'And not developing potential cures to test out on her vampiric monster of a son we keep in the attic.'

Knox chuckles, sweeping the key from his pocket to unlock Andry's room. 'Exactly.'

We find Andry passively staring out of the window, chains draped across the floor, securing his ankles and wrists. He turns slowly, scowling at us. 'Are you actually going to feed me this time?'

'Only if you don't throw a glass at my face,' I say, placing the tray on the table next to his bed. 'I have the elixir for you.'

He turns slowly, eyes darker than the last time I saw him. Skin a touch greyer at the temples, hair a muss of unkempt strands. 'Is this one to slake my thirst, alchemist, or to test if it'll cure your boyfriend?'

'The latter, sadly,' I say, drawing it from my pocket. Knox and I had tried incorporating nonliving matter over the past few days, wanting to rule out any substance we could, as Alden worked with the plant specimens we had gathered. 'Now will you take it, or will I have to hold you down as Knox pours it in your pretty throat?'

'The latter,' he says. Then he sniffs, eyes widening in delight as his mouth stretches into a grin. 'Oh . . . oh this is good. Very good indeed.'

'What?' I ask in confusion, just as Knox freezes at my side.

'We've got company,' Knox says, eyes darting to the corridor.

Footsteps sound on the staircase down the hall and my heart stops.

Andry giggles in that breathy, hideous way of his. 'Mother has arrived.'

Chapter 26

Royal

The footsteps continue along the corridor, the quiet hum of voices peppering their progress. My eyes dart to Knox's, fear drenching me. But he's wearing the same expression, and I know we are likely doomed.

'She likes to make use of the dungeons still, did you know that?' says Andry, grinning. 'There are chains there too, and instruments, oh, so many, and clever people who like to extract—'

'Shut up,' I hiss at him, thrusting the door closed as quietly as I can. Maybe if we can keep Andry quiet, perhaps they'll walk past this room and not look inside . . .

I hear the rattle of the door handles on the next room and realise that plan won't work. Andry draws a breath, as though ready to bellow, and without thinking, I raise my hand and twist. His voice echoes around the walls of this room, but as I create the illusion of silence in the minds of those outside these walls . . . I know it won't reach their ears. To them, there is nothing but the sound of the crashing waves outside.

The wielding begins to drain me, faster than alchemy ever does, and I bite my lip, drawing blood as Andry draws in another lungful of air—

Then the door handle turns. Knox and I exchange a panicked glance as he dives for Andry, tackling him to the ground. And I have to dig deep, deeper than I've ever had to as an illusionist, to wield the appearance of an empty room. I take a step back from the door, hands upheld as I pant and whimper. Every single one of their senses must be ensnared and altered with my wielding. And if there is someone like me with them, a wielder who can sense magic . . . we're screwed. A dull thump begins at my temples and I hear Andry squeal as Knox holds him in a head lock, fierce eyes fixed on the people walking through the door. First two guards, the Queen's guards, just like we saw in the palace. And then . . .

The Queen herself.

She sniffs, this petite woman with fine spidery lines feathering out from around her eyes, the same shape jaw as Andry, the same coloured hair. She's immaculate. Pale smoky grey twin set, a white fur coat draped over her shoulders, sparkling jewels at her throat and earlobes, a skirt and pale boots tapping with impatience. Her eyes stare at me as I shake, then seemingly through me, to the cobwebs and bare walls beyond. 'And the faculty no longer use the hall at all? Not for any purpose?'

'None,' Caroline Ivey's clipped voice states. She pokes her head inside the room, smiling at the Queen and for a moment, unease flits over her features before she gestures to the Queen. 'Let us move on, you have read the reports. The entire place is unstable. I do not like to risk you being here for too long.'

Andry squeals again and my entire being judders from the illusion I fight to maintain. *Absence*, I will. *Silence, emptiness* . . . then without thinking, I reach towards Knox. I call on his magic, his power, and it flows out of him, straight to me. The river of honeyed gold flows through my veins, bolstering the illusion, and I shiver with power.

'Andry is not here,' Caroline says softly, words meant only for the Queen.

The Queen draws in a quiet breath, squaring her shoulders, and nods. For the briefest moment, I catch the heartache there, the disappointment. This is her child, her monster . . . and he is lost to her. What would I do to find someone I loved? Well, I know. I would cross worlds for them. I would walk into the heart of danger and never stop until I found them. She nods, adjusting her features before turning for the door. 'You're right. Let us move on.'

Andry suddenly yells and I gasp. *Silence*, I will, *nothing and no one, absence, neglect . . .*

The Queen pauses. 'Did you hear that?'

'Hear what?'

She turns on her heel, a frown furrowing her brow. Knox clamps his hand harder over Andry's mouth as he struggles against him, bucking and writhing—

'Almost like a . . . No. I'm imagining things.' The Queen scrunches her nose.

Neglect, absence, silence . . .

'We still have Fetlock to cover. The botanists have grown your favourite rose, the spliced species, you recall?'

'The yellow and orange,' she says, nodding. 'Like a sunset. Yes. Can't keep the scholars waiting.'

It's not until I hear them descend the staircase, their footfalls pealing away into nothing, that I release the illusion, sinking on all fours to the floor. Knox swears, releasing Andry, who howls like a dog. 'Bastard bit me,' Knox says, clutching his hand. 'I got the elixir down his throat though.'

I cough, a single drop of blood splattering from my nose to the floor, and Andry gasps in feral delight, reaching for it with outstretched, desperate hands. I shake my head. 'That was far too fucking close.'

★

We leave Andry to his supper and the single drop of my blood I couldn't wipe up from the floor. Knox clings to my arm as we stumble out of Darley, ensuring first that the inspection has moved on. Even though we were nearly caught, even though my head pounds like the worst velvane hangover of my life, I am elated. I did it. I cast an illusion so complete, so all consuming, that not a breath of sound or scent of any of us reached the Crown's party. I look down at my trembling hands in awe. I shouldn't be stronger as an illusionist, it's my lesser magic, my weakest, it makes no sense. After years and years of toiling away, and even under the shrewd guidance of Hester Lewellyn, I could barely scrape by as an illusionist.

Not until my true magic sparked and exploded from me . . .

'Knox,' I say quickly, pulling him towards Fetlock. 'Alden has the book, doesn't he? With Amaria, they're in the lab still?'

'As far as I know . . .' Knox says as I whip through the doorway. 'What is it?'

'I . . . I don't know. Maybe nothing. But maybe . . . something.'

We descend to the lower level where the laboratories are located, finding the one that is locked at the far end. I knock three times and hear a shuffling on the other side, then a key scrapes in the lock and the door opens. Amaria is talking softly to the plant specimens which have taken root, in pots arranged throughout the laboratory. Some coil up to the ceiling, some drape themselves over every surface, and some are tiny in their beauty, winking in every colour, dusting the room with colour. Huge lamps hang down from the ceiling, simulating real light, but it's Alden and Amaria who are wielding to coax these plants into vibrant, riotous life. The whole room is glittering gold in my sight, a wonder of magic. I take a breath, dazzled by the spectacle of so much botany wielding, all in one place.

'Andry playing nicely?' Alden asks, frowning at us in concern as we whisk inside and he locks the door behind us.

'Andry?' I snort. 'The day he's a pleasant person is the day I'll suspect he's about to knife me in the back. No. The Queen has just carried out an inspection of Darley Hall.'

He pales. 'Did she . . .'

'No,' Knox says, wandering towards the book, open on a page in the centre table. 'DeWinter here wielded and the Queen didn't see, smell or hear any of us.' He holds up his hand, which has the imprint of a half circle of teeth marks still. 'A gift from our future king.'

Alden rounds on me. 'But . . . how . . .'

'Illusion,' I say, grinning. 'I wielded an illusion so complete, the Queen and her guards *and* Caroline Ivey just looked inside, then kept walking.'

'You've never been able to do that before,' Alden says in awe.

'Which is interesting, isn't it?' Knox says, turning a page of the book.

'I took Knox's magic, just reached for it instinctively, and it seemed to bolster my illusion. Not only that, but my wielding improved, more precise than it ever was before.' I rub at my nose, frowning as a flake of blood comes away. 'It's still my lesser magic. Still drains me and does not feed me to wield, but it's stronger. I've seen you and Knox do it before, where he lent you his power, and I did it in one of the Ordeals without realising when I touched you . . . I need to know if there's a link in all this. If that's why we need more than one of us to open a portal to their world.'

'Magic feeds magic . . .' Amaria murmurs, walking over to Knox's side to also examine the book. 'There is a story about bridges and portals and gateways. But it's Gallant's story, not Aline's. The tale of the first alchemist.'

I walk over to read the words on the page. Skimming over it, drinking in the details, something clicks in my mind. If magic is the work of the gods, as well as the cold ones . . . I swallow, staring down at my hands. Then they have meddled in more than one world, it seems. 'If the first alchemist was Gallant, it would follow that Aline created the cold ones, and they had a thirst for an alchemist's blood, more than any other. A spiteful twist to their nature.'

'His magic, his gift to our world, the strongest form of wielding . . .' Knox says. 'Is what they crave the most. The blood they seek out on each hunt, above all else.'

'Perhaps others as well,' I say, pushing my hair back from my face as my mind races with the possibilities. But I need to focus. This is not a time for scholarly leanings, to bury myself in research and revel in completing this puzzle. I tap my finger on the part of the tale that talks about Gallant, and how Argus strengthened his magic to step between their own world and into Astrum. How he took a drop of Aline's blood, fashioning it into a compass, to guide their path. 'This may also be why the cold ones could create a portal, but we could not. This is Aline's work, Aline's creatures. She may well have stolen more from Argus and Gallant to give them this ability.'

'Threefold, it says here,' Amaria says, brushing a word. 'It takes three to create a bridge.'

'One secret unlocked, but more questions than answers,' I say, pondering. 'And still no way of curing them . . . but as they are of Aline's making . . .'

'Perhaps one of Aline's tales,' Alden says, already leafing through the pages. 'There is so much here, layers of history, but some tales are symbolic, it's not always clear.'

'Keep searching,' I say, looking at Alden, knowing what he's thinking. Time is slipping through our fingers, the next moon turn is far too soon. 'If we can decipher one piece of this puzzle, we can figure out more. There is hope.'

Chapter 27

Bloodbound

'He's not here,' Knox says as I walk into the maze later that afternoon for my training session with Ezra. 'He's carrying out a raid on Morlagh Manor. Unfortunately, so far he's found nothing.'

'Such a shame,' I say.

Knox shrugs. 'From what I can gather from the note he sent, Celia's enjoying herself. Plying the inspectors with cake and offering tours of the house and grounds. Ever the gracious hostess.'

I chuckle, glancing at the hedges, mist and ice clinging to every jagged twig. 'Are we giving this one a miss then?'

Knox sucks on his teeth. 'Thought we could go over some tactical work?'

'Sure.'

We work through footwork, strategies if we are surrounded, if we get split up and have to act solo. When we take a break, both of us reaching for our water canteens he says we should try target practice, changing our stakes as we throw them from wood to metal and back before hitting the target. Fast, effective and precise wielding, which means that if we find ourselves surrounded, but there are objects around us we can manipulate and use as weapons, we can.

'I will if you will,' he says, striding off to the area of the maze that's been set up with targets.

I freeze. 'What did you just say?'

Dolly. Her eyes, her laugh, her smoking habit. All of it, emerging like a fresh bruise. He pauses, turning, and considers me. 'She was part of my training too, you know. I sparked when I was young but I stayed living with my parents. My mother was a Darley before she married my father. Ezra's older sister. Dolly taught me card games too. I thought you knew.'

'I didn't.' I swallow. 'So that night, when you asked me to meet you in the poison garden, when you talked about her . . .'

'I know when you mean.' He sighs. 'I had to make you believe I was a dispassionate shit. That I didn't know who she was. I thought Ezra would have explained it all by now. I cared about her, we all did. Mother mourned her the most these past few months, she went on a grand tour with her in their youth, gadding about the seaside resorts of the south of Theine. It was Ezra that ran the family business, Mother's not an alchemist. And when I sparked, he insisted that I was trained, for the good of the territory.'

I nod, piecing it all together. 'Your mother . . .'

'She's not at all like Ezra.' He smiles. 'Flamboyant . . . wayward. My father completely adores her. But I suppose I'm more like Ezra than either of them. Not in the way I wield, but I just took to it, the assignments, the strategies, the tactical analysis of the shifting politics. He taught me how to add marks to his map before he sent me to Theine.'

'In case he's killed,' I say, realisation dawning as I look at him. 'You will inherit. The next Collector.'

Knox shrugs. 'I would have employed different tactics to make you spark, if it's any consolation. But he did all that because he couldn't stand to lose you. He's a determined bastard and keeping you alive was his focus. Not keeping you happy.'

I blow out a breath as we reach the clearing between the hedges with the targets set up. 'The more I learn about Ezra, the more I feel like I don't know him at all.'

★

That night, after an afternoon of target practice with Knox, then lectures and actively avoiding the beady eyes of Caroline Ivey and the Crown's visiting party, I fall asleep surrounded by botany books. My dreams are lurid depictions of gods and goddesses, of portals and bridges I cannot cross, however hard I try. In one, it's Knox who forces me into the vault, telling me it's for my own good. Then there's a bright light, salvation, a goddess freeing me from the close dark, crooking her finger, her crimson and gold robe trailing after her like a sunset . . . but it's Dolly, blood blooming from her middle, choking out apologies as I try to reach her in time . . .

I jerk awake, scattering books onto the floor next to the bed, aware of a knock on my bedroom door. Opening it I find Alden, leaning against the doorway. He grins at me, a pile of books under his own arm, hair tousled, top shirt button undone. 'Thought we could research together.'

I rub the sleep from my eyes as his gaze trails over my night clothes, a silk nightdress in deepest navy, trimmed with lace. Now, out of bed, I shiver, a rush of cold air clouding my room from the corridor beyond. The bad dream dissolves instantly, the fog of sleep no longer ensnaring my senses. I'm wide awake. I pull him inside, reaching for my dressing robe, and note the fire dwindling in the hearth. 'Are you not cold?'

'Not in the least,' he says, his grin dropping slightly. 'Must be the vampiric blood in me.'

'Has to be some advantage,' I say, keeping my tone light. But it's just another worrisome sign of what is happening beneath his skin.

We're running out of time. And once it takes hold in two weeks . . . I don't know if he'll be able to keep the monster within leashed.

He walks in, moves the books off my bed and sits down, placing his books beside my own on the bedside table. I sigh as I collapse next to him. 'I don't know if I can focus any more. All the words sort of bleed together after a while.'

He leans on one elbow, facing me, and reaches to skim his fingers over the cord of my dressing robe. 'Perhaps we need to wake ourselves up a bit.'

I smile up at him lazily, casting my gaze over his caramel-flecked eyes, then down to his shirt, where the top button is undone. The fabric shifts over the muscles beneath and my breath hitches. 'What did you have in mind?'

He doesn't reply, instead unwinding the cord of my dressing gown so it falls open, exposing the short nightdress beneath. I shiver, biting my lip as his hand splays over my ribs, just below my breasts. His eyes . . . they're ravenous. Glinting with that hunger that tells of a deeper, more primal need. 'Alden . . .' I whisper. 'Do you need to feed?'

His hand skims the fabric of my nightdress, fingertips grazing the stiff peak of my nipple. My breath hitches again as heat unfurls, deep in my belly. But his fingertips drift further, up to my throat, my jaw. Hunger. Desire. His entire body is taut with it. He clamps his jaw tight and I sense it rippling from him as his gaze hones on my throat. Where my pulse flickers, where blood rushes in my veins.

I reach up to his head, guiding his lips to the side of my neck and angle my head. 'Feed. I trust you, Alden. Feed and be sated.'

He growls against my throat, hand steadying himself, planted on the other side of my head. 'Sophia . . .'

'Remember what I said to you? Mastery comes with practice,' I say, feeling the heat roll over me from his chest. He's scorching hot, as though a fever has overtaken him. The way he is turning . . . the way we are running out of time . . . gods, I want him though. I want him to devour me.

He growls again, but this time I feel the slight pressure of his teeth, scratching against the soft curve of my throat. Then in a rush of stinging pain . . . he bites. I gasp, my eyes flying wide as he sips, as I feel the ribbon of blood leave my body. My heart beats faster and faster, the pull of his hunger guiding me to that strange knife edge between desire and fear. He stops, drawing his mouth away from my skin, and my breath comes a little too quick as I stare up at him. Eyes dark, almost entirely onyx, desire still contorting his features. He licks his lips, swollen and red, everything heightened by his need for me.

'Thank you,' he breathes, watching me intently. 'Now stay very, *very* still.'

I gasp as his knee shifts between my thighs, separating them, opening me for him. Then he sinks to his knees before me, pushing my nightdress up so it hitches above my hips, then slowly drags the lace and silk of my underwear down, down, until I am entirely exposed before him. He parts my thighs as my heart thunders in my chest, heat, desire, all swirling as a storm. His fingertips stroke first and my hips jerk upwards instinctively.

'Still,' he says softy, 'I want you to stay perfectly still, Sophia.'

The first touch of his tongue against me sends flame racing through my veins. I gasp, my hips lifting before he plants his palms on my sides, forcing me down. Then he strokes, again and again, exploring me, teasing me with his tongue. I moan, the desire growing, building and I gasp his name, needing more, needing it faster, harder . . . his breath hitches as I moan his name again. 'You know I love that, Sophia . . . I want to hear it again.'

Then his soft lips suck and pull and I cry out, trembling, it's almost too much, the intensity leaving me wild. 'Say my name again.' He sucks again and I gasp his name, just as he licks and my hips rise again. 'No, no. Stay still.'

He deepens his strokes, finding the very centre, the very apex of my sex, just as he thrusts two fingers inside me. Stroking from the inside, I see white, I see stars, the exquisite climax shattering my mind. I clamp around his fingers, crying out, everything that I am lost in the swirling tempest. Then he removes his fingers, his tongue and nudging my knees so I stay parted for him, he lowers himself over me. I reach down, guiding the length of him inside myself, his guttural sigh of pleasure mirroring my own.

The pressure as he fills me, as he pushes slowly inside leaves me trembling, as he thrusts slowly, as deep as he can and I unfurl around him, gasping. Then he thrusts again, just as deep and I lose all sense of the world around me. All I am is a bundle of sensations, of heat and light and burning desire.

Then he thrusts once more, burying himself inside me, our bodies melting together. He keeps thrusting, deeper and deeper, filling me, consuming me. He says my name as he comes. I cling to him, my body still shuddering from the climax he gave me as his own shatters, as he presses a kiss to my mouth. I wrap my arms around him, my legs, cleaving my body, my very self to his as he falls over the edge and I fall again, with him.

We lie there together, in a pool of pure light, hearts entwined as the storm of us ebbs away. I blink up at him, feeling the delicious ache of the after. He smiles at me, eyes caramel again, mahogany and oak, a spectrum of golds.

'I love you,' he says softly, brushing a strand of hair from my face, searching my gaze. 'So completely.'

'I love you too,' I murmur. 'And if you need to feed again—'

'Let's not talk of it,' he says. 'For now it's just about under control, but what if . . .'

A fist bangs on my door, startling us both. 'Sophia! Get up, it's happening again—'

The bell begins to clatter.

I stare at Alden, my horror reflected in his features.

The cold ones have returned.

We untangle ourselves from each other and I swiftly retie my dressing gown, striding for the door as a fist bangs again.

I wrench open my bedroom door to find Tessa there. She thrusts a stake, laced with metal into my fist. 'From Ezra.' She looks over my shoulder at Alden. 'He said he needs you in the courtyard. Both of you. Ten minutes.'

'Where are we going?' I ask, the heat, that warm honeyed glow rapidly leaving my body.

'Dinas Tar,' Tessa says and swallows, a flicker of fear appearing in her gaze. 'Unprecedented numbers in the heart of the city.'

Chapter 28

Familiar Ground

Tessa hurries off down the corridor. I turn to Alden, who is buttoning his shirt, searching for his shoes. 'Alden.'

'The capital! The absolute bastards, they've never attacked the city, never in great numbers before—'

'Alden!' I say, louder, and he freezes.

'There will be blood. A lot of it,' I say. 'You're turning. You desire wielder blood now and you're resisting . . .'

He blows out a breath, features troubled. 'I can't just sit it out. Not with you there, and Knox and Tessa . . . not with the people I love on the line. I'll control it. I won't turn on any wielders.'

I nod quickly, stomach twisting. I am more afraid for him than of what we are about to face. 'You have to be sure. *Completely* sure.'

'I've just tasted your blood,' he says quietly. 'I do not feel the desire any more. It's under control, I assure you.'

I expel a shuddering breath and go to him, kissing him deeply, passionately. 'I love you and we *will* cure you. And I will not stop you from going. But—'

'I will be careful,' he promises, resting his forehead against my own. 'If I even feel an ounce of bloodlust, of thirst . . . I will run. I will leave. You have my word.'

I reach up, holding his face. 'If anything were to happen to you . . .'

'It won't,' he says, reaching up to grip my fingertips, brushing them against his lips. 'It won't.'

We're both in the courtyard within minutes, stakes and blades strapped to us, wearing boots and clothes to move in. To fight in. I feel the pulse of my magic like a second heartbeat, longing to be unleashed. Those bastards are in my home city, where Banks is, Pewter . . .

Peters and Soames join us, along with Belle, Blake, Knox and Tessa. I haven't seen Peters and Soames in a few weeks, not since before the winter break and I'm shocked at how haggard they look. As though Darcy's death were a plague, ravaging them both. I catch Tessa's eye and she bites her lip, flicking a glance at them and grimacing. We're both thinking it. Are they up to this tonight? Or will they be a weak link in our team that could cost us?

'Scholars!' Caroline Ivey says, stepping into the courtyard, Professor Grant beside her. And behind them . . . behind them is the Queen. We all fall silent and still. 'Two portals, several teams tonight. The cold ones must be stopped and swiftly. The first portal will lead to the palace, the other to Alabaster House for the first teams to step through. Do not split up, we need no rogue heroes tonight. Slay as many as you can and meet back at the portals. Ezra will guide you on the other side if you are entering the city. For those at the palace, you will be commanded by the Queen's guard. Medical teams will be allowed access when you give the all-clear. It's imperative that you reduce the risk to them so they can assess the casualties they're dealing with in a secure environment.'

I notice the medical teams then, standing in the shadows, their features set and grim. They carry bags of equipment and bandages. This is going to be quick and dirty fieldwork. We are effectively entering a war zone.

'Medics, you will assess and any that cannot be saved, you will leave. Again, no heroics.' Caroline hesitates and continues softly, 'You will not be able to save them all.'

A hush falls over all of us as Hess enters, instructing two scholars to place the mirrors in the middle of the courtyard. He looks thinner than the last time I saw him, eyes smudged with exhaustion, but he's determined. Commanding and focused. Either he is being kept busy by the Crown and the college or he has dug deep, beneath his grief for Hester to find his strength. We divide under the careful watch of the Queen, no one daring to make a sound. I'm split from Alden and Tessa, instead following behind Knox and Belle. Peters and Soames are with the others and it's soon apparent they are stepping through a portal to the palace. Knox and I are on our way to the city, no doubt at Ezra's request. It's only the two of us and Belle being sent through the portal into the city so far. There are other scholars waiting to be sorted into teams, hanging back, waiting for their orders.

'We are splitting your training teams. You are going to where you are most needed, according to your wielding and your training,' Hess says, looking at me. He nods and I nod back. The three of us are into the thick of it then.

I brace myself for carnage, for blood and screaming and a barrage of cold ones. But as we step through the portal, finding it closing behind us, only the quiet sounds of the city greet us. No screams, no cries for help, no vampiric monsters waiting to drain us. The snow underfoot muffles everything, drifts of it piling around motorcars and across bonnets. Snowflakes dance in the halo glow of the streetlamps outside Alabaster House and all I can think is that there's been some kind of mistake.

'Surely Ezra should have met us here,' I whisper to Knox as Belle draws a blade, scanning the gated garden and the crescent of houses.

'Looks like he didn't get the invitation,' Knox says. He tiptoes up the steps of Alabaster House, peering inside. But I can see the gloom, spilling out. There's no one in the safe house tonight.

'Stay together,' I say. 'Something's off. From what Caroline told us, I expected a swarm of them.'

'Same,' Belle says. 'Unless they've already passed through here.'

I swallow, eyeing the darkened windows of the houses in the crescent. With the snow still falling in thick drifts, any possible tracks have been lost. We begin moving through the streets, sticking to the edges, listening for sounds of the cold ones and their prey. It's not until we pass the third street that Knox stops and shakes his head. 'I don't like this. We need to find Ezra. Sophia?'

'I agree,' I say. 'To the shop?'

He nods. 'To the shop. Belle, I would ask that you erase what you are about to see from your memory. If you are questioned on your whereabouts tonight, please conveniently forget the place we are about to lead you to.'

Belle eyes us both, then nods. 'All right. I trust you.'

A.A. Benedict and Sons. I stare up at the sign above the door. Never did discover who that was, or what it was before Ezra Darley began to use it as a front for his work. 'How many times have you been here?' I ask him.

'Many,' he says, eyeing me. 'Of course I realise now that Ezra was keeping us apart. Whether because I'm a bad influence . . .'

'Or because he didn't want you asking too many questions. Or getting attached to me, I suppose,' I say. I wish though that I had known Knox. He could have almost been like a cousin, a friend. I could have used a friend my own age.

Knox moves forward to tap on the door, we both expect it to be locked and bolted tonight. But when he raises his knuckles, he finds it already slightly ajar. I draw a stake into my other hand, eyeing the silent shop floor beyond and cross the threshold into my life from before.

Not so long ago, I stepped out through this door for the last time. Before Dolly died, before I entered the Crucible. And now the memories come flooding back. I breathe it in, the scent of her. It still lingers, as though she'll appear at any moment, that silk robe shimmying off her shoulders, the peacock emblazoned on her back. But there's no one here but ghosts. Dust coats the antiques, the desk a shamble of unopened post and missives. Dolly was the glue in this place and now she's gone, it's sagging at the seams.

The sound of voices in the back rooms lures us forward and I nod to Knox as he peels back the curtain divider. Belle moves like a shadow, covering us both, eyes darting to every corner. There's a shout, a glass shatters and I surge forward.

'Sophia, wait—'

But I recognise that voice.

Banks.

Chapter 29
Drenched in Blood

Fuck no.

Not Banks.

Not another person I care about. I whip through the web of corridors, ignoring Knox's pleas to be careful, stake raised in my fist and find three of the bastards, battering the Collector's office door . . . with Banks on the other side, trying to keep them out. Glass sparkles all around them, one of Ezra's cut-crystal velvane glasses, as though Banks has lobbed it at them before prying the office door shut. A cold one, a woman with tousled black hair, has a gash on her cheek, blood spilling down her pale skin. Her eyes find mine and she rubs the blood away, leaving a scarlet smear.

'You get in, kill him and take the map. This one's mine.' Then she moves too swiftly for me to react. Blood thumps in my ears as her fingers find my throat, squeezing out the air with ruthless efficiency. 'Shame I can't savour you—'

I stab up, between the ribs, watching the surprise flare in her eyes. Her fingers slacken on my throat as she scrambles for the stake, lodged in her heart. But before she can do anything more than hiss, she collapses. Ash and dust drift down, just as Banks cries out.

The Collector's office door caves in.

One of them steps over the threshold, disappearing from view inside the office. There's a cry from beyond, another glass lobbed at a wall, the glittering fragments shattering. My chest is a hollow thing as I stumble forward, reaching for the one a few steps away, who leers at me. Not Banks.

Not Banks.

Knox shouts, rushing past me, twisting his hand up and with a rush of his wielding, the door splinters into a thousand stakes. The cold one before me, not much older than a boy, whimpers, trying to get away as all those splinters of stake-shaped wood hover menacingly, then find their targets.

Embedding in their chests.

Knox bowls past the boy, shoving him aside. Not bothering to wait until he's dust. I leap over the shattered wood and glass, the ash, and careen into the Collector's office. To find Knox, hands braced on Banks's shoulders, checking every inch of him. I stifle a sob, running to him as well and throw my arms around him. He's covered in dust. Knox wielded just in time.

'I'm all right, Miss DeWinter, I'm all right . . .'

I nod, breathing in his scent of cigars and books and the city. He's shaking uncontrollably, humming under his breath, and I'm afraid for his heart. I shush him gently, trying to calm the old man. The last thing we need is for Banks to have a heart attack here, not with every medic tied up. 'You're all right,' I say, repeating it over and over. 'You're all right, you're all right.'

'It didn't happen again,' he says, voice cracking over the syllables. 'I didn't let them take the map. They won't— they won't be able to track anyone.'

'You did well,' I say, breaking away from him to peer into his old, kind eyes. 'Just, just sit down for me a minute.'

I lead him to the Collector's chair behind his desk and realise I'm shaking too. I can't stop shaking. He holds my hand as Knox checks the map, then kicks the wall. Belle hovers by the broken door, eyeing the corridor beyond. 'How the fuck they found this place . . .'

'I don't know, Master Darley. The wards . . . he's always been so careful,' Banks says as I pass him a tumbler of velvane. He downs it gratefully, wiping his mouth with the back of his hand, beginning to calm. 'Haven't seen the Collector in a couple of days. Then I heard them, breaking in the front door, and I rushed down, but they saw me . . .'

'Must be a mole,' Knox says bitterly, eyeing the ash and dust on the floor outside. The wood in splinters, the hinges pulling out of the wall. 'There's no way they would have figured out where Ezra kept the map. Or how to get in through the wards. This doesn't feel like a hunt, it's calculated, coordinated—'

'We need to find Ezra,' I say. 'If they broke in now, it means they know he's not here. Which means he's tied up fighting them, or . . .'

'He's been captured,' Knox mutters.

Banks sighs deeply, trembling fingers reaching towards the decanter of velvane. Instead of pouring a tumbler, I pass him the whole thing and he sloshes in a generous pour before downing it. Finally, his shaking subsides. 'I don't know where he is.'

I dart a look at Knox. 'Any ideas?'

'A trick or two,' Knox says, glancing at me. 'There might be a way of locating him that he wouldn't have shared with either of you.' I raise my eyebrows and he shrugs. 'Ezra has secrets upon secrets. Surprised he can keep them all straight.'

'If anyone can, it's him,' I murmur darkly.

'Secrets keep us safe,' Knox says quietly, then he gestures at the room. 'This is what happens when someone knows more than they should. Shit hits the fan. Banks . . . I'm afraid you can't stay here.'

'I'll go to the safe house,' he says, pouring out another glass of velvane and nodding to himself. I swear he's had half the decanter. 'I'll take a few things, you'll let the Collector know?'

'Of course,' Knox says, features softening. 'We'll escort you. The city is not ours tonight. I won't have you travelling across it alone.'

Banks wanders off to the staircase, muttering about finding Dolly's things as well, her keepsakes and such. Then Knox and I both stare at the map, at the tiny dots moving all over the city of Dinas Tar, and the ones of ourselves, standing right in this office. A tapestry indeed of many people and I realise now, many wielders. In the wrong hands, this would be a map of death. A path of spoils for the cold ones to triumph and feast or seek retribution. I close my eyes, scrunching my hands into fists. The thought of anyone close to us helping the cold ones find this . . .

'Do I want to know what that is?' Belle asks from the doorway.

'Probably not,' I say, glancing at her. 'I don't know how safe you would be if you did.'

Belle gulps. 'I'll go and ensure no more of them have snuck in. I didn't see anything, if this Collector asks.'

'Horrific, isn't it?' Knox says bleakly after Belle disappears. 'Not just the map, but all the secrets, the assignments. But it all serves a purpose. I imagine you always thought him a criminal, didn't you? He wouldn't have corrected you. Wouldn't have wanted you knowing who he worked for, would have put you in danger just knowing. I thought him a criminal for a long time, until I learned the truth. Until he began sending me farther afield and allowed me access to some of his secrets. But it took years. He trusts no one but himself really. Not even his own flesh and blood.'

'He's the Crown's man,' I say softly. 'Always has been. And so were my parents. All of them . . . probably recruited straight out of Killmarth all those years ago.'

Knox nods. 'And through him, so are we.' He looks at my wrist, smiling faintly. 'He never offered me a bracelet to keep me safe. That blood bond was for you alone.'

'I hated him for it,' I say quietly.

His eyes meet mine. 'I know. He wanted you to hate him. He thought it might make you spark.'

I laugh humourlessly, shaking my head. 'Why am I not surprised. Ruthless bastard.'

★

We decide to take the map with us and move it with Banks to the safe house. Knox reasons that we know the wards have been breached on the shop, but the safe house is warded too, and with any luck the cold ones do not have knowledge of it. 'Or this mole,' he says, voice steeped in venom as we roll it carefully, placing it in a leather tube. 'If I find out who it is . . .'

'We'll kill them,' I promise, shuddering at what might have happened here tonight. The catastrophic consequences of a map like this falling into their hands. There are so many marks on the Collector's map, people of prominence, power . . . this feels like less of a hunt and more of a targeted assault. The map doesn't necessarily identify wielders for them to feed on, but they can do that with their own senses.

It has to be someone close to the Crown, someone who has knowledge of Ezra's movements and his office . . . that's a very small circle.

The safe house is a few streets away, nearer the leafy, well-to-do district closer to the palace in the north of the city. It's a detached house behind a gate in a street lined with trees. There is barely a whisper of sound, everything muffled by the snow. As we walk in, the wards allowing the four of us through, I suppose because Knox, a Darley, is with us, I wonder why I didn't grow up here. Why in that dusty, dingy shop, when this was the alternative?

'I know what you're thinking,' Knox says, glancing at me as we step inside. 'This was his parents' house, his family home growing up. He saw his sister and his parents murdered here. Barely got out with my mother, his sister. This place is drenched in blood to him. The shop is a refuge.'

I bite my lip, insides churning. The Ezra Darley I know, whom I've always known, is the Collector. Not this man with a past and sorrows and grief. Not the man Knox clearly knows and respects. Even loves. It's unsettling, seeing him in a new light these past weeks, knowing the choices he made were not just to punish me. They were *for* me, however flawed. 'Let's get Banks settled, hide the map for Ezra and find the other cold ones. If they were after the map, there will be more of them poised tonight to use it.'

'Agreed,' Knox says.

'Do you think this is revenge? For us breaking into their world?' I say. 'A warning shot, as it were?'

'Could be,' Belle agrees. 'This doesn't line up with the pattern of attacks from previous hunts.'

Banks drifts off to the kitchen, muttering about finding candles and more velvane and Knox places the map in a vault, so similar to the one in the shop that I have to look away. He locks the heavy door, hides the key and meets Belle and I by the front door. 'The old man will be safe here. Don't worry.'

I nod, looking to where Banks is now getting comfortable in the parlour, a blanket draped over his knees. My heart pangs, as I imagine Dolly sat beside him, where she should be. Not six feet under. My fingers flutter to my throat, to the tender skin that I'm sure is already bruising from that cold one's feral grasp. 'Let's get a move on. Find Ezra, dispatch as many as we can. I don't like the feel of

Dinas Tar tonight. I fear . . .' I swallow. 'Once they know they were unsuccessful with the map, they may turn to a bigger target.'

'Ezra could have moved to the palace, along with the others if there was a bigger attack there, perhaps a diversion for stealing the map . . .' Knox muses, pondering as we move swiftly through the cold streets. 'They've targeted a school already, and there are no schools with boarders in the city. Any young wielders will be in their homes. Where else would many wielders be gathered? It's a high-value target.'

I pause, running today's date through my mind, realisation sinking its claws into me. Have I got it wrong? 'Knox, what night is it?'

He looks at me, then his eyes widen. 'Oh . . .'

'It's the night magic first bloomed in Alloway, isn't it?'

'The anniversary . . .' Belle whispers.

'When Felix Gelding discovered botany in the fields, when all hope was lost as they were starving towards the end of winter . . .' I run a hand down my face. 'There will be a gathering to mark it, but where?'

'The Serpentine Orangery,' Knox says, already turning to break into a run. 'The first ball to mark the dawn of the year. My mother will be there. That's where he'll be, not at the palace. Ezra will have gone to protect her.'

Chapter 30

The Serpentine Orangery

I gaze at the construction of glass and steel with trepidation. The Serpentine Orangery. A domineering structure, it dwarfs the ceiling of the train station in terms of beauty and sheer ingenuity, rising up as a beacon of pearlescent light in the dark. It sits beside the snaking serpentine river, a lawn stretching down to the very bank of the water on the other side. As we approach through a maze of parked motorcars, awaiting the guests to spirit them home, all I can hear is music and laughter, the steady gush of the serpentine a low humming note. No sounds of screaming, of horror . . . yet.

I collar a driver, who is waiting for the family he works for to finish their celebrations, and offer him a handful of florin notes. 'Take these and take this . . .' I hand a hastily scrawled message to him, 'to a man called Pewter at the Pickled Gargoyle.'

The man pockets the florin notes and nods. 'Right you are, miss.'

We watch him drive off into the night and I hope Pewter gets the message in time. Then we turn wordlessly and head up the gravel path to the bouncers and slightly too perky hostess on the front door. 'And the family name of your party is?' she asks in a lilting voice, holding a list of names and a pen.

'Darley,' Knox says, slinging an arm around me. 'And my plus one. And . . . my other plus one.' He slings his other arm around Belle and she laughs, showing all her teeth.

'Darley . . . Darley . . .' the hostess says, a frown pushing down her eyebrows. 'Ah, yes. Never known you to attend, sir, welcome.'

'Why does that not surprise me,' I say to Knox as he leans in, pretending to chuckle at what I've just said.

'He's a recluse but the old families are always on these lists,' Knox replies, guiding me to the edge of the ballroom, surrounded by potted plants, brushing the glass walls with green-leaved fingers. 'My next stab at a name would have been Locke. Or Godolphin.'

'I've used Greevy before,' I admit. 'Old banker I was sent on assignment to collect as a mark years ago. Rich old wielder, total curmudgeon. Had to corner him in an elevator to extract his blood. Name always worked a treat though, like having a skeleton key for every locked society door.'

'We both have a few tricks up our sleeves, it seems,' Knox says, eyeing the gathered crowd then wrinkling his nose. 'This reminds me of the Masquier Ball.'

'The training was worthwhile, it seems,' I say softly as I realise with a jolt, many of the guests of this ball are wearing masks, or deep, velvety capes, hoods pulled low over their foreheads to plunge their features in shadow. With the added allure of soft lighting and the gleam of it reflected in the glass surrounding us like a washed-out mirror, this ball suddenly takes on a new air. Something sinister, watchful. And with the toquay flowing and a band starting a dark, seductive melody, I shiver with unease.

'Belle, I don't think we should split up at all in here. Stay close, keep your stake in your—'

That's when I see him.

Teeth glinting under the glow of a thousand reflections, midnight-coloured cape, hood pulled low to cover all but his grinning mouth. He stands in the centre, watching us, dancers swirling around him, as though oblivious. I stiffen, sensing the otherness of him. The wrongness. Perhaps because I am searching for them and not half cut, but no one else seems to have noticed. I stare at him, catching the flash of canines as he reaches out to one of the dancers swirling nearby, teasing a long lock of her hair through his fingers and holding it up to sniff. Before I can form a warning on my tongue, a scream shatters the happy bubble of the evening.

And that's the moment they all pull back their hoods.

At least a hundred of them, eyes and teeth glinting as they lunge for their prey. Cold ones, so many of them, too many for Knox, Belle and I to ever think of beating back . . . like a rising tide, the blood spatters. Teeth rip into throats, wielders too fond of their drinks and their merriment scramble and raise their hands, but it's far too late. The cold ones have staked their claim on their first victims and there's nothing they can do but scream.

For a heartbeat, I watch as two cold ones wrestle an old woman dripping in gemstones to the ground, her heels kicking as they feed on her throat. She flails, trying to break free, before falling horribly still.

I snap into action.

Calling on the magic buried in that well within me, I hold out my palms, and will the glass dome above us to transform. I feed all of myself into it, this huge, looming structure, needing it to be wood. To be a structure I can draw on. To be my weapon against this tide. I draw in a breath, sensing the magic I need to transform it all. To break it apart, piece by piece into the shards of death I can plunge into every vampiric heart.

But I need more.

I'm not enough.

Instinctively, I reach towards Knox, and I beckon. I crook a mental finger, coaxing his well of magic, his alchemy to join my own. It trickles at first, as though he resists the pull, then it flows, faster and stronger, raw magic I can spin around the threads of my own. It becomes the sea itself as it roars and roars within me and when I can no longer hold it, no longer twine it around my own, I unleash it. The glass dome above us shudders. Then . . . it begins to warp.

Like a cloud, the glass shifts and changes, flowing into wood, running down the sides. The ballroom darkens, the air thickening with screams and gasps as I plunge my will into it, willing it to crack apart.

'Nearly there . . .' I gasp as the dome splinters into shards. Stake upon stake, hovering above all our heads, awaiting the command.

My command.

'Focus, DeWinter . . .' I hear Knox say, but it's as though it's from a lifetime away, a tunnel separating me and him. I hone those stakes, shape them, whittling them down until they're razor sharp. Until they are the weapons I will wield.

I expel the breath I've been holding, attuning my senses to the ballroom. To the gathered crowd, the tearing and whimpering, the feeble magic wielded from rusty palms. Then I sense the vampires amongst them. The monsters. And I will those wooden stakes to drive inside every one of their wretched hearts.

And I unleash.

The stakes hover for a breath, sensing the path, then the magic sparks within them. And they drop, faster and faster, burying into every cold one's chest.

Belle howls, already in her wolf form before leaping back from the cold one she's been tearing into. She transforms back into herself and lunges for a bleeding woman who teeters on impossibly high heels, catching her before she hits the floor.

I drop to my knees, blood gushing from my nose as I swear softly, a numbness creeping over me. Dark stars crowd my vision, the ground tilting up to meet my cheek. I'm aware of a voice, calling my name, a hand on my shoulder, but I cannot move. I cannot run. I blink, seeing a pair of boots as they pause before my eyes, then Ezra's face as he places his hands on my cheeks, calling my name over and over. I try to stay awake as he turns to the side, yelling for someone to hurry. Then I know no more as the world darkens into oblivion.

*

Too many.

There were far too many.

Cold ones everywhere, so many we had no hope of defeating them. The glass ceiling, splintering, the stakes raining down like the last judgement of a cruel god. The light leaving my veins as a flame, extinguished. And then nothing. Nothing but those boots, the fear in Ezra's eyes, the cold floor under my cheek. Just soft, syrupy oblivion.

I wake to chaos around me, screams and moans, the coppery tang of fresh blood. I jerk back, feeling arms around me and stare up into his eyes. 'You found us,' I say.

'Pewter got the note, he came looking at the palace. Ezra was already here though,' Alden replies. 'Looks like they messed with the wrong wielder tonight. Over a hundred at once . . .'

He's carrying me, nestling me in his arms, nodding to someone and talking quickly over my head. I stare blearily around, taking in the carnage, the smashed glass, the splintered wood. The piles of ash, coating everything. And the guests . . . the bodies. Too many on the floor. Too many lying still, blood pooling around them. There are botanists assessing them, those with medical training, but my heart twists at how many are now dead. 'I wasn't fast enough,' I say quietly. 'There were so many . . .'

'You are a fucking hero,' Knox says, appearing at Alden's elbow. 'And now we're taking you home. Caroline and the Crown can deal with the casualties. Ezra's taken my mother away, she was wounded, but not badly . . .' He swallows, as though imagining just how badly she could have been injured. Then his eyes snap to mine. 'A fucking *hero*.'

Alden carries me outside and I'm aware of Tessa's wild eyes, unfocused and scared, her hand touching my face. I try to reach out to her, to reassure her I'm fine, but my limbs are so heavy. Then Alden freezes. 'Looks like there are a few strays to put down before we can leave. Heading for the river.'

I try to focus, try to tell him to put me down, that we have to fight, but he holds me closer, tighter. I crane my neck to look, gazing into the dark, and see the flash of eyes and teeth. If I could just scrape myself together I could finish them, I could . . .

Then a group of wielders charge past us, one blasting vines at them to ensnare them. They all seem to dodge, evaporating like smoke, and I sag against Alden.

'They're retreating, thank the gods,' he says. 'But . . . shit. The way they looked at me. Sophia, I think they know. They know what I'm becoming.'

Chapter 31

Shaping Axe

Word of the attack on the Serpentine Orangery spreads, along with the part I played. Eyes follow me down every corridor, gazes averted when I look their way. Scholars murmur, gossip spreading like wildfire, that I transformed the entire ballroom, that I slaughtered an entire hunt. That I laughed afterwards, bathed in their ash and blood. The embellishments become wilder and I find scholars avoiding me entirely at meal times. Alchemists are rare, but feats like that? Unheard of.

It's not long before I'm summoned to a secret meeting in Darley Hall. Caroline Ivey, Professor Hess and Ezra Darley all stare at me as I walk into the room at the end of the corridor, the night shimmering darkly in the huge windows, casting them in shadow.

'You'll be targeted now,' Ezra says without preamble, breaking the silence. 'Not just for the scent of potent magic in your blood. What you did at the Serpentine Orangery—'

'Which the Crown applauds you for,' Caroline interjects.

'Yes, Caroline, we're all very proud of her display,' Ezra snaps. 'But the next time we send her out, who do you think will be the greatest prize of the hunt?'

'So what, we stop sending a valuable asset into the field?' She gestures at me. 'She could destroy them all, never mind that the nocturnal development has shut down. We send her as bait, and they won't even realise it's a trap—'

'Until I detonate,' I say. 'I find it strange, Ezra, that you don't agree with Caroline. If there's a fast way we can take out many at once with limited casualties to ourselves . . .'

Ezra folds his arms, narrowing his gaze. 'We're getting ahead of ourselves. Surely the Crown will want a full report before any new strategies are formed.'

Caroline sighs, closing her eyes briefly, and I marvel at her restraint. 'Yes. Sophia, please run through, in detail, the exact occurrences that led to the outcome.'

I nod, clear my throat and recount the most recent attack. Ezra's only tell is the slight tic in his jaw when I talk about finding Banks in the shop. Caroline asks me questions about the map, ensuring it is intact and safe, conferring with Ezra about the secrecy of its current location. I describe the details of how I drew on the well of my magic, tapping into Knox's as well, and Ezra frowns.

'Is it not . . . normal to be able to do that?'

'It's becoming rarer. Usually, an alchemist needs to be in direct contact. But you weren't,' Caroline says, eyes widening, then she turns to Ezra. 'It seems the catalyst was Knox, perhaps with them both together, drawing the cold ones to one location . . .'

A hint of pain flits over his features before he nods. 'Perhaps.'

They make me go through everything again, confirming details before I'm allowed to leave. Hess merely watches on, not offering up any opinions until the meeting concludes. 'I know you both see our scholars as assets, but I must remind you both that they are still learning. Still largely untested. You are talking about a strategy that risks their lives knowingly.'

'Did I ever say I agree with it?' Ezra says quietly, darkness flashing in his gaze as it flits to mine, then away. 'Did I ever say I agree with involving Sophia at all in the Crown's response?'

Caroline clears her throat, gesturing to me. 'You may leave, Sophia. Thank you.'

'I will see you out,' Ezra says, looking at Caroline. 'You have enough information for your report to the Crown?'

'Ample,' she says. 'Eddie . . .'

He turns, regarding her. 'What?'

And for the first time ever, I see her hesitate, as though unsure. Then she glances at me and Hess, as though reminding herself it's not just the two of them here. 'Nothing. Hess, a minute more of your time if possible, to discuss the next set of tactical training the Crown has requested . . .'

As we walk down the corridor of Darley Hall, I turn to Ezra. 'You don't seem to agree with anything I do.'

'In what way?'

'The way I handled the Orangery for one, the fact I'm even part of the Crown's response—'

'It's not that I disagree with your methods, or feel you are inadequate in any way.'

'Then what is it?' I ask, hurrying to keep up with him as we hit the staircase. 'If it wasn't for Knox and I, Banks would have—'

'Died, I'm well aware,' Ezra snaps, stopping suddenly. 'And you and Knox could have lost your lives too. Easily. The entire response was a shambles, and all because . . .'

I pause, taking a breath. 'Because you were with your sister. Making sure she was safe.'

He pushes back his hair. 'I didn't know you two were being sent into Dinas Tar, or I would have been at Alabaster House, as agreed with Caroline. I thought you'd be at the palace. And the attack on the shop, that Banks was there, vulnerable . . .' He releases a breath. 'You were all in danger. All of you.'

For a moment, we are quiet. 'Is Banks . . .'

'He's fine. A bit shaken. Drinking all my finest velvane . . .' Ezra shakes his head. 'But unharmed. The shop has been abandoned, however. I— I am sorry if any of your things were still there. Anything you may have wanted to collect later.'

I swallow, picturing the old teapot, the pack of cards, my room, the teddy Dolly gave me, the library books I never returned. And I shake my head. 'Nothing I cannot live without.'

His features soften. 'We have all lost much to them.'

'Alden, he . . . on the lawn, afterwards. We saw three cold ones escaping and he said they knew what he was, what he was becoming. The things, the belongings I can part with. But I don't believe I can . . . I'm not sure if I can lose any more people.' I look down at my feet, amazed I have voiced this to him of all people. But somehow, I know he gets it. More than anyone else, he truly understands the gravity of loss. 'I am afraid.'

Ezra reaches for my hand, and I don't flinch away. He grips my fingers briefly and my heart stills. Then he retracts his hand without a word and turns away to continue down the staircase.

★

My fears are confirmed only the next morning. As Tessa and I are leaving a lecture in Gantry, a scholar is slammed against the wall just ahead of us. My heart sinks as I see who pins Soames against the wall, teeth mere inches from his throat.

Alden.

'Shit . . .' Tessa murmurs, pushing the crowd aside that have suddenly congregated around them. Soames is just grinning at him, as though he knows what he's doing by taunting him. Alden's saying something, one fist twisting his collar, shoving him against the wall, the other pointed at him as he speaks viciously.

'Alden!' I yell and the crowd parts, everyone whispering as Tessa and I get closer. Alden blinks at us, then shakes his head, as though clearing away a bad dream. Then he releases Soames, stumbling back.

'I'm sorry, I'm sorry . . .' he stammers, backing away, then taking off down the corridor.

'Wait!' I call after him, but he's gone. Leaving every scholar in Gantry staring at me. I flush, looking at Soames, who just shrugs.

'All I did was ask him if it bothers him, being the weak link of the team.'

'You're an asshole,' Tessa says.

I bunch my hands into fists, feeling the heady rush of rage, and wonder just how smug he'd be with something wrapped around his throat—

'He's baiting *you* now,' Tessa murmurs to me, taking my hand. 'Come on. It's not worth it. It's his grief, he's spoiling for a fight.'

'Then I'll give him one,' Knox says smoothly, stepping up next to Soames. 'You and me, maze. Ten minutes. Bring that big mouth of yours so I know where to throw a stake.'

Soames's grin drops from his face as he stares down Knox. And I see it, that flash of pain, the grief. Darcy. He's cut up over her and he doesn't know how to express it, or what to do with it. He glances at me, narrowing his eyes, then nods to Knox before stalking away.

'Thanks,' I say to Knox. 'You didn't have to do that.'

Knox winks. 'Always wanted to put him on his ass. Check on Alden, would you? He'll be ashamed he couldn't keep a lid on it today.'

'On what?' asks Tessa, frowning.

'His bloodlust,' I whisper.

★

I search for Alden everywhere, but it's as though he's vanished. Not anywhere in the halls, the gym, even the library. Finally, I check the basement level in Fetlock, going to open the lab we've commandeered. I hear voices beyond and pause, the door only partially open.

'. . . the test tube on the left, Amaria, not that one . . .'

'Honestly, the way you speak to me sometimes . . .'

'. . . honesty, key word there . . .'

'. . . Ezra Darley, you need to work on your manners and use your *kind* words . . .'

I bite my lip, hiding a smile as I push the door open and find Amaria and Ezra in the lab. Alone. They're on the same side of the worktable, which has been almost entirely overtaken by plant specimens, a profusion of flowering vines falling from the ceiling. They both look up as one and Ezra raises his eyebrows, then takes a hurried step away from Amaria. She tuts and looks back down at her notebook, flicking a test tube with a finger. 'If you're after that man of yours, he's gone for a long walk, he says. Wants to be alone with his thoughts.'

I expel a breath, catching Ezra looking up at me. 'Sounds like he'd benefit from you going after him, wouldn't you say?'

Amaria nods. 'I quite agree, Ez.'

Ez?

I bite my lip again, pulling the door closed, and make my way back up to the main floor of Fetlock. Amaria and . . . Ezra? I've never known him to have a partner, or really even a friend. He's always been the stern, glowering uncle in my life . . . although he wasn't even my blood. To hear him bickering like that, to see him so casually close to another human being . . . the Ordeals may have tested me, but this semester is unbalancing me. The things I knew with absolute certainty less than a year ago are crumbling and I still can't quite find my feet.

Can I trust the man I once loathed with my entire being? My parents did. So much so, they gave me to him. To protect. And even now . . . even now he's fulfilling that request, I realise. He's here. He's at Killmarth, using his time to develop a cure. Remaining close to Knox and I. Staunchly protecting us both in the best ways he knows how to.

*

'Knox?' I ask the next day as we walk to a training session with Ezra and Hess. 'Did . . . did your parents entrust you to Ezra ever?'

'You mean for my training?' he asks, raising an eyebrow.

'Yes?'

He smiles. 'You haven't met my mother, his sister. You haven't seen how he is with her, how he cares for her.' He pauses. 'He witnessed the rest of his family's deaths. Just he and my mother survived, and then, much later, he learns that her son, her *only* son, is an alchemist. Like him. And he doesn't dedicate his life to just protecting me and her, now it's more than that. It's about training me, ensuring that I am the best, that I can fight, and well. That I'm cunning, and clever, and strategic . . . and that if I ever face a horde of cold ones in my home, I will be able to defeat them.'

'Because his family couldn't.'

Knox nods. 'He's training you and me not just to protect us, but for that moment when *he* can no longer protect us. Because we attract them, our blood attracts them, just as his did that night when they broke into his home. And through us, through every training session, every hard day, he finds redemption.'

I swallow, my world tilting once more. 'He's trying to make amends . . .'

'It haunts him, that night. Shapes every decision. His blood lured them and it led to their end.' Knox flicks the tip of my nose as we enter Darley Hall. 'Why do you think your parents chose him, of everyone, to leave you with, a girl who they suspected may become an alchemist one day?'

When Ezra sets out an array of different materials on the table before me, I look him in the eye as I change each and every one, calmly and accurately. And I catch it, the pensive look replaced by something else. A flash of pride. When Knox makes a joke with him, he glances over, smiling and chuckling before turning back to me to nod. And it hits me, like a knife to the chest. He's preparing me, protecting me, raised me to be this way, because he couldn't protect my parents. He couldn't do all this for them, but he can for me. His love is a shaping axe, hewn to make me stronger. To force me to survive, when they did not.

Even if it meant in the process, I grew to hate him.

Chapter 32
Confession

The weeks we had left have trickled through my fingers. Now it's just a matter of days. Alden has two more incidents, fighting against his emerging nature, that of a vampiric monster. A cold one. Professor Grant summons him to her office, reminding him that if he cannot keep his fists in check . . . he's out. I don't see him for the rest of that day, he and Knox take it to the maze so he can work through it all in his head.

I find myself ditching lectures, instead spending hours and hours in the lab with Amaria, desperation cloying the air. We don't talk much, just exchanging notes and calculations, but her presence is somehow soothing. Perhaps it's because sometimes, she reminds me of Dolly. One evening, with the night cocooning us in our singular endeavour, she plucks a flower from a flowering plant that's sprouted in the corner of the room. 'My eldest daughter's favourite,' she says softly. 'She loved the deep violet and yellow petals and how it only blooms in the autumn.'

'I love this one too,' I say, coming to stand next to her and drink in the scent. 'They bloom in a park near where I grew up in Dinas Tar. My— my friend and I—' I swallow, feeling that familiar twinge in my chest. 'Dolly. Dolly and I used to take walks there, and she told me how it's native to Alloway. How you can't find it in any other place in the whole of Kellend.'

'Do you know what it's called?' Amaria asks gently.

'No.'

'Iris. Named after a lesser goddess, a messenger between worlds. She would bring messages of hope to us from Gallant. Glad tidings and such.' Amaria passes me the flower. 'Press it. It'll keep if you press it firmly in a notebook. Stack a pile of books on top and let it dry. It'll be delicate, but it's a reminder. Even the frailest form of beauty can bring a message of hope.'

I accept the flower, that twinge lodging in my throat. She's only told us one of her daughters' names. 'What was your other daughter's name?'

'Iris,' Amaria says with a small, sad smile. 'My hope for a better, more beautiful world.'

★

I find Alden in his bedroom, sitting on the edge of the bed, head in his hands. 'I can't sleep. It's like it is when I overuse my magic and burn out . . . the insomnia, Sophia. I can't stand it.'

Closing the door quietly, I go to him, kneeling before him and taking his hands in mine. He stares down at me, a bleakness to his expression that cuts deeper than any blade. We have at most ten days left before the change in him is complete. And he's lost all hope. But I haven't. I just can't, not for him, not for his soul. I need him to still be the man I love, I need this to not destroy him. 'Come with me,' I say. 'Let's leave Killmarth for a few hours. A walk, the woods . . .'

He nods. 'I'd like that.'

I don't mention the fact that his skin is even more feverish than a couple of weeks ago. That this change, it's quite literally burning him from the inside out. Razing all that he is, replacing it with something cooler, more lethal. And I can only imagine what he's thinking . . . will he ever sleep again? Ever dream? I've never asked Andry, but I've never seen him sleep. Another hideous fact of a cold one's life that Alden is facing. A life of permanent insomnia, filling the void of the night, every night. It's like watching someone I love die again but this time, it's slowly. He's dying over a series of weeks, instead of all at once. The light leaving his eyes in almost imperceptible fragments and if I think about it too much, I become frantic. My mind is constantly divided now between spending as much time with him as possible, capturing every last memory like that pressed iris and trying to save him, and working in the laboratory, documenting every plant, researching the components until we find a match and turn the nocturnal into a cure.

Except . . . this unknown plant will not make it a full cure. There is a final step that still eludes us, to make it more potent, to develop it fully. But I cling to the hope that if we can at least replicate the cold ones' potion, then I can capture his soul in the moment before he's fully turned, that I can save a scrap of it . . .

Then discover the full cure and save him completely.

But we still don't have that final component and time is slipping like sand through my fingers. I can offer nothing but a brief reprieve now. And staying still in one place has never offered solutions, I've found. He needs the wilds. This place, Killmarth, his own mind is a cage.

I focus on his bedroom door, changing it into a portal. Then I picture the Morlagh, forming a bridge from here to there, to the deepest part of the woods. I take his hand and we step out near his family's hunting lodge, the fierce chill of winter stinging my skin.

He stares for a moment, then breathes out, his shoulder dropping. 'Can you remember that night here?'

'How could I forget?' I smile, taking his hand, as we walk up to the lodge.

'I wanted to kiss you so badly. But the Ordeals . . .'

'We got there in the end.'

He swings me around, so I'm facing him, and I look up into deep, serious eyes. Hungry eyes. 'Not inside yet, Sophia.'

A thrill of anticipation shivers through my veins and I raise an eyebrow. 'A walk first, perhaps?'

The night is dark and velvet soft beneath the towering trees. I can barely hear a thing, it's just Alden and me here. And his hand is still feverishly hot in mine. I pause by a tree and lean against it, beckoning him. 'You know if you can't sleep, there are other things you can do at night.'

He smiles. 'You're distracting me. Making me feel . . .'

'Human? Like yourself?' I ask, unbuttoning my coat to reveal the sheer nightdress beneath. He goes still, watching my every tiny movement with a preternatural stillness that makes my breath hitch. 'Maybe I didn't bring you here just for a nighttime stroll.'

He prowls towards me, then stops just inches away, reaching out to grasp my hips. His hands smooth over the fabric, over my sides as he takes that final half step, pressing against me. I gasp, the heat of him seeping through the thin fabric, the contrast of heat and chill sending me wild. He dips his head, kissing along my clavicle as I wind my arms around his neck, sighing softly. In these moments when it's just us, I can forget about it all. I can slip inside a bubble where time does not exist, where it's just us, just our bodies, just the liquid heat between us. He reaches down, thrusting my nightdress aside, and slides his hand along my left thigh, sending a shiver all through me. His hand is burning hot, a contrast to the frigid air as he coaxes my leg up, to wind around him.

The tree is hard against my back, my skin where he's thrust back my nightdress exposed to the night air. He kisses me, hard, tearing back my coat until I'm almost naked beneath him. This side of him, this primal side that's growing with each passing day is sending me wild. His hands reach under my nightdress, running the entire length of my body and he groans. 'Gods you feel so good. And your scent . . .'

'Do you want a taste?' I breathe as his hands explore further, tracing slow circles just under my breasts, before circling higher, higher, until his thumb brushes my nipple and my breath hitches.

'It . . . torments me. The taste of you. How I want every inch of you,' he says. 'The intensity of it, the need for you . . .'

'Taste me then,' I say, guiding his mouth to my clavicle.

His low growl, nuzzling my throat, makes me gasp again, as he nips at my skin, licking at the beads of blood that pool there. He reaches down, touching me between the legs as he licks my throat and I moan, the throbbing need for him building, even as he pins me in place. 'I'm afraid I won't be able to stop, one day,' he murmurs against my throat. 'This . . . this curse . . .'

He continues stroking me and I swallow, finding my words, even as the intense pleasure flushes my senses. 'Not . . . a curse. I burn for you too.'

He sighs, his mouth colliding with mine, his tongue sweeping in to claim me. Then he frees himself and in one sure movement, with me pinned in place, he thrusts up. I shudder against him, the intensity of it, as his mouth moves back down, as he nips at my throat, thrusting again and again, feeding as he finds his pleasure. The insistent pull of his mouth on my delicate skin, the knowledge that it's me doing this to him, me making him feral with need, has heat building at my core and he doesn't slow, doesn't stop, and it's all I can do to hold on. His desire is contagious, and I find myself needing more of him, wondering what he'd taste like. When he pulls back from his feeding, I lick up his neck to his lips and nip his lower lip just slightly, the coppery, salty taste of him light on my tongue, and I moan his name, clinging to him as the sheer primal power of what he's becoming, the change in him, takes hold. He doesn't stop, not until we both crest that wave, crashing together, until I'm shaking and weak. He groans into my neck, holding me against him. 'Perhaps the nights won't be so terrible . . .'

I laugh as he steps back, and I have to lean against the tree, catching my breath before he helps me button up my coat, then guides me back through the woods on still shaking legs. We go to the hunting lodge and he lights the fire, the glow of the amber flames dancing over us both. I snuggle onto the sofa watching him. Watching him gaze into the flames. 'I have to tell you something,' he says quietly. 'This . . . what's happening. It's not just the insomnia, or the fear of it.'

'I know,' I say, watching him. 'But we'll work on the full cure, if we can just find that final component, if we can extinguish that bloodlust in you, then we will find a full cure, we will reverse this—'

'Sophia,' he says quietly, glancing at me, then back at the flames. And somehow, I know. Every bargaining chip, every ounce of reasoning I've been clinging to dies. 'I've asked Knox to be the one. He agreed, eventually. It took some time, but he agreed.'

I frown, growing still. Time itself seems to stutter and stop. 'Agreed to what, Alden?'

'He . . .' Alden swallows, reaching for my hand. 'You know I cannot stand this. What may happen, what I will become. The feeding, the temptation, the hideous monster I'll become. It's . . . it's unbearable. Untenable. I've asked Knox to be the one who will end it, end me. If we cannot find a way before . . .'

'Before it's too late,' I say softly. What he's saying, this knowledge . . . my whole world hollows out. Before, it was the reality of a slow death, but now? To know it will be so final, so absolute, to know the moment when his life will slip away . . . I stare at him, the desperation setting in. To capture every moment, every piece of him, to set it all in stone so it can live on forever. Oh gods. He's actually going to die if we don't find the cure. I release a breath, leaning forward slightly, feeling as though a blade has slipped inside my chest. I can't breathe through the pain in my heart.

'The night, finding beauty in the darkest depths of it . . .' He shakes his head. 'I cannot spend a lifetime doing that. I cannot travel further from who I am, I— I cannot live this life. This is not a life. This is torment. I can hardly stand to be near you, near anyone . . . I'll hurt somebody. It's what I'm most afraid of . . . hurting someone. Hurting you. I can't live with this, with the risk whilst we try to develop the full cure.'

We lapse into silence, staring into the flames. And the true nature of this, all of this really sinks in. I will lose him. I am about to lose the man I love. Not just to the change. Entirely. Forever.

★

Alden's words dislodge something in my mind. Maybe because of what he confessed, perhaps because of the flower Amaria and I spoke of, but it reminded me of a story about Aline's servants, one I had leafed past, discarding it as a meaningless tale about beauty. But it was about a flower. A flower that only blooms at night in the gods' world, a flower with luminous, moon-bright petals, so tiny, growing over the ground like camomile. Like a dusting of frosted stars. It was Alden's words, about finding beauty in the darkest depths of the night. When there is no hope, nothing to hold on to.

The book is where Amaria locks it away in the lab when she's resting, a cupboard, behind plants that spill over it. I twist the lock with a mere thought, the metal giving way with the smallest flutter of wielding, and the door opens. I reach for the book, bringing it to the worktable and search for the small tale about the night of flowers, and how Aline gifted a glade to her servants, so they could experience beauty at night, when they had finished their work of the day. So that even when they were tired and sore, they could visit this glade and find peace and hope.

I scoffed at it when I first skimmed over the words, sure it was just a tale for Aline to boast some benevolence. A way of covering up the fact she worked her servants to the bone, then only gave them a few hours off at night, to enjoy this glade and its quiet beauty. But now I find it, placing my index finger on the page to trace the words and truly read it, every sentence. And when I am finished, I am more certain than I've ever been. This flower, these petals, that only reveal themselves at night, like the cold ones' own thirst and wrath, are the key to the nocturnal. A small, almost forgotten tale, something Aline, believing she was oh so clever, would expect anyone to miss. A tale of rewarding her servants by giving them a reprieve. A tale of the epiphinea, beauty of the night.

Chapter 33

Lady's Grace

Within half an hour, I have everyone gathered in the lab. Tessa is still in her pyjamas and dressing gown, sporting a pair of plush, soft slippers. Blake and Knox are dressed much the same, holding matching hot water bottles, and Amaria has stuffed herself into a thick, hole-riddled jumper. Alden is the only one of us wearing a T-shirt, seemingly unconcerned about the cold snap that's arrived overnight. He's got his arms crossed over his chest, muscles taut under his top, and my heart kicks up a beat, with hope and anticipation. We have just ten days, this has to be it.

The missing ingredient.

'Amaria, just read and tell me if you think I'm wrong,' I say, stepping aside so she can scan the tale in the book. She mouths the words and shrugs, looking up at me. 'We'll need to figure out the amount, the concentration . . .'

'But?' Knox asks.

'But it could be what we're searching for.' She smiles and I finally allow myself to smile back. Hope. It feels like a tangible thing tonight. 'But if it is the epiphinea, that doesn't bloom every night. It only blooms on one night a year, the night we celebrate Aline's name day in Alloway. Your botanists may not have even realised it flowered. It's a rare and celebrated thing to witness.'

I release a breath, hope and desperation turning me a little frantic. 'I know this is all circumstantial, that there are still more plant species to test, that we have a methodology, a system . . .'

'We can explore a promising lead. Have we got a sample of this plant?' Knox asks.

Alden opens the notebook he used to document all the plant specimens we gathered in Alloway. He scans the pages and I barely dare to breathe. We have to have gathered a sample, surely . . .

He nods and there's a collective sigh, like we've all been holding our breath for far too long. But now there is hope. At last, we have hope.

'Well, let's get a move on, scholars . . .' Amaria says, clapping her hands. 'Blake, Knox, notebooks. Alden, I'll need your magic to encourage this plant to grow more buds if needed and to open early, before Aline's name day. Tessa, you handle the specimen and Sophia . . .'

'Yes?'

'There's another name for this. In Alloway we call it Lady's Grace. The gift of a benevolent, beautiful god.' She chuckles, shaking her head. 'You're a clever thing.'

'If she's right,' Knox says. And I don't miss it, the flicker behind his eyes. He's given up on hope. He's readying himself for what he has to do for Alden, for the deep well of grief that will come after.

'Jealous?' I ask, goading him gently, trying to drag him out of his mire of disbelief. He looks at me, lips quirking, and I raise one eyebrow in silent challenge. He needs this to work. We all do.

'Of being upstaged by you? DeWinter, if you've got this right, I'll forever be in your debt.'

'The world will,' Tessa says, winking at me.

Alden squeezes my arm, moving past me, and I know this cannot be wrong. I cannot accept a life in which he is not walking beside me.

We all work through until dawn, testing and checking concentrations and dosages against the potion that Tessa pilfered from their world.

'What's interesting about Lady's Grace is that it only blooms that one night a year in Alloway, no other territory,' Amaria says after a few hours of careful work. 'Alden, hold this for me? Yes, keep the beaker steady whilst I add these petals. Botanists have collected samples before and tried to introduce it elsewhere, but it wouldn't flower.'

'So the botanists working on the nocturnal for the Queen . . .'

'Would never have procured a sample to test it, because they hadn't moved on to testing plants in other territories yet,' Blake says. 'It also doesn't fit in with any plant species in our world, that's why it's unique, right, Amaria?'

'Correct. No other species that we know of only blooms one night a year.'

'An enigma,' Alden says quietly, as Amaria drops the last tiny petal into a beaker full of milky liquid. It fizzes gently and Alden touches the beaker, infusing it with his magic. The combined force of the missing component and botany wielding seems to unlock it, heightening its potency . . . and it gleams. We all freeze, staring at it. It glows, moon pale with a viscous quality. Like the epiphinea flower itself made liquid. It isn't exactly identical to the potion from the cold ones' world that curbs their bloodlust.

'What if . . .' I swallow. 'What if it's all in the consistency?'

'You're thinking this could be a full cure,' Knox says, eyes fixed on it.

None of us say anything for a moment, transfixed. As though if any of us dare move, it will no longer be a possibility.

Finally, Alden shoves back his hair. 'Well, there's only one way to find out. And if it doesn't cure me, I can't take the potion you stole.

Because . . . we'll need it. You'll need it. To continue working on the nocturnal. To develop it into a full cure.'

He reaches for the beaker to draw it to his mouth. All our eyes track the movement, no one daring to breathe. But just before he lifts it, I place my hand over his. 'Stop.'

'What is it?' he says frowning.

'This . . . this elixir.' I swallow. 'We don't know enough about the cold ones yet. How they were made, what drives them . . . what keeps them alive.'

'Wielder blood, Sophia,' Alden says, rubbing his hand across the back of his neck. 'It's wielder blood, like the stuff running through everyone's veins at Killmarth. What runs through *yours*. What I can sense more and more, what I crave like some wretched animal.'

'I know, I know,' I say, reaching a hand up to cup his cheek. He's agitated, I realise, on the brink of something. Perhaps the thirst is overpowering him. Maybe he's on the cusp of turning completely. Dawn has broken . . . we have just nine days. We're all on a knife edge. 'But what if it hurts you? Or, or kills you? You take this elixir, and it cures you. It changes you back to human. But what if we're wrong, what if it just takes away your bloodlust? What if it's the same as the potion and there is *still* something else missing?'

'Then I'll no longer look at you like a meal,' he says softly, eyes glittering as they meet mine. The back of my neck prickles, but I forge ahead. 'What if you need that bloodlust to survive? We don't know enough about how they survive in their world. For all we know, the potion Tessa stole is something they take sparingly, or rarely . . . it looks slightly different, the concentration could be off, or . . .'

'She's right,' Tessa says. 'We have to consider every option. Every angle.'

He holds my gaze and I don't back down. I've stared down

worse and in the end, he blinks, expelling a charged breath before glancing at Tessa, then the others. 'I don't see an alternative.'

'I do,' I say, pointing at the lab door. 'Andry.'

Amaria blinks, quickly hiding her shock, whilst Knox and Blake both tilt their heads together, murmuring quietly. Tessa says nothing. I meet her gaze and know she would suggest the same. We've always been alike in this way.

'You would use this on the Crown Prince of Kellend?' Alden says in a hushed whisper. 'No. Absolutely not. We can't risk it. What if the Queen found out? What if it *does* kill him?'

'Better him than you,' I say, meaning it. This is the line, I realise. The one I've danced over, pushing a toe across, testing the boundaries of my own limits. My own monstrosity. Ever since I drove that blade through his hand, I've known I could go further. I could look on, quite heartlessly, as Andry dies before me, but Alden? No. I would sacrifice Andry before him without a moment's hesitation every single time. I grip his arm. 'If that makes me a monster, so be it. Maybe we all have a bit of monster inside of us. Maybe that's what makes us truly human.'

'I am not going to stand back and administer the elixir we've created to another and not step up and test it myself first,' Alden says quickly. Then his features soften, his fingers smoothing back my hair. I lean into his touch, wanting him. Terrified for the change in him to be complete yet equally, just as scared of what might happen should he take that elixir.

'I will take it, and I will bear the consequences,' Alden says, leaning in to kiss me quickly, teeth grazing my lip before he pulls away. 'I cannot stand to be near you, Sophia. Your blood sings like a siren, this torment *must* end, one way or another. Or it will destroy us.'

He grasps the beaker, pulling it free of the clamp it's held in. I press my hand over my mouth, my entire being at war. Desperate to stop him and knock it from his hands, but at the same time, knowing I must respect his decision, his choices, that he is doing the noble, good thing, and I am the one who would drag him down and make him less. I am the one who would readily give it to Andry and test it on him. His eyes meet mine and my heart twists. But his soul. His heart. All that is beautiful and good within this man, everything I love about him, what if it's about to be torn away? What if, what if—

He mouths *I love you* and before I can so much as gasp, he knocks the elixir back.

Chapter 34
Schemes

Alden chokes on the nocturnal elixir. My breath stutters as he claws at his throat, trying to swallow. He slams his palms down on the worktable, head dropping, and I crash across the room, reaching out to him. But when his head snaps up, his eyes bloom dark, like ink blots. His teeth flash in a feral grimace and I hesitate, terror sweeping through me as Knox shouts for me to back away.

Then he draws a long, laboured breath.

'Alden?' I ask, taking a tentative step towards him.

He coughs, waving one hand as he grips the table with the other. 'I'm all right. Potent stuff.'

'Does this mean . . .' Tessa asks.

'I'm not sure,' Alden says straightening up. 'Ask me what I'm thirsty for.'

Knox pulls in a breath. 'Velvane?'

He smiles tentatively. 'Hold the wielder blood.'

The relief hits me and I clap a hand over my mouth. I feel like my chest just got a stone lighter, a weight lifting off it that I didn't realise I had been carrying. Knox turns away, wiping at tears, as Blake rubs his arm and I know we're both thinking the same thing. There's hope. The promise Alden extracted from Knox might never have to come to pass. After weeks and weeks of bleakness and misery since the great hunt began, the deaths, the devastation, this finally feels like a victory.

'Test him, please,' I say and swallow, clearing the lump in my throat. 'Test his blood and— and mine, analyse it when compared to Andry's.'

Amaria nods, moving to pick up a needle and vial, as Knox begins to move, finding samples of mine and Andry's we've been testing, analysing, recording . . . he also pulls out the sample taken just yesterday of Alden's. Between them, we can see if it's changed. If it's more like mine, or like Andry's.

Amaria draws his blood and we're silent as she lines up the samples. Knox assists her, sorting the samples, moving them under the lens. I'm barely breathing. The air in the room has thickened, charged with so much hope, it's electric. Alden reaches for my hand and I lean into him. Then Amaria straightens, blinking slowly.

'Amaria?' Knox asks.

She looks at Alden and I know before she says it. 'I'm sorry, Alden. So sorry.'

He exhales, like he's been punched, and closes his eyes, pinching the bridge of his nose. 'No change at all?'

'None,' she says softly. 'What you're feeling right now is a lack of bloodlust, I would say. So a partial success, a very useful step forward.'

'But not the cure,' I say, my voice echoing in my ears.

She shakes her head. 'Not the full cure, no. Alden is still changing.'

He drops his hand and opens his eyes. 'It's all right. Really, it's all right.' He takes a breath, looking at all of us. 'This is a breakthrough. We have to remember that. I'm not going to lie, I got my hopes up . . . but Sophia hit on the final component and now we have a working elixir that completely curbs bloodlust.'

'But you'll still, you're still . . .' Tessa swallows.

'Yes. I'll change fully in nine days and still need to feed on wielder blood,' Alden says quietly.

'Nine days,' Knox says, placing his hands on the worktable. 'Alden's right, we aren't out of time. And we *have* made a breakthrough.'

★

After spending the day monitoring Alden and snatching sleep in fits, we all gather in Darley Hall. I'm trying to hold it together, for him, for all of us. But nine days. We have just nine days before he turns completely.

'He's going to be an arse about taking it,' says Knox grimly.

'But at least we know it won't kill him,' I say.

'Well . . . probably won't,' Tessa adds, staring at the locked door. 'I mean, we've only tested it on Alden and he hasn't fully turned yet. Only one way to find out though. And if it makes him more of a palatable person . . .'

I snort. 'That's asking a lot of an elixir.'

Amaria reaches for the door handle. 'I'm glad he's not my future king, is all I'm saying.'

Andry's eyes light up in feral delight as we all troop in and close the door. 'The full complement today.' He crosses his legs and clasps his hands on his knee. 'To what do I owe the pleasure?'

'We have an elixir for you to try,' I say, attempting to smile and realising my features are arranged all wrong. 'It's worked on Alden.'

'Curbed the bloodlust, like the cold ones' own potion does,' Tessa says. 'It won't cure you, but it will mean you no longer thirst. A good solution, I think.'

Andry's stare turns to a glower. 'You *think*?'

'It's a risk we're willing to take,' Knox says darkly.

Andry splutters indignantly, the veneer of civility gone. 'You're feeding me your half-baked concoction that you've tried on *one* person? Absolutely not. I demand to see a professor. Or— or Ezra Darley. Yes. Bring me Ez—'

'Shut up,' Amaria snaps. 'All you do is whine.'

'Can you tell he's royal?' Knox drawls.

'How could we forget with the constant reminders,' mutters Blake, raising an eyebrow.

Andry glares at all of us and I smile grimly. We're all on edge, we were all so hopeful . . . 'Andry, either we force it down that pretty royal neck of yours, or you take it like a good boy and we'll reward you with treats.'

Tessa snorts but says nothing.

'It's Prince Andry to you, alchemist,' he grumbles darkly. 'To think I've been nice to you, and now you're going to poison me.'

'If we wanted to poison you, I would have raided the poison garden and knocked you off long ago,' Alden mutters. 'We are mostly sure this will not harm you. There's never a guarantee though.'

Amaria exchanges a look with Tessa. 'We could just feed it to him and see what happens? I was going to suggest a smaller dosage, but I don't feel like spending any more time with him. There must be a spare heir somewhere.'

'Agreed,' Knox says with a nod. 'And if it kills him, then at least our ears will get a break.'

'Mother will hang you all,' Andry says and I chuckle. Andry can say whatever he likes today, be as furious as he likes, the whole college could burn down around us, and I wouldn't care. Not when we still have to cure Alden.

★

We convene in a common room in Fetlock, the one most of the other scholars don't bother using. Alden insists that we toast with a bottle of toquay that Knox smuggles out of the professors' stash in the Keeper's Hall, but it falls flat. As Blake stokes the fire until it's roaring, we all sip our drinks, the bubbles fizzing on my tongue. This feels like a corner's been turned, but we're not there yet. And once we've drained the bottle, we move on to velvane, swirling the forest green liquid in our octagonal glasses. Knox extracts a notebook and pen and we toss around ideas, devising our next steps. It's just Tessa, Knox, Alden, me and Blake tonight and I wish, not for the first time that Greg was here with us. When I catch Tessa's eye and she smiles sadly, I wonder if she's thinking the same.

'Andry isn't dead and Amaria will let us know if he takes a turn for the worse,' Knox says. 'She's volunteered to watch over him. I'll go and relieve her in a few hours so she can sleep.'

'I'll take the graveyard shift with you,' Blake offers.

'Good man,' says Knox with a wink.

I shift on the sofa, leaning against Alden, and consider our next move. 'If it seems like it's worked on Andry, we need to gather more Lady's Grace. Do we have enough of the other ingredients?'

'We do,' Tessa says. 'And most are common plants, gathered in the woodlands of Kellend, so we can gather more if we need a bigger batch.'

'What are you thinking?' Alden asks.

'That we need enough to create a weapon the next time any of them cross over. We could really change their planned feeding frenzies into a tame affair, if they have no bloodlust. If we could somehow administer it en masse . . . and we need more so we can change the consistency. What if it just needs to be thicker, more potent to act as a full cure?'

'Hmm,' Blake says, leaning forward. 'Consistency may be the

key. And in the meantime, developing it into a weapon isn't a bad idea. In its current state as a liquid dosage, that's tricky, but perhaps as an aromatic?'

'Exactly.' I nod and swallow, glancing at Alden. 'We'll need you for this, you know. You're very much needed.'

Alden's features are unreadable as he seems to ignore all thoughts on developing the cure, only focusing now on using it as a weapon. 'You know we'll need to test an aromatic on a greater number of cold ones. To check the dosage, the spread . . .' Alden considers. 'Andry is good for testing on one, but we need a room of them, all frenzied and ravenous.'

'One of their parties,' Tessa says. 'In Astrum, they have parties at the great houses, all decadence and sin. If we time it right . . .'

I shiver, repulsed by the thought of it. But as a solution to test our elixir and also to send a warning to the cold ones planning their next great hunt . . . do we dare? But if I can keep Alden focused on this, if we can continue our work on developing a full cure . . . I don't know what his nature will be when the change is complete. He doesn't know and he's afraid. He hasn't mentioned what he told me in the Morlagh again, but I hear his words like a second pulse. They haunt me. His decision haunts me. I look at Tessa. 'Are you thinking what I'm thinking?'

She smiles back, a glint in her eye. 'I'm thinking the cold ones of Astrum need a lesson in true warfare.'

'It's a dangerous ploy but could yield the results we need. Two birds with one stone. And if we then cut off their routes into our world . . .' Knox says. 'I've been thinking about the portal, these thresholds of the gods that they use. What if we could destroy them, like the one in Darley? Even if we miss one, it creates a bottleneck when they're returning here.'

'A trap,' I say, leaning forward, the thrill of a plan forming in my mind.

‘Which means me and you, DeWinter.’

I knock back my velvane and nod. ‘I’m in. Although you do realise who we need to bring in on this plan . . .’

‘Ezra,’ Knox says, leaning back, hands braced around his knees. ‘What are the odds he’s going to praise us for our ingenuity?’

‘I’d say slim to none,’ I reply. ‘But I’ll look forward to seeing his face when you present the nocturnal to him.’

No one mentions the full cure again, but I know we’re all thinking about it, skirting the subject, gazes flitting to Alden. It could be a question of concentration . . . or it could be an entirely missing ingredient. We’re close, but not close enough. We need to figure out how to reverse this curse of vampirism entirely.

★

That night, I lead Alden back to my room and we say nothing. No words are needed, not with everything that’s at stake. I take off his clothes slowly, unbuttoning his shirt, planting soft kisses over his chest. Then I pull down his trousers before removing my own clothes. I capture his gaze as I strip down, wanting him to know that I love him. That what he is, what he craved does not define him. It’s what he is to me, what *we* are that matters. I kiss him deeply, allowing the heat to build between us, the want. Then, with his arms around me, he walks me backwards to the bed, one step, two, three, all whilst dusting me with kisses.

Then with moonlight streaming over our bodies, we move together, slowly, languorously, revelling in this moment of being us.

Being human.

I will find the cure. I will.

I won’t lose him.

Chapter 35

To Take a Life

Ezra stares at the beaker, expression closed and unreadable. The nocturnal glimmers faintly inside, imbued with Alden's botany wielding, the milky liquid seeming to almost ripple up the glass's sides. Alden finishes explaining the properties of the nocturnal, winding down into silence. Andry, for the first time unchained and still, clears his throat and we all turn to look at him.

'I didn't appreciate their methods, but I must say, I'm grateful to them. I'm not cured, but my bloodlust has gone. I can consume normal foods without longing for it to be a wielder's blood, even though wielder blood still sustains me, sadly. It's a fact of my anatomy I may have to live with forever. I do still have the heightened senses, for instance, I can discern each of you by the patter of your pulse and the scent of your blood . . . but still. The Crown applauds them.'

Ezra runs a hand over his face and turns those stony eyes on Andry. 'It matters not what you think, boy. What matters is the repercussions. You do not speak for the Crown. Not yet at any rate.' Then his eyes travel over us. 'You have done well, all of you. When I first told you to fix it, I'll admit I was desperate. I didn't think . . . not for a moment . . .'

'Desperation breeds hope,' I say, eyeing Alden. He's staring at Andry, a small frown on his face, and I wonder what he's turning over.

'It's the biggest breakthrough we've had in some time,' Ezra concedes. 'Although you all realise you cannot ever take credit for it. If the events leading up to this discovery were ever made public . . .'

'Nor can my involvement ever be known,' Amaria says, looking at Ezra. 'I must return.'

They share a look and Ezra nods. 'Of course.' He clears his throat. 'I can plant files indicating that the team of botanists had already figured out this missing component in the nocturnal. We are the shadows behind the Crown. I'm afraid none of your names will be marked in the history books.'

'I can live with that,' I say.

'As can I,' Knox agrees.

Ezra sweeps his gaze over us all before nodding and leaving the lab. Pride. It's unmistakable. My heart beats a little faster and I stand a little taller. Ezra Darley is proud of us.

⋆

Sunlight patters down through the towering trees of the Morlagh Woods, dappled light thawing the frost and snow. We gather, all of us, having slipped through a portal the night before. Field assignments, Ezra has excused us from lectures for. I only hope it doesn't raise any suspicions, particularly with the Crown. To avoid the Queen's retribution, our plan must be executed faultlessly. There is no room for error. And this time, Ezra is accompanying us to Alloway.

'Allow me to carry the book for you. It's heavy, cumbersome—' Ezra mutters to Amaria as she shoulders her pack once more, shrugging to distribute the weight.

Amaria raises an eyebrow. 'You think me incapable because what, I'm a woman?'

'That is not the case. I was merely offering—'

'Such a poor, weak female . . .'

Ezra makes a kind of strangled sound and shoots her a look as they continue to bicker. Amaria is clearly enjoying herself. I raise an eyebrow at Knox, who hides a smile. Neither of us has ever seen him this ruffled. In Amaria it seems, he has truly met his match. He walks beside her the entire way, as though he is not yet ready to part with her. He likes her. Ezra Darley, who never seems to like anyone, likes Amaria.

Knox and I work together, Amaria feeding us coordinates a little closer to Castle Caryn this time. I picture the grove, the melting frost, the quiet and eventually, a portal ripples in the air before us, a bridge from the Morlagh, to the northeastern woods of Alloway. We all step through, Alden, Knox, Ezra, Amaria, Tessa and I, and I close it behind us with a swipe. Andry we've left in the care of Blake and Belle, whom we decided to bring in on our schemes. Andry has promised not to cause trouble, or expose himself before the plan is complete, despite his restless need for freedom. For that at least, I am grateful. He is less of an arse now, at least.

'Castle Caryn is an hour in that direction,' Amaria says, indicating the densely packed trees. 'And we can forage around here. Gather what we can of the plant, then return there. It won't be flowering, you'll have to wield to coax it to bloom once picked. But look for pale, star-shaped leaves.'

By midday, we've exhausted the local vicinity and Amaria takes us farther west. A valley stretches out, drenched in wintry sunlight and in between the folds of two mountains, the tiny plants drift in droves of star-shaped leaves and pale buds. A huge field's worth, left to spread in the wilds, a bounty of the plant we need.

'You're quiet,' I say to Alden as we begin our work.

He shrugs, that same frown furrowing his brow. 'Just thinking, that's all.'

We work along the edge, plucking and placing each plant in the sacks we brought for the purpose, Knox keeping watch as we fill them. But the whole valley is silent, peaceful, save for the sound of birdsong. Gradually, we venture farther from the line of trees, filling up sack after sack with the plant. The sun warms the back of my neck and for the first time, I feel real hope.

I look over at Alden, opening my mouth to call over with a joke, when I spot a shifting of light, fifty or so feet away. Then a crack, and my shoulder judders backwards. I glance down to find a hole and a spray of blood.

My blood.

Shock ties me in place as the valley erupts around us, Allowayans rushing down the valley with cries in their throats. With weapons. Then the pain in my shoulder connects with my mind and I see white-hot, blazing stars. I breathe quickly, aware and yet unaware of everything, my instincts kicking in.

There's a piece of metal lodged in my shoulder, spiked and shaped like a six-pointed star, a thrown weapon, designed to dismember. Or kill. A little further to the right, and it would have been my heart.

As the Allowayans clash with my group, Ezra leading the counterattack, I wield. I dig into the well within me, willing this weapon, this metal to dissolve. To become something necessary, a bandage. It transforms far too slowly, becoming a wad of bandage that I reach over with shaking fingers, stretching around the wound. I can do nothing for the pain, but as I look up, narrowing my gaze, I ignore it. These people are here to kill us, or capture us.

They will not take my friends.

Ignoring the throb in my shoulder, spreading through my chest and down my arm, I lift my other hand, willing my magic to form a portal. In desperation, I picture those gargoyles, the foreboding, ancient bulk of them as they crept ever closer, and I wield.

My magic streams, gold and steady from my outstretched fingers, desperation and fear fuelling it—

Then instinctively, I reach for Alden. I grasp the raw magic from his own well, conjuring it from his veins, gripping it. Reweaving it with my own. Terror tunnels my vision as I will the portal to form. Then when I see the gargoyles, across the bridge I have created, I release a moan, low and guttural, the pain throbbing from my shoulder almost eclipsing me completely.

'Get through!' I call, spinning wildly, pulling my blade from its holder. 'Retreat! Amaria! Knox! Tessa!'

Amaria bolts, ducking under the blow of a blade, jumping through the portal with the book in the pack on her back. Tessa flies through next, then Alden stands beside me. He chokes, beholding the blood gushing through my makeshift bandage and I shove him, pleading, 'I can't hold it, please . . .'

Ezra and Knox are last, holding back a wave of Allowayans bent on a massacre. Their features contorted, they rush at them, but Knox and Ezra wield as one. Creating a web of magic, they feed each other, forcing the very air to transform into a weapon. Metal bullets form, pelting the advancing Allowayans as I scream at them to hurry. In one swift movement, they dive for the portal and I feel a shift in the air at my side.

I whip around, a gasp wrenching from my lips, and find the throat of the person about to murder me.

A boy.

He can't be older than fifteen, eyes wide in surprise, his own blade held aloft, angled at my heart. We both freeze, eyes locked, inches apart and I know I should do it. I know I should slash and end this life, this boy bent on killing me and taking my own life.

But I can't.

In one swift movement, I kick him back and he falls to the ground. Then I leap, straight through the portal, a blade slicing through at my back. And as I fall to the ground, it flies past my hair, embedding in the stone wall of Castle Caryn. I turn, seeing the boy stood there, hand raised before him, the blade just thrown from his fingertips. Our eyes lock, and all I see is hate. Ezra slashes at the air, the portal collapsing between us and him.

Chapter 36

Weary is the Head that Bears the Crown

Dread steals over me as I lie there bleeding. He saw our faces. They heard the words ripped from our throats. Those Allowayans could have been watching us for some time as we gathered those plants before they attacked. What if that boy saw what was beyond this portal? What if he noticed the gargoyles, the stone walls? I roll onto my side, the pain radiating out in waves from my shoulder. I've compromised us all by not killing that boy. By withholding the killing blow, I may have damned us all.

'Get her inside the castle!' Amaria calls and I feel hands underneath me, hauling me up. I groan, red and white exploding behind my eyes, fingers turning numb as the life drains from my limbs. Alden murmurs in my ear, a faint brush of warmth that I try to turn to, try to tell him I'm all right; to warn him about that boy . . . we are at war with Alloway. And we may have just caused an escalation that will end far more lives. I must tell him what that boy saw, that the people here may no longer be safe—

But the next thing I'm aware of is a cold table beneath me, biting into my bones.

'Hold her still,' a voice says and I look around blearily, trying to fix on someone, anyone familiar. Then I see Alden, his eyes, caramel flecks in a world gone awry. His mouth is a grim line, blood speckling one side of his face. As though an arc of blood sprayed up from a body. I open my mouth to speak, to ask him where the others are but then a hand clamps down on my arm, another on my shoulder and I bite back a cry as they unwrap the bandage and press something cold and slick into the wound.

The world tumbles into a well of agony and all I know are flashes. When it's over, when I'm stitched and bandaged, they lead me to a sitting room where the others are waiting. I assess them quickly, casting a glance over each of them, finding them all whole, some sporting bandages like me, cuts and bruises and torn clothing. Kadie is there, the elder from before, and I realise Ezra is talking rapidly, features drawn with worry.

'This could be seen as an act of war. A furthering of the strife.'

'Your Queen . . .'

'. . . find out. They saw our faces. They watched us for some time, I'm sure of it now. Foolish.'

Kadie rises, exchanging glances with the two men who helped me in here, and nods to Amaria. 'When you can, it's best you all leave. Thank you for returning the book, and Amaria to us. We wish you well, we will help all we can with your elixir, with information . . . but we cannot involve ourselves with the politics of the territories. Staying hidden is how we survive.'

I catch the exchanged glance between Ezra and Amaria, a softening in their features, a vulnerability. It's fleeting, there and then gone, but I know I didn't imagine it. They don't want to part. But her world is here and his is elsewhere, and until this is over, Ezra cannot easily contrive a reason to return. Amaria looks down in resignation, as though her whole life has been an exercise in defeat, in loss. And my heart bleeds for her.

⋆

Ezra carves out a portal, then a bridge linking the castle to Killmarth. We step into Darley Hall, all of us subdued, despite the haul of Lady's Grace we managed to find and bring back. Ezra turns to us, saying, 'Not a word.' Before ensuring that we all return to our rooms, our schedules. The work on the elixir, producing it in batches, will take time, until we know the ratios for producing it in bigger quantities. Alden grows quieter, hours of sleep stolen by the laboratory between studies. And with my bandaged shoulder healing slower than I'd like, even with Alden wielding over it, I suffer even more whispers in the halls as I pass. Rumours abound over our absences, the dark smudges under our eyes, the injuries we're still sporting. Blake starts to put it around that we're part of an elite group, being sent to Alloway in the night. The whispers dwindle, but the stares follow me everywhere. And still progress feels achingly slow.

Yet despite our careful tiptoeing, no word reaches us in three days and we begin to relax, even recognising it as a win. My shoulder heals and I can roll it, use it in training, it doesn't ache when I do something minor like pull a shirt over my head. I begin to sink into lectures more, spend time in the library and engage again in my pursuit of learning. We've got away with it, I'm sure of it. I stop thinking about that boy in Alloway, about the repercussions. Perhaps Ezra has smoothed the way, maybe we can get away with it all. We begin to plan our mission to Astrum, and I dream of the days after this is all over.

Until the day the messenger arrives, summoning us to the palace.

And this fragile peace shatters like glass.

Caroline Ivey collects me herself from a lecture on the great wielders of our age and their achievements, her index finger crooking at me, then Tessa beside me. We meet her in the corridor outside as those silvery eyes regard us coldly. 'Either you have done something very good to please the Queen, or insurmountably stupid. Either way, you have thirty minutes to pack some things and meet me by the gatehouse. We're travelling in the royal carriage of the 11:04 train from Marazia and we cannot be late.'

The air has a bite to it as we all walk to the train station in Marazia, across the long and winding path through the sea and past the huddles of shops, cafés and homes that make up the town. I stare through the window of the Copper Spoon, wishing I'd had the chance to go in there. We still haven't been given permission to visit Marazia on a weekend, the great hunt too raw and current in everyone's minds. What if this is the last time I see this place? How much does the Queen know? We board the royal carriage, at the back of the train, in silence, Tessa and I barely glancing at each other. I expected opulence but instead find a long carriage full of seating and tables that wouldn't be out of place in second class. Alden and Knox are already seated, Knox drumming his fingers on the table before him as Alden's gaze bores into mine. I give him the smallest nod, I'm all right. He nods too and I release a breath.

'The Crown reserves this carriage for the people who work across Kellend on its behalf,' Caroline explains, gesturing for Tessa and me to take a seat too as the train whistles, steam billowing from the sides. I exchange glances with Alden, Tessa and Knox, my relief short-lived that Blake has been spared, and therefore can keep an eye on Andry. 'The Queen requested an audience on arrival. You will see her tonight, once we reach Dinas Tar. And don't try to lie,' Caroline says with a small smile. 'She can smell it from a mile away.'

'Then let's hope she doesn't ask the right questions,' I murmur to Tessa.

As we pass through the countryside of Kellend, stopping at the towns on the way up the country to the capital city, I flip between staring out of the window, reflecting on the difference between this journey and the one I first took to Killmarth, months ago, and trying to lose myself in a research book about portals and bridges, the collected theories of an alchemist who died a decade ago. The train rattles and whistles; sandwiches and slices of cake and tea are given to us at intervals as the sun eventually sets, the windows darkening. One of the staff lights lamps throughout the carriage and my own reflection peers back at me from the window. Do I look guilty? Do I look like someone who is harbouring a Crown Prince, who has possibly landed us in an escalation of the conflict with Alloway? Do I seem . . . monstrous?

I should have killed that boy.

No . . . no. Of all the things I regret, that cannot be one of them.

Caroline remains mostly silent throughout the journey, reading what appear to be a series of typed reports, making tiny notes and sipping her tea. I catch her eye as she looks up at one point, but she doesn't smile. Those silvery eyes flash, as though she knows the inner workings of my very soul.

'There's been an incident in Dinas Tar,' she says, eyes flicking to Knox, then back to her report. 'Just to give you a picture of what we're facing now. One of the Queen's assets, killed in our very own capital city.'

Knox sucks in a breath. 'How?'

Caroline's smile is tense. 'An Allowayan poison. We'll catch them. We have eyes everywhere.'

They're getting closer. I share a glance with Knox and know he's thinking it too. To take out one of the Crown's own in Dinas Tar, no less . . . that's a warning shot. Perhaps Caroline is telling us this to warn us of the Queen's mood. Or maybe she's fucking with us so we're not quite so good at lying when we arrive.

The palace looms from the fog coating the streets of the capital. We are transported in two motor cars, Caroline and Knox sat beside me on the back seat. Gravel crunches under the tyres, the woodland beyond curtaining the world in pitchy black. I realise my hands have formed fists as we approach and I loosen them, trying to quell the frantic beat of my heart. If the Queen knows everything . . . no. I can't think like that. I will hold my head high, answer her questions and walk out of here. We all will.

Get in, get out, don't get caught.

But where is Ezra? Has he tried and failed to smooth things over with the Crown? Worse . . . has he been remanded in custody already, to be tried along with us? My mind won't stop spiralling and it takes an effort to remember my training. Not that of Killmarth, but of the Collector. Of armour and masks and cooling my blood so I could be impassive. Calm. Unruffled in any situation.

We are escorted down corridors to a receiving room. I pictured a dais, a throne, guards lining the walls. But the Queen sits on a sofa before a fireplace, hands clasped in her lap, surrounded by similar sofas and armchairs. And as the door clicks closed behind us, I realise it is only us in the room with her. And Ezra Darley, standing before the fireplace. Caroline Ivey approaches first, bowing then taking a seat in the armchair the Queen indicates she may sit in, to her left. Alden, Tessa, Knox and I stand in a line and the air around us seems to thicken and churn like butter. We're all coated in guilt, it's cloying the air. This Queen, the woman who represents the Crown of Kellend, is in complete command. She doesn't need guards or pomp or ceremony. She *is* the Crown. And every mask and piece of armour I hastily built to deceive, simply falls away.

For a moment she says nothing, merely studying us. Then she sighs, fingers tightening in her lap. I realise she is holding a letter. 'I received this from the territory of Alloway, wielders. An account of a skirmish, of a threat to their realm, one they threaten to meet with force. A party of wielders, gathering plant specimens in a valley to the northwest.' She narrows her gaze as the silence stretches, as though time itself has stopped. 'I will ask once and only once. Where were you all three nights ago?'

Chapter 37
Aromatic

Suffocating silence warps the room. My thoughts spiral as I try to gather them together, knowing with startling clarity that one word from her will signal our deaths. None of us responds, not one of us so much as breathes under her direct scrutiny. Her lips twitch, as though she knows one of us will speak up and try to deny it, or spin a tale designed to mislead. But which of us? Who is most adept? Should it be me?

But before any of us can speak, Ezra clears his throat.

'The answer is quite simple. I charged them with an assignment on behalf of the Crown.'

The Queen turns slowly, regarding Ezra. I am reminded of a venomous snake, the kind that slithers before it strikes. 'Explain.'

'I have been identifying portal locations across Kellend, the points at which our enemies have entered our world. Hess has been working on this project for months, dissecting reports from the last three great hunts, lining them up with maps, analysing the terrain. These scholars,' he says, indicating us, 'are the team I entrusted the Morlagh to. I sent them there five nights ago to stake out two locations and ward them, should the cold ones choose to enter there again. The cold ones will now find a ward to navigate, which also acts as a warning system for myself and Caroline should they attack from those entry points again.'

The Queen blinks slowly. 'Interesting.'

'What is more interesting, my Queen, is why Alloway would send a damning letter with such wild claims,' Ezra says smoothly. 'It appears to me that they wish to sow dissent.'

'They have no reason to lie outright, particularly if their claims can be proven.'

'They're trying to create cracks in our defence. Turning us on each other to weaken us,' Caroline Ivey says. 'Could be an excuse by their current administration to invade Theine. We can't rule out that they're planning a campaign of expansion, they're out for blood, after all.' She clears her throat. 'Not that I have any knowledge of these scholars' whereabouts personally. I was not privy to Ezra's assignment.'

'Hmm,' the Queen says. She breathes in sharply through her nose, eyeing us all in turn. 'I will give this all some thought. But one matter remains . . .'

'Yes?' Ezra asks.

'Portals,' she says, stirring in her seat. 'Some of the scholars present are able to create portals, are they not?'

Caroline's gaze flicks to mine. 'Two of them. Knox Darley and Sophia DeWinter.'

'Alchemists,' the Queen breathes, a smile twitching her lips. 'A dying breed. Is this the wielder who triumphed in the Orangery?'

'It is indeed.' Ezra nods.

The Queen's gaze meets mine and I am reminded of the day I had to hide Andry from her. And I have that feeling now, of her really knowing everything. Of her peeling us all back, layer by layer, discovering the truth in our hearts. 'A great service to Kellend. A woman worthy of working for the Crown. Sadly, there were still too many deaths that night. The people of Dinas Tar require answers, wards, perhaps even blood . . . a tricky time.'

'Sadly,' Caroline agrees.

'I have a question that's been nagging at me for some time now. A missing prisoner, who escaped from this very palace.' She indicates the room with one hand, changing the subject so swiftly, I have to blink to keep up. 'No sign of a struggle. No indication of how they escaped. And yet they are missing. And I keep thinking about . . . portals. And the alchemists, the strong alchemists of Kellend, who are able to create them.'

My heart slows, pounding like a fist. She locks her eyes with mine and I stiffen under her direct, assessing gaze. My skin is flayed raw in her searing search for the truth. I am doing all I can to throw up a wall, to seem impassive, even surprised. To keep Andry and the events of that night, of everything that has transpired after, hidden.

'The missing prisoner has indeed raised questions about palace security,' Caroline remarks. 'But our investigation is ongoing. No stone will be left unturned.'

'Hmm,' she says again, that searing gaze still locked on me. 'As we have discussed, I believe there is a mole. An informer, a betrayer in our midst. Ezra has suspected it for some time, pieces and details seem to fall into the wrong hands far too frequently.' Her eyes grow colder, icing over as they finally sweep away from me, gliding over Alden, Tessa and Knox. 'If I discover one of you has lied today, even by omission, know that the wrath of the Crown will be final and absolute.'

Then her gaze rests on each of us in turn and I know for certain, she knows it was us. She knows we took Andry, she probably realises we also went to Alloway, she just cannot prove it.

Yet.

★

With the Crown turning its unflinching gaze on us, Alloway threatening the stability of the three territories, and the cold ones poised to resume their hunting again at any moment after the events of the Orangery, I feel the walls closing in on all sides. Time is running out and if we do not act swiftly, it won't just be our heads the Crown severs. It'll be the whole of Kellend that suffers. We are at war, a hidden, secret war, as well as the one with Alloway, and the Crown cannot afford to continue this fight on two fronts. It is decimating us. We must enact our plan, and we cannot fail.

We spend every unaccounted for moment in the laboratory, producing the elixir. Without Amaria's steady head, there's more sniping at one another. But still, we turn up. No one abandons the team.

On a night webbed with clouds, illuminated by a brimming moon, we burn through the last of the plant specimens we gathered in Alloway and Kellend. The elixir has filled bottle upon bottle, enough of the nocturnal, we hope, to neutralise the cold ones that plague us when they next attack. And to curb Alden's and Andry's bloodlust.

'In liquid form, we would need to gather them in one place. Trick them into drinking it,' Tessa says, arms folded, eyeing the rows of bottles containing the milky, viscous nocturnal. 'Or be able to inject it in them as a weapon.'

'When they attack again, we can coat our stakes in it. Our blades,' Alden says. 'We wouldn't need to aim for the heart, it would be more about striking them, getting the elixir in their blood to eliminate their thirst and their frenzy. But the aromatic we discussed before is still the better option.'

We all stare at each other, knowing what that means. Testing. If we manage to change the state of the elixir from liquid to aromatic, we need to test the potency on a crowd of them in a controlled environment, not whilst we're in the throes of an attack. Which means visiting their world.

'Ezra will not like this,' Knox says, running a hand through his hair. 'The Queen suspects us, at the very least. For all we know, the tale he spun about wards in the Morlagh could have been entirely true. A warning to us, spoken in front of the Queen.'

'That he'll know what we're up to,' I say.

'Still . . . it's a good plan. The best we have,' Alden says quietly. 'We've never discarded something because of the risk before.' He's exhausted. Of all of us, he has worked the most, wielding over and over to ensure the elixir is in its most potent state. And yet, he still fights for what he knows to be right. I reach over, gripping his hand. I'm in awe of him. Despite the burden he carries, what he must now feed on to sustain himself, he continues. He prevails.

'They hold their parties in their houses, so we would need to infiltrate one. But we'll be working with one bloodline,' Tessa says. 'Put it this way, would you drink something served by a rival house? Or worse, an unknown host? They only drink blood at their own house parties. Seldom seem to mix with those in other houses. Unless . . .'

'What?'

Tessa bites her lip. 'There is one night a year when all the great houses have a party. A celebration. Aline's name day.'

A shiver of anticipation trickles over me. 'Her name day?'

'There will be great gatherings. Many cold ones in each of the five great houses,' Tessa says. 'It's three nights from now.'

We all look at each other, the date and our fate sealed. I don't say it, but Knox and I share a glance. It's also the night Alden will change completely.

'It has to be an aromatic,' I say, eyeing the liquid, suppressing the trickle of cold down my spine. 'To ensure it's spread and absorbed. Without breaking down the effectiveness of the elixir though . . . that's complex wielding, Locke.'

'Afraid I'm not up to it, DeWinter?' Alden asks, raising an eyebrow. 'I'll need you and Knox. If you have enough in your wells for me to combine with my own power . . .'

'That sounds like a challenge,' I say, grinning at him, ignoring the bitter twist in my stomach of what that night means. How he could still ask Knox afterwards to end him. 'I'm going to ignore the fact you're clearly *baiting* me.'

He chuckles, shaking his head. 'The audacity.'

'Indeed,' I say. 'Well, Darley, Locke and I will be getting fuck all sleep for the next few days. Anyone else got any fun plans?'

'I have a plan, not sure if it's particularly fun though . . .' Tessa begins. 'I need to bring someone else in on this, a masquier. Someone who can spread the aromatic with me in Astrum. Belle.'

Everyone shifts, considering. 'She's been trustworthy so far,' I point out. 'And she's a wicked masquier.'

'Better than me, I reckon,' Tessa agrees.

'No way, T,' Alden says, bumping her shoulder. 'You're the original cold one here.'

She smiles at him and my breath catches. Moments like these, moments with all of them . . . I will stake my life for this. For us to continue like this at Killmarth, as long as we can.

'Then we're agreed,' I say. 'Alden, Knox and I will work on stabilising the elixir as an aromatic and Tessa will rope in Belle to perfect the appearance of a cold one.'

⋆

Of course, it is never as simple as it seems. The nocturnal twists away from Alden as he wields on it, Knox and I feeding our magic to him, bit by bit for him to draw on. And when Alden strengthens it, the aromatic collapses. Every. Damn. Time. And there's the issue of the portals themselves . . . I can open one into their world, but only with a cold one. I need Tessa and Belle to wield so immaculately, it can trick the very rules of portals to create a bridge from here to Astrum. I don't think about what can go wrong over there. If they don't return from the city . . . I will be trapped in Astrum as well.

The fact is . . . we need Andry. A true cold one to open a portal. But the thought of using the Crown Prince again, of moving him to the Morlagh, which could now be warded and watched . . . such risk. We are practically walking into a trap. I'm not sure if using Alden as a cold one will work, if it matters that he won't be fully turned until the end of that night.

On the final day, Alden finally shares the truth. He waits until it's just the three of us, Knox, myself and him, and he reaches for a bottle of the elixir. Then he sighs deeply and downs it before wiping his mouth.

Knox freezes, features blanching as he stares at the empty bottle, then his gaze rises to meet Alden's eyes. 'That didn't last long. You've been tempted?'

'Today,' he says. 'I need to feed again. I can't . . . Knox. I just can't. After we return from Astrum, if we do . . . that's it for me. I'll be fully turned and it's over.'

My stomach twists sickeningly as I realise what this means. What he's not saying.

'Fuck,' Knox says, pushing his hair back from his forehead and turning away from us.

Alden shakes his head, staring down at the worktable. 'I'm sorry. There is no one more sorry than me.'

Knox places a hand on the worktable and for a moment, I think he's going to retch. Then he straightens, dusting himself off, and looks over at me. 'I need a minute, sorry, DeWinter. I'm— I'm sorry.' Then he turns on his heel and leaves the lab. The ringing silence between Alden and me is deafening as we look at each other.

'You can't make him,' I whisper. 'I'll do it.'

His smile is a sardonic twist. 'You'll stake me through the heart? You have to really mean it, that's the problem. It has to really be driven in.'

I gulp, clutching my throat with my hand. 'This isn't fair.'

'None of it's fucking *fair*,' he snarls. 'It's war. It's an endless war that we are going to lose. This, all this . . .' he indicates the table, 'a clever ploy, but we need more than cleverness. We need a weapon that'll wipe them out. And we're not even close, Sophia. We— we haven't got a cure. We've got another blade, spread out on this table. That's all.'

'Then let us use you, test *everything* on you, find the cure—'

'Stop trying to save me,' he says, seeming to deflate. 'There is no saving me this time. Just stop.'

*

Knox returns later that night without a word to either of us. None of us make for our beds, not even as Killmarth wakes around us. My thoughts become muddied and cloying, until they are nothing but a pool of darkness. And Alden keeps coaxing the elixir. Trying to get it to bend to his will, using our raw magic.

Until finally, it does.

The bottle Alden holds becomes smoke, a silver fog enclosed within the glass. I release a strangled cry and slump against the work-table, eyes burning with fatigue. Alden has done it. He's changed it into an aromatic. But as his gaze locks with mine, there's not a hint of triumph there. All we have, as Alden pointed out, is a clever ploy, another blade. If it cannot cure him, it's not enough. It never will be.

I return to my bedroom, stumbling up the steps to the courtyard to find it's full night again. I put on the jacket with the deepest hood I own to conceal my features. Then I create a portal, wielding through my exhaustion, determination and knife-sharp fear shaping every movement. And I step through from Killmarth to the gates of Castle Caryn.

The gargoyles regard me with cold indifference, not bothering to ask their three questions. I take this as acceptance and step forward to open the gates myself. They don't make a move against me, one even sighs, as though bored. 'Good little monsters,' I whisper and close the gates in my wake. I find Kadie waiting for me in the entrance hall, as though she knew the very moment I would seek her out. Relief washes over me to find this place exactly as the last time we were here. The Allowayans haven't managed to find it. They're still safe and hidden.

'I need your help,' I say, taking Kadie's hands. 'We've turned the nocturnal elixir into an aromatic and we plan to test it on a large group of cold ones by breaking into their world. It's not a full cure, but it will curb the bloodlust if it works. We could use it at their portal locations as soon as they enter our world . . . it would cut down on our losses. Perhaps turn the next great hunt in our favour.'

'It sounds like you have a pretty concise plan. Why do you need me?'

'I . . .' I hesitate. 'Something's been nagging at me. About Aline's story, and about the origins of the cold ones. Aline, Gallant, Argus . . . they're all real. If the story is to be taken as truth, then those gods are really trapped. And we are forming a plan to seriously meddle with Aline's creations.'

She nods. 'You are worried about incurring her wrath. Of her noticing your ploy.'

'There wouldn't be anyone to stop her, if the gods who could defeat her are trapped,' I say quietly. 'This is bigger than us. Bigger than the cold ones. It ends with them, doesn't it? If we want an end to the great hunts, we need a god on our side.'

She watches me for a moment, considering. 'You realise what you speak of? What could happen to you?'

I swallow, thinking of Alden. This has to end. I have to cure him. If it means freeing a mightier power than her, if that is the only way to free *him* . . . so be it. Maybe her death will be the cure. Or surely a god would be able to cure him. I'll be damned if I stand by and allow this to be the death of him without trying everything I can think of. 'I do.'

She nods thoughtfully. 'It is one thing to fight against her creations, quite another to meddle in the schemes of the gods. Come with me.'

Chapter 38

God Trap

Kadie turns to a page in a different book to the one she allowed us to borrow. She hands it to me, pointing to the top of the page. 'The lesser gods do not feature so much in the recordings of our ancestors. But I recorded the stories passed down orally, nevertheless. This is one of Gwydion's tales.'

I look at her sharply. 'The lesser goddess of trickery?'

She nods. 'This may be the information you seek. It was not just Aline who conspired against Argus and Gallant, as you know. Although she is known to us as a lesser god, that may be a trick in itself. For she is just as powerful, if this tale is to be believed.'

I lean over and fall into Gwydion's story.

★

Gwydion, the youngest of seven siblings, grew up fighting for every scrap. She learned quickly that trickery was a shortcut to a full belly and that lying came as easily as breathing to her. The one thing about having so little is that she never forgot the ache in her heart and the dirt she emerged from. She didn't just dream of more in some polite, distant, pleasant way. A fire burned in her stomach, consuming her whole until she clawed her way out, leaving the life she was born into far behind.

Leaving her family to the narrow, winding road of their lives, she cut her way out with the finest weapon at her disposal; her liar's tongue shaped by the whetstone of her endless hunger. Gwydion tricked her way up and up, all the way to Aline's side. But she never forgot that ghost, her past self that haunted her at every step, ready to drag her all the way back under.

So when Aline is scorned, as women so often are, Gwydion is ready with a whisper in proud Aline's ear. One of revenge, one of trickery. One fitting for two gods who left Aline behind.

Aline, proud as Argus, allows the seed to grow in her heart. It takes root, unfurling shoots and leaves, until Gwydion's idea eclipses all her senses. She desires revenge. She longs for vengeance. But most of all, she wants to rise. For she is a goddess and she does not belong beside some hearth. She is not the goddess who simply waits.

So with her forged weapon of steel and war, she crossed into this other world and Gwydion's delight knew no bounds. For Argus had betrayed Aline not once, but twice, finding an otherworldly wife to bed in Aline's absence. Gwydion whispered of a new scheme, seeing her chance and seizing it. For in this world, she could be the shadow behind the throne, with Aline as a queen, here she could leave that ghost of her past self far behind. If only she could rid them of the two domineering gods.

She transformed into Aline's likeness and tricked Argus and Gallant into visiting another world, one she promised contained multitudes, all the bounty they surely deserved to claim. They followed the sweet cadence of her voice, lured by Gwydion's greatest weapon, her liar's tongue. Then when Gwydion fastened the god shackles on their wrists, the real Aline appeared, their power joined, enough to contain and trap two gods, and the trickery was complete.

Gwydion transformed back, leaving Argus and Gallant with one final, exquisite whisper. 'You underestimated me.'

And there they stay, trapped in another world, shackled and bound. For now, one god may enter, but it takes three together to leave, and they are only two and chained, whilst Gwydion revels in the thrill of the hunt. For she is the huntress and the great hunts are hers, whilst Aline delights in all the glory of a dread queen.

Now Gwydion, with her band of cold ones, Aline's blood in their veins on her wild, thrashing hunts, believes she is untouchable. And her life before, along with the trapped gods are locked away as nothing more than memory. For who would triumph against a dread queen and a huntress? Especially when the dread queen herself must be slain to rid the worlds of her cold ones. Or for another to control them.

★

I lean back, stunned as the story unspools in my mind. 'If all this is to be believed . . . if this account is true . . .' I say, thinking aloud. 'Then Gwydion and Aline still exist in Astrum, and Argus and Gallant truly *are* trapped in another world.'

Especially when the dread queen herself must be slain to rid the worlds of her cold ones . . .

Kadie nods. 'And true to form, Gwydion's tale was nearly lost. For who looks to the accounts of the lesser gods? She truly is under-estimated. Perhaps even by Aline.'

'Proud Aline,' I murmur and rub a hand over my eyes. 'The dread queen. But tricking a god, that's the first step. A mortal cannot slay a goddess. But a god . . .'

'What does Gwydion desire most?' Kadie asks.

I think for a moment, turning over her story. Then I realise, of course . . . she is me. The girl who clawed her way out, who longed for freedom, who wanted more than the cards she'd been dealt.

Or for another to control them . . .

'Power,' I breathe. 'Gwydion wants power. And Aline has given it to her. Gwydion has never turned on Aline, never slain her, because without Aline, there are no cold ones for her to have power over.

But now her weakness is that desire, the hunt itself . . .' I swallow. 'She desires more and more, doesn't she?' My gaze tracks to my own veins, to the blood of an alchemist, flowing in a steady stream. 'More power. More distance between herself and her past. And with Aline alive and well, she'll always have that. Because the cold ones are linked to Aline . . . but she will never have complete control. Complete power. Unless *she* overpowers Aline. The dread queen.'

'And Aline, what does she desire?'

'To be loved. To be worshiped,' I say with a small smile. 'By the people of Astrum, the cold ones . . . she is where their power flows from, so they adore her.'

Kadie nods. 'I believe you have your answer.'

'Yes, I believe I do,' I agree.

★

Killmarth slumbers deeply, waves grazing the rocks in a constant push and pull of tide as I cross the courtyard like a shadow, darting through the door to Fetlock. Hope is a wild thing. It beats in your chest, sometimes only a murmur, but tonight, it suffuses every chamber of my heart. I have to see him. Can't sleep without him, consumed with thoughts of his arms surrounding me. This time, I knock on his bedroom door and he answers, torso bare, rubbing the back of his neck. My breath catches as I behold him, hair tousled, lips and cheeks flushed, eyes languid. His smile grows slowly as he tugs me across the threshold, his mouth finding mine in the cold, quiet dark.

I step back, closing the door then locking it, smiling up at him as his forearms rest against the wood, either side of my head. 'I hope you weren't planning on actually sleeping in this room, DeWinter,' he says, voice husky and thick from sleep.

A shaft of moonlight falls over us and I stare up into his eyes, desire all twisted up in something deeper. Something richer. I stand on my tiptoes, kissing him gently, cradling the back of his head to pull it down to my own. His tongue flickers over my bottom lip and I gasp, the knot in my chest unravelling. I needed this. Needed him. With the weight of the gods and our future upon me, I know I must do more than test the aromatic. This is a fight without end if I do not act, the great hunts slowly gutting our world until we die out completely. Then Gwydion and her hunt will move on to the next, Aline forever sated by power and glory.

And Alden will be lost to me.

He is my strength. The person I've fought for, and who has fought for me. He gives me courage when it's waning, hope when it's a mere flicker. He's the first person who truly saw me, every piece of me, and wrapped his arms around me, embracing the dark and the light in my soul. This moment with him is a beat, a moment to take a breath before the end. The end that is inevitable, that could go either way.

I run my hands down over his back, feeling his muscles shift beneath his skin. Then I graze my fingertips over his broad shoulders, just as his own hands come down, finding the soft fabric of my leggings. He tugs them down in one swift movement, my underwear coming down with them to my thighs and I shiver. Then he smiles, kissing me again, deeper this time, pinning my head against the door with his mouth, his desire. His fingers find the core between my thighs, rubbing gently, coaxing a moan from my lips. He plunges a finger inside me, working me gently, until I'm slick and wanton, until I burn for him. 'I'm going to take you right here, up against the door. Any objections?'

'None,' I breathe, heart pounding harder. Right now, I want him to blot out the world, the future. I want to exist here, in this moment, only with him. 'Take me.'

His smile curls over his mouth as his gaze drops to his finger, still inside me. 'Kick off your boots, take off your clothes.'

He steps back, watching me as I toe off my boots, eyes locked with his. Then I shrug out of my jacket and unbutton my shirt. Finally, I strip off my underwear and leggings completely, standing naked before him. I glance down and swallow, seeing him bulge in the jogging bottoms he's wearing. But he shakes his head. 'You came into my room, DeWinter. I'll set the pace.'

Then he reaches around my body and lifts me, hands clasped around my thighs, sliding my body up against the door. I gasp again, straddling him, arms draped over his shoulders. 'Set the pace then, Locke,' I manage to whisper. What I don't say, what I can't, is I can't lose you. I *won't* lose you. This is not the end, this is our beginning and I will become a monster if it means he lives.

He grins at me, removing one hand to yank his jogging bottoms down, then repositions me against the door and his hips. Then in one smooth movement, he sinks into me. I groan as he does, the full length of him settling inside me. I part for him, allowing him deeper than ever before, his body angled to thrust up inside me. He looks into my eyes as he moves inside me, thrusting gently, the movement sending wave after wave of delicious, golden heat. The whole world stills around us, honed on this moment, on the movement of him inside me, as that glorious ache builds in my centre.

I love him. I love how he worships me, how he coaxes me open, unfurling me at my core, until I am entirely his. His body rocks against mine, stroking that sweet, perfect spot inside me until I'm clenched around him, until the waves grow higher and higher. The power of it, the slow build inside me is overwhelming, and all I feel is love. And that's when I realise . . . we're glowing. The threads of magic, glittering all around us, over our skin, in the air, our magic, combining. Unleashing as we build to climax, together.

Love. I'm almost swept away by the power of it, not by desperate hate or fear that usually unleashes the deepest pieces of my raw magic, when I can usually reach for another's – but *love*. The deepest, rawest of all, what has cleaved my heart to his. He thrusts even deeper, seeming to grow inside me and the glitter all around us explodes. I moan his name as my handle on the world around us fractures, as my entire body, my very self, comes undone.

And he's right there with me.

With a final thrust, he grips me harder, roaring into the quiet of the night. I cling to him, feeling every wave, soaring up and up as we crescendo together.

Then all those glimmering glints of our magic disappear, leaving only me and him. He lowers me carefully, dusting kisses over my mouth, my cheeks, my eyes, whispering, *I love you*. Then we move to his bed, Alden pulling the covers over us both, wrapping me in his arms. I snuggle into his chest, hearing the beat of his heart and wonder if we can stay here forever, cocooned, my own heart a sated patter behind my ribs.

As Alden slips into slumber, a rare thing for him now he is nearly fully turned, I go over the plan in my thoughts. The one that's formed since reading Gwydion's tale, since knowing what she is, the essence of her. I think again about blood, about my gold, honeyed, alchemist-rich blood and hear the chilling sound every time a cold one has breathed in the scent of me. The way their pupils dilate, the euphoria transforming their gazes. And I know how I will trick Aline, how I will release two trapped gods.

I will lure her to me.

I will be the bait.

Then I will offer her what she desires most.

Part 4

Better to reign in Hell than serve in Heaven.
~John Milton

Chapter 39

Get In, Get Out, Don't Get Caught

Get in, get out, don't get caught.

The one rule, the *only* rule. The one I lived by for so long. And now, it blasts on repeat in my ears. When Knox glances over at me, I swear he's hearing those words on an endless loop too. We're back in the Morlagh Woods, on one of the gods' thresholds, as it's written in Aline's tale. A place where we can build a bridge between worlds, which we now understand is created through the blood of a goddess. The blood running through a cold one's veins, one of Aline's own creations.

Knox, Alden and Tessa stand beside me. Belle has transformed, snarling softly at Andry every few minutes, the innate part of herself that is werewolf revolting against the wrongness of him.

'If I snarl back, will she bite my head off?' Andry asks, glaring at her as she stalks back and forth.

'She's got bigger teeth than you, I wouldn't bait her,' I say then shiver. Bait. I've told no one of my real plan once we arrive in Astrum. I know they will stop me, and I cannot be stopped. Not this time.

Not if I want to end this once and for all.

'And you'll give me a fresh dose of the nocturnal after this?' Andry says. 'Or you can just offer up a vein now, alchemist—'

I fasten my fingers around his throat, staring into his eyes. 'I'm on edge, prince. I really hope this side of you abates with your thirst or you and I are going to have a problem.'

'It's just my charming personality . . .' he manages to choke out with a grin and I consider tightening my grip.

'Sophia . . .' Tessa says. 'You know it's not worth it. You know he makes terrible jokes.'

'Terrible?' he squeaks. 'Rude. I'm very funny.'

'You'll get your dose when you prove yourself useful,' I say, pushing him away and ignoring his chuckle. He's getting to me. It's *all* getting to me.

Tessa pats my arm as Alden takes a breath. 'You're sure you don't want me there with you?'

I shake my head. 'Just Tessa, Belle and me. I can't risk . . .' I swallow, choosing my words carefully. If he even suspects my real plan . . . 'I can't risk you. And you have to protect Knox. If this goes wrong, you can open a portal with him and Andry, or close it if . . .'

He brushes the hair back from my temple and brushes a kiss over my skin. 'We will be here. The plan will work.'

Belle moves suddenly, rushing for the tree line. We all still, weapons in our hands, and the trees part, Ezra walking through. Then Amaria. Belle trots behind, head down. I pinch the bridge of my nose. Of course he would work it out. And this time, we really didn't want him to.

'What would a Crown Prince, two alchemists, a botanist and two masquiers have to do in the Morlagh tonight?' Ezra asks softly, flicking his fingers. Amaria stands beside him, mouth set in a grim line. I suppose Kadie must have told her, and she somehow got a message to Ezra. Traitor. I try to hate her, but her features soften, a look of fear in her gaze. I sigh, knowing what she's doing. Protecting. Protecting me when she couldn't protect her own daughters.

'Sophia? Knox? I thought the Queen made everything quite clear. You're all on thin ice.'

'We're sending a warning,' Tessa says before I have the chance to answer. 'And gathering information. We know the repercussions if we're caught.'

'I don't want to be here—'

'Shut up, Andry,' I growl. 'One more word and the deal's off.'

'Deal?' Ezra says, eyes widening. Then he crosses his arms. 'Let me guess . . . a portal to their world. A carefully orchestrated plan to eliminate the thirst of as many as you possibly can, to test the nocturnal you've developed into an aromatic. I take it you have got that far? Then another team on this side in case it goes to shit.'

'You missed out Belle,' I mumble.

His eyes dart to meet mine. 'A solitary werewolf won't stop a horde of cold ones pouring through a portal, even if they are no longer in a frenzy—'

'No,' I say, tipping my head to the side. 'But her pack will. And Belle, in her werewolf form, has been in touch with them.'

A howl shivers through the clearing, another one joining it and I smile gravely at Ezra. 'This is a reckoning. If they follow us back here, we'll pick them all off. We knew that no one would take our plan seriously. And we also knew that if we suggested it, it would be confirmation of what the Queen suspects. Especially as we need Andry here. So we had to do this without your blessing, yours or Caroline's.' I take a step closer, saying softly, 'You're not the only one who is allowed to protect those around you. If you sanctioned this, then you would have had to admit you knew where Andry was.'

For a moment no one moves, no one speaks. Then he sighs. 'The Crown would never approve a mission like this, you're correct. So off the record it is.' He eyes me calmly. 'I will join you, headstrong, infuriating girl, on one condition.'

'Name it,' says Alden.

'You tell me every detail.'

I catch Knox's eye and incline my head. And he takes a breath, then walks Ezra through our plan. No one interrupts and he nods, running a hand down his face then points at Tessa and Belle. 'Show me.'

They transform under his assessing gaze, an immaculate wielding weaving before our eyes. Tessa winks at him and every hair on the back of my neck rises. I even *sense* that she's a cold one. Her masquier wielding is horrifying in its perfection.

Then he turns to me. 'And you'll stay in the woods until the aromatic is fully unleashed in the great houses?'

I nod once.

'All right,' he says. 'Then I will stay with you. And he comes too.'

I whip my head to Alden. 'No.'

'Let me guess, you want to protect him?'

'I cannot . . . not again.'

Ezra narrows his gaze on me. 'Is that not the very thing you fought against with me? And in fact, with him in the Ordeals? But it's different when the shoe is on the other foot, Sophia?'

'I . . .' I expel a breath, lacing my fingers over the back of my head. 'This is different. I'm not protecting him to manipulate or control him.'

'It's not, Sophia,' Alden says quietly. 'It's not different at all. I wasn't trying to control you, ever. But I respect your decision all the same this time.'

'I don't,' Ezra says. 'He comes with us. He's a talented botanist and we may need him. We need every asset.'

'As a sacrifice?' I hiss.

Ezra raises a cold eyebrow. 'If it comes to it. Amaria, we'll need you too.'

She bobs her head, arms folded across her chest. My own chest tightens as she avoids my eyes.

'DeWinter, enough discussions,' Knox says, his cold hand closing over mine, drawing my focus. 'You can fight it out with Ezra afterwards. Right now, we need to move. Belle stays with Andry, he won't get far with the werewolf pack harrying him. But Ezra's right . . . we could do with a strong team. The strongest we can assemble.'

My rage simmers from flame to ice as I stare daggers at the man who kept me trapped in his protection. I can't trust myself to speak, blood pulsing in my ears like a battle cry. Assets. We're all assets.

Then Alden's hand wraps my other hand and he whispers in my ear, 'I love you. Trust me.'

I bite my lip and nod, hoping that when we're on the other side, when I tell them the truth . . . well, I hope he'll still trust *me*. Alden releases my fingers, stepping back as Knox grabs Andry's hand. 'Last time, my prince. For Crown and territory.'

Then I extend my fingers to that space in the centre of the clearing, the threshold to another world. Their world. And I feel Knox's raw power and Andry's cold fire douse my veins. Now I can parse them apart, I can sense the cold one's will alongside my own. The deadness, the thirst. And I channel it all, willing the portal to open. Willing that bridge to extend across to the one on the edge of Astrum. The space ripples, then the mirror woods appear. And without hesitation, those that are crossing step over that threshold, into the cold world beyond.

When we're all through, Knox and I collapse it. Before Ezra can begin barking orders like this is his show, I turn to them all, spreading my palms wide. 'I need to tell you something. All of you. Before we continue, there's a change of plan.' I swallow, meeting Alden's gaze. 'The aromatic is a tonic for this world, but it will not stop Aline. It will never tear out this curse of cold ones at the root.'

'Sophia . . .' Alden says, closing his eyes as though he somehow knew all along that I was up to something. That I had one last trick up my sleeve, an ace I needed to play.

'I am going to bait her into freeing Argus and Gallant. I mean to put a stop to all this forever.' Then I explain what I have learned from Gwydion's story, about the trapped gods and the role both goddesses play in this world. How in order to cure the cold ones, Aline must be powerless. And the only way to do that . . . is to free Argus and Gallant.

For a moment, no one makes a sound. Then in a torrent, they all speak at once.

'Gwydion's tale, of course . . .'

'Lost your mind . . .'

'Foolish, foolish . . .'

'. . . of all the things!'

'Shit . . .'

I hold up a hand. 'I know. I know it seems impossible, starting with leaving this woodland and all of us venturing closer to Astrum. Tessa said normal people live here, they won't just attack us—'

'They'll eat you alive,' Tessa says, her own eyes blazing through the cold one's face she wears. 'I can't support this, not if it's a— a *death* mission! I may be able to blend in, so can Alden . . . but you cannot. You have magic in your veins. You're a wielder! The humans here are not wielders. They're not anything.'

'Were you really not planning to return?' Alden asks quietly and it's the crack in his voice that nearly slays me.

'I was,' I promise, reaching for his hand. 'But I didn't want to subject you to this part of my plan. I mean . . . to be taken to her. For Tessa and Belle to pose as my captors and bring me before her.'

Ezra frowns, then his features clear. 'So you're close to her. So you can play on her pride and need for adoration. Clever, ruthless girl.'

'And I didn't want to subject anyone else to that.' I look at Alden. 'Especially you. Not after what you've been through. This could still go very wrong.'

Alden sighs, shaking his head. 'And you think I would have let you walk this path alone?'

'I was afraid you'd walk by my side the whole way,' I say to him, placing my hands on his chest. 'That was my deepest fear.'

He catches hold of my hands, staring deep into my eyes. 'I will walk at your side anywhere, across territories, across worlds. There is nowhere else I want to be. For you, I would cross the burning stars. With you, I would do anything.'

'That is what I am most afraid of,' I whisper. 'That you would step so willingly into the path of death for me.'

He smiles sadly. 'I can handle it. What I can't handle is you concocting a plan to make me human again and not involving me in it. Let us end this. Together.'

I nod shakily, my resolve cracking. To carry this burden alone. To not involve any of them, to keep them safe, to protect them. 'All right then. Together.'

'No,' Ezra says, crossing his arms. 'This plan is foolish, there are too many variables, there's too much at stake—'

'Ez, really—' Amaria starts.

But I turn to him, holding out my hands. 'What more must I *do*?'

'What?' he says, a frown pinching his features.

'What more must I do for you to trust me?' I ask, and it's as though I'm that little girl again, holding out my wrist. Feeling the bracelet encircle it, not realising that door to the vault was snapping shut. 'You put a bracelet on my wrist so I couldn't die. So I was tied to you, so I could never leave. You trained me in your image, to be ruthless and cunning and calculating. You pushed me and pushed me, just to see if I would spark. If I *was* the wielder my parents hoped I would become . . . and now I've proven myself. *Again and again*. I beat the Ordeals. My magic sparked. I created a portal into another fucking *world* . . . and *still* you have no faith in me.'

'It is not a lack of faith!' he snaps suddenly. 'Your parents died in this world, Sophia! Died! I have mourned them ever since, and Caroline would never allow me to even try to come after them—'

'You're afraid of more death,' I say quietly. 'But death is beyond our control, Ezra. We have to fight to *live*. Even if we fail. We have to try, or in the next few decades, we will all be hunted anyway.'

He seems to deflate, his mouth pinching into a thin line. 'I never gave you all the details, did I? Of your parents' demise. That final mission, when they entrusted you to me.' I freeze, barely breathing. Hanging on every single word. 'The Crown ordered an assault, trying to drive them back, to seal the portals. There was one in Darley Hall, here, the Pendle Woods . . . but those that entered those portals, that chased them through, never returned. Including your parents.'

His features crumple, his gaze suddenly far away.

'I regret, more than anything, obeying the Crown that night. It is not that I do not have faith in you. It is not that I do not trust you or believe in you. I am afraid of history repeating. Of being powerless once more. Of seeing you now, following in the footsteps of your parents, brave and full of fire . . . and those gods tearing you apart. Of you sacrificing yourself on the altar of their battles. Your mother entrusted you to me. And now I must watch as you go to a place where I can no longer fulfil her wishes. Where I can no longer keep you safe.'

I close my eyes, the tears clawing up my throat. And finally, I understand him. Fully and completely. Something cracks inside me, fracturing and falling away. And maybe that bracelet was clamped around my wrist. But it was also around my heart. And now . . . now I can breathe.

I am truly, finally free.

'Thank you,' I say, opening my eyes. Then I walk to him, placing my hands on his arms. 'Thank you, uncle.'

He pulls in a breath, placing his hands on my own arms. 'Go, now. They would have both been so proud of the woman you've become.'

I turn from him, wiping at my eyes, and feel it all. The wielders that have come before me, the wielders surrounding me. The power to tear down the very gods.

'First, we go to Astrum,' I say, looking at them all. 'The tables have turned. It's time to capture our own cold one.'

Chapter 40

She's a Ten, but She's a Cold One

We stalk through the night-quiet woods. Ezra and Knox, Alden, Tessa, Amaria and I, all of us in a blur of shadow and will. Belle and Tessa are in front, scouting in plain sight, talking loudly of the hunt, of thirst, of the smell of wielders in the mist as they wield to appear as cold ones. We need to know where Aline will be tonight and we need to know before we enter the city of Astrum. It doesn't take long to rake three real ones from the trees surrounding us.

Two women and a man, all with darkened, glazed eyes, staring at us like a feast to devour.

'Strange night for a wander between worlds,' one of them says, sniffing the air.

'We heard there's a party tonight,' Knox says, twirling a stake in his fingers.

'Several,' I say with a smile.

The two women look at each other, uncertainty lighting their features before Ezra comes up behind them, plunging twin stakes in their backs. The man blinks down at the ash, then up at us and turns to bolt. Straight into Tessa and Belle. He struggles and pleads as Ezra wields, pinning him to the ground with his stakes.

'We have a question for you,' Alden says, crouching beside him.

'If I answer, will you spare me?'

'Probably not,' I say.

He pants quickly, then strains against the stakes before unleashing a loud, desperate cry. Knox quickly stuffs a handkerchief in his mouth, crouching down as well. 'Where is Aline tonight? If I take that out, answer me, or I'll stuff it back in.'

Of course, he screams again.

It takes three attempts before he answers us. And several more threats before he tells us the truth. It's only when the fear drenches him that Ezra and I nod to each other, believing him. She's in a house of glass, on the edge of Astrum.

His pleading is cut short by the stake Ezra drives through his chest. Then we turn as one to the faint lights of Astrum and for the first time ever, I can sense the tide turning on the gods. For the first time, we are no longer the hunted, no longer the playthings of Aline, or the target of the relentless hunts led by Gwydion.

We are the hunters.

Five main houses, five lairs we will fill with the aromatic before seeking out this glass house to find Aline. Alden believes this will incapacitate most of them in Astrum, the nocturnal sating their desire for several days at least. As long as we've got the potency right. Tessa mutters directions to each of the great houses as we make our way to the outskirts of the city, the lights dragging us into a web of streets and alleyways.

It is Dinas Tar and yet . . . not. A distorted version, as though a mirror has cracked, darkness and lurid light bleeding around the web of fractures. Sirens blare, music blasts from bars alive with bodies, cackling laughter hounds us around every corner. And groups, stumbling, shouting, drinking from bottles, flashing pearly, sharp teeth, roaming eyes . . . I swallow, keeping my gaze low. They aren't all cold ones, and yet they're not all human either. Tessa was right. This world is a symphony of otherworldliness, of creatures and monsters I cannot fathom. In this place, Aline has carved her throne. A world apart from her safe, cosseted hearthside.

I spy eyes burning red with flame, pointed ears and tucked-in wings, both feathered and membranous. There is one group of young women that seem to glow luminous, trailing a path of water in their wake.

'Sirens,' Tessa murmurs. 'If they start singing, don't follow them.'

'There are . . . werewolves here,' Belle says, sniffing. 'But they don't smell the same as the ones in our world.'

Humans hurry past too, eyes darting everywhere, shoulders hunched, as though they wish to disappear and become shadow itself.

'They seem to have some protection, but they also have a curfew,' Tessa says, tightening her grip on my arm and baring her teeth at a cold one that slinks past, eyeing us. 'Belle, make it clear they're ours. Let's hope we're not challenged.'

'You're taking us to Aline, remember?' Ezra mutters. 'A tribute.'

'And we're searching for her, yes,' Tessa says, then snarls at another cold one, who is all hunger and big eyes and sallow skin. 'It's the lesser members of the houses I fear most. They've got nothing to lose.'

We reach the first house, laughter and music spilling out of an open doorway, cold ones flanking it, tilting their heads to everyone walking in and out. It's a huge building, windows with narrow, glinting panes, tall, towering spires, gaunt dark stone. The kind of building that in our world, would be a place of the gods, a church, a cathedral, a sanctum in the heart of Dinas Tar. But here . . . here it is a wild, reckless place. And yet not a godless place. Aline just extracts a different kind of adoration here. Instinctively, I slow my pace, fixing a mask of fear over my features. This feels all too similar to the assignments I would go on for the Collector . . . for Ezra. Walking up to a society gathering, pretending to be something else. I dart a glance at him, and I wonder if he and Knox are thinking it too. How the work hasn't changed, not really.

Tessa skips up those steps first, bold as brass, winking at the cold ones on the door. The one on the left, hair black as pitch, grins at her, winking back. Then he breathes in, eyes snapping to us. 'Visitors?'

'They're for Aline,' Tessa says. 'She here tonight?'

The cold one scrunches his nose. 'She's gracing another house tonight. The Ravens. But Gwydion may favour us with her presence . . .'

We all step through after Tessa, looking suitably terrified as Belle barks at us. I hold my breath, sure it's about to go to shit, that there'll be blades and teeth and a swarm of them descending on us for a taste . . . but we slip past and just like that . . . we're in.

'Made friends when you were here?' I murmur to Tessa.

She shrugs. 'A few. The ones I didn't kill anyway. Stay close, all of you. Word will spread that you're a gift for Aline so they shouldn't nibble . . . but let's not tempt them.'

The house beyond is in the throes of a decadent party. High-ceilinged rooms filled with cold ones, draped over armchairs, lounging in groups, clinking glasses and listening to the music wafting from somewhere near the back of the house. We wander through the rooms, curious eyes following us as we pour ourselves drinks and cross into the back room. It's far more crowded than the other smaller reception rooms at the front, lined with glass-panelled doors at the back, giving way to a terrace. They're all thrown open to the night, a band playing in one corner, hundreds of feet spinning as the cold ones dance. It's like a ballroom, but with the ceiling extending up into those lofty spires, the sound echoes and collects, the music clashing and distorted. I wince, feeling off kilter, unbalanced by the music.

Tessa sashays off to a staircase, leading us up to a higher level, a mezzanine looking over this dancing hall as Belle jabs me in the back.

'They're all half cut,' Knox says dryly. 'I suppose this name day is a celebration of their victories.'

'Victories . . .' Ezra says stonily. 'Perhaps this house sent the most cold ones across to our world.'

'Comforting,' Tessa remarks then nods to another staircase. 'I'm going up there, did you notice the grates? There must be an air system.'

'Good thinking,' I say. 'Alden, if you go with her, the rest of us can be paraded by Belle and meet you by the entrance.'

'Fifteen minutes, tops,' Alden says, checking no one is watching us before leaning in to kiss me. I relax into it, the crush of his lips, his hands spread over my lower back, the feeling of falling into him momentarily distracting me from where we are, *what* we are . . . until he pulls back, eyeing me quietly. 'Don't get into trouble.'

I nod, my gaze trailing after him and Tessa as they ascend to the next level to find a quiet place to release the aromatic. And I realise . . . we cannot be here when it's released. We need to all be out so we are not implicated. I clutch Ezra's arm in apparent terror as Belle jostles us forward. 'Shall we?'

The following three houses are similar in shape and stature, as if each great house is an ancient dynasty, competing with all the others. Word does indeed spread that we are a gift for Aline and I know she will be expecting us. Dread and anticipation fill me, we are balanced on the edge of a blade. The fifth and final house is a different kind of beast. On the outskirts of Astrum, where the streets trail away, leading to fields and trees, there is a house that sits atop a small hill, entirely made of glass.

'Where that cold one said we'd find Aline,' I say.

'The Ravens' house,' Tessa says. 'Careful, here. They're the dominant ones amongst the great houses right now. Gwydion's favourites.'

Lights glitter within, cold ones drinking on the lawned hill surrounding the house, the door open to the dark. No one stands on it, checking who is going in and out. And yet there are many gathered within, that same strange, otherworldly music weaving through the cold air towards them. An odd prickle of foreboding sweeps over me as we step closer, and I want to pull everyone away. Tell them we should abandon this great house, that we should hurry back through the portal, to our own world. But we are so close now. So, so close.

'You sense it too,' Knox says softly. 'Don't you? That feeling of . . .'

'A swirling void of otherness, a divine glory, ichor and ambrosia . . .' Ezra murmurs thoughtfully, quoting a poem I remember him reading in his private collection, long ago. I shiver, the memory of then colliding with the unease of now, sending my senses skittering. 'No splitting up. Let's not lose heart in the final act of this desperately reckless ploy.'

'Agreed,' I say, running my fingertips over my blade, secured at my thigh. Wishing I could hold it, hoping I am faster than the sharp sting of teeth. Hoping Aline will believe me.

We cross the threshold of this great, glass house, and step into another world entirely. Glass panes set in frames divide the rooms, and all we can see are pools of shadows beyond as cold ones shift and move. That foreboding intensifies as we walk deeper into this glassy maze, as the music lures like a temptress and the press of eyes is everywhere.

'No grates,' Tessa murmurs. 'Here, it'll have to just be left in a corner. Ezra can wield before we leave, ensure the bag securing the aromatic is torn.'

'There are some outside still,' I say, biting my lip. 'We're not going to get them all, are we?'

Tessa meets my eyes and shakes her head, regret and sorrow pooling at the corners. 'But this is not a failure. And if you—'

But a gasp cuts off her words. We all turn as we enter a larger room right in the centre, surrounded by those colourful, twisting panes of glass. And at the far end, on a glass throne atop a dais, a woman sits, one arm dangling over the arm of her throne. I pull in a breath, every instinct telling me to bolt, to flee, to *run*—

'Aline,' Ezra says. 'I believe we've found our god.'

'And there,' I say, watching a slight woman with the allure of a goddess slink through groups at the sidelines, cruel, narrowed eyes like a hawk, fixed on us. 'That has to be Gwydion.'

Chapter 41

House of Glass

To call Aline beautiful would be blasphemous. She is beyond human depictions of beauty. She is glory incarnate; she is luminous, divine. And as her gaze wanders over the dancing cold ones, the thrash and leap of frenzied bodies, her eyes settle on me. As though a searchlight beams upon me, I shrink away, taking a shuffling step back, her gaze so intense, it's as though she's stripping me down to my marrow. Then she smiles, the slightest quirk of her lips, before her gaze passes on, over our heads. I shudder, gooseflesh raised along every inch of my skin. Ezra cannot be wrong. She is beyond any mortal or creature, she is truly otherworldly.

Suddenly, my plan seems reckless indeed.

How can I trick one such as her? An immortal, a god?

And suddenly it's more than just foreboding eclipsing my plan as I watch the trickster goddess, Gwydion, melt away into the crowd. To trick one god . . . but two?

'We should leave,' I say behind a hand to the others. 'Drop the nocturnal, Ezra can wield to burst the bag and we'll hotfoot it out of here.'

'Agreed,' says Alden. 'Did you see the way she stared?'

My stomach churns. 'This doesn't feel right. It's so staged, so . . . unlike the other houses. But it's not just Aline I'm worried about . . .'

I don't want to abandon the plan. It's the only way Alden

becomes human again, it's the only slight chance we have . . . but what if I get him killed in the process? What if we all end up dead? Now I'm faced with the actuality of a god, reigning over this great house of monsters, I don't think I can do this. I can't see how I can trick Aline so I can open the portal and free Gallant and Argus.

We turn to leave as Tessa kicks a leather bag of the nocturnal into a corner, weaving between the cold ones seemingly in rapture. And that's when it clicks . . . this is different to the other houses, because of Aline's presence. They are frenzied because of her influence. My plan suddenly seems so ludicrous, something that could never possibly have worked. How could I trick a goddess of trickery? Someone who has tricked the gods themselves, lining them all up like her pawns. Gwydion will see through me in an instant and warn Aline.

Just as I am about to step over the threshold, a woman steps from the open doorway. She grasps the glass door, stained in colours of blush to magenta, and sweeps it closed in her wake. Her hair is a russet brown, her creamy skin splattered with colour from the stained glass. And her eyes . . . they are gold. The eyes of a cat, watchful and cunning.

And my breath catches.

Gwydion.

She smiles at me, her canines glinting. 'Leaving so soon? My lady requests that everyone stays. Perhaps you need a drink? You must be so *very* thirsty.' Before I can form a retort she clicks her fingers and two cold ones bearing trays rush over. Only . . . they do not seem to be cold ones. Eyes vacant, necks bruised and riddled with puncture marks, wrists the same as they hold their trays aloft. And in those glasses, thimblefuls of viscous red liquid. I can smell it from several feet away, the desire shaking me to my core.

Wielder blood.

A glass is passed into each of our hands and when I glance at Tessa and Belle, I note the disgust before they quickly conceal it. They don't have that instinct nagging within them like the real cold ones they appear to be. To them it is truly abhorrent.

'A toast, friends to our god, our divine,' Gwydion says, gold eyes shifting over each of us in turn. 'And when you've had your fill, join her. She longs to witness your devotion, your love.'

The woman flutters her fingers, sending the wielders with their trays to the next group. Power ripples from her, darkly power, like the night itself, chasing back the sun. 'But wait . . .' She sniffs delicately then stills with preternatural grace. Then a smile spreads slowly like melted butter across her cruel, pinched mouth. 'You are the gift . . . indeed, five of you are, aren't you? A gift of potent wielder blood for our benevolent Aline. Perhaps she will give you to her best hunters . . . perhaps I may hand out the prize . . .'

She blinks slowly, eyes never leaving mine, and I feel an age passing. I fight back my instinct to bolt, knowing what she is. That if I flee, she will chase. And I will die.

'Come, come,' she says, crooking a finger. And even though every instinct within me screams, I am compelled to follow. We all are. The throng of dancers parts, revealing Aline atop her dais. Gwydion leads us to a set of steps at the side and we ascend to where Aline is waiting. Now we are closer, I can see a sheen over her skin, a manic quality to her gaze. She is desperate, I realise. For adoration, for love, for worship . . . and Gwydion is playing on that. The power behind the throne, guiding her hand.

'My goddess, a gift for you,' Gwydion says, her hand on the small of my back, pushing me forward. 'Wielders, strong ones. Full of potent, raw magic.'

Aline sniffs, her eyes darkening, just like a cold one's. It seems they are made partially in her image. The darkest parts of her, the thirst and hunger, the desire for more, the monster lurking in this god's heart. 'A gift you say . . .'

I kneel before her, bowing my head. Now my hand has been forced, now we are here, this has to work. 'I have a request, a wish. But now I am before you, I find myself lost for words. Unworthy.'

'Oh,' she says and chuckles. 'You do smell good. A potent mix to be sure. Is this the one your hunters have spoken of, do you think, Gwydion?'

'It is possible, my lady.' Gwydion nods. 'Not only alchemy.'

'Illusion, I believe,' Aline says and I look up to catch that spark in her gaze. 'How delicious. And you crossed over here, all by yourselves?'

'We worship you in Kellend. We are your most devout,' I say fervently, eyes wide. 'To be in your presence now . . .'

She preens, smiling with benevolence. 'You mortals, how wonderful you are. Gwydion, aren't they a delight? I can just feel their love. It's washing over me like a wave.'

'A delight indeed,' Gwydion agrees. 'Will you take this gift and give it to your most loyal followers? The Ravens have been the most successful in each great hunt, strengthening their bloodline.'

'Give them away?' Aline frowns. 'No, no. They are a gift for me, Gwydion.' She beckons me forward. 'Come, sit by my side. Tell me what you would request of a god.'

'I almost cannot ask, I am so unworthy,' I say, tripping over my words.

'Ask,' she breathes.

'I wish . . . I wish for you to turn me into one of your chosen. A cold one. For you to do it, the goddess Aline.'

'Ahhh . . .' Gwydion says quietly. 'Now we get to it. You want power, is that it?'

'I understand hunger,' I say, turning to her, the words hovering in the air between us. 'I know the bone-deep desire for power, for freedom. For choices. And to not be tied to another.'

Gwydion blinks in surprise but quickly shifts the shock from her features. 'Do you now?' She steps away, circling so she stands beside Aline. 'And you believe you are worthy because you hunger for more?'

'She's allowed to desire, Gwydion,' Aline chastises. 'As you once did, if you recall.'

Gwydion looks at her. 'If you turn her, you offer her a drop of your own blood—'

'I know, I know,' Aline says, waving her away. 'I may offer this when I will it, not when *you* will it. Remember that. I can make and unmake a creation. Whenever *I* choose.'

I blink.

Did she just . . . ?

'You can unmake a cold one as well . . .' I breathe out. 'You are truly all powerful.'

The cure. Her blood, *Aline's blood* is the cure.

And if I have but a drop of it in my veins, will the portal recognise me as a god?

For now, one god may enter, but it takes three to leave . . .

There are two gods trapped. Two gods I must free. My mind explodes with possibilities, with strategies, with a way through . . . I'll need to be the third god. Which means I truly need Aline. I need her blood in my veins.

I need her to believe me.

Gwydion's shrewd eyes narrow. 'This is unwise. Give them as a boon to your best hunters, give them to the Ravens as a feast—'

'Gwydion,' she snaps, her gaze swivelling to the lesser goddess, who flinches. 'I grow tired of being told what to do. You are sounding a little too much like *him*.'

Argus, she must mean Argus. I can work with this, play on her need to be the most beloved, the one in control, in power . . .

'Only you can bestow this great gift, my lady,' I say, as though in rapture, bringing my palms together. 'May we, with our own power, fortify you through our blood.'

Aline smiles, her features relaxing. 'Gwydion, check the rest of my followers are enjoying my name day. I want my name to be on the tip of every tongue this night. I will gift this wielder's blood to who *I* choose. Who *I* deem is worthy. Remember that.'

Gwydion bows her head, concealing her frown, and stalks off the dais. Leaving us and only us with Aline.

She offers me two vials. An empty one, and one glinting with her blood. Honey toned, like sunlight. I take them from her with a shuddering breath that isn't fake, the relief of having a cure for Alden in my hands, so close, so close . . .

'Drink my blood, dear mortal, and offer me your blood in return, so I may bestow it.'

I turn away from her, towards Alden and conceal my movements as I pour a drop of her god blood into the nocturnal elixir he has stoppered in his pocket. He cuts my skin and I hiss, my own blood dripping into the empty vial. Alden's jaw tightens, his eyes darkening and I'm aware of the entire room growing still. I'm a feast. A feast of magic-laced blood in a room full of desirous vampires.

'I love you,' I murmur to him then look at the others. Tessa, Ezra, Knox, Amaria and Belle. This has to work. I cannot have their blood on my hands, the guilt of their deaths marring my soul. I cannot lose them.

Then I drink Aline's blood, feeling it fizz in my veins. The blood of a god, directly from the source. I offer her my own and she sighs with joy, reaching for it. And in that slight contact, that moment when her fingers brush mine, I feel them. I sense the hidden portal, the one she is keyed to. The one she would never dare open, for she would never be able to get back out alone.

I'm aware suddenly of a blur stalking through the room, Gwydion, all gold eyes and pinched, knowing features, moving towards us, opening her mouth to warn Aline . . .

I look back at Aline, at her vulpine features, her too wide smile, the manic gleam to her eyes.

And as though a veil has been thrust back, I see her.

Really see her.

The hunger in her, the greed, the loneliness, the pride. She is power, she is grace . . . but she has been scorned. She is selfish and cruel, she is not whole. She wants to be adored, but it does not appease the real hunger within her. To be loved. To be cherished. So I plaster a beatific smile over my features and beckon my friends forward as I step back. Gwydion reaches the dais steps, eyes fixed on me, and I know it is now. It has to be now.

I pour everything I have into it. The portal. The bridge from this world to the one where they are trapped, the one I sensed as our hands brushed, the one keyed to her god blood, now in my own veins. Then I call on the raw magic, the power of every wielder gathered on the dais. Amaria. Tessa. Ezra. Knox. Alden. Belle. And with the power of every type of wielder, with the blood of a god, I picture Argus and Gallant. I picture two trapped gods, bound and shackled. I focus on a portal that will lead me to them.

There's a roaring in my ears, an unearthly, wild shriek.

Then all I see is gold.

Chapter 42

Made/Unmade

Endless, pure gold. The gold of magic, of light, a symphony of every type of wielding. Botanist, illusionist, masquier, alchemist . . . all combined in one almighty weave with the honeyed blood of a god. I push everything into it, binding it with my will, ripping a portal open.

But I can sense it, as this divine god turns her gaze on us, realising what I am taking from her. What I am using her for. She is the key to unlock a world. The place on a map I would never be able to find.

A god trap.

Her lips part in shock as a portal opens beside us, a bridge reaching for another portal, in another world—

Before she can close it, before she can slam the vastness of her power down on me, I leap through that portal, closing its maw at my back. And I can only hope that Ezra and Knox, combined with the others, can hold her power in check, can stay alive whilst I am gone. Then I fall, endlessly, forever, down a bridge to another world.

A world no one should have ever found.

A world of two gods, trapped for eternity.

A scream rakes up my throat as I descend through the portal on the other side. Colliding with the ground in a cloud of smoke and ash, I blink, dazed as the world settles around me. Grey. Everything is grey. No light, no dark, no stars. Only shades of shale and slate. The sky above, the earth below, an endless sullen sea.

But that isn't what unnerves me. It's the absolute lack. Of sound, of scent . . . of any form of life. Mist eddies around me, puffing up from the ground and I place my hands beside me. It's soft like dust, like the corpses of cold ones . . . for any being to have been trapped here . . . I shudder. This is not life, this is death. When they were trapped in here, this was their ending.

I take a breath, forcing myself to focus. Carefully, I rise, finding my feet in this ever-shifting soft grey and do not immediately tumble back down as it flows away from my boots, a constant current that seems to want to drag me under. As I cast around, wondering which way I should turn, feeling the edges of this world begin to pull at me, as though it wishes to absorb my very essence, an outline appears on the horizon. A dark shape in the swathes of mist, a huge structure, almost like . . .

'Killmarth,' I breathe. Or a world that contains a version of Killmarth. Everywhere else is indefinable, dead and distant and cold. So I strike out towards it, the ground shifting like waves of sapping sand beneath my feet as I struggle towards that silhouette, beyond the dreary folds of fog. For a while, I walk. Without any way of measuring time or distance, it seems that this silhouette is only ever just beyond my reach. Neither growing, nor becoming more defined, I begin to fear that I am chasing a shadow, a ghost of what might have been, but is no longer.

My mind unspools. I try counting under my breath as I traverse the bleak, shifting landscape, but soon lose track, my thoughts muddied and unsure. I dwell on the past. On the lost. I feel the slow trickle of my energy as my limbs and throat ache, then burn. It could have been hours, or days. But there is no sun, no moon, no way to quantify my progress. I wonder if this is some kind of test, or a barrier I must overcome. This world attempting to push me back, when all I need is to press forward.

Then as I roam closer, the mist slowly, like a truculent child, begins to relent, releasing its insubstantial grip. I stumble, gasping in an almost trance-like state, and find something hard beneath my boots. A path. A stone path through the sea, then a tidal island with a huge structure clawing up from it. I try to swallow, my throat and lips cracked and dry, as though this world is a desert. I look back, and all I see is lifeless grey. The ground and sky blurring into one and I fear it more than anything else. I was lost in there. I could have been lost forever. Before me the sea is ash and shifts only with the occasional gust of wind, the only sign of life and movement I have found in this world. The stone path is worn down entirely in places, as though this ashen sea has chipped away at it over thousands of lifetimes. And the island at the end of the path . . .

An ink blot. A dark star, captured at the point of implosion. Less a building made by man, more a carved rock, bloated like a washed-up carcass. It lists to one side, smaller rocks surrounding it, and I wonder if it's been worn away by whatever passes for time in this world. Perhaps the ash and the wind create spectacular storms, ones I have yet to witness and have buffeted and chiselled it, dragging it down on one side.

I set off gingerly, knowing somehow, that this island is a place to trap the gods. This world is dead; there is no life to draw on. No devotion or rapture to coax from these stones. Anathema to a being that craves those things. As I reach the end of the winding path of stone, I find that the rock has a simple opening in its side, a gaping mouth darker than the rock itself. I hover on the lip of it, imagining the shadows within sprouting wings and limbs and clicking claws . . . then I hear it. A song, the kind sung in rounds in a pub, one I'm sure I've heard before, or at least the tune of. The voice is deep and sorrowful, at odds with the pithy tune, yet each note echoes in my chest. I feel a pull, a drag, like the hungry tide, as though I'm in a net, drawn out of this ashen sea. Onto a boat, the catch of an ancient, desperate god.

Before I realise what I'm doing, my feet carry me inside.

My eyes do not adjust. It's more that the rock adjusts around me. Pale light emanates from the walls and ceiling, throwing stark shadows across the ground. I follow the song, the deep baritone like a call to arms, to glory, and know it for what it is, the voice of a god. A god of justice and might.

Gallant.

The rock suddenly falls away, leaving me in the centre, walls of the dark stone looming up and up. And in the centre, sat on the cold ground, the swirl of fog above them, like a ceiling of smoke, are two trapped gods. The ones I seek.

My heart flutters at my victory, triumph spreading through my veins. I've found them. Gallant and Argus. But as Gallant ends his song, he turns his gaze on me and I stagger beneath it. They are . . . real. All the stories, the Attestations, the teachings of the church . . . and they are just feet away. So real I could touch them, I could simply lean forward and brush my fingertips over theirs. Immortal beings that no mortal should simply be able to gaze upon like this. And yet here I am. In the presence of two more gods. After meeting Aline and Gwydion, it's almost too much. These beings shouldn't be real, not tangible, breathing beings . . . and yet.

Awe overtakes me and I fall to my knees. This moment is unlike meeting Aline, although the power and beauty are the same. With Aline, it was a moment of pure fear, of witnessing a being who had caused great harm, whom I had to trick. But these are gods who have been wronged, cut down and trapped. Reduced to appear as mortal men. Surely they are different to Aline. Surely they will want to do good. I do not agree with how Argus treated Aline. But in all the stories, he never created monsters in his image. Her reaction to his misdeeds far outweighs the original sins.

'Approach then, mortal,' Gallant rumbles and I feel the command in my chest, a tug that forces me back on my feet. 'You are tired. Your body aflame with thirst and pain from your journey across the ash way.'

'Aline, she . . .'

'Sent you here?' the other god, Argus, says, a sorry twinge of hope in his voice. He raises his eyes to mine and all I can feel is pity as I shake my head.

'She did not,' I say. 'I tricked my way here, tricked her into giving me her blood so I could open a portal keyed to a god's blood. And I mean to free you both. So you can put right their wrongs and end the hunts in my world.'

Gallant's gaze turns thoughtful. 'I believe this mortal woman is from that world we visited, once.'

'The one bent on consuming itself with war over the gifts we bestowed,' Argus agrees. 'The one with magic we imbued in some of them. You are a wielder?'

'I am,' I say. 'An alchemist.'

Argus blinks, then, as though I've delivered the best news he's heard in a thousand years, he smiles. And I can barely behold it, the luminous good, the shining beauty of such an immortal face. Then he lifts a hand and I see why they are both still sat here. Chains. Chains to bind the gods themselves, around their wrists and ankles, securing them to the ground. Heavy and thick as my neck, I would not even be able to lift them, let alone free them with my strength alone. 'We wove that gift so that you may alter metals and rocks and other things that do not grow and breathe. What is your name?'

'Sophia,' I say, and swallow, approaching them slowly. They are tired, lines etched deep beneath their eyes, a gaunt hue to their bronze skin. 'How long have you been here?'

'Too long,' Gallant says. 'More than your mortal lifetime. Gwydion, the vixen—'

'Tricked you,' I say. 'I've heard the story now. I expect she shared it herself.'

'A fickle creature, that one,' Argus says. 'She once was soft on you, do you recall?'

Gallant chuckles. 'Me and half a dozen others. Who knows where her interests truly lay.'

'Did she forge these?' I ask, reaching out to touch the chain securing Gallant's wrist, and instantly recoil. 'It— it drained me.'

'Hmm,' Argus says. 'Why do you think we've never broken free ourselves? And no, she did not. They were forged by Aline, in my forge. They drain us so even if there were three of us here, three gods, our power could not be used. Not whilst we are chained. We only have a small amount of our power left.'

'Well,' I sit beside them, studying the chains, 'she certainly didn't want you breaking them.'

'She made them thirsty,' Argus says.

Thirsty . . .

I angle my head, getting a closer look at the chains. They glow faintly, perhaps with the magic I've just unwittingly fed them, perhaps with a god's power . . . but what if I channelled these gods? If they are not depleted entirely, I could transform these chains into nothing more than air, I could mould their raw power and make it my own . . . then I remember. As though it happened many years ago, my mind catches on a snag, like a fly in a web. Something I carry, something that was given to me . . .

'Are you willing to trust a mortal woman?' I ask them both, drawing it out. A vial containing the last drops of Aline's rich god blood. The key to the portal to this world, and I suspect now, their chains as well. 'I believe that the three of us can leave this place together, but the two of you cannot. I've consumed a drop of her blood already and it meant I could form the portal to reach this world. I would bet anything she's also forged these chains with her blood. To make and unmake . . .'

They exchange a look then both nod. 'We have nothing to lose,' Gallant says. 'That vial you hold smells like her, faintly. Like wheat and storms and the sweet cloy of poisonous envy.'

'Along with my wielding, it could work. I suppose we'll find out.' I pour the last drops on a link in the chain, watching the metal absorb it greedily. 'All right,' I say, holding out my palms as my heart thrums like thunder. To make and unmake . . . I need this to work. I cannot stay in this place . . . an immortal may cling to a life here, but I will be dead all too soon. 'Place your hands in mine and if you feel more of yourselves being leached away, don't resist. Don't fight it. Lend me the last of your strength. Your power.'

Then I close my eyes, reaching for their power as a moth to a flame. And when it flows into me, when I feel the full force of even the scraps of what they have left, I cannot breathe.

Light and magic and pure raw life flow into me, melding with my magic, with my will. I open my mouth, trying to haul in a breath, my lungs constricting, resisting . . . so much power. It's like metal, not blood, now twists in my veins, like every piece of me is filled with something I cannot contain. My very skin feels ripe and raw, as though I will burst open, as though I have a star at my centre, and even now, it strains against my earthly form.

I open my eyes, release the gods' hands and reach out to grip the chains in my fist—

My lips part in a bellowing roar. All at once, all that power, all my own, I shove into these chains. I give everything. Everything

I am. Everything I will be. I give all that these gods gave me, and with a feral shriek, they crack. They are unmade. I gasp, my fingers slackening as I tip sideways, onto the cold, hard ground.

The last thing I see are Gallant and Argus filling with luminescent brilliance, before the fog descends and my world shrinks to nothing.

Chapter 43
A Kernel

I fed everything into the chains. Every last drop of my power, my magic, my life force. All that remains is my soul. How can a mortal body, a fragile skeleton enclosing soft, shreddable organs, coated in viscous blood and paper-fine skin, ever hold the wrath and will of gods? I sensed my mind crack, like the shell of a bird's egg, the fizz of my thoughts and memories disintegrating before sparking no more. Perhaps I left that shell of a body. Perhaps briefly, my soul evanesced. There was no hunger, no thirst, no tiredness anchoring me to the earth. Only a symphony of senses, of colour and light and warmth. It was dark. A darkness of satin and the soft nap of velvet, of swirling night, like a cloak cocooning me. I was nowhere. Everywhere. I was no longer what I was before. And that was Aline's last trick of spite. She ensured those chains would take everything from the person who sought to break them. Draining their power entirely.

I fought for that power.

I broke myself for it, shattering the Collector's bracelet, pushing and shoving until my power sparked. I dug so deep, I found the heart of it, buried for so long beyond my desperate reach. It's my source of freedom. My hope for a life of my choosing. And now . . . I gasp. Now it is ripped from me.

Everything I fought for, gone.

And yet even in the deepest darkness, even when everything has gone, there is always light. When I blink, or what I believe is movement in my eyes, that sense of seeing, of experiencing, there are stars. Glittering endlessly, splayed out across my vision. Suddenly I am aware of my body. Myself. I lift fingers to my lips and feel a mouth, nose, skin. I draw in a breath, focusing on the slip of air over my tongue. It tickles and I cough, then smile. I blink again and awareness fills my being, the world aligning around me in shapes I can understand. This world, this god trap is no longer shale and flint.

'She's awake,' rumbles Gallant.

'I'm awake,' I whisper, smiling into the starry sky. And in a rush, that absence is filled. I feel . . . *wonderful.* That dipped-in-toquay feeling but better, deeper, my limbs a frisson of crackling light. My heart beats slow and steady, my mind expanding, as though every whisper of knowledge has been placed there, book by book, just at the tips of my fingers. I am the vastness and the knowing. And I realise . . . this is a mere taste of the world of these gods. I can sense it, the power I tapped into still glittering in the hollow of my chest, a fleck left behind, a kernel. Now, all mine. My secret to carry. It warms me, infuses my magic with lightning. Illusionist, alchemist . . . now with the tiniest glitter of a god's power, setting it all aflame. Not just a god's blood, no. A piece of them, fused with me.

'You nearly died, mortal,' Argus says. 'We brought you back, just before your final heartbeat, hopefully the exact same as before.'

'But there may be differences, subtle, perhaps undetectable . . . the chains extinguished all your magic. You were no longer a wielder and we had to gift it back to you,' Gallant says, impossibly gently for a god.

'I nearly died,' I echo back. Wondering at that fact. I feel the furthest from death. I feel so completely *alive.* They gifted it back to me. All of it. And yet . . . why does it feel like so much more?

I sit up, looking at the two gods, stood side by side, peering down at me. Towering, broad, handsome in a way that is more myth than man. Their features are limned in the glow of stars, ethereal and wondrous. And yet with that hidden kernel within me, I do not shy away from them, as I did with Aline, or indeed with them, when I first beheld them. I can meet their gazes without flinching. Gallant holds out his hand and I take it, rising to my feet, marvelling at the feel of my skin against his skin, the way it moves and puckers, the indented whirls in our fingertips. Senses. My senses are heightened beyond anything that is human. That kernel . . . oh gods.

In a seamless motion, they both place one fist on their chests and bow their heads to me. A mark of respect, of deference. And in that moment, I am one of them. I am a god amongst gods.

'The chains . . .' I say as they straighten, all of us eyeing the mass of coiling metal at their feet. Blood speckled and already rusting away, they're no longer glowing with imbued power. 'They were alchemised.'

'Gwydion bound us with Aline's chains,' Argus says, reaching for them. 'They may yet still be useful to us though. We, as fools, trusted her when she brought us here to this new world. I truly thought it was Aline. But Gwydion . . .'

'She is the first masquier,' Gallant says. 'The woman of many faces, she can turn her magic into any other kind. You must have masquier wielders that are able to do this?'

'No,' I say, frowning. 'Not that I'm aware of. This is new.'

But what strikes me, looking at those broken chains as Argus coils them and secretes them on his person, is that they're so similar to that bracelet I wore. The one binding me to the Collector, the one I broke by passing through the warded gates of Killmarth. And now, I have broken the chains on these gods. It seemed impossible, a last resort, a desperate prayer screamed into the abyss when I left Dinas Tar for Killmarth that day. But here, now, I am more.

So much more.

'Ready to face your scorned wife?' Gallant says, raising an eyebrow to Argus.

Argus cracks his neck. 'I am ready for justice. I admit it was my own folly that led us to this place, Gallant. For that I apologise.'

'Wait.'

They both look at me, and I meet their stares. 'Gwydion. What will become of her?'

'She will be tried and measured, as is our way,' Argus says. 'Alongside Aline, she is culpable. Perhaps even more so, for she was not first scorned. I will take that into account.'

'I am Gallant the just for a reason, Sophia,' Gallant adds.

I smile, inclining my head. 'That's fair.'

Allowing them to leave this carved-out rock first, hidden on a tidal island on the edge of this forsaken world, I gesture to the stone path, winding through the shifting sea. 'Shall we?'

Argus and Gallant seem to know innately where their god threshold is in this world. And as we draw closer, I can recognise it too now. The outline of it, a haze of a doorway that shouldn't be there. I have never been able to see a portal location before. But perhaps now . . . or maybe this one is different. Needing three gods to open it. 'Do you have these in every world?'

'Just every world we have visited,' Argus says. 'To forge a portal is a rare skill, even among gods. Once it is forged, then we can step through and create the bridge to the portal we wish to cross to.'

'What will happen to this one? Will you collapse it?'

'No,' Argus says, his mouth a grim line. 'This world has served a purpose. The portal will remain for that same use. Although the rules will need tweaking, perhaps from three to two to leave this place.'

A prison then, for the gods. Perhaps for Aline herself. I shiver, a breeze ruffling the ashen landscape, and hope I never see this world again. 'On the other side, Aline has created a house of glass, my friends are there and her . . . creations.'

Gallant and Argus exchange a look. 'She has a penchant for adoration. I am unsurprised she's created more. Are they a danger to us?'

'I doubt it. Only to human wielders.'

'Hmm,' Gallant says. 'Another strike against fair Aline.'

Argus grunts in agreement, waving his hand at the portal. The edges brighten, and for the first time, I can see it truly is a door that opens, a mighty one, made of air and power, of alchemy. Then a bridge beyond, carved from nothing and everything, a way between worlds. 'Back doors, if you will. And hidden passages.'

'That's an interesting way of describing this way of travelling,' I say, examining it more closely. I have never been able to see detail before, or even so much as an outline. But they are indeed doors and bridges. 'Like you aren't moving between worlds, but between houses. Or rooms.'

Gallant smiles knowingly. 'You must forever boil it down to something you can grasp.'

'I have such a small, human mind,' I say with a shrug.

'Indeed,' Gallant replies, a small frown dimpling his forehead as he regards me. 'Perhaps not so small . . .'

Argus clears his throat, impatience marking every movement as he strides towards the portal. 'Time is wasting, Gallant. Arm yourself. Aline will no doubt have a trick or two awaiting our return. And Gwydion . . . she'll writhe and wriggle away if we do not stop her.'

Gallant sighs, tearing his gaze from me, a sword appearing in his hand. A mighty blade, which he strikes on the ground, the chime like a melodious bell sweeping out. And the long sword is suddenly alive with white flames. 'At your side, old friend.'

I follow them through the portal, these gods, these fables made flesh, and stutter on the threshold as I witness the first stirrings of their true power. We step through onto the lawn before the glass house, towering up before us. And with a swipe of Argus's hand, it simply shatters. I gasp, fear hollowing out my thoughts, as the glass splinters outward then simply . . . stops. Hovering in midair, entire walls of broken glass are caught, as though in a huge, splintered web. And standing in the very centre where these rooms had walls and doors is Aline with my friends.

Chapter 44

God Battle

Gwydion is conspicuously absent. As though she knew this would not end well for her if she stayed to see it through, and that it was likely I would succeed in breaking out Argus and Gallant. She's a survivor, a manipulator and the first masquier. I imagine she is already far from here, waiting to see how this plays out between the gods. Ready to form new allegiances that benefit her and only her. Hoping, perhaps, that these gods destroy themselves in the process, leaving her to sweep up the spoils of victory. Entire worlds. It may still come to that, if Aline does not back down. If the tales in the Attestations and the book passed down by the elders of Alloway are anything to go by, these gods can indeed be monstrous when it comes to war.

Reaching into my pocket, I feel the vial which contained Aline's blood. If Aline is not defeated today, the cold ones will still abound, and it will be up to us to replicate her blood in the nocturnal. The ultimate cure. Will my blood work now? Will it create the effect we need now it holds a god's kernel of power? Gallant and Argus may be almighty and powerful, but I have learned never to put my full trust in the gods. They have their own schemes, their own battles to win.

'Gallant,' I call and he cocks his head. 'I ask a favour of you. The blood of Aline can unmake the cold ones. Please do not destroy her completely. We will need her. I will need her blood.'

Gallant nods, showing he heard, and even as I watch, he seems to grow taller, wider. Wilder. And I can only hope that he makes good on the favour I've asked of him after this is over.

My friends . . . they are dwarfed by these immortal beings. I do not trust them to view my friends as any more than tragic casualties in this battle. Their focus is on defeating Aline, but that is not mine. My focus has always been on the people I love most. Saving them and saving myself.

I look them all over, Alden, Tessa, Amaria, Knox, Belle and Ezra, relieved they are all still standing. Their hearts still beat. But I can sense the hold Aline has over them, stopping them from fleeing. Cold knowing washes over me. Aline has been scorned once more, and she will not allow those who scorned and tricked her to live. If she lives, if she triumphs, she will hunt me down.

'Aline,' Argus says and his voice booms, shaking the very earth beneath my feet. 'This is between just us. Allow the mortals to leave.'

'Husband dearest,' Aline says, clasping her hands before her, a vision of beauty and homeliness, or so she wishes to be perceived. 'I've truly missed you.'

'Lies do not suit you, Aline,' Gallant says, his voice a rumble like thunder. Lightning splits the night in the distance and even I cower back, sensing Gallant's wrath. 'Gwydion,' he says, that wrath even more apparent. 'Where is she?'

Aline shrugs one shoulder. 'It appears we were all deceived, Gallant.'

'Deceived? You?' Argus's laughter rumbles like thunder. 'If you have fallen victim to her trickery, then more fool you, Aline. But I doubt that, somehow. She is not your scapegoat.'

Aline blinks quickly, shifting under their gaze, appearing smaller, eyes widening like a doe. 'You didn't like the new world she gifted you?'

'That *she* gifted us? We did not like the chains *you* forged for us,' Argus says, seeming to grow in stature as he speaks. 'Gwydion may have been the one who led us there, but you were instrumental in the trap. I ask you once more Aline, allow the mortals to go and we will settle this matter between us.'

'That's the thing . . .' Aline says, reaching over to trail her fingertips over Tessa's cheek. I stiffen, Tessa's gaze snagging on mine as I try to communicate to her that I will get her out of this. Whatever happens, we will make it through. 'These mortals interfered in a way I did not find amusing. They created an elixir and unleashed it, removing all my creatures' devotion. Their passion. Do I not deserve passion? It's my name day, Argus, or have you forgotten? I deserved so much more, and they made me feel like the goddess I am. They worshipped me. But these mortals with their elixir . . . they took away their lust on my special night. Made them hideous. Boring. The music across Astrum has stopped, can you hear the jarring silence? They were devoted, Argus. The kind of devotion *you* failed to give me.'

'You call us pathetic . . .' I say under my breath and Aline's gaze snaps to mine, her lip curling in a snarl.

'You are a liar. The worst of all.'

'Let them go, Aline,' Gallant says again. 'Allow them to walk away. You do not need a mortal shield. We *will* have our reckoning.'

Aline opens her mouth to argue, then slowly, delight spreads across her features and she nods. 'Yes . . . yes. Why not? Go, mortals. Leave my side and walk to your fierce protectors. Walk to Argus and Gallant. Walk to a long, untroubled life, mortals.'

Sensing the trickery, Argus and Gallant raise their swords, painted in luminous flame and take a step towards her. They grow taller still, four times my height, armour cladding their chests. But Aline lifts a single finger. 'No, no, boys. *They* must walk to *you*.'

Gallant falters, gaze swinging between them all, and I realise why he is a force for good, for the people. He is our protector, the one who loves all mortal lives. But Argus . . . he is here to smite a foe. To rain justice down on an errant god, a deceiver. His sword crackles, lightning pulsing over the flame, and he swings it wide, the splinters of the glass house shattering to the ground. I turn to my friends in horror. Alden's eyes lock with mine and all I see is his end.

I can't accept that.

I *will not* accept a life without him.

Without thinking, before Argus can swing that mighty sword again and start a war afresh, I wield. I create a portal, then a bridge that takes me to them . . . and I step sideways.

Between blinks, I'm at Alden's side, tipping my head to them all to step through. Aline doesn't notice at first, too caught up in the tempest Argus is calling, but just as Amaria slips through, she stills. With a small, breathless laugh, she turns, gazing at me. And my heart stops.

'Little rabbit . . . what are you doing?' she says softly, taking another step. She's now only a room's width away, and I falter, fear crawling all through me. But . . .

She doesn't know that I kept that kernel of power from the gods.

I close the portal, sensing my friends on the other side of the lawn as thunder booms closer, lightning forking down towards Astrum. It strikes a building, screams and cries eddying towards us. The gods' battle has begun. And I am Aline's first target.

I flick my fingers, a portal shimmering in the air before Aline as she grows, tall as the trees surrounding the lawn, and stumbles, falling through it. But an instant later, she walks out of the other side, through a portal she carves with half a thought, to my right. I whip around, finding her bearing down on me, growing taller and taller, a giant like figure, just as Gallant and Argus now are, eyes alight with rage. She holds twin blades, shorter than Gallant's and Argus's, but glinting silver, sharp as whips.

'How dare you . . .' she says and the sound screams in my ears, enough that I clap my hands against them, the discordance of a thousand glasses shattering in my ears. 'To wield against a god is *blasphemous*.'

She thrusts those twin blades in the ground and from them, tornadoes erupt. Spinning wildly, cones of wind and storm, stealing my breath and dragging me towards her. I try to scream, but no sound comes out. Then I hold out my hands, wielding with no plan, no purpose, just power. And those twin blades, once silver, begin to bubble and melt into a pool. The tornadoes abate, cut off from that root of power in the blades and she bares her teeth.

Aline thunders towards me, a small dagger appearing in her fingers, perfect for spearing my mortal heart. I'm sure in that moment that I am dead. Then in a mighty rumble, lightning cleaves the sky, shooting from the clouds above, straight at her. She is alight for a second, her mouth agape before the lightning ends and she falls to one knee. The ground shudders from the impact. I look up, finding Gallant's eyes on me as he nods. I nod back, unnerved, wondering what this means . . . am I now further indebted to a god?

'Sophia!' Ezra calls and I glance back, finding him on the lawn behind me, a portal open at his side. He holds his hand out, beckoning me. 'Leave them to their battle, this is no place for us!'

I stumble back, scrambling for the portal that Knox is holding open with him a few feet away. On the other side of the bridge they've forged, I see the woodland on the outskirts of Astrum, the god threshold shining just beyond, our way home. But then a shriek rattles the air and I turn just in time to see her—

Aline.

She rises to her feet, extending her arm to Gallant, and from her fingertips, celestial light explodes. It strikes him in the chest and he groans, falling backwards, his mighty sword setting alight a copse of trees. They burn like a pyre as Argus grasps Gallant's hand, pulling him up. Then Aline's dreaded gaze turns on us. Her lips curl back in a guttural snarl as she palms another blade, shining like the deepest velvet night.

And as though this is the signal, the cold ones pour onto the lawn. My breath catches, the sheer number of them racing for us, the flashing teeth, the manic eyes, the whoops and cries . . . murder. We will be murdered here, right here on this lawn on the outskirts of Astrum, this grass flecked with glass, trees burning, the storm wailing overhead, crashing around us—

Aline reaches a hand towards that burning copse of trees, uprooting them with her might. She points at Gallant and they thrash towards him, flame and root and tree, drowning him.

'*No*, Aline!' Argus cries, but she does not heed him. This— this is a god scorned. A god bent on vengeance.

The first cold ones reach us and Ezra and I square off against them. They cannot get to the portal, to Knox holding it open, to my friends, Alden . . .

I stake one, watching as Ezra commands those flying stars, hitting three in the chest at once. Ash explodes just as Argus's blade crashes down upon Aline's shield, a shield she now holds aloft, as vast as a rooftop.

Gallant roars, those burning trees tumbling off his shoulders, and the clouds burst open with a torrent of rain. It douses them, smoke filling the air and I can barely breathe, barely see through the smog of ash and soot and rain.

'Wield, Sophia! Find anything to turn into stakes, into wood—'

A cold one grabs Ezra's arm, wrenching him into that smog and I cry out, wielding in a rush of raw fear, every glass shard surrounding me becoming wood, becoming sharpened stakes. I lift them all to hover, calling his name until he appears suddenly, coughing and bloodied, and I send them into that dense mist to find their targets. As many as they can.

'We can't hold them back!' I say, standing my ground, stake in my hand as Aline trades a blow with Argus, the sound of metal on metal shrieking louder than a dozen bells. They tower over us, these three gods and if we are not killed by the cold ones, we will be crushed by them . . .

Then Aline shoves Argus back, tumbling into Gallant. And her furious gaze turns on us. No longer beautiful, she is rage and hate and death.

'You,' she bellows and every part of me freezes in pure, primal terror.

With a shriek, she flings that midnight blade, and I watch in horror as it careens towards Knox . . . the one keeping that portal open. Our means of escape from her. The blade flies through the air, Knox's features paling, not moving, refusing to let go of his hold on the portal, our only means of escape, but before it reaches him—

Ezra leaps in front of him.

The blade burrows deep inside his chest.

'Go,' he breathes, eyes fixed on mine. '*Please*.'

There is a roar of fury and I fling myself at Knox, shoving him through the portal and falling over the threshold after him. I twist, striking the air with my hand, closing it behind me as I fall down the bridge, to the adjoining portal. On the other side I land in a twist of limbs, feeling my wrist give way with a snap. Pain lances up my arm as the portal shuts in my wake, leaving me panting, trying to gain my bearings. Then, as I look up, meeting Knox's gaze, I see reflected in his eyes the horror of what just happened. The person we have lost.

Ezra Darley, uncle, Collector, keeper, protector . . . is dead.

And the gods' battle rages on.

Chapter 45

Mother First

Thunder rumbles over Astrum, lightning catching our shared horror in flashing bursts. The pain in my wrist flares, the dull thud of pain beginning to sharpen. I cradle it to me, staring at the city . . . now consumed by smoke. Another explosion tears apart the sky, light flaring suddenly, burning my eyes. Whole buildings are aflame. Soon, Astrum will be a furnace if Aline is not defeated.

'We have to leave. Now. Before Aline searches for us. Whilst they're distracted,' Tessa says, placing a hand on my arm. I nod, turning, trying to scrape myself together, but my mind is a blaring mess, that blade, the horror . . .

Knox is bent over double, a choking sound coming from his throat. Alden crosses to him, kneeling beside him, speaking quickly and quietly.

I'm reeling. Ezra just . . . he's . . . I turn quickly, away from Tessa, as bile builds in my stomach and I heave. Heat writhes inside me as I expel a breath, wiping my mouth with the back of my hand. Thunder cracks again, the sound of distant sirens beginning their shrill blare. Chaos. The gods battle . . . they will rip this world apart in their war. We have to leave. There's nothing more we can do here, not for those people in Astrum, not for this world . . . I control my breathing, ignoring the pain in my wrist, the death I've just witnessed and like I've been taught, like I've learned over years and years of practice . . . I lock it all away. I lock away my shock and straighten, placing on that practised mask of calm. Letting it wash over me.

Amaria's arm is around Belle, who is moving from foot to foot, staring at Knox, still bent double, not functioning. I have to take control, I realise. We have to return to Kellend. Even now, the cold ones may be fleeing Astrum towards the portal location in these woods, looking to cross over. And they will hunt. Before we can work on a full cure, they would kill too many, they would decimate us. I cannot allow them to follow us into our world.

'Alden,' I say softly and he looks at me, stricken. 'Get him on his feet. We have to leave and I need to collapse the portal. Now.'

He runs a hand down his face and nods. 'All right, Knox. We have to move.'

There's a bright flash, lighting up the woods around us, as bright as daylight. Then the world stills, as though it's holding its breath . . .

Then an explosion rents the world.

The ground judders violently and I stumble, crashing to one knee, the impact jolting my wrist. I cry out, pain radiating up to my shoulder, and have to bite my lip, tasting blood. When I look up, I see Aline approaching from Astrum, striding across the fields between the city and this woodland. Proud and tall, more god-like than before. She steps across the distance as if it is nothing, bellowing for us, chasing after us—

She's not going to let us leave.

I gather myself together, calling upon that kernel now at my centre, wrapped in the golden, honeyed light of my magic. Forcing down the pain in my wrist, the bleating panic of a god coming to crush us, I trace the outline in the air, like I saw in that cold, grey world. The portal. It's there, right there, hanging as a door in the clearing. Clearer than ever before, an actual door, a threshold of the gods.

Then I sense the snap of twigs, the rustle of movement. Someone approaches. It is not just a god chasing us now. There's no time for any more grief, any fear. I pour my will into the gods' portal, shoving it open, like it truly is a door. And beyond, the bridge, or the passageway as they call it, lining up with the door in the Morlagh Woods. It ripples, reflecting that woodland back to us and I nod to Amaria and Tessa first. Tessa sniffs, stepping through, Amaria then Belle after. She places her hand on my shoulder and I suppress a shudder, all that I'm feeling only just skin deep. I hated him. I loathed him. I couldn't stand him for so long. Then I began to understand. And I even started to like him, to respect him, to see a new relationship we could forge from the ashes of the old. My uncle.

And now . . .

Now he is dead.

How do I rage against him, challenge him and begin to move forward with him when his heart no longer beats? Despair claws at me, dragging me downwards. The only thing we needed to repair, to rebuild, stolen from us. Time.

I place my hand over Amaria's, then her fingers slip away as she too steps through, back to our world.

'Alden, it's time,' I say, sensing the presence of cold ones, not far from here. My voice cracks. 'Please. I can't— I can't lose either of you.'

Alden bends, shouldering Knox and half carries, half drags him through the portal. I turn before I too step through, casting my gaze over the swirling devastation, the gathering clouds, the whistling trees and celestial, burning light. I breathe out, allowing that mask to slip away, and take a gasping, rattling breath. A sob escapes me, uncoiling from somewhere deep inside, somewhere even I cannot pretend.

Why does it hurt so much? Why do I care so gods damn much?

Then I hear them again, too close now. I have to go.

Stepping back, I see their eyes in the dark, the cold ones, fleeing the gods' wrath and thunder. 'There is nowhere for you in our world,' I shout. 'Be gone. It will never be your hunting ground again.'

The ground shudders and I look beyond them, beyond the whistling woods to Aline, bearing down on me. And there, there is Argus, and Gallant, great chains in their hands, chains only the gods can hold, once imbued with Aline's power and now, with their own. Argus swings it around and around his head, a great loop of metal . . . then he throws it. It encircles her chest and arms and she cries out, louder than the storm, then Argus tightens it with a mighty roar and she stumbles, crashing to the ground. She is hidden from the trees, but I can hear her, the violent screams of rage, Argus and Gallant securing her, telling her she has lost. Then she's hauled up and for a moment I see them all above the tree line, three gods, towering over us all. She cries out her hatred as those chains soak up her power. As they take away the strength of a god.

Gallant and Argus pull on her, through a portal, out of this world. And suddenly, the storm abates. The rain ceases. And the only sound is the crackle of flame across Astrum, the sirens blaring. The cold ones surrounding us shift and I see one, stepping into the clearing. A woman, the same age as me, with dark brown hair, a slight frame, wide dark eyes. She blinks, unmoving, and I hesitate.

I hesitate.

Despite the killing, the horror, their lack of humanity . . . they were made. They were made by a scorned god and a trickster, their purpose nothing more than to serve the will of two gods. They can be unmade.

'Do you want to be cured?' I whisper. 'To be human again?'

She tilts her head to the side, more animal than human, then shakes it slowly. 'Not in this world. Not when it's the only form of power I have . . . to be human here, without a form of wielding is to be weak. Even when this curse of thirst is a steep cost. Others may, though. Perhaps if those gods return . . .'

I stare at her, then nod. 'All right. Your choice. But you cannot hunt in my world.' I raise my voice. 'None of you. The tide has turned and if you cross over, we will hunt *you*.' Then I reveal a glimpse of that kernel within me, lighting up the clearing like a star. They shrink back, gasping, and the girl shields her eyes before I let the light dim.

A smile flickers over her mouth. 'It's not for me to speak for all of us . . . but I'll ensure the head of my house knows of . . . that.'

I nod, stepping backwards through the portal, I wonder if any of them will wish to be cured, the favour I have asked of Gallant. Then I reach the bridge, collapse the portal, wielding with that kernel of the gods' power, smudging the lines of their doorway, until it disintegrates forever. I keep walking, along the bridge between worlds, slower than ever before, sensing the vastness between worlds. The molten stars and pitchy expanse, how it's endless and forever, how if I just tipped over the edge of this bridge, I could fall and fall and never reach another world. There are many, I can feel the press of them. Is this what it is to be a god? To wander between worlds, to meddle as you wish?

My heart catches up with my head in those few precious seconds of quiet, as I contemplate what it is to exist at all. And I walk back into the Morlagh.

Knox looks at me with bloodshot eyes and I put my arm around him, knowing his pain. Our mentor, our protector is gone.

★

Just over a moon turn later, when I am sure, I send her a message. Just three words, the three that I know will snare her. And within hours, I am summoned by Caroline Ivey. I walk into Darley Hall with my head held high, knowing this is what must be done. Ezra has not returned, but there is someone else that can. And as I bow my head to the woman at the end of the hall, I know I am doing the right thing by sending Andry home.

Cured.

Alden left a drop of that blood Aline offered me. A single drop, after he had drank from that vial of nocturnal, for Andry. For the promise we made to him. After he drank it, he broke down and wept. Recounting a memory of a ball his mother had thrown when he turned eighteen, how he danced and danced, how he cared for nothing, how he felt so alive and young and eternal . . . and then he was bitten in the next great hunt. And his life, his youth, ended. But now . . . now he is free again. I had to leave the room, the pain of it too much. His life of confinement has been like living in the vault, I realised. He believed he would never be let out. That this was his eternal death.

'Choose your next words wisely, Miss DeWinter,' the Queen says now, every inch the living embodiment of the Crown as she holds my note in her fingers. 'For they will condemn you or liberate you.'

I smile. 'Andry is on the upper floor, in the fourth bedroom. He's waiting for you.'

She pulls in a sharp breath, and that slight sound tightens around my heart. Then she composes herself, blinking furiously, the guards in the room already moving to grip me. As she sweeps past me, a guard before her to check it's safe, she whispers, 'Keep her here.'

Caroline Ivey eyes me quietly before walking out after her and I remain there, in that dusty hall with the guards' hands clamped on my shoulders. It's a lifetime, and yet no time has passed when the Queen walks back in, Andry beside her. They both stand before me and I note all the ways they are the same. The heavy brows, the golden red hair, the proud noses. 'Release her and leave us,' the Queen says, then she glances at Caroline. 'All of you.'

I await her judgement, clasping my hands at my back. I will not flinch, not from this. What I did, all that I have done has been monstrous. I kidnapped and locked away her son. I tormented him, tried to break him, all to end what I saw as a greater threat. A greater evil. For as I stare back at him, I know the truth of it. He may have been a cold one, but I was the monster. I was the one who was relentless. And now there is death, on my hands and in my heart. And death cannot be washed away.

'Andry has explained everything,' the Queen says softly. 'And I am grateful to be reunited with him. I owe you a debt, it seems. For he is whole and cured. He is my son once more.'

I bow my head.

'You have collapsed the portals between their world and ours?'

'As many as I could find,' I say quietly. 'There may still be some I am unaware of.'

'And these . . . *gods* can open a new one, any time they like,' she says.

'Aline, for now, is pacified, I believe.' I raise my gaze to meet hers. 'But I have not been back to see the aftermath. The last I saw, Argus and Gallant had captured her, rendering her powerless.'

She is quiet for a moment. 'Ezra? We have had no word from him for some time now.'

'Dead,' I say and swallow, that now familiar ache in my heart overwhelming me for a moment. 'He died so we could live.'

The Queen nods, eyes suddenly brighter. 'Well.'

'Mother,' Andry says, turning to her and taking her hand. 'You always told me that the hardest path to tread is the loneliest. And the one that is right. Sophia trod that path, right to this hall, to stand before you now. She has ended the hunting, the massacres.'

'I agree,' she says with a small, tight smile. 'I may be the Crown, but I am also a mother. And I know the hard choices. I have made them myself.' She exhales and nods, as though reaching a decision. 'I need strong wielders. Strong counsel. The people who will challenge me, who will be honest. Who will not take the easy path.'

'Like Ezra,' I whisper.

'Like Ezra Darley, yes,' she says. 'He trained you, didn't he? You are steel, I see it in you. He shaped you and hid you from me. I can't imagine he condoned *all* your actions.'

I smile faintly. 'Some things I hid from him too.'

She smiles back, a knowing thing. 'I will need you, and your accomplices in the days and years ahead. We are still three territories and Alloway is a thorn in our side, becoming a greater threat than I have ever had to face. The terror of the cold ones may be gone, but an enemy has many faces. Many forms. And these gods . . . they are at the root of it all.'

'Work for the Crown,' says Andry. 'Finish your training here, at Killmarth, and work for the good of your territory. You owe us that.'

I eye them both, the Crown in human form, and I know that no is not an answer I can offer. I left a threat hanging over the cold ones if they ever find a way to cross again, but I cannot be sure that threat will hold. And Alloway, I know of their hatred. The wounds I bore still ache sometimes on the coldest, dampest days, a reminder of what I chose. The people I choose to love.

So I accept. I step over the firm line that Ezra painted around me, the protection he so carefully constructed to hide me from them. 'All right.'

'Good. Now . . .' The Queen clears her throat and Caroline enters the room, flicking me a curious glance before handing her a document. 'There is also the matter of the mole we believed was in my closest circle. Caroline is investigating the disappearance of a botanist, a woman who worked on the cure, but who we believe was not in attendance at the wedding on that tragic night.'

I frown. 'But I thought they were all accounted for?'

Caroline blinks quickly, what she does when she's ruffled. 'We have reason to believe she wasn't a botanist at all, but a masquier.'

My thoughts tumble, appraising my memories. Then the words the gods spoke, of Gwydion. The god who is the first masquier, who can wield all forms of magic. The trickster god . . . could she have been in our midst right from the beginning?

'We will trace her,' Caroline says in her clipped tone. 'But we may need your assistance. Yours and Knox Darley's. We understand you are both adept at finding people. At . . . assignments.'

I consider for a moment, then nod. 'I have a request though. On behalf of a friend.'

'Yes?'

'A lab, a dedicated one. And resources.' I raise my chin. 'The cure given to Andry was blended using the blood procured from Aline herself. Some more was used for . . . other members of our team. But we need to use any more we may procure for testing, for research. My partner, Alden Locke, will need the use of these resources to develop the nocturnal into a full cure, to replicate that key ingredient . . . should the cold ones ever resurface.'

I don't mention the favour I asked of Gallant, but I believe, somehow, I will see him again. I believe he will make good on his word. And then we will be ready with the resources, the means to develop a final, lasting weapon.

'Done.' The Queen smiles, waving her hand. 'Consider yourself an agent of the Crown now, Miss DeWinter. With all the resources you and your team require.'

Chapter 46

Divine Interventions

Tessa links her arm through mine as we round the corner of Killmarth, the sea wind blasting us. My eyes stream and I giggle, wiping at them as we make our way to the path that skirts the cliffs. Our first visit into Marazia was only a few days ago, but Tessa and I are already planning our next afternoon in the small town.

'Two scones with jam and cream at the Copper Spoon—'

'No, three. A pot of tea, then that little bookshop . . .'

'Yes! And then a pint at the pub.'

Tessa laughs. 'It's a date, DeWinter.'

We come to the path and pause, gazing out over the restless sea. 'T, when I was with the gods . . . they talked of something. Of what Gwydion could do. Of what a masquier is capable of.' I turn to her. 'It made me wonder . . . what you might be capable of.'

'Oh?'

'A masquier apparently can also imitate more than just a wielder. But also *how* they wield.'

Tessa's breath catches and she looks at me sharply. '*Oh*.'

'Yes.'

'Well.'

'Interesting, right? I haven't told the professors, or the Crown. Thought you and Belle might like to figure it out yourselves first.'

She chuckles. 'It does rather open up my options.'

'Explodes them, more like.'

She shakes her head, thrusting her hands into her pockets as the icy wind gathers, billowing around us, smelling of the sea. 'Greg would have loved it. It would have tickled him, the idea that he could be more powerful than half the scholars here.'

'Can you imagine the illusions he would have created?'

Tessa chuckles again. 'The tall clown.' Then she exhales. 'I miss him. Every day, I miss him so much. It doesn't ever really fade.'

I lean into her, squeezing her arm a little tighter. 'Me too. He was actually the best of us.'

'He really was,' Tessa murmurs. We continue our walk, looking out to sea, at the waves as they tumble and crash, the frolicking nature of the weather around Killmarth on a sunny winter day. 'I've been thinking about this more, what he would have said to me. What he would have wanted. And I think he'd want me to pick myself up and carry on. He'd want me to be a full scholar, to improve as a masquier. To unlock more of myself. He'd want me to take risks, be brave, but also stick to my convictions. Work for the Crown, yes, but only if it's truly in service of our territory. To protect what we are, what we have and leave that legacy.' She smiles. 'I know he had all the talk, he was such a joker . . . but his heart was so full. He was my compass point, and I miss that. I miss his presence, his warmth. I never realised that he was the sun in my life until it was gone.' She pats my arm and looks at me then chuckles again. 'I'm not getting morose, I promise! Just reflecting. There's life after Greg.'

I nod and sniff, wanting to hold her forever. My brilliant friend. 'There's life after Greg.'

'Just as there's life after Ezra,' she says softly.

Her words pluck a chord in my heart and I nod again. 'You're right. It's . . . complicated when it comes to him. But you're right.'

She wipes away a tear from my cheek, that I hadn't realised had spilled. I laugh, rubbing hers away, and she takes a deep breath. 'I'm going to walk around the gardens. I'll see you back at Gantry for dinner?'

'Yes,' I say. 'Thank you. Honestly, thank you so much, Tessa.'

She smiles, her whole face melting with the kind of buttery warmth that only real love, shining through from beneath, can create. Then she wanders off, towards the gardens on the other side of the building, leaving me to gaze out at the wide expanse of sea.

'Your world is one of my favourites, I've realised.' A voice rumbles to my left. I gasp, finding a man beside me, someone with a strange likeness to a rather powerful god.

'Do you make a habit on sneaking up on mortals?' I say, crossing my arms.

He cocks his head. 'Only the ones I like,' Gallant replies. 'The rest get my all-powerful, I-am-a-great-god booming voice.'

I chuckle, shaking my head. 'You've recovered from your entrapment, it seems.'

'I have,' Gallant agrees, looking out to sea. 'I'm calling this my holiday. You take those here, don't you? Holidays. I quite like the sound of them.'

'People do like to visit the sea,' I agree. 'Or the mountains. Take the air, go for a swim. Frolic. Have an afternoon snooze. That sort of thing.'

'A novel idea,' he muses. 'A novel! There, I could read a book. Enjoy some of your mortal words.'

We both contemplate the froth and roar of the waves for a few moments. 'Any other reason for your visit?'

'Yes, now you mention it. To thank you. Properly,' Gallant says. 'Argus would have visited too, but he's had his hands full, dismantling Aline's schemes. And keeping Aline from escaping that world of grey.'

'You've locked her up?' I frown.

'For a spell. Not for eternity though, as we've threatened. Aline would find some foul thing there to worship her,' he says. 'And then it wouldn't be a punishment at all. But her face was a picture when I forced her in there.' He laughs. 'Argus built her a hearth to sit beside and contemplate her follies in that hideous outcrop of rock. I gifted her a sewing needle and thread. I was sure she would gouge my eyes out with it, but perhaps she will find something to sew.'

I snort-laugh, covering my mouth with my hand. 'You gods are funnier than I imagined you'd be.'

Gallant grins. 'Aren't you meant to be made in our image?'

We're both quiet again for a moment. Then he holds out his hand and in the centre of his palm is a vial, filled with honeyed liquid. 'The favour. Aline's blood. In case you have need of it. It's been offered to the cold ones, some taking up the cure, some not. Vampirism is rather on trend in that world. We've had to work on this tonic they drank to sustain themselves, ensure it's a reliable food source for them so they don't become frenzied and attack the wielders there. A balance, as ever. And we cannot remain always to monitor them.'

I take the vial and pocket it. 'Thank you. So . . . I suppose I owe you now?'

'Not exactly,' he says, pressing his lips together. 'After what you did, we felt it fitting to offer you something more. No strings, no repercussions, for any of it. Simply an offer, a gift of thanks.'

'Oh?'

'In recognition of what you did. What we believe you could become. To join us,' Gallant says, facing me fully. 'Immortality, power, all the trappings of the gods. In fact, Aline's power. We stripped her of it and now it must be bestowed on one we feel is most deserving. It's how it works.'

My breath stutters in my chest. 'That is . . . that's quite the offer, Gallant,' I manage to get out, turning to look at his serious, perfectly formed face. The sculpted face of a god. 'Not like a cold one?'

He smiles. 'No. Not like a cold one. Sophia, god of bravery, truth. Conviction. Messenger between your world and ours. Taking Aline's pride, her scorn and fury and crafting it into something good. Has a nice ring to it, doesn't it?'

'And you cooked this up with Argus?' I ask faintly.

'Him and the other gods. We take this offer seriously. It has only ever been offered to one other mortal.'

I swallow. 'Did they accept?'

Gallant smiles for a moment, the sea ruffling his hair, a thousand memories and thoughts and moments seemingly flitting before his eyes as he answers. 'He did.'

'It's not power from us, you understand. Although I do hope you're enjoying that little kernel . . . no, don't look at me like that, of course I know. Argus doesn't, so best stay quiet. But you are worthy of that, and more.'

'I . . .' I hesitate, then look up at Killmarth, the granite walls, the lichen stealing over them like pale lace. Then over to Hope Hall at the edge of the island, a gaunt figure standing sentinel against the tide. Then to the sea itself, the rough tumble of it. How very small my lifespan is. In a few short years, I will be gone, erased by tide and time, lost to the folds of history. I may not be remembered. I may live out my days with the same people, achieving things that are not considered noteworthy, at least not by any grand historian of the time. I might just . . . fade away. Taking my passions, my loves, my memories and moments along with me.

But . . .

What a life. What a short firework of a life. A chance to hold on to every passing second, to revel in each small moment. Would

I love as deeply, as fully if I knew my time was endless? If I knew Alden was a mere chapter in my vast existence, would I cherish him as I do now? Or would I become restless, agitated by the banality of quiet? Would I long for wars and oceans, for storms and might . . . for more power?

Aline grew greedy, wanting devotion, wanting adoration. She may have begun as simply Aline, a loving wife, a woman content with the passing moments. But for the monster inside her, that was never enough. And what of Gwydion, with her devouring needs and wants? Her trickery, her lack of morality? She was born with so little and fought to rise amongst the gods. I look at Gallant and I see only good. But what if there is a little monster in him too, prowling just beneath the surface? Who can resist the tug of so much almighty power at their fingertips?

I have not always been good or fair or wise or brave or any of those other qualities. At times I have lied, I have fought tooth and nail, I have done anything, *been* anything to get what I believed I deserved.

What of Andry? What of the way I treated him? It was all too easy, my dislike tipping over into calm cruelty. I tortured him. And I did it with a slice of ice in my heart. That . . . that's monstrous. And I don't regret the outcome. I would do it all again for my friends, for those I love . . . and perhaps that's the issue. That lack of care, of humanity would be magnified, the further I moved from mortality. I may not be the god I would want to be. What the many worlds may need. I might step over the lines I drew again and again. Just like Gwydion. Always desiring more.

A shiver runs a finger down my spine, the wind picking up its wild cadence. I want to live. I want this life I have fought for. I want it to be enough. To not desire more and more.

If I took this offer, it never would be. I know myself. I know I would crave, endlessly. And that monster inside me, the beast roaming beneath my skin, would awaken. As it does in all of us.

I expel a breath, raising my gaze to meet his. This god, Gallant, in the form of a man. And I do the bravest thing of all. I shake my head. 'I'm afraid I cannot accept your gift, as lovely as it is. But I will be your messenger, if that aids relations between us. Consider our lines of communication forever open, Gallant. If you wish it.'

Surprise flits over his features before he nods. 'I accept. Sophia DeWinter, I offer you the role of messenger, emissary, between our world and yours. Without all the . . . trappings.' He chuckles and shrugs. 'Which is why you would have made a great god, Sophia. Your acceptance of the work but refusal of the gift of immortality, of godly power speaks volumes. You know we will have to bestow it, I suppose I will have to figure that out. A god's power cannot be left to fester, or it becomes a darkly thing. But . . . I do have another gift. One I believe you *will* accept.'

The world seems to shift, as though the air has been displaced and then refilled, and I look down to see a coffin beside us on the ground. Walnut-coloured wood, sleek and simple, a name carved into it in glinting gold.

Ezra Darley

'Now you can mourn the man who raised you.'

I choke out a sob, clapping my hand to my mouth. 'Th-thank you. This, this is everything. Thank you.'

Knox. Knox will have a chance now to mourn. He'll have a proper burial. Perhaps I'll also now be able to part with some of the weight on my own shoulders, the memories and feelings I've carried. And let them go. Step forward, on my own terms. As I always wanted. As Ezra, ultimately, wanted.

Gallant raises his hand, placing it on my shoulder, and I stare up at him, through a film of tears. 'I am only sorry he died. A great man. Complicated, yes. But there is a reason why he protected you, Sophia. Not all men have the tools to carry out the work that must be done, but they find a way.'

I cry quietly as Gallant lifts his hand from my shoulder, then raises it, in a gesture of farewell. When I look up, he is gone. And I am left to mourn the man who loved me in his own way, through it all.

Chapter 47

Love Fiercely

'You've used an illusion twice now,' Alden says, facing me. We're in the poison garden, the walls high, the sea a faint murmur beyond, and Knox is lounging in a garden chair next to Blake, like this is an afternoon show. They've even brought a bottle of toquay, uncorking it to pour glinting glasses of fizz which they sip at, whilst providing a rolling, rather opinionated commentary. 'I can practically hear Caroline Ivey's disappointment . . .'

'You think . . .' I pant, dodging a streaking vine, intent on wrapping around my throat that Alden shoots at me, 'that I . . .' I roll, reaching with my will to dislodge one of the cut granite rocks from the top of the wall, planning on toppling it into Alden's path . . . 'give a fuck about her disappointment?'

Alden chuckles, sending three vines my way, more rumbling and bursting from the ground to snare me. I grit my teeth, focusing on breaking apart that granite, slicing through the vines chasing me between the poison beds. Full of plants that are also snapping at me, intent on devouring my mortal flesh . . .

Then I stop, eyeing Alden, and a small smile licks up my lips as I twist my wrist, ready to show him what I've figured out over these past few months. What I can do now.

The ground rumbles beneath him and his own smile falters, before my own vines burst from the ground, slithering around his wrists and middle. I flick my fingers as two more secure his ankles and he huffs a laugh, straining against them.

Knox and Blake begin to clap, Knox whistling before pouring another glug of toquay into Blake's glass. 'She's got you this time!'

I saunter towards Alden, eyeing him in triumph. That kernel of power, from the gods themselves, has been more than a little fun to play with this spring. A god's power, even the tiniest glimmer, can be moulded and cajoled to do many things. Take many shapes. Tessa and I have revelled in it, she as a masquier discovering the full spectrum of her potential and I with this.

'Are you going to release me then?'

'Perhaps. After I've claimed my prize,' I say. Then I stand on the tips of my toes and plant a kiss on his lips. 'I win.'

He grins, kissing me back, and a flicker of heat ignites in my chest. 'Or do *I* win, DeWinter?'

★

After practice, Knox, Alden and Blake head back to their rooms before the evening lectures. We have a series of them now, all from recruits of the Crown, delivering more than just the theories and practice of wielding. Battle tactics, the history of war, strategies . . . all part of Andry's efforts to better equip all of us in the days after we graduate as scholars. Especially with the rumbling threat of Alloway, the stirrings beyond their closed borders. They calmed for a spell, and we withdrew from Theine's borders. But then they began launching a spate of attacks. And it was clear, this wasn't over. Not even close.

Knox travels back to Dinas Tar frequently now. He debated it, taking on the role of the Collector, using the map. But in the end, I encouraged it. He employs Banks still as his driver, and Banks has found a new lease of life by residing in the Darley family home. He's taken up gardening. Sends me letters with progress reports of what's beginning to grow in the greenhouse. He never mentions Dolly, but I can picture her there, with him. Enjoying what might have been a retirement of sorts, although I wonder if she would have continued with an assignment here and there for Knox. Enjoying the thrill of collecting the odd mark.

I have a bedroom there too, if I wish it. As an adopted Darley, a ward of the family. The deeds of my parents' house, I've since learned, passed to the Crown on their demise, after they never returned from Astrum and their final mission. It's a house near the Pendle Woods, used now as a retirement home for members of the Crown's forces. I rather like what it's become. What it's used for. I enjoy learning snippets about them and their lives, but I have no need to dig about particularly. I have my place in the world now, my path that I've forged. I'm looking forward, not behind me and mourning the loss of a path untrodden.

I watch the others go back, as I always do, striding back up towards Killmarth proper, where we'll all be for the next couple of years, and walk down a couple of levels of the walled gardens. To the bench beside the sea. It was impractical to keep visiting the churchyard in Marazia, although I do like to go there every few weeks with Tessa to visit Greg. And Hester. But we all felt it only fitting to have a space here for Ezra. So Grant installed this bench. Something to remember him by. Ezra Darley. For all he gave to Killmarth, Kellend and the Crown. I sidle up, as I do a couple of times a week, placing a flower beside me. A private joke that I think he would appreciate. Carrow, that can still any poison before it takes hold.

And I talk to him, as I usually do. I tell him about my day, like I wish I could have done in person. There are many things we should have done differently, me and him. I've told him, sat on this bench, that the bracelet possibly wasn't the best move. Even if he was deathly afraid of a six-year-old girl dying before she had a chance to really live. To spark. And the punishment of the vault . . . also a terrible decision. I imagine him elsewhere now, maybe some world the gods have carved out for our souls. Another place. And he'll either be chuckling or raising an eyebrow or telling me to be better. Work harder. Be smarter. Use the advantage of this small piece of the gods' power to benefit myself, and the people I care for.

We didn't understand each other. We never saw eye to eye, that much was clear. But in the end, he was the parent I needed. The one who stuck by me, who tested me, who pushed me. The one who ensured I lived. I tested him too. Pushed him to his limits, as a stand-in parent, as a mentor. A protector. I pat the bench, feeling the true warmth of spring wash over my face after the bleakness of winter and wonder what his life would have looked like, without the cold ones. Without my parents dying. Without so much heaped on his shoulders. I suppose I'll never know.

All I know is this; what he taught me. Get in, get out, don't get caught. But also love fiercely. Love completely. Even if you don't have the tools to do the job well. Even if you are out of your depth, you are greater, more powerful than you know.

Love anyway.

Acknowledgements

This book was an absolute joy to write from beginning to end. There's something very special about closing a final chapter and concluding a series, and it has been wonderful getting to write this duology for you, my readers. Thank you for following Sophia's journey. I hope it's been a welcome distraction on the hard days and helped give you the courage to fight for more good days.

To my brilliant agent Maddalena Cavaciuti, thank you for being the ultimate champion of all my stories, always. Forever grateful for your time, energy and wisdom and Taylor Swift knowledge. Thank you also to Allison Hunter for finding the perfect US home for this series.

To my editors, Seema Mitra and Alicia Clancy, you have gone above and beyond for this duology. Your guidance, wisdom, care and love for the books have shone in everything you both do. I'm forever grateful, thank you.

Huge thanks to my team at DHA, notably Rachael Sharples, Zara Petranova, Rhian Kane, Clare Israel and Danni Parkes, every time I hear from you it's always more amazing news. I am so incredibly lucky to have you all in my corner.

To my team at HQ, Emma Pickard, marketing mastermind, Georgia Hester, PR extraordinaire, and Caroline Lakeman, creator of the most gorgeous, perfect covers, thank you so, so much. Thanks also to Eldes Tran and Rhian McKay for your work on the book.

Thanks to my US publisher for everything you do to get my books ready and into the hands of readers, particularly Jean Slaughter, Emily Seigmund, Taylor Noel, Cindy Berman, Sarah Bereta and Megan O'Leary. Sarah Horgan, thank you for another stunning cover design.

And finally, last but never least, my family. Joe, Rosie and Izzy, I love you all to the moon and back, and all the stars in between.